Patricia Highsmith (1921–1995) was born in Fort Worth, Texas, and moved to New York when she was six, where she attended the Julia Richman High School and Barnard College. In her senior year she edited the college magazine, having decided at the age of sixteen to become a writer. Her first novel, *Strangers on a Train*, was made into a classic film by Alfred Hitchcock in 1951. *The Talented Mr Ripley*, published in 1955, introduced the fascinating anti-hero Tom Ripley, and was made into an Oscar-winning film in 1999 by Anthony Minghella. Graham Greene called Patricia Highsmith 'the poet of apprehension', saying that she 'created a world of her own – a world claustrophobic and irrational which we enter each time with a sense of personal danger', and *The Times* named her no. 1 in their list of the greatest ever crime writers. Patricia Highsmith died in Locarno, Switzerland, in February 1995. Her last novel, *Small g: A Summer Idyll*, was published posthumously the same year.

Novels by Patricia Highsmith

Strangers on a Train
Carol (*also published as* The Price of Salt)
The Blunderer
The Talented Mr Ripley
Deep Water
A Game for the Living
This Sweet Sickness
The Cry of the Owl
The Two Faces of January
The Glass Cell
A Suspension of Mercy (*also published as* The Story-Teller)
Those Who Walk Away
The Tremor of Forgery
Ripley Under Ground
A Dog's Ransom
Ripley's Game
Edith's Diary
The Boy Who Followed Ripley
People Who Knock on the Door
Found in the Street
Ripley Under Water
Small g: A Summer Idyll

Short-story Collections

Eleven
Little Tales of Misogyny
The Animal Lover's Book of Beastly Murder
Slowly, Slowly in the Wind
The Black House
Mermaids on the Golf Course
Tales of Natural and Unnatural Catastrophes
Nothing that Meets the Eye: The Uncollected
Stories of Patricia Highsmith

PEOPLE WHO KNOCK ON THE DOOR

Patricia Highsmith

Introduced by Sarah Hilary

virago

VIRAGO

First published in Great Britain in 1983 by William Heinemann Ltd
This paperback edition published in 2016 by Virago Press

3 5 7 9 10 8 6 4 2

A CIP catalogue record for this book
is available from the British Library.

ISBN 978-0-349-00497-6

Typeset in Goudy by M Rules
Printed and bound in Great Britain by
Clays Ltd, St Ives plc

Papers used by Virago are from well-managed forests
and other responsible sources.

MIX
Paper from
responsible sources
FSC® C104740

Virago Press
An imprint of
Little, Brown Book Group
Carmelite House
50 Victoria Embankment
London EC4Y 0DZ

An Hachette UK Company
www.hachette.co.uk

www.virago.co.uk

To my Mother

INTRODUCTION

Those in glass houses, we're taught, shouldn't throw stones.

Patricia Highsmith – brittle, breakable – flung stones like Arthur in the opening line of *People Who Knock on the Door*, with calculated aim. We feel an urge to duck as we turn her pages. Or else we wrestle with our moral compass, thrown out of whack by her absolute deviation from the novel-writing norm. Highsmith is not in the business of allaying our fears. She wants us to dodge and swerve and come up short, to ask awkward questions of everyone, especially ourselves. *Dear reader* is not in her vocabulary.

'Art is not always healthy,' Highsmith said, 'and why should it be?'

We don't read her books to feel better about ourselves, nor yet to pit our wits against hers. Whodunits were just 'a silly way of teasing people' when she wanted to seduce, perhaps even to pervert. She frees us from the confines of moral certitude to grant us an hour or three of leisurely ambivalence (some would say *sin*; plenty have said *evil*). Her theme is the grotesquerie of the everyday. Her monsters are you and me seen from an odd angle – across the dazzle of the Aegean sea, or in the sliding doors of a U-Bahn train. Her great joke was to write a crime novel without a crime (*The Blunderer* is perhaps her best example). Her great skill was to make us, dear readers, complicit. We squirm because her books are full of broken bits of mirror where we keep finding our own faces.

Every writer enters into a pact with their readers, asking that we keep step and keep faith, suspend our disbelief to this or that degree, and of course pay attention. Highsmith demands close attention, repaying it in the dubious coin of discomfort. We're deep inside the heads of her characters, seeing the world through the dark lens of their delusion, or desire, or indifference. When at the end of each book we emerge blinking and off-balance we find our reality skewed a little to the side, as if that lens has fused to our eye. Sooner or later, and usually sooner, we have to return to her world. Highsmith, let's face it, is addictive. She tempts us, time and again, to the place where we feel uneasy if not sleazy, and subversive. We come to crave what Terence Rafferty in one of her favourite reviews called, '(her) annihilation of our comforts.'

Do not look for heroes in these pages. David Kelsey is jealous and delusional. Chester MacFarlane is a drunk and a conman. Rydal Keener is feckless. Arthur Alderman, a saint by Highsmith's standards, nurses a quiet loathing for his father that sidles close to patricide. Each man stumbles repeatedly, even shamefully. Yet these are the men who will guide us through her stories, our 'sole access to the fantastic' as Sartre (Highsmith was a fan) puts it. And her outsiders appeal to us. Those bits of broken mirror are awfully bright.

Highsmith's existentialism reached its zenith in *This Sweet Sickness* (1960). We inhabit the same strange skull space as David Kelsey, unreliable narrator par excellence, a man driven (and driven mad) by jealousy. Dedicated to her mother, with whom she had a poisonous relationship, this is a fevered tale of what happens when we fail to separate our fantasy life from reality. David, tirelessly optimistic in his pursuit of Annabelle (who twice marries under his nose), must learn the harsh lesson that, 'Nothing was true but the fatigue of life and the eternal disappointment.'

Rubbernecking the car crash of his ambition is a guilty pleasure spiced by the knowledge that Highsmith believed we all have fantasy lives – imagined worlds where we retreat from reality. Writing *This Sweet Sickness* she was struck by a sudden, disorientating awareness of her creative impulse, describing the place her stories came from as, 'this abyss in the middle of myself.' No one escapes the mirror, not even Highsmith.

The Two Faces of January (1964) invites us inside the heads of not one but two outsiders. Rydal and Chester are morally ambiguous, ultimately dangerous men, who circle one another for much of the book. And we dog their footsteps, feeling as they feel – angry, aroused, humiliated, gleeful, destructive. Chester's wife, Colette, nurses her husband through his hangovers while finding time to seduce Rydal in what is surely the seediest of Highsmith's many *ménages à trois*. This love triangle soon morphs into a deadlier shape as Chester and Rydal race and chase their way from the Acropolis to the Grand Bazaar of Istanbul. Highsmith leads us a merry dance, first dividing and then routing our sympathies, as she perfects her peculiar brand of catoptrophobia.

Having left the US in 1963, Highsmith returned nearly twenty years later to immerse herself in revivalist propaganda – research for *People Who Knock on the Door* (1983) – an acid-bath immersion for a woman repulsed by the way in which Reagan's conservatives had hijacked organised religion. The result is a corrosive story that strips the pious veneer from suburban America. Highsmith played her ace in this quiet little novel where deep-rooted ethical transgressions are served up as mere everyday and we pine impenitently for a dash of psychotic sparkle before realising that, as in *Edith's Diary* (1977), the horror isn't about to crash through the doors because it's been living in the house from the start. We want to be the ones throwing stones as Highsmith exposes the petty tyrannies of a society that evangelises gun ownership yet throws up its hands in horror when shootings occur, which resents the price it pays for its own squeamish condemnation of sexual relations, pokes its nose into its neighbour's business then withdraws help when it is most needed. Confronted by his father's shallow piety, Arthur 'felt as if he were absorbing guilt through his pores, like radioactive fall-out.'

Guilt is Highsmith's great gift to her characters. And it's the gift that keeps on giving, passed down from father to son, and from author to reader; we close her books with a desire to wash our hands and cleanse whatever passes for our soul. And we imagine Highsmith, from above or below, watching with approval. She has entertained us (always her first purpose) while ridding us of our conceits.

Her biographer Andrew Wilson put it like this, 'She celebrated irrationality, chaos and emotional anarchy.' Plenty of people have tried to protect us from Highsmith's anarchic tendencies. *The Two Faces of January* was rejected by one publisher because of its 'unhealthy air', and the revulsion it inspired in the publisher's reader to whom no one had thought to explain Highsmith's uniquely profitable talent for revolting us. The critics, unsurprisingly, loved the book for exactly the reasons it had been rejected. At the time of writing, Highsmith had been reading Dostoevsky's *Notes from the Underground*, and confessed herself struck by the nihilism at the heart of the story. She was, in her own words, exploring 'the ultra neurotic' with which she identified so strongly. What was more, she didn't care whether or not the reader got it – 'to hell with reader identification in the usual sense, or a sympathetic character.'

Hell is Highsmith's business. Not just the hell of other people but ultimately, intimately, of ourselves. Her characters, pursued and pursuing, may often evade capture or justice but they cannot escape themselves. As Sartre so neatly says, 'There are many ways of holding a man prisoner. The best is to get him to imprison himself.' David Kelsey poured his heart and wallet into an expensive prison. Chester and Rydal confront the consequences of their rivalry in the epic ruins of Athens, while Arthur returns to a home made happy by the devastation of his family. This is a very real, rather tender and entirely plausible version of hell. One where we must, as Arthur Alderman resolves, 'Tread carefully, speak carefully, and hang onto what you've got.'

Hang on because Highsmith's cut the guide ropes, set us in freefall. None of the paraphernalia that helps us through a novel – sympathetic heroes and despicable villains, heroic quests and resolution, a linear structure – exists here. Just those sly little slices of mirror, everywhere. And Highsmith's sure hand, lobbing rocks to rid us of our complacency, our apathy and our hubris.

Violence, like chaos, is everywhere in Highsmith's stories. It underpins her style, attracting and repelling us in equal measure. Yet her books represent the antithesis of sensationalism. By making violence remarkable, we draw its sting. Highsmith wants us to suffer that sting, to seek out its cause and consider its cost. At our most vulnerable, on the brink of violence, she seems to say, we are also at our truest. If we find few heroes in her books it's because they're full of humans – full of us.

Sarah Hilary, 2015

expensive prison. Chester and [illegible] contemplate the consequences of their rivalry in the epic [illegible] of Athens, while Arthur returns to a home made happy by the destruction of his family. This is a very real, rather tender and [illegible] plausible version of hell. One where we must, as Arthur Alderman [illegible], 'Tread carefully, speak cheerfully, and hang onto what you've got.'

Time to [illegible] Highsmith [illegible] the [illegible], [illegible] in her [illegible]. None of the [illegible] that helps us through a novel – sympathetic heroes and despicable villains, [illegible] and resolution, a linear structure – exists here, just [illegible] little slices of [illegible], very short. And Highsmith [illegible] [illegible], [illegible] us [illegible] our complacency, our [illegible] and our [illegible].

Violence, like chaos, is everywhere in Highsmith's stories. It [illegible], [illegible] and [illegible] us in equal measure. Yet her books represent the [illegible] of sensationalism. By making violence [illegible], we draw its sting. Highsmith wants us to suffer that sting, to seek out its cause and consider its cost. At our most vulnerable, on the brink of violence, she seems to say, we are also at our [illegible]. If we find few heroes in her books it's because they're full of humans – full of us.

Sarah Hilary, 2015

1

Arthur flung the stone with calculated aim. It skipped six, seven times over the water before it sank, making golden circles on the pond. As good a throw as when he had been ten years old, he thought, ten being the age at which he had been more proficient at certain things, such as roller-skating backwards. Now he was seventeen.

He picked up his bike, and rolled on toward home. Today was different. This afternoon had totally changed him, and he realized that as yet he was afraid to think hard about it.

Was Maggie happy now, too? Less than ten minutes ago, she had smiled at him and said, almost as usual, 'See you, Arthur! Bye!'

He glanced at his watch – 5:37. Absurd and boring hour! Absurd to measure time! The May sunshine touched his face; the breeze cooled his body under his shirt. The time 5:37 meant that dinner would be in an hour or so, that his father would come home around 6, pick up the afternoon newspaper and plop himself in the green armchair in the living room. His brother Robbie would be either sulking or bursting a vein with a story of some injustice at school today. Arthur jerked up his front wheel and eased the back one to hurdle a fallen branch on the street.

Would he look in some way different to his family? Was Maggie wondering the same thing about herself?

This afternoon was only the second date that he had had with Maggie Brewster, if he wanted to think in terms of dates, and today hadn't been a date before five past 3, when Maggie had said to him, after biology class, 'Do you know what Cooper means about that Plasmodium drawing?' 'The life-cycle,' Arthur had replied. 'He doesn't want it from any diagram, in case we find one. He showed us the shape of it. He wants to make sure we understand spore reproduction.' So Arthur had offered to help her, and had ridden to Maggie's house on his bike. Maggie had her own car and arrived ahead of him. In Maggie's room upstairs in her family's house, Arthur had drawn the life-cycle of this malarial parasite in about ten minutes. 'I'm sure this'll do,' Arthur said, 'and I'll reverse my own drawing when I make it.' Then he stood up from her table, and Maggie had been standing near him. The next moments were too surprising or incredible to try to go over as yet. It was easier to recall his first date with Maggie six days ago; they had simply gone to a movie, a science fiction movie. During the film, he had been too shy to try to take her hand! But that was the kind of girl Maggie was, or the way she made him feel. He hadn't wanted to ruin everything, possibly, by taking her hand during the movie and having her withdraw her hand because she wasn't in the mood. Arthur felt that he had been in love with Maggie, from a distance, for at least two weeks. And judging from this afternoon, perhaps Maggie was in love with him too. Wonderful and incredible!

Arthur put his bike in the garage and entered the kitchen, 'Hi, Mom!' He caught the smell of baking ham.

'Hello, Arthur. – Gus just phoned.' His mother turned from something she was stirring on the stove. 'I said I was expecting you back any minute.'

Arthur was thinking of buying a bike from Gus. 'Not important. Thanks, Mom.' In the living room, his father was already installed in the armchair, Arthur saw. '*Good* evening, brother Robbie, and how're you today?' Arthur asked the skinny figure in shorts whom he met in the hall.

'Okay,' Robbie said, gasping. He was wearing one black flipper and had the other in his hand.

'Glad to hear that,' said Arthur, and went into the bathroom. Arthur washed his face in cold water, combed his hair, and checked himself in the mirror. His eyes, of a dusty blue color, looked the same, he thought. He straightened the collar of his shirt and went out.

'Evening, Dad,' Arthur said, going into the living room.

'Um-m. Hi.' His father barely glanced at him over his right shoulder. He was reading the spread pages of the *Chalmerston Herald*.

Richard Alderman was a life-insurance and retirement-plan salesman for a company called Heritage Life, which had its offices on the other side of Chalmerston, four miles away. He was a hard-working and well-meaning man, in Arthur's opinion, but in the last year or so, Arthur had come to think that his father was selling dreams to his clients, promises of a future that might never be. His father's pitch, Arthur knew, was that diligent work and conscientious saving paid off, combined with tax shelters and tax-free retirement plans. Lately Arthur was much aware of inflation; he heard the word from his mother almost every time she got back from shopping, but whenever Arthur said anything along these lines, his father would point out that the people who invested with Heritage Life were saving on taxes and had spouses or children to whom they would bequeath their holdings, so nothing was lost. Except the value of the dollar, Arthur thought. Arthur believed in buying land or art objects, neither of which detracted from the virtue or necessity of working hard and so on. Some of these thoughts drifted through Arthur's head now: Suppose he and Maggie liked each other enough to want to marry one day?

The Brewsters had more money than his family had. That was an uncomfortable fact.

A yell from Robbie interrupted his reverie.

'I can do it if you just *let* me!' Robbie shrieked in a still unchanged voice.

'Ar – thur?' his mother called. 'Dinner's ready.'

'Dinner, Dad,' Arthur relayed, in case his father hadn't heard it.

'Oh. Um. Thanks.' Richard got up, and for the first time that evening looked straight at his son. 'Well, Arthur. You look as if you've grown another inch today.'

'Yeah, really?' Arthur didn't believe him, but was pleased by the idea.

The dining table stood at one side of the big kitchen, near a bench fixed against a partition between kitchen and the front hall. There was a chair at one end of the table and one on its kitchen side.

Arthur's father talked about business, because Lois had asked him how things had gone today. His father talked also about morale – how to maintain 'morale and self-respect,' a phrase that his father uttered frequently.

'There are lots of tricks,' said his father with a glance at Arthur, 'telling yourself you've had a pretty good day, congratulating yourself – trying to – on some minor achievement. It's the nature of man to want to make progress. But that's pretty thin air compared to money in the bank and a backlog or an investment that's growing year by year . . .'

Or a girl in your arms, Arthur thought. What could compare with that, speaking of morale? Opposite him, his mother looked her usual self, her short brown hair something between combed and uncombed, her roundish face without makeup, showing the start of wrinkles, little pouches under the eyes, but a bright and happy face all the same, concentrating politely now on his father's dull monologue.

Robbie ate doggedly, shoving his fork under morsels of baked ham which he had cut up in pieces. Robbie was left-handed. His fair eyebrows scowled under a smooth, babyish forehead, as if eating were a chore, though he had a fantastic appetite. His torso was narrow; his ribs showed in summertime when he wore shorts with an elastic waistband, and threadlike muscles appeared on his abdomen when he grew angry or when he yelled.

'Dining in flippers tonight?' Arthur asked his brother.

Robbie lifted his gray eyes and blinked. 'So what if I am?'

'Going to practice in the bathtub tonight?'

'Need them for swimming class tomorrow,' Robbie replied.

'I can see you getting on the school bus in them tomorrow. Flop-flop-flop.' Arthur wiped his lips with a paper napkin. 'You'll sleep in 'em, I suppose, or you can't get 'em back on tomorrow!'

'Who says I can't?' Robbie said through clenched teeth.

'Arthur, do stop,' said their mother.

'I was about to say,' Richard went on, 'the *stock* selling – in real estate for community projects – is coming in nicely for us, Loey. Good commissions, need I say.'

'But I don't understand to whom you sell them,' said Lois. 'The same people who have life insurance buy these stocks?'

'Yes. Often. What you'd call little people, not millionaires. I was about to say my people are the little people, but that's not always true. Fifty thousand dollars here and there, you bet they can afford it – or pledge it – if my approach is right and the terms are right for them.'

His mother asked another question, and Arthur's mind drifted. The conversation seemed just as boring and forgettable as details of American history around 1805, for example. His father was talking about 'security' again.

Arthur felt extremely secure at that moment, maybe not because of his savings account in which there was just a little over two hundred, but money wasn't the only basis of security, was it? 'Dad,' he said, 'isn't self-confidence a form of security, too? It's close to self-respect, isn't it? And you're always talking about that.'

'Yes. I agree with you. Part of it's mental. But a steady and rising income, however modest—' Richard seemed embarrassed by his own seriousness, glanced at Lois and squeezed her wrist. 'And a quiet, God-fearing life or home life – that's security, too, isn't it, Loey?'

The telephone rang.

Both Lois and Arthur started to get up, but his mother sat down, saying, 'Maybe Gus again, Arthur.'

''Scuse me,' said Arthur, sidling out from the bench after Robbie had got up. 'Hello?' he said into the telephone.

'Hello,' said Maggie's soft voice, and Arthur felt a pleasant shock of surprise.

'Hi. You're okay, Maggie?'

'Yes. Why not? – I'm phoning from upstairs, because I have a minute before dinner. I—'

'What?' Arthur was whispering.

'I think you're very nice.'

Arthur squeezed his eyes shut, 'I think I love you.'

'Maybe I love you, too. That's a very important thing to say, isn't it?'

'Yes.'

'See you tomorrow.' She hung up.

Arthur went back to the kitchen with a solemn face. 'Gus,' he said.

Before 9 o'clock, Arthur was in his own room. He was not interested in the evening's TV fare, a Western that Robbie was avid to see. His mother was going to do some mending, she said, and his father would half-watch the Western for a while, then go off to his study adjacent to the living room and fuss around with his office papers till nearly 11.

His room struck him as ugly and untidy, and he picked up a

pair of socks from the floor and hurled them in the direction of the closet. Pennants on the wall caught his eye as if he had never seen them before. Soon time to get rid of the Chalmerston High School orange and white, he thought, and why not now? He pulled the three thumbtacks out carefully and dropped the pennant in the wastebasket. The blue and white Columbia could stay up, because he was going to Columbia in September and Columbia looked serious and adult. He was going to major in biology or maybe microbiology. He was just as interested in zoology, however, and in the evolution of animal forms. He would have to make a decision in order to specialize, and he regretted that.

Maggie! The thought of her sent a blissful shock through him, as her voice had on the telephone. Arthur had thought in the past weeks, since he began noticing Maggie in school, that she was standoffish, possibly snobbish, hard to approach. Ninety percent of the girls at Chalmerston High looked fantastically boring; ten percent slept around and flaunted it; perhaps another twenty percent did and were quieter about it. The greatest flaunter of them all was Roxanne, who looked half-Gypsy but was not even half-Italian. Then there were a few snooty girls from such rich families, one wondered why they weren't going to a private school somewhere. Maggie wasn't like any of these; she had the advantage of being pretty, very pretty in fact, and she certainly didn't sleep around. This afternoon with Maggie had been quite different from going off with Roxanne, for instance, after a soda at the drugstore, with a couple of other girls and fellows who happened to know that the parents of one of them would be out of the house that afternoon. Half the time at these silly free-for-alls nothing much happened anyway, and it was all silly, to be forgotten.

But Maggie was not to be forgotten, because she was serious.

Arthur undressed, put on pajamas, and lay on his bed with his geography text open. He had an oral exam tomorrow.

From the living room, he heard Robbie wail defiantly, then a sharp crack, and silence. His mother would never slap Robbie, but maybe his mother had slapped a magazine on a table with impatience. A scene came from Arthur's memory: Robbie about seven, wailing like mad because a little girl had stepped smack into his sandwich at a picnic. There'd been no comforting Robbie, even with another sandwich. His face had turned red; he had danced on his bare feet and brandished his fists in his tense, jerky way, and Arthur remembered the veins standing out as if they would burst on either side of his neck.

Arthur took a piece of paper and a ballpoint pen and wrote:

Dearest Maggie,

Thank you for calling me up tonight. I wish I could kiss you again. I love you. I mean what I say.

A.

After writing that, he felt calmer. Tomorrow he could pass the note to her easily, not that anyone was spying on him and Maggie, or making rude comments. That was another pleasant realization.

Chalmerston High School was a rectangular beige stone building set amid oaks and tulip trees that had been there longer than the building. A gymnasium with an arched roof projected from the back of the building like the apse of a church, and was in almost constant use during daytime hours by boys or girls, and on at least three evenings a week for special basketball practice or for games between Chalmerston's and other high schools' teams.

Arthur left his bike in a rack among a hundred or more others.

'Stevy? Hi!' said Arthur, waving a hand at a tall, curly-haired boy. He loped up the wide stone steps and entered the poster-covered front hall, which was now full of noisy boys and girls passing the time until the warning bell at five to 9 sent them off to their homerooms for attendance checking.

He did not see Maggie until just before 11, when students

crowded the corridors, changing classrooms. He spotted Maggie's light brown straight hair, her erect figure with shoulders held back. She was taller than most girls, nearly as tall as he. 'Maggie—'

'Hello, Arthur!'

They walked along. 'How are you?' Arthur's free hand – his other hand held books and notebooks – fumbled with the folded note in his pocket.

'Fine. And you?'

He had expected her to say something unusual. His eyes dropped past her breasts, held in a brassiere, he knew, under her white shirt, down her rust-colored corduroy slacks, then rose to her face again. 'Brought you this.' He pushed the folded paper into the hand she extended. 'Just a couple of words.'

'Thanks, I'll—' A passing student bumped her shoulder. She put the note into the pocket of her shirt.

'Going to the drugstore at three?'

'Maybe. Yes, okay.'

It seemed to Arthur that her smile was merely polite, that her quick glance at him was shy. Was she ashamed of yesterday, regretting it? 'See you at three then.'

Arthur could have spoken to her again at noon in the lunch hall, but by the time Arthur had his tray, he saw that Maggie was installed with at least four other girls at a back corner table. Arthur found an empty spot at one of the long tables in the center of the hall and sat down.

'Hiya, Art,' said Gus, suddenly standing by Arthur with a tray in his hands. 'Move over, would you?' Gus said to a fellow on Arthur's right. 'You didn't call me yesterday,' Gus said, sitting down.

'I got hung up. Sorry, Gus.'

'Still interested? Thirty bucks?'

'Sure!'

They agreed that Arthur would come that afternoon at 5

to Gus's house to pick up the bike. Gus had to go directly from school to work for at least an hour at someone's house. A repair job. Gus even did some housecleaning sometimes, Arthur knew. There were five children in Gus's family, of whom Gus was the oldest, and those old enough had to do odd jobs to bring in some money. Arthur had a lurking admiration for that, even though it was just the thing his father would praise: old-fashioned hard work and knowing the value of a dollar. If Arthur had ever done odd jobs for neighbors, he had been allowed to pocket the money. Arthur envied Gus his height also, though otherwise Gus was plain enough: lank blond hair, an unremarkable face with a rather gentle expression, and he had to wear glasses all the time. Physically, Gus was strong, but Arthur knew that girls never looked at him twice. In that last respect, Arthur felt better off than Gus Warylsky. Impossible, really impossible, to imagine Gus with a girl!

Arthur was at the Red Apple, called the drugstore by everyone, just after 3. Maggie had not arrived as yet, but the other old stand-bys were here – certain dumb fellows like Toots O'Rourke, who was a football player, and of course Roxanne, flouncing around the counter stools, showing off a pink ruffled skirt that looked appropriate for *Carmen*. Fellows guffawed and pawed at her, and silly Roxanne laughed as if she were listening to some joke that never stopped. Neither Arthur nor Maggie, he was sure, came often to the drugstore. The ice-cream sodas cost a dollar, a slab of apple pie eight-five cents, though it was good and homemade. The coffee was weak. The Red Apple was shaped like a round apple, painted red outside and topped with a stem, in a painful effort to be cute, which was why everyone called it the drugstore. Finally Maggie came in, carrying a book bag, wearing a denim jacket.

'How about here,' Arthur said, indicating a corner table that he had been guarding. He took her order, a strawberry soda, and asked the counter boy to make it two, though he did not care much for strawberries. 'You're looking very pretty today,' he said to Maggie when he had sat down.

'Thanks for your note.'

Arthur shuffled his feet under the table. 'Oh, that!—'

Maggie looked at him as if she were pondering something, as if she might be about to tell him that she wanted to break it off.

'Something happen?' Arthur asked. 'With your parents?'

Maggie took the straw from her lips. 'Oh, no! – Why?'

A girl's shriek rose over the jukebox music. Arthur glanced over his shoulder. A boy was hauling Roxanne up from the floor, where she'd evidently fallen.

'That Roxanne!' said Maggie, laughing.

'She's nuts.' Arthur felt a pang of shame. Several months ago, he had been quite hung up on Roxanne – for a couple of weeks. The town whore! Arthur cleared his throat and said, 'Are you free Saturday night? There's a film – maybe not so great. Or we could go to The Stomps.' That was a disco.

'No. – Thanks, anyway, Arthur. I need some time to – by myself to—'

Arthur took it as a rejection. 'Maybe you just don't want to see me anymore.'

'No, I don't mean that. It's just that yesterday – Nothing like that ever happened before. To me.'

How was he to take that? She was sorry? Shocked somehow? Nothing like that had happened before to him either, but he wasn't going to say *that*. 'So – well – doesn't matter when I see you, but it'd be nice to know I can see you again. I mean, to go out.'

'I don't know. But I'll tell you.'

That sounded even more ominous to Arthur. 'Okay.'

2

On Tuesday of the following week, Robbie came down with (of course) the most flaming case of tonsillitis that Dr Swithers had seen in his many years of practice, and he had to go to Chalmerston's United Memorial Hospital. Arthur took his brother extra ice cream, riding to the hospital on his newly acquired secondhand bike. Arthur glanced at Maggie in the school corridors, not wanting his glances to be noticed by her lest she be annoyed, but his eyes seemed to find her in a crowd against his will. Then on Friday afternoon, he met her almost face to face in a corridor, was about to murmur 'Hi' and walk on, when Maggie said:

'I will go out with you, if you want to. I'm sorry I was so—'

'Never mind. You mean – maybe Saturday? Tomorrow night?'

She agreed. He would call for her at 7, and they would go out to eat somewhere.

Arthur's spirits rose again as high as they had been on that afternoon ten days ago. The memory of Maggie's pretty room with its blue and beige curtains, its blue-covered bed, took on renewed life.

'Never saw you so chipper with exams coming up,' his mother remarked on Friday evening.

Arthur was sure his mother thought he was happy because of a girl. His eyes met his mother's across the dinner table, but she smiled and looked away.

Robbie was coming home tomorrow. He had had to stay an extra day so that the doctor could be sure he was out of danger.

'Robbie reminds me so much of the little Sweeney boy at the Home. You know, Richard?' Lois said.

'No,' said Richard, jolted from his food as if from a newspaper.

'Jerry Sweeney. I've told you about him. Five years old and always worried about *nothing.* He's a dear little fellow, scared of the dark just like Robbie used to be. And Jerry's parents fuss over him like wet hens. *They* get therapy sessions with Dr Blockman and poor little Jerry gets the tranquilizers! Imagine, at his age!' Lois blinked her eyes. 'Really, there's quite a similarity.'

'Lois, you take those kids too personally,' said Richard, pushing his plate back. 'You said you were going to stop that.'

'No, I—' His mother shrugged. 'Arthur, you don't tease Robbie too much, do you? When I'm not around to hear you?'

'No, Mom. – Why should I waste my time doing that?'

'I'm only asking,' said his mother pacifically. 'Because Robbie's nearly fifteen – and insecure enough as it is. I don't know if that's the right word for him.'

'These terms!' Richard said. 'Who isn't insecure? Robbie hasn't found his set of values yet. Few people can, at fifteen.' By way of hastening the appearance of dessert, he got up and removed his dinner plate and also Lois's.

Set of values. Just what did his father mean? Selling insurance to scared-of-the-future clients, putting in an appearance at church a couple of times a month, mainly so that people of the town could see him there? It was still bound up with money, Arthur felt, his father's set of values. And his father wasn't the type who would ever make a big pot of money, in Arthur's opinion, because he hadn't the flair or the push. His father had had to quit college and go to work, as many a successful man had, but there was something ordinary about his father. Even his not very tall figure looked ordinary, and Arthur hoped that when he became forty-two or forty-three, he would be able to stave off the paunch his father was acquiring.

His mother worked four or five afternoons a week at the Beverley Home for Children. It was half a hospital, half a clinic and day nursery for out-patients, and a lot of the babies and children were retarded or mentally upset, or they were being parked there because of family uproar. Lois did voluntary work, as she had no degree in pediatrics, but she was given some money for car expenses and she could eat her midday meal there, but Arthur knew she seldom did. As soon as she entered the Beverley Home, her attention was taken by one of the small children who might be walking around the downstairs hall on his own, or might be with a nurse. Arthur had seen the Beverley Home several times. One might think the children were his mother's own, or related to her. His father called it 'highly commendable work,' and Arthur wondered if his father had urged his mother to do it? She'd been working there about four years, and Arthur couldn't remember how it had begun. Was his mother too easily pushed around? Sometimes she could be independent and high-spirited, in contrast to his father who never seemed happy, and she'd hold her head up and say, 'I want to have some fun in life before it's too late!' and she would persuade his father to take a vacation to Canada or California for a week or so.

The next day, Saturday, Robbie was worse instead of better. When the hospital telephoned during the morning, Arthur was the only person in the house, as his mother was out shopping and his father was visiting a client in town. The female voice informed Arthur that Robbie could not go home today and maybe not until Monday.

'Oh? Well, how serious is it?'

'He has a fever. Your parents can call back if they want to.'

Arthur went back to his bike in the garage. He was cleaning a bit of rust off, but the bike was in fine condition, because Gus was a good mechanic. Gus had no doubt earned by the sweat of his brow enough money to buy a better secondhand bike, though Gus's father let him use the family car now and then, Arthur recalled with a twinge of envy. Arthur knew how to drive, and driving was allowed at seventeen with a test and a permit, but his father wanted him to wait until he was eighteen in September. Arthur recognized the sound of the Chrysler at a distance. His mother was back. Arthur stood by the open garage door as his mother drove in.

'Hospital called,' said Arthur, opening the hatch where the groceries were. 'They said Robbie can't come home today, maybe not till Monday.'

'What?' Alarm was all over his mother's face.

'They said he has a fever and that we could call back.'

His mother went into the house to telephone, and Arthur began unloading the groceries. Robbie's condition probably wasn't serious, Arthur thought, but Robbie was the type who resisted every pill and tied himself in knots at the approach of a needle for an injection.

His mother came back from the living room. 'They say it's an unusually high fever and they're giving him antibiotics. We can visit after four.'

His father came home at noon. When they telephoned again at 2, the hospital reported no change.

His parents were still not back from the hospital at a quarter to 7, when Arthur set out on his bike for Maggie's house about a mile away. The Brewsters' house was finer than his family's with a bigger lawn and a tall blue spruce to one side in front, a couple of burning-bushes of a lovely red color, and a handsome front door painted white with a short roof over it. He set his bike at the side of the front steps.

Maggie opened the door. 'Hello, Arthur! Come in. – It's cooler, isn't it? Raining a little?'

Arthur hadn't noticed.

'Mother – Mom. Arthur Alderman.'

'*How* do you do, Arthur?' said her mother, who was kneeling in front of a record shelf in a corner of the living room. She had light brown hair like Maggie's, but with a wave in it. 'I'm not going to play anything, just looking for a record I'm sure is here somewhere.'

'Cold drink, Arthur?' Maggie asked.

Arthur followed Maggie across a dining room with a large oval table and into a vast white kitchen. 'Your father's here, too?' Arthur somehow feared meeting him.

'No, he's away now.'

'What does he do?'

'He's a pilot. Sigma Airlines. He has odd hours.' She was opening a can of beer.

Maybe Maggie's father was over Mexico now, Arthur thought. 'You can leave it in the can. Stays colder.'

A few minutes later, they were in the car, Maggie driving, heading for the Hoosier Inn, Maggie's idea. Arthur considered the Hoosier a rather stuffy place for older people, but the food was good and abundant. Maggie wanted to split the bill with him, but Arthur wouldn't let her. And she didn't want to go to The Stomps or even to a movie.

'I feel like going up to the quarry,' she said.

'Great!' Maggie could have proposed anything, and he would have thought it was great.

Maggie drove as if she knew the way very well. They passed some of the long, two-story dorm buildings of Chalmerston University, their U-shaped courts lined now with students' parked cars. Cozy lights shone in several windows. Arthur wished he were eighteen, with a car, with a dorm apartment of his own such as these people had, except that it was not his ambition to attend Chalmerston U.

They stopped beside a quarry which Arthur knew was abandoned. All was dark here. Maggie cut the car lights, took a flashlight from the glove compartment, and they got out on a rise of gritty land. The breeze blew harder. A couple of hundred yards away, a rectangle of white dots of light outlined the form of a quarry that was in use. A half-moon sailed in the sky, giving not much light. Arthur knew this quarry. Standing near the edge, he could feel the emptiness, the black pit below. Great slabs of limestone, neatly cut by machines, lay in disorder around the quarry's edge. Maggie climbed up onto a slab and focused the flashlight downward.

'See any water?' Arthur scrambled up beside her.

'No. The light doesn't reach the bottom.'

The hollow darkness seemed to make a sound, like a chord of music. Arthur put an arm around Maggie's waist, smelt her perfume, opened his eyes and regained his balance. He kissed her cheek, then her lips. She took his right hand and jumped down to the ground, and he with her. When she took her hand from his, Arthur leapt onto another slab, then onto a higher one that lay across it. He imagined dashing up it and leaping into space.

'Hey, watch it!' Maggie yelled, laughing, holding the flashlight so he could see to descend.

Arthur jumped off the higher slab to the ground. One foot hit something uneven, and he fell and rolled once. He was sliding downward, and he spread his arms. His hand found something, maybe a projecting piece of wire, and he checked his fall. He began scrambling upward, clinging to sharp rocks, toward the light Maggie was holding for him, but she was not able to shine it where he needed it. Face down, he reached the rim and stood up.

'My *gosh*, Arthur! Are you okay?'

'Sure.' He took a step inland, not wanting to look behind him at what he had escaped.

'What if that had been a sharp edge there! – You tore your pants. Did you cut your knee?'

'Na-ah,' Arthur said, but he felt a trickle of blood down his left shin. They were walking toward Maggie's car. Arthur sucked a cut on the palm of his left hand. The taste reminded him of Robbie. 'My kid brother's in the hospital tonight.'

'The hospital! What happened to him?'

'Tonsils out. He was supposed to come home today, but he got a little worse.'

Maggie asked how old he was. Did he want to call his parents from her house? Arthur agreed to that. It was nearly 11.

His house did not answer.

Maggie brought a paper tissue soaked in surgical alcohol, she said, and a wide Band-Aid for the cut on his palm. 'Want to phone the hospital? – Or were your folks going out tonight?'

'Don't think so,' Arthur said. He looked up the hospital's number and dialed it. After his inquiries, a female voice said:

'Yes, your parents are here. There's no change.'

'Can I speak with my mother, please?'

'We cannot connect you with the rooms upstairs . . . No more visitors are allowed tonight, I'm sorry.'

Maggie was standing near him.

'Maybe by the time I get home, my folks'll be there. Or else they're staying there all night.' Arthur was suddenly worried.

'Want me to drive you to the hospital?'

'They won't let anybody in now.'

Just before midnight, Arthur got home to an empty house. The cat meowed hopefully in the kitchen. Arthur fed him.

During the night, Arthur woke up suddenly as if from a bad dream, but he hadn't been dreaming. It was after 3 a.m. Arthur went barefoot into the hall, put on the hall light, and saw that his parents' bedroom door was still slightly ajar, as it had been. He opened the door to the garage. His father's car was not there. He went back to bed and lay awake a long while before he fell asleep.

The telephone awakened him in broad daylight, and he went to the living room to answer it. It was their next door neighbor, Norma Keer, calling to ask how Robbie was, because she had heard about the high fever.

'No change, the hospital said last night. My folks spent the night there, and they're not back yet. What time is it, Norma? I just woke up.'

'Nine thirty-five. Let me try the hospital and I'll call you back.'

Norma's voice was comforting. She was about sixty, slow-moving, and nothing seemed to upset her, though she often said she was dying – of something awful like cancer. Cancer of what, Arthur had forgotten. She had no children, and her husband had died when Arthur was about ten.

Arthur put some water in the kettle for instant coffee. While he was pouring hot water into a cup, his father's car approached the house. Arthur opened the door in the kitchen that gave on the garage.

His mother looked pink-eyed, his father grim.

'How's Robbie?' Arthur asked. 'Is he okay?'

She nodded, so slightly that Arthur hardly saw it. Her eyes looked shiny, as if she had been weeping. His father came into the house silent, his gray eyes dark with fatigue.

'Yes, Robbie pulled through. Pretty close thing, though, I think,' said his mother. She had drawn a glass of water at the sink.

'Really, Mom. – Hospital didn't tell me anything – except "no change."'

'And you were with a girl on a date,' said his father, sighing.

His father's tone was reproachful, and Arthur ignored the remark. 'What happened with Robbie, Mom?'

'Very dangerous fever and a strep throat,' said his mother. 'The hospital said they'd never seen anything quite like it. They had him in intensive care; oxygen, everything. We had cots in a room down the hall. But he *will* be all right.' She sipped the glass of water and leaned tiredly against the sink. 'The crisis was around five this morning, wasn't it, Richard?'

'And we prayed,' said Richard, swinging his arms in a downward motion. 'We prayed and our prayers were answered. Isn't that right, Loey?'

'Uh-hm,' said his mother.

'Christ answered us. I prayed to Christ,' said Richard, filling the kettle, setting it on the burner.

The telephone rang.

'That's Norma, Mom. I'll get it.' Arthur went to the telephone. '*Yes*, Norma, thanks, I just heard. My folks just got back.'

'Now isn't that wonderful? He's out of danger.' Norma asked if she could speak to his mother, and Arthur called her.

Arthur didn't want to go back into the kitchen with his father in his present mood, but he did, and picked up his coffee cup.

'I had a great experience last night,' said his father. 'Maybe one day you'll have one like it, too. I hope you will.'

Arthur nodded. He knew that his father meant that Robbie had pulled through because of his praying. 'I phoned the hospital last night around eleven. They just said there was no change, not that he was worse. Maggie even offered to drive me to the hospital, but they wouldn't have allowed visitors then.'

His father might as well not have heard, and his smile was dreamy. 'You've been in a daze for a week or more. A girl. More important than your brother or a human life.'

That was not true. Or was it? At any rate, Arthur took the remark as a rebuke, which was plainly the way his father meant it. He wasn't going to say that he loved Maggie and loved his brother too. Now he was sorry that he had uttered Maggie's name. 'I don't know why you're – scolding me.'

'Because you're selfish – thoughtless about the things that matter in life.'

Since Arthur felt that his eyes had been opened to life in the last week or so, he shook his head and remained silent.

His mother had come in and heard part of this. 'Richard, we're both tired. Haven't we something to be happy about now? What if I make us all some scrambled eggs and then – both of us could use a little shut-eye, I think.'

'Scrambled eggs, fine,' said Richard, removing his jacket. 'But I don't feel like sleeping. Too keyed up, too happy. Today's Sunday. I may take a stroll around the yard.'

Lois looked at Richard with faint surprise as he headed for the living room. A door opened from his study into the backyard.

Arthur went to his room to get dressed. He didn't want to sit and eat breakfast with them now, but he knew his mother wished him to, so he did. His father ate in silence, and with his usual good appetite. His mother only picked at her food and shyly said she was going to lie down for a while before they left for church.

Of all days, Arthur thought, to go off to church at 11, when they'd had hardly any sleep. Then his father said:

'I would like you to come too, Arthur.'

Arthur took a breath, ready to make an excuse about studying before exams, even to lie about a date with Gus for studying, but a look from his mother kept him from speaking.

3

So that Sunday became, in Arthur's mind, the day his father found God, or was 'reborn,' as his father put it. The hour in church had been almost embarrassing. His father had knelt with head bowed almost the whole time, except when the congregation had stood up to sing something; then his father had boomed out in rather good baritone, though so loudly that a couple of people in pews in front of them had turned around to see who it was. Then at the good-byes at the door afterward, when the preacher, Bob Cole, always shook everyone's hand, his father had made a speech to the Reverend Cole which several around had heard, even paused to listen to, about his younger son Robbie having recovered, been called back from death by his prayers to Christ. 'I know the doctors had given up. I could see it in their faces,' his father had told the attentive Bob Cole. 'He'd even developed a strep throat . . . '

Arthur told some of this to Maggie on their next date, which was the following Thursday evening. They'd had a date for Wednesday, but Maggie had canceled it, for no reason that Arthur could see, and she had been unwilling to make another date either, so Tuesday evening, when he had heard from Maggie that the Wednesday date was canceled, Arthur had felt a bit gloomy.

And his father, with his new-leaf-turning, had made a speech in regard to Arthur's doing part-time work this summer, like Gus, to make him less dependent on his twenty-dollar-a-week allowance, and finally even his mother had said, 'Let Arthur finish his exams right now, Richard. They're important this year, because Columbia's going to look at his grades.'

Robbie had come home Tuesday morning, and Lois had taken the afternoon off from the Beverley Home for Children to be with him. Robbie for once looked happy and content, tucked into bed and living on ice cream and caramel custard. He smiled, and his brows were unfrowning. It occurred to Arthur that maybe he *had* been near death, and then saved, and that Robbie realized it.

On that Tuesday afternoon, Arthur had taken his history exam and was sure he had passed, but he was aiming for 85 or better.

The next morning, when he saw Maggie in a corridor, her face had been glowing, and she asked him if he was free the next evening. Arthur said he was. He had to brush up for Friday's English exam, he thought to himself, but he would squeeze that in somewhere. Maggie herself was inspiration.

Thursday night, they were alone at Maggie's house. It was her mother's bridge night, and she mightn't be back till 1 a.m., Maggie told him, because Arthur asked.

'My cooking,' Maggie said, pulling a tray of broiled lamb chops from the grill over the stove. 'Doubt if I'll win any prizes.'

Typical Maggie! She wasn't fishing for compliments. She was really shy, in some situations. Arthur felt in seventh heaven, alone with Maggie in her kitchen, in the whole house! That day he had taken his biology exam (and so had Maggie taken it), looking forward to coming to her house this evening, and all the genera and phyla names had flowed from his pen with no effort on his part, and he had made a beautiful drawing.

During dinner Arthur described Sunday morning to Maggie, his parents coming home tired after Robbie's crisis, and his father announcing that he felt he had found God because his prayers had been answered.

'Easy to see he could think that. – I suppose it was like a miracle to them.'

Was Maggie making a polite comment? Arthur felt that he hadn't made himself clear. 'Yes, but – you don't believe that Christ personally heard somebody's prayer, do you? That's what my father's saying.'

Maggie hesitated, then smiled. 'No. That I don't. – It's a personal thing, I suppose, if someone believes that or not.'

'Yes. And I wish my father would keep it to himself. – Now he wants to drag me to church. I hope not every Sunday. I just won't go.'

They were eating in the kitchen at a plain pine table.

'Suddenly reminds me,' Maggie said. 'About two years ago my father had a drinking problem. *He* thought he drank too much sometimes, even though my mother didn't say anything. So a friend of my father's gave him religious things to read. About the evils of drink. Then' – Maggie laughed – 'we had college students knocking on the door trying to sell us subscriptions, and there was suddenly junk mail as if we'd been put on mailing lists. My mother hated it! So my father said, "If I can't lick my problem without these people, I'm not worth much." Then he made a resolution and kept it. Never more than two drinks a day and never on the day he's flying.'

Maggie put on a cassette. Duke Ellington at Fargo, 1940. 'Mood Indigo' was on it. Even the music, which Arthur knew well, sounded better in Maggie's house. Would he and Maggie ever have a house like this together?

'Why'd you break the date with me for Wednesday?'

'Oh—' She looked embarrassed. 'I dunno. Maybe I was scared.'

'Of me?'

'Yes. Maybe.'

Arthur didn't know what to say, because the phrases that occurred to him were either trite or too serious. 'That's silly.'

A little later, Arthur said, 'Do you think we could go up to your room again – like the other afternoon?'

Maggie laughed. 'Is that all you think about?'

'No! Have I mentioned it? – But since you ask, yes.'

'Suppose my mother came home early?'

'Or your father!' Arthur laughed as if in the face of catastrophe. 'But – when then?'

'Don't know. Have to think. Maybe you'll want to give me up.'

'Not yet,' Arthur said.

That night, he walked the mile back to his house, as he had walked to Maggie's. Maggie had said tonight that she had wanted to become a doctor or a nurse when she was about twelve. She had had a baby brother who had died around that time. And she had talked about puppets. The doll on her bed, Arthur remembered, had been a two-foot-long wooden puppet in a fireman's uniform, and Maggie said she had made it when she was fifteen. She had more in the attic. She had used to write plays for them.

'That lasted about a year. I'm always getting enthusiasms and then dropping them,' Maggie had said. 'You're lucky, being so sure of what you want to do.'

Arthur began to trot down East Forster, causing a couple of dogs to bark in people's backyards. He trotted around the curve into his own street, West Maple, then slowed to a walk. He could see the dim glow that meant the living room light was on in his house. Norma Keer's light was on next door, behind her living room curtains. Norma was always up late, reading or watching TV. Arthur went softly up her front steps and knocked with two slow raps.

'Who's there?' called Norma.

'Burglar.'

Norma unlocked the door, smiling broadly. 'Come in, Arthur! – My, you look nice. Where've you been?'

'Out on a date.' Arthur walked into her living room, where the TV was on with no sound, and a book lay open on the sofa under a standing lamp.

'What's your news? – Would you like a drink?' Norma was in stockinged feet as usual.

'Um-m – maybe. Gin and tonic?'

'Sure thing. Come with me.'

They went to her kitchen at the back of the house, and Arthur freshened Norma's drink and made one for himself. Norma watched him, looking pleased by his company. She pushed her fingers through her thin, orangy-colored hair, which was short and stood out around her head like a vague halo in certain lights or like the idea of hair instead of hair. She was dumpy and shapeless, perhaps one of the least attractive women Arthur had ever seen, but he liked to be with her, to answer her questions about school and family life. Norma's dinner dishes lay unwashed in the sink.

'I'm so pleased Robbie's home again,' Norma said, 'leading the life of Riley, I gather, after his ordeal.'

'Ah, yes.' Arthur relaxed in an armchair. *I've met a wonderful girl*, Arthur wanted to say. Norma would listen with interest while he told her about Maggie, all except that they had been to bed together once. 'And Dad – has found God. Did he tell you?'

'Wha-at? Well – he did say something. I forgot. What does he say?'

'Well, he's thankful Robbie pulled through, and Dad thinks it's because he prayed. He's reborn.'

'Oh. You mean Richard says he's born-again. Town's full of 'em. They don't do any harm. Very honest people as a rule. Hah!' Norma gave one of her slightly out-of-place laughs.

'So,' Arthur continued, 'there's a new law in the land next door. Church every Sunday and a grace before dinner every night. We have to thank the Lord for our bread.' Arthur smiled, realizing that bread meant money, too.

Norma tucked her feet up on the sofa with a whisking sound. 'What's your mother say?'

'Puts up with it to keep the peace.' But would she rebel about church every Sunday, when she needed her free time for paper work for the Home, and wasn't that doing God's work, too?

Norma took a delicate sip of her gin and tonic. 'Does Richard want to make born-agains out of you and Robbie?'

'I'm sure he'd like to.'

'I heard you have to have a personal experience for that, like a revelation. – Well, honestly, as boys go – I think your father should be pleased with you compared to some of the kids I hear about, wrecking cars right and left, on drugs and dropping out of school.'

Arthur took no comfort from that. He felt vaguely uneasy, and glanced at his wristwatch.

'Not late for me, but maybe for you.'

'No. Got an English exam tomorrow, but in the afternoon, thank goodness, so I can sleep late if I want to.'

Norma's bulging eyes explored the corners of the room thoughtfully, as if looking for something. Arthur was reminded of fortune-tellers' eyes gazing into crystal balls in cartoons. He had a sudden and unpleasant thought: Would his father try to block his going to Columbia, somehow? Was his father jealous of him because of Maggie? Crazy thought, since Arthur was not sure his father would know Maggie if he saw her, but his father knew of the family.

'News from your grandmother?' Norma asked.

'Oh – yes. She'll come for a visit this summer. I'm pretty sure.' Arthur's maternal grandmother lived in Kansas City, Missouri, and had a school for ballet and ballroom dancing.

'Love to see her again. – And I'll sure miss you when you take off in September, Arthur.'

Norma talked on, and Arthur's mind drifted. If for some reason his father balked at paying his Columbia fees, his grandmother

Joan would certainly put in a good word for him, even probably contribute to the cost, which would be about ten thousand five hundred for the first year. It would be more, but Arthur had a fifteen-hundred-dollar grant on the basis of his biology grades. His grandmother was indeed different from his father, and even from his mother. Arthur suddenly remembered a fact he seldom thought about: His mother's family, the Waggoners, had not been pleased about her marriage to his father. The Waggoners were better off and had been against her marrying a young man with no money and whose prospects were vague. However, once they had married, his mother had once told Arthur, her family had accepted Richard and even come to like him and respect him, and Arthur could see this in his grandmother's attitude.

'Went over this evening to see Robbie,' Norma said. 'Took him a *Mad* magazine, which seemed to please him. He looked well. Happier than usual – in the eyes. In bed, but so full of pep your mother had to tell him to shut up. – Another drop, Arthur?'

'No thanks, Norma.' Arthur stood up. 'I'll be shoving off.' He smiled, waved a hand and departed.

4

Arthur ran smack into his father in the front hall. His father, in pajamas and bathrobe, had evidently just come from the living room, where the only light in the house showed, and Arthur was so startled he almost fell back against the door.

'You're out late – for exam week,' said his father, who had stopped, hands in robe pockets, so that Arthur had to turn sideways to get past him in the hall.

Arthur put on the kitchen light. 'I hope you weren't waiting up for me.' Arthur opened the fridge. 'As if I were a girl.'

'You've been drinking, too?'

Arthur felt quite sober enough to hold his own. 'Yes. I had a drink with Norma just now.'

'And before that?'

'Two beers, I think. Big evening.' Arthur poured a glass of milk to the rim and sipped without spilling a drop.

'And you want to go to Columbia.'

What was his father getting at now? That he wasn't worthy, that he was having a good time, that he was silly?

'Before Norma, you were out with your latest girlfriend, I gather.'

'Latest? Since when do I have a harem?'

'Fine time to be drunk,' said his father, nodding his big head. His straight brown hair was graying. Some strands of hair bobbed over his heavy, creased forehead.

Arthur kept Maggie in his mind, her beautiful cool, and he faced his father with equanimity.

'Nothing to say for yourself?'

Arthur took a couple of seconds to answer. 'No.' His father wore his sandal house-slippers with crossing leather straps, which Arthur knew his father didn't like. A present from Arthur's mother. Was his father wearing them now because they looked sort of biblical? Arthur repressed a smile, but saw that his father had noticed the start of it.

'You'd better change your ways, Arthur. Or you can put yourself through college.' His father nodded, then relaxed a little, having fired his guns.

Big news! Very hostile. 'I don't see what I've done to—'

'In the time that you waste,' his father interrupted, 'you could be doing something for your own good. Studying or working at a job to bring in a little money. That's my point.'

Arthur had supposed that that was his father's point.

'I shall speak to your mother about this.'

About what? Arthur nodded, with a brisk but polite air, and watched his father enter the living room and put out the light. Then his father disappeared into the bedroom on the left in the hall.

Arthur was awakened the next morning by a gentle rap at his door. He had left a note on the floor outside his room last night: 'I can sleep till 10,' and this was service, his mother arriving with a mug of coffee!

His mother came in quietly and shut the door. 'I'm making Robbie stay in bed, because the doctor's coming at noon to look at him and I don't want him to run up a temperature.' She was whispering. 'I hear you and your father had a row last night.'

Arthur sipped the coffee. 'Not a row. He said I was out late. Hardly midnight.'

'He's still a bit wrought up, Arthur. You know, about Robbie.'

'Sit down, Mom.' Arthur removed a shirt from the seat of his straight chair.

His mother sat. 'You saw Maggie last evening?'

'Yes. But don't mention her name again to Dad, would you?'

'Why?' His mother smiled.

'Because I have the feeling Dad's against her. Against my seeing anybody in the evenings now.'

'Oh, that's nonsense.' Already she looked about to get up from the chair. 'Richard sees the world in a different way now. I'm not sure how long it'll last. Maybe not long.'

The English exam that afternoon lasted two hours. Maggie was taking the same exam, and Arthur glanced at her a couple of times across the room. She sat far to his right, so he saw her in profile, her head bent, her lips slightly parted. Arthur chose a four-line poem of Byron's of which to complete the last two lines, and as 'a poem you have memorized' one of Robert Frost's. He supplied one title each for James Fenimore Cooper, Washington Irving, and Theodore Dreiser, a writer whom he rather liked, and completed the title of Willa Cather's 'O,—!' Then a one-page 'essay' on the influence of the media on American speech. Grammar: multiple choice, and one was supposed to check the right one. At the end of the exam, when those who hadn't already departed stood up, stiff, grinning with relief, frowning with dread, Arthur headed straight for where Maggie had been sitting and could not find her, not in the corridor either, or when he ran down the stairs to the main hall.

Had she deliberately tried to avoid him? Maybe. But why?

Arthur rode home on his bike. Robbie was walking around in the backyard in pajamas and bathrobe, which was probably against his mother's wishes. He drank a glass of water, then went to the telephone and dialed Maggie's number. She lived nearer the school than he, and had a car besides. The telephone rang seven or eight times, and finally Maggie answered.

'Me,' Arthur said. 'Looked for you just now.'

'I wanted to get home.'

Long pause. Arthur didn't want to talk about the exam. 'Well – I'll see you tomorrow night?' They had made a date for Saturday night.

'I don't think so – after all. Because I'm going away tomorrow morning for the weekend. With my family. – I'm sorry, Arthur.'

Arthur was baffled when they hung up. Maggie had sounded distant. Had he done something wrong last night? Nothing that he could remember or imagine.

He resolved not to telephone Maggie on Saturday or Sunday, in case she hadn't gone away with her family, because it would look as if he were checking on her. If she stayed in town over the weekend, it was easy enough for her to call him.

On Saturday afternoon, Robbie was up and dressed, still in a sunny mood, and maybe he'd been born again too? Their mother made Robbie sit bundled up in a blanket in the sun every afternoon, and the sun had put roses in his cheeks and bleached the cowlick over his forehead. Robbie had missed his final exams neatly, which didn't bother him.

'Why're *you* so down in the dumps?' Robbie asked Arthur.

Arthur was sharpening the spade. The telephone had just rung; his mother had summoned him, and it hadn't been Maggie but a girl acquaintance called Ruthie. She had asked him to a party tonight, one of the 'grad parties' that were taking place all over town in the next days. Chalmerston's Main Street was bedecked with orange and white streamers saying 'Congrats Grads!' Arthur had thanked Ruthie and said he would come. But he was not sure whether he would or not.

'I'm not down in the dumps,' Arthur said.

'You're sorry because I got well,' Robbie said like a flat statement of truth.

Arthur leaned on the spade handle. 'Wha-at? Are you nuts, little brother?' Had their father been feeding Robbie some kind of crap, Arthur wondered, some kind of anti-Arthur propaganda? Arthur got to work on the spade again. 'What's Dad been telling you?'

'He just said – God touched me.'

'I see. Wa-al, you just keep that in mind,' Arthur drawled like a Westerner. 'You be a good boy from now on.'

Arthur went to the party at Ruthie's at half past 10. It was good to get out of his house's atmosphere. Rock music pulsed half a block away from Ruthie's. Three or four bikes lay on the grass near the front door, and several cars were at the road edge and in the driveway. Arthur walked in the front door, which was open.

People were dancing in the living room. At a glance, Arthur recognized a lot of faces from school, and there were a few older boys whom he didn't know, probably students from C.U.

'Hi, Arthur,' said a girl named Lucy, in blue jeans and T-shirt, barefoot. 'By yourself? Where's Maggie?'

He was surprised that Lucy knew about Maggie, but at the same time pleased. 'Away. She's—'

Roxanne danced in, snapping her fingers over her head, twisting. 'Hi there, Art!'

'Out of town this weekend!' Arthur shouted to Lucy over the music.

'Right, she is,' said Roxanne, still dancing, and winked at Arthur.

'She told you?' Arthur didn't think Maggie and Roxanne were at all chummy.

'Ye-es,' said Roxanne, and with a sweep of her dark eyes past Arthur to Lucy, she twirled into the thick of the dancers.

'Get yourself a Coke or something in the back!' Lucy said, drifting off.

Arthur tossed his jacket on a sofa which already held a heap of outer garments. He didn't feel like dancing. He looked around for Gus and didn't see him. A fellow and a girl were smooching on another sofa. Dull as all hell, Arthur thought, without Maggie! Might as well be another classroom, except for the booming music and the shrieks of the girls and the big laughs from the fellows. Arthur made his way to the kitchen at the back.

A husky fellow in a white sweater was trying to persuade a girl – Sandra Boone, an idiot in Arthur's English class – to take off with him, probably to his C.U. dorm room.

'—nobody there *this minute!* My roommate's out and won't be back till four; I know him.'

Sandra giggled, plucked at the boy's sleeve, and seemed unable to make up her mind.

Lout, Arthur thought about the husky guy, who looked maybe twenty-one and hadn't bothered to shave, probably because he thought stubble made him look older.

Then a little while later, Arthur was dancing, because the music was good and someone had said, 'Aren't you gonna dance tonight?' and Arthur didn't want to look sour, because that reminded him of his father.

Then he was riding home on his bike, having drifted out when the serious eating started in the kitchen. Ruthie had boiled a couple of cauldrons of frankfurters.

Amazing that it was already nearly 2, and amazing that Norma's living room light was still on behind her drawn curtains, but Arthur didn't feel like calling on her tonight. He felt more like cruising by Maggie's house, to see it silent and black – yet belonging to Maggie and familiar to her – but he didn't do that either.

5

There was no school the following Monday or during that week. The exam results were due next Friday, and graduation, the ceremony which Arthur considered ducking out of, came on the Monday after.

Sunday had brought, of course, the churchgoing, with Robbie, though Robbie would have fitted in better at Sunday School, Arthur thought. In the past, when his parents had gone to church perhaps twice a month, Robbie had been parked in the Sunday School class in an adjoining room of the church. Arthur had wriggled out of Sunday School around the age of ten, and his parents had not been difficult about it, but now things were different. It crossed Arthur's mind that his father was bringing Robbie to the adults' service as if to say, 'Behold my son, alive and well!' Robbie squirmed and twitched during the Reverend Cole's sermon, which could last half an hour or more. Robbie glanced at his mother as if to ask when would it be over, twiddled the hymn books in the slot on the back of the pew in front of him, and that Sunday he dropped a book flat down on the floor with a loud bang just when the Reverend had paused for a few seconds. It sounded as if somebody in the congregation had had enough, and Arthur had to stifle a laugh.

Then after church, his mother worked with a little extra speed in the kitchen to prepare Sunday dinner, which was always more elaborate than their evening dinners. His father, inspired by just having been to church, brought a glossy magazine called *Plain Truth* from the living room and looked through it, searching for something to read aloud, Arthur feared. Arthur was in the kitchen to set the table, swing the lettuce, to keep the sink clear for his mother's work. They hadn't a dish-washing machine, as had Maggie's family. Arthur imagined Maggie and her family at this minute installing themselves at a nice table in a hotel dining room after a morning of tennis or swimming.

'Listen to this,' said Richard, leaning against a sideboard from which Arthur just then had to get paper napkins from a drawer.

Arthur made a gesture with his finger, and his father stepped aside.

'A quote from Isaiah,' said Richard, '"The earth shall be full of the knowledge of the Lord, as the waters cover the sea." A simple thought, but a profound one, happy one,' Richard said, glancing at Lois who was lifting a roasted chicken from the oven. She had partially cooked it before church. Richard looked at the roasting pan, its edges garnished with browned potatoes and onions, and smiled his appreciation.

'Call Robbie, would you, Arthur?'

Arthur walked through his father's study, and saw his brother running like a colt, whipping a long twig against a leg as if beating himself onward. 'Hey, Robbie! Dinner!'

Heels down, Robbie jolted to a halt and tossed the switch aside. He had put on sneakers, but still wore his Sunday best suit.

When Arthur returned to the kitchen, his father was moving toward the table but had found another passage. 'This is funny. They're talking about the time when Christ returns. "Think – what will be one of the worst problems people will have in the millennium? It will probably be the tendency to gain weight!

There will be such an abundance of food and drink that some people are very likely going to grow a little too fat. Of course one of the laws of health is that gluttony is wrong." Fine thing to be reading just as we're sitting down, isn't it?' Richard beamed at his wife.

They seated themselves on benches and chairs. Heads bowed.

'Father, we thank Thee for our bread and meat. God bless those who walk in Thy name. Let us be – thankful for yet one more day of Thy loving care for us. Amen.'

'Amen,' murmured Lois.

When the plates were served, Lois said, 'Robbie, you shouldn't be running around like a wild Indian, when just a couple of days ago you were in bed. You should see your face.'

Robbie's face was pink. And his lips were already shiny with chicken fat, his mouth so full, he couldn't reply.

Richard had laid *Plain Truth* aside on Arthur's bench and was concentrating on his plate. Then he lifted his face and said to Lois, 'No comment from you on our gluttony?'

Did he mean that as a joke, Arthur wondered. Nobody was plump in the family except his father.

'When they say, "when Christ comes again" in that magazine, does the writer mean it literally or someone resembling Christ?' Lois asked. 'I find it vague, phrases like "plenty to eat". All over the world do they mean?'

Arthur felt like laughing, it was so ridiculous. Was Christ or somebody going to drop sacks of wheat or rice in the middle of a desert in Africa or wherever a million people were currently starving? Arthur had taken a look at *Plain Truth*, on his father's orders, and found the articles so naive they might have been written for children younger than Robbie.

His father took a long time swallowing.

'It doesn't *read* as if it's symbolic, I mean,' Lois added. 'I read that part about the danger of too much food and the need of experts to tell people how much rich food is good for them. Well' – she laughed a little – 'some people patronize the experts now! – And how is Christ going to reach the people who aren't Christians?'

Arthur could hardly have said it better himself. He glanced at Robbie, who was listening attentively.

'Oh, symbolic mainly,' said Richard. 'And *yet* – with the right attitude and confidence in a superior God, all the fruits of life come, there's no doubt about that. It's just that the majority of people don't give God's laws a chance. Even many people who were in church today.' He looked at Arthur, then back to Lois. 'Many trust entirely in material things – money – to bring in material goods.'

And so did his father, Arthur thought. Did this chicken on the table drop from heaven?

'What're you doing with yourself this next week, Arthur?' asked his father during dessert.

Arthur had thought of taking some books to a secondhand place and selling them, of going to the public library to take out some books to read just for pleasure, and he had also thought of going to the Grove Park tennis courts in the middle of town, maybe with Maggie, to bang a ball around for a couple of hours.

'Done anything about finding a part-time job?' asked his father.

'Not yet.'

'Richard, he's just had a whole week of exams,' said Lois.

'And he's got a free week ahead and the whole summer free as far as I know,' said Richard.

And a few people Arthur knew were going away on vacations with their parents or by themselves. Burt Siegal and Harry Lambert were going to Europe together.

'There's Mrs DeWitt over on Northside,' Richard said to Arthur. 'She's always in need of yard work.'

Mrs DeWitt was a widow who did nothing, as far as Arthur

knew, except take in stray cats and bake cakes now and then for the church or the Red Cross. 'All – right,' Arthur said quietly and grimly. 'I can ask Mrs DeWitt.'

So after dinner, Arthur telephoned Mrs DeWitt and asked if he could do any work for her in her yard.

'Well, there's always *something* to do.' She rambled on. When could he come? Today was a nice day. And how much would he want, because she wasn't prepared to pay more than two dollars an hour, though some young fellows were demanding three or more.

Arthur so detested even her voice, he seized the job with a bitter enthusiasm. 'Two is *fine*, Mrs DeWitt. Today? Four hours of daylight left, at least.'

She demurred at four hours and suggested three.

Arthur took his bike and departed. The DeWitt house was past the college dorms on Northside. The houses here were more modest than those on his parents' street. He saw two of Mrs DeWitt's cats on her front porch. Mrs DeWitt herself was an eyesore, and when she answered the bell, Arthur literally avoided looking at her more than he had to, which maybe gave him an evasive air, but he couldn't help that. She wore flat old house-slippers, no stockings, and even her loose blue dress was dirty and full of food spots. A minute later, Arthur was gazing at her backyard, which looked like a city dump.

'Oh, just stack some of the stuff to one side,' Mrs DeWitt said, when Arthur asked her what she wanted him to do with the broken dog kennel, for instance. He was glad that she went back into the house and didn't stand there watching him, though perhaps she was watching him from the kitchen window.

Arthur hauled a few pieces of old wood and metal, a lawn mower blade rusted beyond salvation, to one side against a fence, as Mrs DeWitt had suggested, then did the same with a few rocks whose position seemed to have no purpose. After a quarter of an hour of this, he investigated the toolshed for a change of activity, and found a hand mower covered with dust and cobwebs, pruning clippers, hedge clippers, all in need of brushing and oiling. The grass needed cutting, but it wasn't very high, indicating that whoever had cut it last must have brought his own mover, because Mrs DeWitt's hadn't been used in many a month. There was a broom. Arthur swept. This led to the discovery of rags, 3-in-1 oil, a whetstone. He oiled and sharpened what he could, then took the pruning clippers to the rosebushes. Appalling, he thought, that any human being could let roses get into such a condition.

When Arthur looked at his wristwatch, it was after 6. He had trimmed the hedges, and he realized that they looked quite pretty now. He began putting tools away, knowing this job always took longer than he thought it would.

'Arthur?' Mrs DeWitt called from her back porch. 'Come in and have a Coke!'

He went into the kitchen. Mrs DeWitt opened a bottle of Coca-Cola for him, but first Arthur took some cold water from the sink, drinking out of his hand. Even Mrs DeWitt's glasses on the drainboard looked slightly dirty.

'Yard looks marvelous, Arthur. I think you did wonders,' she said, smiling.

Arthur could almost bear to look at her as he lifted the Coke bottle. She was fishing for loose dollar bills in an old leather purse and asking him if he could come again soon. She gave him eight dollars.

'Thank you, ma'am,' said Arthur, and promised to telephone her Tuesday when he knew how his week was shaping up. Her kitchen smelled of cat dung, and he was eager to leave it.

Now, he thought, he might try calling Maggie.

His mother was in the kitchen preparing supper, and Arthur saw her typewriter on the coffee table, where she had been doing work for the Beverley Home.

'You've got a streak of grease across your forehead,' his mother said. 'Was it tough work? You look as if you've been at it.'

Arthur laughed. 'Just a plain mess! Anybody phone?'

'No.'

Arthur took a quick shower, then went into the living room and dialed Maggie's number. Maggie's mother answered. Arthur identified himself and asked if Maggie was there.

'No, she's away till tomorrow evening.'

'Oh. – I thought she was away with you and—'

'She said that?' Betty Brewster laughed. 'No, she's with Gloria Farber. Went to visit Gloria's aunt in Indianapolis. Shall I tell her you'll call her again tomorrow night?'

'Yes. Yes, thanks.' Arthur hung up, puzzled. Gloria Farber's *aunt*. What a boring way to spend a weekend! And why should Maggie have told him she was going away with her folks? Was she lying to him and her parents, and was she away with some other fellow?

At supper, Richard asked Arthur about his work that afternoon, and his pay.

'Two dollars an hour. Gus Warylsky takes four, I think.'

'Put that aside toward your college,' said his father.

'Where'm *I* going to college?' Robbie asked, frowning.

'See how good your grades are,' said Lois gently. 'What do you want to be, Robbie?'

Robbie wriggled and thought.

'Still want to be a fireman?' asked Richard.

'No. Maybe I'll be – a *brain* surgeon.'

Arthur guffawed. 'A brain surgeon! Where'd you get that idea?'

'I read it,' said Robbie, and his brows came down again in his old defensive-belligerent style as he looked at his brother.

Arthur kept a pleasant manner. 'Well, you just might be one one day,' he said, and was pleased by the approving glance that his mother gave him. Then the telephone rang, and Arthur felt sure it was Maggie, Maggie back suddenly, and wanting to speak with him. Richard anwered in the living room, and Arthur listened from the hall, dish towel in hand.

'Ye-es – well, good. Glad to hear that. – Yes, he is, when he wants to be,' said his father, chuckling. 'Not quite the same around our own house, I'm afraid. Ha-ha.'

It was old Vera DeWitt, Arthur realized, praising him to the skies so she could have a little more of his slave labor.

His father came into the kitchen smiling. 'That was Mrs DeWitt. She said you wrought a miracle in her yard, Arthur.'

The afternoon of the next day, Arthur rode his bike to the woods on the town's Westside. His mother had left for the home at 12:30 without lunch, and Robbie was lolling on the floor of his room amid *Mad* magazines and religious pamphlets, the latter given to him by their father. Something called *The Waylighter* had arrived on Saturday, a drab black-and-white publication, and Arthur supposed the family had a subscription to that now, too.

He leaned his bike against a tree and walked on. Then he kept his eyes on the ground. Sunday at Mrs DeWitt's, he had found a fossilized sea urchin the size of a golf ball and he had pocketed it. He had five or six such lined up on the table in his room behind his typewriter. When he had been younger than Robbie, he had found two ammonites, of which he was rather proud.

Arthur wondered what he would be doing one year from now, even six months from now? Walking on some sidewalk in Manhattan? Would Maggie still care anything about him? Even remember him? That was a yes-or-no question, with nothing in between. Four more years ahead for both of them, if they both finished college! And at least two more for him, if he made anything of himself! Would any girl in her right mind wait for that?

It was after 4 when Arthur got back home. He had a dead and dried out insect to look at under his microscope, a couple of mushrooms, too. Robbie's cassette played *Peter and the Wolf*. Arthur closed his door, put his acquisitions from the woods on a corner of his table, and picked up a book by Jacques Monod, borrowed from the public library. He liked Monod's combination of science and philosophy, even though he felt he did not understand it completely. It was interesting to imagine nothingness as *something*, as an entity, even though nothingness might never be proven to exist, except of course by theory.

The telephone rang, and Arthur got up.

'Hello, Arthur.' It was Maggie's voice, with a smile in it.

'You're back?'

'This afternoon. Mom said you phoned.'

'Nice weekend?'

'Ye-es,' she drawled, sounding oddly shy, as she often did.

'Well – when can I see you?'

'Tonight? At seven?'

By 6:30 Arthur had showered, scrubbed his nails with care, scraped at his jaws with his razor, and put on white poplin trousers.

'Maggie again,' said his mother as he strolled into the kitchen.

His father was in the living room with the newspaper. 'Don't tell Dad I've got a date with her, would you, Mom?' Arthur whispered, frowning.

'He's got nothing against her! Bring her for dinner sometime.'

Arthur got on his bike.

Maggie looked prettier than ever in a pink and white shirt and blue slacks with a crease in them. Arthur found plump girls in sloppy slacks repellent. Maggie looked like a fashion model. She gave him a rum and Coke.

'My dad's home tonight,' Maggie said. 'You probably won't meet him, because he's sleeping till dinner.'

They had just returned to the living room, when Arthur saw a man coming down the stairs in a bathrobe and slippers.

'Oh, sorry, Mag,' he said, stopping at the foot of the stairs.

'Evening,' he said to Arthur. 'Just looking for Sunday's paper. Is it anywhere around?' He was tall and broad-shouldered, with blondish hair now tousled as if he had just woken up.

'Kitchen. I'll get it. – Dad, this is Arthur Alderman. My dad.'

'How do you do?' said Arthur.

'Hello, Arthur,' said her father, politely enough, but looking asleep on his feet.

Maggie came back with the bulky *Herald* Sunday edition.

'Have a nice evening. I'm going to fall asleep again with this.' He waved a hand and climbed the stairs.

'He's often like this – the day he gets home,' Maggie said.

Arthur nodded. Her father looked less forbidding than he had feared.

An hour later, when they were at Hamburger Harry's, Arthur asked, 'Why'd you say you were with your folks last weekend?'

'Oh – I dunno. Just to be secretive, maybe. We didn't do anything interesting. I just wanted to get away for a couple of days after exams.'

'Three nights at somebody's *aunt's*?'

'Her aunt's got a swimming pool. – We took walks – and talked.'

With a girl, Arthur thought. 'Why can't we do that some weekend? How about the Log Cabins Motel on Westside? Nice woods around there for walking.'

Maggie laughed. 'Not sure what my family would say to that!'

Arthur wasn't sure how to go on from there. But what did it matter if Maggie was in a happy mood, which she was?

'I'll know about Radcliffe in a month,' Maggie said. 'It depends on the math course that I start this week. There's an exam on that at the end – natch.'

Arthur's heart dipped as if this were the first time he had heard about Radcliffe. Maggie wouldn't be coming back to Chalmerston often, if she went to Radcliffe – four times a year, maybe. And he wouldn't be able to afford a lot of trips back either.

'You don't look very pleased,' Maggie said. She gave a laugh, a bit shrill and unlike her. 'My father just donated a thousand dollars to Radcliffe – as a Harvard man, but he mentioned that his daughter expected to go to Radcliffe. Isn't that shameful? Almost like bribery.'

'No. I've heard of it.' But Arthur felt bitter, because his father certainly wasn't giving a thousand dollars to Columbia. 'Know what I wish,' said Arthur, as a beer he had signaled for arrived in record time. 'That I had an apartment in the university dorms right now and I could invite you and—'

'You're always talking about the same thing!' Maggie's cheeks were pink.

'No! I was about to say we'd sit on the sofa and watch TV – the way hundreds of students must be doing *this minute* – over on Northside.' He had not been thinking specifically about going to bed with Maggie, but he was suddenly inspired to say, 'By the way, I can take precautions – next time.' He had prepared this phrase at home and thought it more polite than to suggest that Maggie take the pill. He meant condoms, and he had acquired some.

Maggie glanced down at the table.

'Did I say something wrong? Sorry if I did.' The jukebox was playing now, and no one could possibly have overheard.

'No, but – I don't want to talk about that now.'

Change the subject, Arthur thought. He thought of Mrs DeWitt and laughed. 'Shall I tell you how I spent Sunday afternoon? Oh, and Saturday night a rotten party. Not rotten, just boring without you. Couple of people asked why you weren't with me, in fact.'

'Whose party?'

'Ruthie's. Very ordinary batch. Roxanne – I didn't stay long. Don't know why I went.'

Maggie said nothing. Then she wanted to leave.

Maggie was already outside. Then, to his surprise, she took his hand and smiled at him, and Arthur felt easier. He had thought she was annoyed by what he had said about taking precautions, but it was wiser to be definite about it, Arthur had read in quite a few books on the subject. However, Maggie wasn't cooling toward him, or she wouldn't be holding his hand, walking along in a happy way, looking up at the June bugs that circled the street lamps. His optimism lasted the rest of the evening, which was short, because Maggie said she wanted to get some sleep.

Arthur walked to her front door with her, and suddenly they were embracing, kissing each other under the little roof there. Arthur went down the steps weak-kneed and nearly fell.

'Arthur!' Maggie whispered. 'See you tomorrow?'

'Sure! What time?'

'Phone me after ten tomorrow morning?'

6

Arthur did the shopping at the supermarket the next morning. His mother was clearing the spare room chest and the closet for his grandmother, who was not coming till the end of June, but his mother liked to start early on a task, drop it, then at the last minute finish it.

The Chalmerston supermarket stayed open day and night, even on weekends. Arthur rather enjoyed its Aladdin's cave atmosphere. Suddenly he saw Gloria Farber beside him, pushing her cart in the opposite direction.

'Well, Arthur! – And how are *you*?' She looked him up and down with a smile that Arthur felt was cool, even unfriendly.

'Okay thanks.' He might have said, 'Hope you had a nice weekend,' but Gloria had passed him. Slightly snooty type, Arthur had always thought.

Arthur cycled home with groceries in the front basket of his bike and in sacks on either side of his back wheel.

Mrs DeWitt had telephoned, his mother came into the kitchen to tell him, and asked if he could come over this afternoon around 3 to work for an hour or so. 'I told her you probably could, and if she didn't hear from you, you'd be there.'

'I could, sure. But I was going to look around town this

afternoon for a job.' Arthur knew his mother was thinking of Richard, of how virtuous his father thought it, that Arthur worked at such low pay and at such a low labor, too. Arthur shook his head nervously. 'I'll go. That job is definite and what I'm looking for isn't.'

His mother said softly, 'It'd please your father if you went once more.'

He nodded and started to leave the kitchen, when he noticed a new copy of *Plain Truth* with its glossy cover plus a black plastic leather-covered Bible at the end of the bench by the dining table. Had his father been quoting at breakfast? Arthur hadn't been up for breakfast. There was even more stuff in his parents' bedroom, Arthur knew. His father had pushed some magazines on him, just like the people who knocked on the door, giving you something free at first, then you were supposed to subscribe. His mother had said they had started to turn up at the door, just as Maggie had said they had at her house. Robbie actually enjoyed the stuff, Arthur knew, but Robbie had only recently stopped being afraid of the dark and being able to sleep with his light out, and he had devoutly believed in ghosts at the age of twelve. Arthur glanced at his wristwatch, saw it was not yet 10, then saw his mother standing in the doorway of the living room, watching him.

Arthur felt suddenly angry, annoyed by his own thoughts, and he said in a level tone, 'I wish Dad would keep this stuff out of the kitchen, at least. It's already all over the living room.'

'You mean the Bible?' his mother asked, and laughed.

'The other stuff. – These magazines are even anti-evolution. You must've noticed, Mom. Can't even call them anti, because they don't even bother to argue about it.' How could his mother not have noticed that his father had decided to be 'anti,' because that had been the subject at dinner one night. His father had been maddeningly vague, not exactly denying the evidence provided by fossils, just hanging on in a fuzzy way to the possibility that God had created Adam and Eve instantly one day about six thousand years ago, because the Bible said so. At repeated signs from his mother, Arthur had shut up that evening.

'Don't worry so much about it, Arthur. Richard'll cool down. We both should keep calm and act like grown-ups, don't you think so?'

His mother wasn't swallowing hook, line and sinker all the stuff his father was spouting, Arthur knew. She simply wanted to keep the peace, 'to compromise' as she had once put it, but to Arthur there could be no compromise, no ground-yielding, about such an obvious fact as the age of certain forms of life.

That morning, Arthur tackled the clothesline pole in the backyard. His anger or unease had not left him, even though his telephone conversation with Maggie at half past 10 had been entirely positive. He was invited for dinner at Maggie's, and her father would be there. 'Just a family dinner. My dad has to leave at ten for Indi, so can you come at a quarter of seven?'

When Arthur turned the clothesline pole on its side, the bottom of the metal base reminded him of a girl's sexual organs, the hole in the centre, the four supports splayed around like limbs. Why should an unattractive idea like that pop into his head? Aesthetically ugly! And he had thought of Roxanne at once. Well, she was the splayed type, all right, and what fellow hadn't been to bed with her, except maybe Gus? Good for Gus, if he hadn't been! If anything was a stupid 'sin,' as his father would call it, it was his own brief roll in the hay with Roxanne, maybe fifteen minutes, or even ten, of silly grappling and fumbling, finally laughter, thank God. Roxanne had had gin and tonic that afternoon at her house, Arthur remembered. It had seemed very dangerous and sophisticated. Arthur tightened the bolts with all his strength and set the thing upright again, poured a bucket of water on the ground, wielded a fork for a minute, and finally hammered the circular base in as hard as he could.

After lunch, Arthur put on a clean shirt and trousers and rode his bike into town, down Main Street, which had a lot of small shops. He walked his bike along the sidewalk, finally leaned it against a lamppost visible from the inside of a haberdashery, and went in to inquire in regard to the SALES HELP WANTED sign in the front window. The manager told him that they had hired someone an hour ago and hadn't yet removed the sign.

A shop called simply Shoe Repair, but which also sold shoes, had a sign in the window, and Arthur went in. This was a shop not much bigger than his family's living room, with shoe bargains on two tables, shoe boxes against the walls all the way to the ceiling, and a tiny repair shop at the rear. Arthur spoke to the balding man in shirtsleeves and vest behind the cash register, whose face Arthur vaguely remembered, because the Aldermans had bought shoes here. Within two minutes, Arthur had an afternoon job: three dollars and fifty cents an hour, with a promise from Arthur to work at least four hours a day, five days a week, and he could work all day Saturdays at the same rate, if he chose. The balding man said:

'I remember you when you were a much smaller boy. Got a younger brother, haven't you?'

'Yes, sir.'

'Finished high school now?'

'This summer, yes. I'll be going to college in September.'

'My name's Robertson. You can call me Tom. Makes things easier. See you tomorrow at one, Arthur.' He said the last words hastily, because a woman was asking him if he had a size smaller of a shoe she held in her hand.

Arthur felt cheered. What would it be like to have a father like that, a man who looked at you with some interest in his eyes when he talked? There was *his* father, looking on the fence now about whether to give in to middle age, which Tom Robertson had certainly given in to, or to try to stave it off by buying fancy striped shirts and remembering to hold his waistline in now and then.

The thought reminded Arthur that he wanted a new shirt for this evening. He had looked over his shirts after his phone call to Maggie, and none had seemed right or good enough for tonight. His eye fell on a conservative, good-looking navy blue with white buttons in the window of a men's shop. Seventeen ninety-five, reduced price at that, and it was a Viyella. Arthur again placed his bike within view and entered the shop with deliberate cool, as if price were of no importance, though he had barely twenty dollars with him. And would his father stop his allowance, now that he had a part-time job? Very likely.

'I'll take it,' said Arthur, looking at himself in the mirror in the square-tailed shirt.

When Arthur looked back on the evening at Maggie's, he wondered why he had been so anxious. The atmosphere had been quite unsticky. Maggie's mother Betty had put a gin and tonic in his hand, and then laughing, had excused herself, because she hadn't asked him if he wanted it. Maggie had told her that he liked gin and tonics. Arthur kept it. Maggie's father had come down at the last minute before dinner, in his uniform trousers and white shirt without tie or jacket, and he had paid little attention to Arthur, which in a way had been a relief. Warren had been expecting the telephone to ring (it did not) to inform him that he had to replace another pilot on a short late flight tonight. If not, he was going to sleep at the hotel owned by Sigma Airlines near the Indi airport, as he usually did before a flight in the morning. A happy element in the evening was Maggie's attitude: She acted as if she wanted her parents, especially her father, to like him. After her father left at 10, Arthur even helped in the kitchen. Then he and Maggie had been alone in the living room for a while. '... Most boys are joking and pretending all the time ...' The words before that and after, Arthur couldn't remember. But Maggie had said she liked him because he was serious.

On his bed that night, Arthur found one of his father's

little pamphlets whose title in bold black letters was FOR DISBELIEVERS. Well, not tonight. Tonight he believed in a lot of things, even in himself, in himself and Maggie, but not in this crap! And what had he done wrong today?

He carefully unbuttoned his new shirt. 'All signals go,' he said softly, picked up the pamphlet with two fingers, and dropped it on the floor by his closed door. Tomorrow it could get lost among the other stuff in the living room.

7

June spread itself over the town, making lawns green, the woods lush, gardens bright with flowers, in day after day of sunshine. Sometimes at 6 p.m. when Arthur cycled home from Shoe Repair, there would be a half hour of light rain, as if nature were doing the exactly correct watering that year. Arthur felt it was the happiest month of his life. His grades had averaged 88, a 75 in French having pulled him down and a 96 in biology having pulled up the average of six subjects.

He had even attended the Chalmerston High School graduation rites in cap and gown, after hesitation. A stuffy ceremony with beaming parents was Arthur's idea of hell and absurdity, because if you passed the exams, you made it and that was that. But Maggie was going, with an attitude of 'sure it's silly, but it doesn't take long and people expect it.' So Arthur went, and his family was represented by his mother and a slightly reluctant Robbie in the auditorium audience. His father said he had important clients to see that Tuesday morning and couldn't get away. When Arthur came home with his mother at noon, she told him there was a surprise for him on the table in his room. This was a new typewriter, a beautiful blue Olympia portable, clean and shining, lovely. Arthur had had his present typewriter since the age of ten, though it still worked perfectly.

'I thought you could use a second to take with you east,' said his mother. 'Then you'll have your old one here when you come home on visits.'

He had sent off his report card to the Columbia admissions officer, a Mr Anthony Xarrip, with a letter reminding Mr Xarrip of the favorable comments six months ago of Mr Cooper of the biology department of Chalmerston High School. Arthur wrote the letter twice to get it right and showed it to his mother before he sealed it. His mother was now not a hundred percent sure that his father would agree to pay all of Arthur's Columbia fees, or not without a little more groveling, Arthur gathered, but he could also see that his mother was hopeful.

'There's such a thing as paying a family back,' Arthur said to his mother. 'I said that to Dad. I don't like the idea of a part-time job while I'm at Columbia. I suppose Dad'll think that sounds lazy.' College was a full-time job, Arthur thought, and he had said that before to his mother.

'Well – we'll see,' said his mother.

One evening Arthur overheard his father saying to his mother in the kitchen, 'But what does he do with his mornings? Sleep? He's never even out of bed when I leave the house.'

'He's at the library a couple of mornings a week. He reads science books there – the ones people can't take out,' his mother replied.

Arthur was tempted to linger in the hall to hear more, but he went on into the living room, where he had intended to go. So his father wanted him to take a full-time job now, or maybe another part-time in the morning. And his father had stopped his allowance. Arthur did not think Tom Robertson had enough work for him on an eight-hour-day basis, because one of the repair shop boys helped out as salesman whenever there were a lot of customers.

Maggie came twice for dinner, and his mother liked her quite well and said so, though his father had been merely polite and made no comment later. Robbie had only stared at Maggie, hostile or curious, Arthur couldn't tell.

'My grandmother's coming the last week of June,' Arthur said to Maggie. 'I want you to meet her. She plays golf. And she doesn't let herself get pushed around by my father.' He told Maggie that his grandmother had been a dancer in several musicals in New York and that when his grandfather Waggoner had died ten years ago, she had opened a dance school in Kansas City, which she was still managing. 'Tangos and stuff, what she calls ballroom dancing,' Arthur said. 'But she has ballet classes for kids – and they go on from there or not.'

The atmosphere in the Alderman house improved as soon as his grandmother arrived. She had presents, a striped cotton bathrobe (dressing gown, she called it) made in England for Arthur, a pressure cooker for his mother, an electronic game for Robbie, something for his father who was not yet home. It was not quite 6 o'clock.

'You've grown – oh, two inches since I saw you, Arthur.'

Arthur smiled, knowing it wasn't true, since Christmas.

His grandmother Joan had brown wavy hair which she kept free of gray with some kind of rinse, she had told Arthur, but the result was nice. She was shorter than his mother, sturdier in a fit and athletic way, though there was a resemblance between them in their blue eyes with their sharp-cornered lids. It was hard for Arthur to realize that his grandmother was sixty.

In the few minutes before his father's arrival, Arthur told his grandmother about his 88 average on his finals and his afternoon job, and since his grandmother asked about 'any girlfriend,' Arthur said he quite liked a girl called Maggie.

'I told Maggie you were staying a week. Hope it's longer.'

'Oh, we'll see,' said his grandmother cheerfully.

They were in the kitchen, Arthur making the salad, and Robbie had gone to his room with the new electronic game.

'And – I'm doing some yard work for a woman called DeWitt,' Arthur said. 'Dirty old dump full of cats. You'd have to smell it to believe it. Bet she's got twelve!'

'Didn't I meet her once, Loey?' Joan asked. 'Four feet square and a lot of white hair?' Joan laughed and turned her blue-mascaraed eyes toward Arthur. 'Seems to me I met her at a church thing here. She was going on about cats then.'

'Speaking of church,' Arthur began, smiling.

'Now, Arthur,' said his mother. 'Yes, Mama, I've got to tell you, Richard has discovered God, as Arthur puts it. Maybe that's the best way of—'

'He's a born-again,' said Arthur.

'I wrote you a little about it, I know, Mama. Now we say grace and it's church every Sunday – since Robbie pulled through with that tonsil crisis, remember?'

Joan was listening attentively and had glanced at Arthur. 'Ah, yes, I've heard of these things. So Richard talks about walking with God, things like that?'

'Yes!' Arthur said.

'Yes,' said his mother. 'So we've bought an ecclesiastical encyclopedia and subscribed to a few magazines that keep turning up in the mailbox—' She laughed a little. 'Just wanted to warn you that—' She broke off, because Richard's car at that moment was visible out the kitchen window, turning into the driveway.

'You should see these magazines, Grandma,' Arthur said. 'They're anti-everything, anti-liberal, anti-abortion, anti-women's rights – really anti-Catholics and Jews, but they don't exactly say so.'

'All *right*, Arthur,' said his mother.

Arthur heard his father's car door slam in the garage. 'Have to add,' Arthur said to his grandmother, 'when Christ comes again, we'll all speak one language. English, of course.'

The kitchen door opened. 'Well, Joan!' said Richard. 'Welcome to our homestead! How are you?'

They kissed cheeks.

'Just fine,' said Joan. 'You're looking *very* well!'

'I've put on three pounds, don't tell *me*!' Richard said, tugging his seersucker jacket down. 'All having drinks? Where's mine?'

'In the fridge, dear.' Lois swung around to open it for him.

Arthur watched his father take the Alexander from the top shelf of the fridge. His mother always made him this sweet drink on special occasions.

'To you, dear mother-in-law!' Richard said, holding his glass aloft. 'We're pleased as can be to see you!'

Half an hour later, his father was saying, 'Now we will all bow our heads for a moment.'

His mother's laugh at something died abruptly. They were all seated, the five of them, at the pretty table in the kitchen. Arthur's grandmother bent her head obediently, even clasped her hands.

'Father, we thank Thee for the blessings spread before us.

'Enable us to be worthy of Thy love and kindness. Protect our home and fill – fill our souls as You have filled our – table.'

Arthur tried to suppress a laugh, but still it came out, because he had thought his father, at a loss for a word, had been about to say filled our bowls or bowels or even stomachs.

'*Arthur!*' said his mother.

His father gave him a look.

Robbie, unperturbed, gazed with interest at the big steak that his father had begun to slice.

'What've you been doing today?' Joan asked Robbie.

'Experimenting with worms,' said Robbie.

'How?' asked Arthur. 'Sticking pins in them, I suppose.'

'In water.' Robbie looked at his brother with the sudden seriousness that his lean face could take on. 'They drown.'

'They're land creatures. Of course they drown,' Arthur said. '*Phylum Annelida, lumbrica terrestris*, amen. Why'd you do that?'

'Pass me your grandmother's plate, Arthur,' said Richard with impatience.

'Because I'm going fishing again,' said Robbie.

'Where do you go fishing?' asked Joan.

'Delmar Lake. Fellows I met at the swimming pool. *Older* fellows,' said Robbie with a glance at Arthur. 'Men.'

'How old? Twenty? Gosh! Any girls?' asked Arthur.

'Robbie, what kind of boat were you in? Ordinary rowboat?' Lois asked.

Robbie hesitated. 'A canoe.'

'That's not true!' said Arthur. 'Never seen a canoe at those boat houses on Delmar Lake.'

'Arthur, cool down,' said his mother. 'All right, Robbie, I want you just to tell me next time you go. *When* you go. Do you understand? I've heard of people—'

'You're collecting worms for the next fishing trip?' asked Joan.

'Not yet. I was experimenting to see how long they'll keep wiggling if they're under water for so long.'

Arthur groaned. Submersion, drowning, and then their limp forms would be stirred on the hook by the water. That was the way it would go in fishing. 'How many times has he been out fishing?' Arthur asked his mother, mildly interested, because Robbie was accident-prone. Robbie would lean over a boat's side, reaching for something, and just fall in.

'*I* don't know.' Then Lois said to her mother, 'We're treating Robbie like a big boy this year, leaving him on his own in the afternoons, and he promised not to go off anywhere without telling me. Didn't you, Robbie?'

'I did say I was going fishing last Friday, and you said okay,' replied Robbie, and his face grew a little pink.

'Just always say where you're going, Robbie,' said Richard, 'and tell your mother who you're with. These older fellows, who are they?'

'Reggie Dewey – He's eighteen. St—'

'School drop-out,' Arthur put in. 'I know him.'

'Steve and Bill,' Robbie went on. 'Bill and a man named Jeff are much older.'

'How do you get to Delmar Lake, on your bike?' Arthur asked. The lake was nearly three miles away.

'Reggie or Jeff picks me up. Once I went on my bike.'

'I don't think I like the sound of that,' Richard murmured in Lois's direction. 'You're not the best swimmer in the world, Robbie, and you can't depend on another fellow in the boat – risking his life just to jump in after you.'

'Maybe I can count on *God*,' Robbie said.

Arthur laughed and almost swallowed something the wrong way. He looked at his grandmother, who was smiling and listening to all this with interest.

'Now, Robbie, God helped you through one really – bad – spot,' said Richard, trying to make every word sink in. 'Don't you tempt Him by your own foolish behavior. God might not be ready with a second miracle just to save *you*.'

Robbie's blondish brows drew closer together. 'I dig worms for the fellows. I bait the hooks. The fellows like me.'

'Sure,' Arthur said. 'I bet you're their slave.'

'They say I can keep quiet when everybody's got to be quiet,' Robbie continued to his father. 'That's why they like me.'

Around midnight, his grandmother rapped on Arthur's door. He had been hoping she would do exactly that and had left his door the least bit ajar. He was in bed, reading.

'Come in,' Arthur said with a big smile. 'Close the door. Can you find a place to sit?' He jumped out of bed, but he had already cleared his armchair and turned it facing his bed.

'Well, well, nice to be here, Arthur,' said his grandmother, sitting down. She was in slippers and nightgown and a pretty robe of blue and yellow.

Arthur put on his new dressing gown and sat on the edge of his bed. 'So – you didn't hear as much about religion tonight as I'd feared, but – what do you think?'

'About Richard? About life?' She leaned forward and laughed heartily but softly. 'Does it bother you so much? – You're looking well, Arthur. Happier than the last time I saw you.'

Had he been moping over a girl at Christmas? He couldn't remember. 'I told you I met a nice girl. I *have* a nice girl. She's different – from most girls.'

'How different?'

Arthur looked at the ceiling. 'First, she's quite pretty and she doesn't use it. And she's reliable.'

'I see,' said his grandmother. 'And what's she interested in? She's going to go to college, too?'

'Radcliffe. Interested in puppets. Stage designing. Something to do with people, she says, but she doesn't know exactly what yet. So she wants to start with liberal arts at Radcliffe until she – decides. Oh, you'll meet her, maybe this week. – But what did you think of the prayer tonight, the blessing? Doesn't it make you feel sort of stiff?'

'Well—' His grandmother let several seconds pass. 'Harmless, though, isn't it? If it makes him feel better. I forgot my cigarettes and I'd love one. One minute while I—'

'Allow me!' Arthur said before his grandmother could rise from her chair. He whisked his pack of Marlboros from the top of his chest of drawers. 'These okay?'

'Perfect. I limit myself to five a day, but I love every one.'

'It's this holier-than-thou stuff that bugs me,' Arthur went on, returning to the edge of his bed. 'Dad walks around as if he's holding God's right hand. Well, maybe so am I – in a way. But I'm not telling other people to read a lot of – nonsense,' Arthur said instead of the word crap. 'I'm talking about the pamphlets around the house. And I don't tell other people to work their fingers to the bone.'

'Is that what he's telling you to do?'

'Yes. Not that I mind so much. – I might've taken a summer job without *his* pushing, because I have to set some money aside for Columbia, I don't think Dad's going to finance me. Not for all of it, anyway. That's something new, too.'

'Well, well!' She drew on her cigarette thoughtfully, then leaned forward and whispered, 'Did they join a new church?'

'No, it's the same old church, First Church of Christ Gospel.' Arthur could see that his grandmother was relieved at this, because some of the churches in town were pretty wild and there were gatherings at least twice a week at places in town with gospel singing and public confessions, something like the Holy Rollers, and certainly his parents hadn't gone that far. 'Church every Sunday now, as Mom said. I have to go sometimes to please Mom. I—' Arthur realized that he would not be going to church, if it weren't for Columbia. He was sucking up.

8

Arthur and his mother decided on Thursday as the evening to ask Maggie for dinner. He telephoned Maggie, and to his surprise she seemed shy about coming.

'I'm not feeling very social these days,' Maggie said. 'Don't know why.'

After another effort, Arthur persuaded her, however. Arthur had telephoned from Shoe Repair, and he had hoped to be able to see her that evening, even if only to take a walk, but she said she had to stay alone and finish her homework for the math cram course. Arthur offered to help her with it, but Maggie declined that, too.

That afternoon, his grandmother looked in on him at Shoe Repair, as she had promised to do. Yesterday and today she had driven his mother to the Beverley Home for Children around 1, then kept the car to cruise around in with Robbie or go to the Chalmerston Golf Club, which was not really a club, because anyone could play there.

'I think this is charming!' Joan said, looking around at the shoebox-lined walls of the little shop. 'So old-fashioned!' She was whispering, so that Tom Robertson, who indeed looked like the owner and was near them at the repair counter, wouldn't hear her.

'Doing a lot of business!' Arthur whispered back.

'I'll look around,' his grandmother said, when Arthur was accosted by a woman carrying a pair of white shoes.

Arthur took the shoes and the money back to the cash register. Often he worked the cash register too, and in fact since he now knew the stock, his and Tom's work was very similar. Arthur put the white shoes in one of their plain brown bags and gave the woman her change. 'Thanks, and have a nice day,' said Arthur.

His grandmother had sat down in one of the two chairs of the establishment and was trying on house slippers. She wore her black and white golf shoes with stockings, a cotton skirt and blouse, and Arthur thought, as he often did, that she looked amazingly young, hardly older than his mother.

Arthur said to Tom, 'I'd like you to meet my grandmother – Joan Waggoner. Tom Robertson.'

'Well! Arthur's grandmother! A pleasure, Mrs Waggoner!'

'How do you do, Mr Robertson,' Joan replied. 'I've been admiring your store. It looks human.'

'You're here on a visit, Arthur told me.'

'Yes, a week or so. – I think I'll take these slippers. They're so cozy! I haven't had anything like them since I was ten years old.'

The slippers were entirely rabbit hide with the fur inside. Tom looked on the brink of making a present of them, but Arthur spread his hands sideways and frowned to convey that his grandmother wouldn't like that. Arthur took the slippers and the ten-dollar bill his grandmother gave him. The slippers were eight dollars and ninety-five cents.

'How's Arthur doing? Satisfactory?'

Arthur didn't hear Tom's reply. There was a man at the repair counter with a pair of shoes to be half-soled.

That evening during dinner, his grandmother told Arthur that Tom had given quite a good report on him. She added to Richard,

'He said Arthur had been quick to learn the stock and hadn't once been late for work.' She gave Arthur a smile.

'Umph,' said his father.

They were dining at El Chico's, a rather swanky Mexican restaurant where the food was excellent and the beer came in huge, cold, stemmed glasses. The dinner had been preceded by pink tequila highballs all round, except for Robbie who was now on 7-Ups. For Arthur the dinner was unusual for two reasons. His father had not said grace before they all fell to. Maybe Mexican food wasn't worthy of being blessed? And his brother's voice underwent a transformation at the table. When he had sat down, Robbie had said in his squeaky, usual voice, 'I don't know what I want yet. Sure, I know what it means, it's written underneath in *English*!' Then during Arthur's second beer, Robbie said:

'Jeff caught a bass today. Big one. The one I caught was – much littler.'

Arthur noticed the deep tone, and noticed that his mother had almost jumped. 'Well, well, a *bass*,' Arthur said solemnly.

'Is that the – questionable item I saw wrapped up in newspaper in the fridge?' asked their father.

Robbie was now at the plate-scraping stage of his repast. 'Yup,' he replied in the same new voice and reached for another tortilla.

Well, Arthur thought, Robbie was almost fifteen, after all. And he seemed to be growing visibly, like bamboo. Robbie was going to be taller than he. Arthur was a bit envious of that.

On Thursday evening at dinner they had to hear grace said by Richard, and Arthur stole a glance at Maggie's bowed head. Her lips were serious, her lightly mascaraed eyelids quivered over her closed eyes. At the end, Arthur straightened up and smiled at Maggie, pleased that he had managed not to hear one boring word of what his father had said.

'Have you visited Radcliffe and seen the campus there?' Joan asked Maggie.

Maggie said she had, when her father had gone to a Harvard reunion a couple of years ago. His grandmother talked quite a lot with Maggie and in an easy manner. Maggie looked as beautiful as ever and kept the calm that Arthur so admired, but he thought underneath it she was nervous and that she looked even a little sad. Was that stupid math course bothering her this much? He was aware of a June bug bumping at the screen door between the kitchen and the garage. His mother served the raspberry sherbert dessert. Then there was coffee in the living room. Maggie and his grandmother sat on the sofa.

'Arthur tells me you haven't decided what your major will be, Maggie,' his grandmother said.

'No. So far, English literature and composition. I know that sounds vague – because what do you do with it afterward? I think – after the first year or during the first year, I'll make a decision.'

Then Arthur's father put in a few droning words that made Arthur shrink into his chair. His father didn't use the word God, but something like the hand of Providence that would guide Maggie into the right path herself. Arthur was aware of Maggie's shyness for a few seconds at finding herself the center of attention. To Arthur's relief, she made no reply.

It was hardly 10 when Maggie said she should be leaving. Arthur didn't mind, because he was going to be alone with her in the car when she drove home and maybe she would want to go somewhere. Maggie thanked his mother, said good night to his grandmother, then to his father. Robbie had disappeared.

Arthur walked out with Maggie, and they got into her car. 'Going to play golf with my grandmother?' he asked, smiling. He had heard his grandmother asking Maggie if she played.

'Doubt it. I'm better at tennis. Anyway just now – not much time.' She started driving toward her house.

'Something the matter, Maggie?'

She took a long time to answer. 'Oh – I'll tell you tomorrow.'

'Tell me now. – What happened?'

Maggie drew her lips back from her teeth, and Arthur glanced at the road ahead to see if they were about to hit something, but the road was clear. Near her house, Maggie turned a corner into a darker street and stopped at the edge. Then she sighed, like a gasp. 'If you want to know – I'm pregnant.'

He stared at her. She was looking down at the lighted dashboard. 'Are you sure, Maggie?'

'Positive.'

It was his fault. Arthur felt that a bomb had hit him. Two months ago. Arthur remembered the date, May second. They hadn't been to bed together since. 'Not – not impossible we could get married.' It seemed a simple and happy solution at that instant.

'Don't be silly, *I* can't – and you can't. Got a cigarette? I left mine at your place.'

Arthur whipped his cigarettes out of his pocket and dropped them on the floor of the car. He lit her cigarette with a slightly shaking hand. 'Why didn't you tell me before?'

'Because I thought the abortion would *do* it,' she replied with impatience.

'What abortion?'

'That weekend I went away.' Maggie glanced at him and he saw a flash in her eyes. 'I told my parents I was with Gloria at her aunt's and told Gloria I was with – a boyfriend, and in case my parents phoned her aunt – well, they didn't. But I went to Indi by myself.'

Arthur felt stunned. 'You had an abortion?'

'*Yes*, the operation and – I paid him, but – I've heard of these things. They just don't do a good job.' Maggie looked through the windshield and drew on her cigarette. 'Now you know why I'm nervous. Got to find another doctor.'

'Your mother knows?'

'No.'

Arthur's heart was beating as if he were running. 'I'll find a doctor, Maggie, don't you worry. I'll pay for it. What does it cost?'

'Five hundred. That one did. – I sold a gold bracelet in Indi, and if Mom notices I haven't got it, I'll tell her I lost it!' Maggie tried to laugh.

'Son-of-a-bitch doctor in Indi,' Arthur muttered.

'Bum steer from Roxanne, that doctor.'

'Roxanne?'

Maggie reached for the ignition key, then let her hand fall in her lap. 'I couldn't ask our family doctor – Dr Moodie – for the name of someone who'd do it.'

Arthur winced. Now he knew why Roxanne had given him a sly look at Ruthie's party that Saturday. Roxanne must have supposed he knew why Maggie had been out of town. 'I'll find a good doctor, Maggie. I'll try at the Medical Building tomorrow. Reliable place. How about that?'

'All right, try it.' She was backing around the dark corner. 'You won't say my name, will you? They don't care as long as they're paid.'

'I won't!'

The Brewsters' living room light was on, and Arthur looked dismally away from the house, fumbled with the door handle and got out. He had wanted to embrace Maggie, but had been afraid she would push him away. 'Can I call you tomorrow at noon?' he whispered.

'Twelve-thirty. I'm in that math class till noon.'

Arthur walked into the darkness, frowning, clenching his teeth. Five hundred dollars? Sure! Sell his microscope or pawn it, get his savings out of the bank. And hide the situation from his father! Suddenly Arthur was on home ground, almost. Norma Keer's light was on. This was not an evening to visit Norma.

The lights were on also at his family's kitchen window and

in the living room. Arthur crept in via the unlocked front door, passed the living room whence came voices and laughter, and went to his own room. He was in pajamas and about to turn his light out, when he heard his grandmother's tap at the door.

'Yup?' Arthur said.

His grandmother opened the door. 'I saw you sneaking in. Just wanted to say I think your friend Maggie is lovely. I thought you'd like to hear that.' She had come in but not quite closed the door. 'What's the matter, Arthur?'

'Nothing!' Arthur said, sitting down nervously on the edge of his bed. He knew he wasn't going to fool his grandmother, so he added, 'Little quarrel. Not important.' He jumped up again. 'Sit down, Grandma!' Arthur moved his armchair a fraction and reached for a cigarette. 'Like one?'

His grandmother accepted. 'And Maggie's very fond of you, I think.'

'Do you?' said Arthur automatically, politely, though at the same time he felt tears about to pop out of his eyes, and he blinked. 'Well, too bad I'm not twenty-two or so – and she weren't going off for four years. Think of all the older guys she'll meet in the east. Ha-ava-ad men.'

Joan smiled and adjusted her long black skirt over her crossed legs. 'Worry about that – later, maybe. Be happy while you can.' She looked at him with narrowed eyes and drew on her cigarette.

Arthur blinked again. 'Anything fascinating happen after I left tonight?'

'No-o. We were talking about Robbie – after he went off to bed.' She laughed a little. 'He was switching on the TV and he knocked over the little vase on the table there. So I got a sponge from the kitchen, and it was nothing at all, because nothing broke. But Robbie blew up in a rage as if we were scolding him!'

'I know. He'll die of apoplexy before he's twenty.'

'Where'd he pick up this anxiety? Or inferiority? – I don't

remember you teasing him a lot when he was little. You didn't, did you, Arthur?'

'No, Grandma. Just ask Mom. And now – why does he hang around these older guys? Never kids his own age. I can't figure him.'

'Mm-m.' His grandmother looked at the ceiling. ''Tis odd that he likes sitting in a rowboat without moving for hours on end.' She laughed again. 'Without moving or saying a word, he tells me with a certain pride. And tonight I thought we'd have to give him a sedative. Red in the face—' She lowered her voice, in case Robbie in the next room could hear. Then she got up and kissed Arthur on the cheek. 'Good night, dear boy.'

Arthur put out his light and lay face down with his hands clenched in fists under his pillow. What a good show Maggie had put on tonight for his family! It was his fault! Why hadn't he taken precautions? And Maggie had the bother of it, the shame, the pain, the trouble, the expense, the secrecy! Starting now, he had to help her and stand by her. The difficulty came from other people, the outside world. Tomorrow he couldn't even tell a doctor Maggie's name.

9

The next morning just after 9, Arthur was walking down the marble-floored corridor of the Medical Building. He stopped at the white-on-black panel of doctors' names between the elevators. The Alderman family doctor, Dr A. Swithers, caught his eye unpleasantly, and so did the name of Dr F. Moodie, whom Maggie had mentioned. He decided to try a Dr G. Robinson, because the name reminded him of Tom Robertson, who was decent. Arthur went to the receptionist's desk, where the girl was quite cool, because he had no appointment.

'It's just to ask a question. Five minutes – or less.' The girl telephoned somewhere, then told Arthur that Dr Robinson's secretary could speak to him in room 809.

Arthur rode up to the eighth floor. A girl secretary sat at a desk in room 809, and there were four doors in the room, all closed, with doctors' names on them.

'If it's short, you can see him now. Your name, please?'

Arthur gave it, and the girl wrote it in a ledger, then pointed to a room behind her.

Dr Robinson was washing his hands at a basin when Arthur went in. A high, white-sheeted table stood on the left, and there was also a desk in the room. The doctor sat down at the desk, indicated a chair opposite, and Arthur sat obediently.

'What can I do for you?'

'I would like the name of a doctor who can do an abortion – reliably.'

'I see. Yes. Prepared to pay?'

'Yes, sure.'

Dr Robinson looked about thirty and had a suntan. 'Age of the girl or woman?'

'Seventeen.'

'Any health problems? Drug-taking?' he asked with a bored sigh.

'No.'

'Parental consent?'

Arthur's heart dipped. 'I'm sure she could get it. But it isn't necessary, is it, if she's over sixteen?'

'Right,' said the doctor, as if it didn't matter one way or the other. 'Unmarried? . . . And how long has she been pregnant? . . . Seven weeks. Yes, I know a doctor who could do it. In Indianapolis. – Dr Philip Bentz.' Dr Robinson was writing on a pad. He consulted an address book and copied out something, then tore off the page and handed it to Arthur. 'This is for you. But I'll telephone for you. And the name of the girl?'

'Can you see if Dr Bentz can do it – soon. Then I'll give the name?'

The doctor gave a tolerant laugh. 'I'm pretty sure he can do it; it only takes a few minutes, even though it means an overnight stay. But look, young man, I can't spend all day on this; I've got to give a name.'

'Stevens,' Arthur said. 'Alice.'

'Fine,' the doctor said, wrote it, and stood up. 'Phone my secretary around three.'

Arthur had hoped for an appointment, but was afraid of being thrown out if he tried to press the doctor. 'Do you know what it'll cost?'

'Between five and seven hundred. It depends.'

Arthur nodded, and felt white-faced as he and the doctor moved toward the door. Outside, the secretary stopped Arthur and asked him for twenty-five dollars. Arthur had feared even more and had left the house with forty-nine, all he had in cash just now.

As he dropped down in the elevator, it occurred to Arthur that Dr Robinson was getting a rake-off from Dr Bentz. Still, Arthur thought he should consider himself lucky on this first try, because he had read about absolute brush-offs that left people in quest of the next doctor.

Arthur cycled homeward, thinking. It might be simpler to pawn his microscope than to sell it at the right price. And he had better count on the doctor's bill being closer to seven hundred than five, because things were never cheaper for any reason. When he got home, his grandmother was in a corner of the backyard with Robbie, and he heard his mother's typewriter in his parents' bedroom. Two hundred and ninety in his saving account, he was thinking, and maybe he'd get two hundred at a pawn shop for his microscope, which had been secondhand when his parents had bought it for him years ago, but they'd paid two hundred and fifty then. His wristwatch was so ordinary, it was a joke to think of hocking it.

He set his microscope on his writing table and removed its beige cloth cover. There was a pawn shop, the only one in town that Arthur knew of, just two blocks from Shoe Repair.

Another thought came, and it was like a black hole into which he dropped: All this would wipe out his proud contribution toward Columbia in September. And so much for his parents' contribution toward Columbia, if his father ever found out about *this*. Arthur almost laughed with terror. Would old holier-than-thou Richard demand that he marry Maggie? That she have the baby, because abortions were against God's will? Well, he could think of worse fates than marrying Maggie!

Arthur could arrive at a figure no higher than six hundred and eighty dollars, as to ready assets, and some of that was hypothetical. He carried the microscope in a plastic shopping bag in his waste-basket, under the pretext of wastebasket-emptying, to the garage, and this worked. He had had to pass his mother in the kitchen. He put the heavy bag in the wire basket at the front of his bike.

'Got time for lunch with us, Arthur?' his mother asked. 'Just some baked beans and bacon.'

'Not hungry today, Mom, thanks.'

His grandmother came in, Robbie behind her. 'Are you in tonight, Arthur? I'm inviting us all to a film.'

'Thanks, Grandma. I think I've got a date with Maggie.' Arthur felt a curious unreality about the scene in the kitchen, as if they were all playacting, except him: Robbie barefoot and topless in khaki shorts that hung so low his navel showed, describing a garden snake that he had just rescued from the cat, a snake two feet long, illustrating with hands apart, though Arthur knew their garden snakes were no more than ten inches long. And his mother, rather silent as she opened two cans of beans, probably already thinking about some kid at the Beverley Home for Children, where she would go in an hour. All the scene needed was his father saying blessing over the beans in a few minutes. Was his father due home? The table hadn't been set. His father had used to come home once or twice a week for an early lunch with his mother, but lately he didn't. He now said he often had lunch near his office with some 'young person' or 'someone in spiritual distress' whom he had met in church. One Sunday his father had stayed after church to meet someone the Reverend Cole wanted him to 'counsel,' while Arthur and his mother had gone home in the car. There was always someone willing to drive his father home later.

When Arthur got to the pawn shop, he found it manned by a boy of about his own age in shirtsleeves, reading a paperback while a transistor played. The place was full of dusty junk, hanging wristwatches, guitars, and old clothes. Arthur said he had a good 50× microscope to pawn, worth two hundred and fifty.

'The boss isn't here today. Maybe tomorrow.'

Arthur had the plastic bag in his hands. 'Can't you take a look? Advance me something on it today?'

'I'm not allowed to take in any goods. Sorry.'

That was that. 'I'll come back tomorrow morning.'

Arthur went into the next public telephone booth he saw to call Maggie. It was now half past 12.

Maggie's mother answered. 'Oh, Arthur. Just a *min*–ute. Maggie! For you.'

Then Maggie said, 'Hello, Arthur.'

'Hi, darling. I got what I wanted. This morning. The name of somebody. Indi.' His grip on the telephone tightened. 'By yourself now?'

'Yes. But Mom knows anyway,' Maggie said softly.

'My God! – She *knows*?'

'Well, she guessed it and I couldn't lie to her. She noticed I was nervous, so she asked.'

Arthur felt shame, recalling her mother's polite but annoyed tone seconds ago. 'She's angry with you?'

'N-no. She just says I have to do something about it. She said these things happen or something like that.' Maggie's voice sounded almost the same, calm and even.

'Maggie – I'm supposed to call at three for an appointment. I'll try to make it for this weekend. Is that all right? And don't worry about what it costs.'

'My mother wants our – It's not our doctor, but somebody he knows. And we have family insurance, Arthur. As long as my folks know anyway—'

Arthur felt further alienated, and detested. 'I feel it's my responsibility.'

'No! – Oh, we'll talk about that some other time.'

His fingers writhed on the receiver. 'Can I possibly see you tonight?'

'I can see you after dinner. My dad comes home today around five.'

Arthur suffered another jolt. 'I suppose your mother's going to tell him.'

'Um-m – I suppose, because otherwise why'd I be going to the doctor? You shouldn't worry so, Arthur. It's not the way you think.'

A father was not going to take it so casually, Arthur thought.

'You still there? I asked my mother not to tell him tonight. We might go away this weekend, Mom and I, and get it done.'

Arthur said that his family was going out to a film tonight, and could she come to his house after dinner? Maggie said she could be there a little after 9. Arthur left the booth shaken and walked his bike along the sidewalk instead of getting on it.

'Present for your girl?' Tom Robertson asked when Arthur arrived at Shoe Repair with the plastic bag.

Arthur was putting the microscope in a safe place, under his coat hook at the back of the shop, next to an old raincoat of Tom's. 'Um – yes,' said Arthur. The plastic bag, he realized, came from a women's shop in town. Since when did Tom know he had a girl? Tom was probably assuming.

The day was bright with sunshine, and the one tree in view outside the shop bent its branches in the breeze like someone dancing slowly. Maybe the day was a lovely one for a lot of people, just not for him and Maggie.

Arthur was very aware of 3 o'clock when it rolled around, and he did not call Dr Robinson's secretary. It was a pretty safe bet that the secretary wouldn't bother to telephone his house. Arthur hadn't given his address, though his family's was the only Alderman listing in the book. He worked till nearly 6, when Tom usually closed, though Tom was always lenient about late-coming customers. When Arthur picked up the plastic bag, Tom Robertson said:

'You look as nervous as if you're going to pop the question tonight. I'm very curious what's *in* that. Looks heavy enough to be a wedding cake.'

'Angel food,' Arthur said, letting the bag slip nearly to the floor as if it weighed a ton.

'Ha! Good luck, boy! See you tomorrow.'

Arthur was alone in the house when he heard Maggie's car at nearly 10, and he went out to meet her. They went into the kitchen, because he thought Maggie might want a Coke or coffee, but she didn't. Arthur asked the question that was on his mind:

'Does your father know yet?'

'Well, yes. My mother told him just now. A few minutes ago.' Maggie sat down on the sofa.

Arthur remained standing. 'I can imagine what your father thinks of me. You may as well tell me.'

She shook her head and sighed. 'It's not like that. Maybe my family's different from yours. – Did you say anything to your mother?'

'Good gosh, *no*!' Arthur hit his forehead. 'And if my dad ever found out, he'd throw me out of the house!'

Maggie smiled nervously, took a cigarette from her jacket pocket, and Arthur sprang to light it. 'My mother spoke with a doctor recommended by Dr Moodie. He can do it Monday morning – in Indi.'

Arthur knew this was better, surer, than anything he could have come up with. 'I'd really like to pay for it, Maggie. You don't have to tell your folks that, just tell me what the bill is.'

'But I told you, we've got insurance.'

'All right, but don't you still pay *something*?'

'Honestly – I wouldn't worry, Arthur.'

Arthur suddenly thought that her family probably wanted to see the last of him, therefore didn't want a cent from him. 'Your father annoyed with you?'

'Oh, he said why didn't I have the pill like a bright girl. But he's not angry. – He's right.' Maggie sat leaning forward. Her eyes met his a couple of times; then she looked down at the floor.

The minutes were slipping by. His family might be back in half an hour. 'Maggie—' As he approached her, she stood up.

His arms were around her, and he heard her gasp. She seemed to hold him just as tightly, and he shut his eyes, as he did when he spoke to her on the telephone. 'God, I do love you, Maggie.'

'For how long?'

Arthur laughed. 'Maybe always.'

'Mom says—' Maggie stood back, but Arthur gripped both her hands. 'She says I'd better be realistic. You, too. That we have four years ahead if we both finish. Four years when we're mostly separated. She wants me to finish college and so do I want to.'

'But we will!'

Maggie pulled her hands away. 'Sometimes you look so serious, I get scared.'

'Oh, Maggie!' Arthur ran his fingers through his hair, turned in a circle, and faced her again. 'I have to ask you a question. Are you going to be sorry about this – the—'

'The operation. No. I've thought about that. – I know, I've read about girls being depressed – afterward. I don't think I will be. I know it's best if I have it done.'

And if they ever married, Arthur thought, there would be a time for children, but he found he hadn't the courage just now to say this. He saw Maggie glance at the front door, though the house was silent.

'We could take a drive now,' Maggie said.

'Yes, sure. – Or would you like to go over and meet Norma next door? Norma Keer.' Arthur went into his father's study.

'Who's she?'

Arthur looked through the study window and saw a glow of light at the side window of Norma's living room. 'Our next-door neighbor. Widow about sixty. Likes people to drop in. She's sort of—' He couldn't think of a word for Norma's good nature. 'She's supposed to be dying of cancer or something, but she's very cheerful.'

'Gosh!'

'Shall I call her and see if we can come over? Just for a couple of minutes. You give me a sign if it's boring.'

'Sure, if you want.'

Arthur dialed. 'Hi, it's me. I'm right next door and—' He laughed. 'Yes, all right! I'm with a friend – girl called Maggie, and I wondered if we could come over for a couple of minutes?'

It was fine if they came over.

Arthur turned out the lights, except one, lest his father remark on his wastefulness, and locked the front door.

'Well, you kids! Come in,' said Norma, in stockinged feet. And the TV was on with its sound turned off, and a book lay open on the sofa – just as usual.

Arthur introduced Maggie.

'What pretty girls you have, Arthur!' Norma murmured.

'Girls plural?'

'Come in the kitchen. What'll you folks have? Seven-Up, ginger ale, gin and tonic – rum – and no beer, because I'm trying to watch my weight.'

Maggie asked for a gin and tonic. Her eyes seemed to take in the entire house, while Arthur, who knew the one-story house well, simply enjoyed the change of scene, the safety it offered from the imminent arrival of his family next door. They sat in the living room. It dawned on Arthur that Norma was the least bit tipsy tonight. Forgivable, maybe, if she wasn't going to live another whole year, as she frequently said.

'I think I've seen you – in the First National,' Norma said to Maggie. She gently touched her hair, which looked like translucent reddish fluff. 'You've finished high school, too, like Arthur?'

'Yes, just now,' Maggie said.

'Arthur's one of my favorite beaux. Hope you appreciate him, Maggie.'

Arthur laughed.

'What'll I do when all the nice young people are gone away to college this fall,' said Norma, sadly.

'Meet some more,' Arthur said. 'Gus Warylsky's staying, going to C.U. You know him – tall blond fellow? We did some work together in your yard a couple of times.'

'Oh, yes, Gus! Another nice one, true.' Then Norma asked Maggie about her college. And what was she going to study?

Arthur didn't listen. He was thinking about Maggie, and Monday. Maggie declined another drink, but went with Norma back to the kitchen when Norma freshened her glass. Arthur stayed where he was. Then Maggie followed Norma out of the kitchen and bent to look at a table, Norma's dining table, in the area between kitchen and living room.

'Beautiful,' Maggie said, touching its surface with her fingertips.

'Thank you, Maggie,' said Norma. 'Inherited it from an old aunt. It's from Italy.'

Arthur had never paid any attention to the table. It was handmade and probably a few hundred years old, he realized. And Maggie liked it very much. From his armchair, Arthur looked at the X-legged table as if he had never seen it before. If Maggie liked this – one day he and Maggie would have furniture like this, he promised himself. Nothing with varnish on it, nothing of formica, nothing of chrome! Maggie wanted to leave.

'I'm supposed to be home by eleven,' Maggie said. 'Thank you for the drink, Mrs Keer.'

'I'll come with you,' Arthur said.

'You'll just have to walk back!'

'And so what?'

Arthur declined Norma's invitation to come back later if he wished. He wanted to be free to stay with Maggie, because he couldn't predict her: She might want to go to the quarry tonight. But she drove toward her house.

'What time are you taking off tomorrow – you and your mother?' Arthur asked.

'Sometime in the morning. We're all going to the Sigma Port Hotel where Dad always stays. Then Sunday afternoon I'll be in the hospital, because they want me to sleep there the night before. All very proper.' Maggie gave a nervous laugh.

He bit his lip. 'I'll be thinking about you every minute – Monday.'

In her driveway, he said a quick good-bye, afraid to linger, and set out at a trot for his house. Maggie had said he could telephone her at the hospital Monday afternoon, the All Saints Hospital. She knew there would be a telephone in her room.

His family was home and in the living room, all except Robbie, whose room light was on and his door open. His father was standing with a glass of beer, wearing one of his new shirts, a boldly striped blue-and-white that hung outside his trousers. It seemed to Arthur that his church activities had inspired him to buy flashier clothing. Very strange.

'Hello, Arthur, where've you been?' asked his grandmother.

'Went in to say hello to Norma for a few minutes.'

'And she gave you a couple of drinks I suppose?' He added to Joan, 'Round the clock bar next door.'

'Oh, Richard—' said Arthur's mother. 'You had a phone call a few minutes ago, Arthur. A girl named Vera – no, Veronica. She said there's a party on at her house and Gus is there. She thought you might like to come over.'

Arthur sucked his lip. 'No. But thanks for the message, Mom.'

Robbie entered the living room just as Arthur was about to leave it.

'Here they are, my specials,' Robbie said. He had both fists clenched and extended. 'Bought five.'

These were fishhooks with double and triple barbs, which Arthur gazed at with fascination, as did the others. They lay on Robbie's open palms, and in his enthusiasm, he had stuck his palm with one, and a little blood came, which Robbie dismissed as 'nothing.'

'With this one here, a fish *can't* get away,' Robbie said, as if it were imperative to catch a fish.

The hooks made Arthur think of the operation Maggie was going to have Monday morning. Hook it and tug it out. But from what he had read, the operation was rather a scraping. He had read about desperate women using coat hangers, however, and dying from it. Arthur did not care to look at the hooks any longer and went off to his room. He felt even slightly faint.

10

The sunshine early Saturday morning, beautiful as it was, struck Arthur as a curtain rising on a first act of tragedy, or doom. Maggie was going away this morning with her parents. Arthur had to keep telling himself that it was for 'the best,' that it was what Maggie wanted.

He was inspired to buy Maggie a present, and the one he had in mind wasn't a big one: a beige and blue scarf he had seen in a window the day he had visited the pawn shop. The forty-nine-dollar scarf had been out of the question then, but now it wasn't. He left the house around 10. His mother had been ironing, his father poring over papers in his study. His grandmother had taken his mother's car to do an errand. His grandmother could stay another week, which pleased Arthur. He cycled toward the street of the pawn shop, then to the street in which was the rather expensive shop for women's accessories. Arthur bought the scarf. It was of heavy silk. The beige and dark blue, set in an irregular diamond-shaped pattern, were the colors of Maggie's bedroom, the colors of her curtains, anyway, and he supposed that Maggie liked them. The salesgirl put the scarf into a pretty, flat square box. Then Arthur, with his spirits lifted a little, rode on his bike to the Chalmerston public library to change books and browse in the science shelves for an hour or so.

It was nearly noon when he got home. His grandmother was back, and Arthur's mother told him that she and his grandmother were going to make curtains for the whole house.

'Isn't that nice?' His mother turned with a large spoon in her hand to look at Arthur. She was making an orange cake, she had told Arthur.

'Sounds great – curtains.'

Arthur went to his room and put the box for Maggie in his second drawer, which contained folded shirts. He felt unhappy, vague about everything. Even Maggie. Would the operation somehow change her and turn her against him – next week, by Tuesday? Was his father going to put up the nearly nine thousand dollars for Columbia or not? Arthur wanted very much to speak with his mother about the Columbia money now, to find out his father's attitude through her, if he could, but his grandmother was in the house and might overhear, and Arthur did not want to appear to be hinting for money from his grandmother. His father, at best, would make him aware of every dollar, every hundred dollars that college would cost, even though his father was now poking ten-dollar bills into the limp purple bag that they passed around in church, Arthur had noticed, instead of his former couple of singles. Columbia might be a dream. And so might Maggie, he realized.

He didn't want to see or speak to anybody in the kitchen, his mother, grandmother, and now Robbie, back from fishing, so he left quietly by the front door and no one noticed. It was near enough to 1 to go to Shoe Repair.

That afternoon, Gus Warylsky came into the shop with a pair of shoes that needed new heels.

'Good party last night?' Arthur asked.

'Yeah. Veronica's birthday. – Greg wrecked his car afterwards. Did you hear?'

'Where would I've heard?' Not the first car Greg had smashed up, Arthur knew. 'Hurt anybody?'

'Broke his own nose. The girl with him was okay, but the car's a write-off. Dumb show-off. That guy ought to have his licence taken away for a *year*.'

Arthur didn't comment. Greg's father had political influence in the town, and Greg would be driving again as soon as he got another car.

'Might buy some shoes, too,' Gus said, looking around.

'What kind you want for them big feet? – What size do you take, twelve? Fourteen maybe?'

'Ten and a half. I was thinking of something – for dress,' Gus said a bit diffidently.

'Wedding? Funeral maybe? Try this section, the ones on the floor. See you in a minute, Gus.'

A man with two small children was waiting for service.

A few minutes later, Arthur found just the kind of shoes that Gus had had in mind, shiny black leather that kept its shine but was not exactly patent leather and didn't crack either, and with a buckle at the side.

'Wow, are these comfortable!' Gus said. 'They don't *look* so comfortable but they feel like house-shoes. How much?'

'Eight ninety-five.'

'It's a deal.' Gus was admiring himself in the full-length mirror. 'Snazzy,' he commented. Gus wore a limp white shirt, black cotton trousers and a leather belt that looked like a hand-me-down from a grandfather. He put his old shoes back on and gave Arthur a five-dollar bill and some singles. 'Coming to the barbecue tonight?'

'Whose barbecue?'

'Nobody's. Big collective thing at Delmar Lake. We're all supposed to bring something like a sack of beers or franks and the entrance is one dollar. Goes to the summer recreation center at Chalmerston High. They're trying to keep it open, you know, with a cut budget.'

Arthur wasn't interested in the Chalmerston High recreation center. 'Sounds boring. Doubt if I'll go, but thanks for telling me.'

Gus was standing by the cash register. 'What're you doing tomorrow? I've got the day sort of free.'

Arthur handed him the paper bag with his new shoes. 'I'm over at Mrs DeWitt's doing yard work. Starting around ten tomorrow morning. Didn't I tell you I was working there lately? Gets me out of church Sunday mornings.' Arthur smiled.

'Maybe I'll cruise over and see you. Round eleven?'

'Okay. Fine.'

'Got to fix somebody's busted dishwasher starting nine-thirty, ten. If I get it fixed—' He waved a hand and departed.

To Arthur's surprise, Robbie was going to the Delmar Lake barbecue that evening, and was to be picked up by his fishing pal Jeff at 7. At 6:30, Robbie was in the living room in a new red-and-white-checked shirt and new blue jeans – genuine Levi's, standing out now like Dutchman's-breeches – presents from Grandma, Robbie said. With his new deep voice, Robbie was at last ready to crash the teenage social set, Arthur supposed.

'You're not going?' asked Robbie.

'Nope. – Have a good time, Robbie,' Arthur said.

Robbie was duly called for at 7, and went striding down the front walk toward the waiting car. In the new Levi's, he reminded Arthur of a bird, maybe a swallow walking on a split tail.

'Robbie's so pleased – going out tonight. Did you notice, Mama?' asked Lois.

'Of course I did. – It'll be good for him.'

Arthur's mother and grandmother were in the kitchen, his father, too, drinking what looked like Tom Collinses. Arthur made himself a gin and tonic. It seemed to Arthur that his father deliberately avoided talking to him or even looking at him, though he was smiling a lot this evening. His grandmother had persuaded his father to play golf with her tomorrow afternoon.

Arthur said he would be working, when his grandmother had asked if he could join them, and Lois begged off because she wanted to check the curtain measurements again.

'If I measure them all again when I'm alone, I can be sure I didn't make any mistakes. Or if I do make a mistake, then it's my fault entirely.'

'Where're you working tomorrow, Arthur?' asked his grandmother.

'Same old place. Mrs DeWitt's cathouse.'

'Arthur, do you *have* to use that expression?' said his mother, but she was smiling a little.

'Your grandmother's coming to church,' his father said. 'Why don't you come along? Work in the afternoon.'

'No, it's ten o'clock again at Mrs DeWitt's and she's pretty fussy,' Arthur said as if it were a pity.

That evening, Arthur read a book he had borrowed from the public library on deep sea exploration. It had a section of color photographs, some of phosphorescent animalcules which had always fascinated Arthur. A group of scientists had dived in something like a glass submarine off the Galapagos Islands and discovered geysers of unusually warm water at great depth. The warmth of the water had enabled huge worms and foot-wide red clams to live down there, all of the life forms having adapted themselves to the terrific pressure, so that now they never came even halfway to the surface. Arthur wondered if he would ever make it to a ship like the one the book described, to be one of a team of scientists diving in glass bells to look at the bottom of the Pacific Ocean? The deep sea book was the only thing that kept his thoughts from Maggie that evening. Usually he loved daydreaming about her, but now anxiety seized him when he thought of her. Something could go wrong, and she could die.

By 10 the next morning, Arthur was at Mrs DeWitt's. Her pink and yellow roses were in bloom in their newly cleared beds. A big apple tree stump remained in the center of the backyard lawn, and Mrs DeWitt had said she wanted it removed, but Arthur had dodged the task, because the two-foot wide stump would take an electric saw and a tractor to get out. Funny, Arthur thought, that though he didn't own the place and didn't want to, he looked on the work he had done with a certain pride. Mrs DeWitt had told him a friend of hers had called it a 'transformation.'

Arthur was inspired to tackle the toolshed for the second time, and to sort out what was usable and what wasn't. There was an old frame barely recognizable as that of a bicycle, dried-up cans of paint, empty glass jars, and old rags full of spider webs. Arthur amassed a heap on the lawn.

Mrs DeWitt came out with a bottle of cold ginger ale for him. 'That's a step in the right direction,' she said, meaning the heap of junk. 'I'll speak to the garbage man, give him a tip, and he can carry that off.'

Arthur was working without his shirt. Sweat ran down his sideburns and his neck. 'Thank you, ma'am,' said Arthur, taking the ginger ale bottle. Mrs DeWitt suddenly reminded him of an old-fashioned striped mattress. Today her bulk was shrouded in a blue-and-white-striped dress, plain as a nightgown; she wore house-slippers on her bare feet, and her white hair looked as if she hadn't touched it since she got out of bed.

'Have some lunch with me today, if you'd like to, Arthur. Got some cold fried chicken and potato salad. Ice cream, too.'

That sounded rather good, worth putting up with the cat smell for. Then he could work another hour or so in the afternoon. 'Nice of you. I'll say yes.'

Arthur was sweeping the toolshed floor with a worn broom when Gus's old four-door car came up the driveway. Arthur raised his right arm in greeting.

Gus got out of his car and came over, looking around. 'Give you a hand with something?' he asked, looking from the heap of junk to the back of Mrs DeWitt's house, where at the moment she was not to be seen.

They decided to tackle the tree stump. With Gus pitching in, it became fun, maybe impossible to get out today, but that wouldn't matter. There was a pick-axe in the shed and an old saw that was usable. They took turns with the pick-axe, getting enough earth out for the other to attack a root with the saw. Gus removed his T-shirt. His skin was pale and there were freckles on his back, fine as cinnamon powder. His gold-framed glasses, which looked so delicate, stayed on his nose despite his exertions.

'Bet this so-and-so's fifty years old if it's a day.' Gus suddenly jumped on the stump at an angle, causing a root to give a little, and Gus bounced backward onto the grass. He rolled over and got up.

Arthur took the saw to a root. 'How was the barbecue last night?'

'You didn't miss much. Reggie Dewey had some hard stuff and he was whooping it up with Roxanne and they both fell off the boat dock – dancing. Then we all went swimming in the dark. Big deal.'

Arthur kept on sawing, shaking his head now and then to get the gnats away from his eyes.

'Since my car's here,' Gus said, 'want to run some of this junk off? I know a dump near here.'

Gus's car had a hatch door. They loaded most of the junk in and dumped it at the place Gus knew, then returned to the stump with renewed enthusiasm, because it was nearly out. The last thinner roots Arthur was able to clip, and then with a few pushes and pullings they got the stump out and onto the lawn. Panting, triumphant, Arthur began raking the displaced soil back.

'Well, howdy-do?' said Mrs DeWitt's voice nearby, startling both of them. 'You've got *that* thing out!'

Mrs DeWitt's joy was gratifying. Gus assured her he was 'just passing the time.' Arthur introduced them. Gus's face was pink and damp with sweat. He put his T-shirt back on.

'And all that junk cleaned up and gone! – It's twelve-thirty and I was going to ask you to come in, Arthur. Lunch is ready. Maybe you'd like a bite with us, too?' she asked Gus.

'No, thank you, ma'am, my folks expect me before one. I just came by to see how Art was doing.'

She insisted that Gus come in to wash his hands and face and have a cold drink. Arthur was already washing at the hose tap, letting the water run over his chest and back.

Gus went hesitantly into the kitchen, out of curiosity, Arthur felt, because he had told Gus about the cats. The oilcloth-covered table looked quite nice with its glasses of iced tea, plates, and green paper napkins and a big bowl of potato salad that a black and white cat had been licking at when they walked in. Gus washed his hands at the sink at Mrs DeWitt's suggestion. She made another glass of iced tea.

'Got the fried chicken in the oven to keep it away from the cats,' she said.

The telephone rang. Mrs DeWitt went into her living room to answer it.

'Arthur?' Mrs DeWitt called. 'It's for you. Your father.'

Arthur was surprised. 'Hello?'

'Arthur, I'd like you to come home as soon as possible. Now.' His father sounded grim.

'What's the matter? Something happen to Robbie?'

'Robbie's fine. Just get yourself home.'

'Mrs DeWitt asked me to lunch here, and I intended to work this afternoon,' Arthur said.

'Will you come home or shall I come and get you?'

Arthur stood up straighter. 'Can I speak to Mom?'

'No. I'm giving you orders.'

'R-r-right,' Arthur said with equal grimness and put the

telephone down. He went back into the kitchen. 'I'm supposed to go home right away. Sorry about lunch, Mrs DeWitt.'

'Something happen at home?' Gus asked.

'No! I don't know what's the matter.'

'What a shame!' Mrs DeWitt said.

'I'll run you home, Art,' Gus said. 'Stick your bike in the back of my car.'

Mrs DeWitt gave Arthur five dollars. Arthur said he would be back before 2 to work a while more.

11

Arthur went into his house via the kitchen, which was empty, though the table was set. Voices murmured in the living room; then his mother came into the kitchen, looking worried.

'Well – what's up?' Arthur asked.

She raised a finger to her lips, and went near the door into the garage, out of hearing of the people in the living room. 'It seems the – Bob Cole spoke to your father after church. Bob said he heard – something about a girl. That a girl had to have an abortion. Is that true, Arthur?'

'Who said that?'

His father was coming in. 'I'll handle it, Lois.'

'I was only asking him if it was true,' his mother said calmly.

'I'll ask him. Is it true? Is it the Brewster girl? – Never mind your grandmother, because she's heard it,' his father added, as his grandmother came through the broad door of the living room.

'Hello, Arthur,' said his grandmother as cheerfully as ever. 'This is family business, so I'll get out of your way. See you later.' She went down the hall toward her room.

Richard looked at Arthur. 'I suppose you know if it's true or not?'

Arthur felt like saying, 'Yes,' but Maggie had kept it quiet and wanted it to be kept quiet.

'Arthur—' said his father.

'I don't think it's your business or anybody's business,' Arthur said, and his father slapped him hard in the face. Arthur at once pulled his right fist back.

'Arthur! *Richard*, really!' His mother looked about to step between them.

'Hey, Mom, when're we eating?' Robbie was coming in from the hall.

Their mother sighed. 'Take some potato chips, will you, Robbie? She got a cellophane bag from the cupboard. 'We have to talk for a few minutes before lunch. Can't you go out in the yard for a while?'

'I don't feel like it.' Robbie carried the potato chip bag back to his room.

'Are you saying it's true?' his father asked when Robbie was out of hearing.

Arthur's fist was still clenched, but at his side. 'I'd like to know the so-and-so who said this. Who told Bob Cole.'

'It's true, though, isn't it?' Richard said to his mother, 'Just look.'

Arthur detested his father at that moment. 'Yes. And what's all the fuss about? – Gossips!'

'All – right, Arthur,' said his father with an air of triumph and patience combined.

Arthur made an effort to sound calm. 'Maggie's keeping quiet, her family's quiet. They don't even – dislike me, by the way.'

'They should,' said his father quickly. 'A nice girl and a nice family.'

'Yes, and they said – these things can happen.' Arthur suddenly could have cracked up then, so he stood carefully straight.

'They happen because people *make* them happen.'

'If you're blaming Maggie, you can go to hell!'

'Arthur! – Let's not talk like that – any of us.' His mother raised her hands in a peacekeeping gesture. 'Let's continue this discussion after some dinner, if we have to continue it. I mean that,' she added with a look at Richard.

Arthur wanted to go to his room, but was afraid he would appear to be retreating, so he stayed where he was.

'Could you call your grandmother, Arthur?' his mother asked.

Arthur walked down the hall and did so. Then he went into his room. He wiped sweat off his forehead and whirled around when he heard a knock on his door. It was his mother. 'I can't sit at the table, Mom. I think I'll go back to Mrs DeWitt's.'

She came in and closed the door.

'Who told Bob Cole, Mom?'

'I don't know. But news gets around this town. You know that.'

Arthur thought suddenly of Roxanne. She didn't go to that church, but she might have said something to a few people like Greg or Reggie Dewey, who could have passed it on to someone who might attend that goody-goody church.

'I've got to serve dinner. Your father's going to want to talk to you again and I want you both to keep your tempers – if you can.'

'You can tell him he's the one making the fuss. Is he going to tell the neighbors now? Make a speech in church?'

'Of course not,' his mother whispered. 'And Bob Cole spoke to your father in private, in his office there, after church. – Just when did this abortion take place? Before Mama's visit, I gather.'

'Hasn't yet; it's tomorrow.'

'Oh? Your father thought it was a couple of weeks ago.'

'That didn't work – to be exact. But don't tell Dad, will you? Don't say anything else about it. Just let it – die down.'

'Your father tried to phone the Brewsters this noon.'

'Oh, my *gosh*! They're not home, so he can stop wasting his energy.'

'Would you like me to bring you a plate of something?'

'No, Mom. No, thanks.'

As soon as she was gone, Arthur gasped. He clenched his fists and swung his arms a couple of times, then went quietly into the bathroom, which was the next room, and washed his face in cold water. He thought to get out of the house by the front door, possibly unseen, but his father saw him.

'Oh, Arthur,' said his father, getting up from the table. He came round into the front hall, carrying a napkin in his hand. 'I'd like you to tell me where the Brewsters are this weekend.'

'I don't know where they are,' said Arthur, and walked out.

To arrive at Mrs DeWitt's again was a pleasure, a little like arriving at old Norma's cosy house, even though Mrs DeWitt's house meant labor. Arthur didn't see her as he leaned his bike against the toolshed and thought perhaps she was still eating lunch, because hardly forty-five minutes had passed. Arthur started picking up the sawed roots from the grass. He worked slowly and steadily, hardly thinking about what he was doing. By this time tomorrow, the operation would be over, Maggie's ordeal. She was due home Tuesday midday. And Maggie still liked him – it seemed – just as much as ever! That thought, that fact, was like a fortress to Arthur, a mighty defense against his crackpot father.

Arthur jumped when he heard Mrs DeWitt's high, thin voice near him.

'Back already, Arthur! Come in and have some ice cream. You can't have had a big dinner in that short a time.'

He begged out politely.

A few minutes later, Mrs DeWitt came out with a glass of iced coffee and a big piece of coconut cake on a tray. Arthur had a little of both and finally tossed the rest of the cake where Mrs DeWitt wouldn't see it. It was nearly 5, when he returned the tray to her kitchen. He didn't see Mrs DeWitt, so he took off, sweaty and tired.

He thought of going by Gus's house, which was almost on the way, but he wouldn't be able to talk freely to Gus. He couldn't talk to Norma Keer either, though Norma would probably be the most understanding of all the people Arthur knew. It wasn't fair to Maggie to talk to *anybody*, and that was exactly why his father was being unfair. Maybe even Robbie knew now.

As soon as Arthur got home, his mother met him in the kitchen and beckoned him back into the garage.

'Your father spoke with the Brewsters. I didn't want it to surprise you,' she whispered. 'Richard's trying to—'

'Dammit, how'd he find them?'

'He phoned Sigma Airlines. He knew from somewhere that Maggie's father is with them, and they said – I don't know, Arthur, but your father said it was urgent and they told him Mr Brewster was at their hotel this weekend. So your father reached them and said – said he didn't approve of the abortion,' his mother finished in a still softer whisper.

And his mother had told his father that the abortion hadn't been done yet. Arthur felt near exploding. 'Well, well, he doesn't approve! Who is he? Isn't that the Brewsters' business? Has he gone *nuts*?'

'Sh-h. You might as well say that – about this. He's said so much, even Robbie knows. I tried to keep it from Robbie, naturally. And I did try to persuade Richard to keep out of it.'

'Hope the Brewsters told him to go to hell.'

'Well – in a way they did,' his mother replied with the start of a smile. 'I spoke with Maggie's mother for a minute. She sounded nice, I must say. Told me not to worry. And Maggie wants to speak with you. Wants you to call her.'

'You mean now?'

'The number's by the phone. Call her before eight,' his mother said and went back into the kitchen.

Arthur followed her. It was not yet 6.

Since his father was in the living room, Arthur did not glance in that direction, though his grandmother was there, too. Arthur went into the bathroom, dropped his clothes on the floor and stepped under the shower. He also washed his hair. Then he grabbed his dirty clothes in one hand, checked the hall, and nipped into his room. Naturally, his father wasn't going to quit the living room to give him any privacy to phone, he thought as he put on clean clothes, but Norma would let him phone from her house. She would be delighted to render that little service.

Arthur went into the living room to get the number his mother had mentioned. He greeted his grandmother.

'Hel*lo*, Arthur,' she said with a sigh, as if she'd had enough of something, maybe of his father.

His father sat hunched with folded hands on the edge of an armchair seat, and Robbie sat in another armchair, straightening out a tangled mess of cord in his lap, looking all ears. Arthur picked up the piece of paper and started for the front door.

'Oh, Arthur! I'd like a word with you.' His father stood up, arching his back as if he had had a hard afternoon in the armchair. He beckoned Arthur into his parents' bedroom.

Arthur pushed the paper into his back pocket, and followed his father.

His father closed the bedroom door. 'I've found out that operation won't take place till tomorrow. There's time for you to stop it or help to stop it right now. Tonight.'

Arthur was aware of his father's bulk, of his aggressive chin jutting forward as he bent close. Arthur stepped back.

'It's your duty to say your word about it. I've said mine to both the Brewsters.'

'It's for Maggie to say – and for nobody else to say.'

'Maggie's hardly more than a child! Seventeen. – I'm talking about the importance of *life*, Arthur.'

'I'm not going to do it. And it's not your business,' Arthur went on, when his father started to say something, 'to tell the Brewsters what they should do. It's embarrassing to me.'

'*You* dare talk about embarrassment?'

Hopeless, Arthur thought. He turned toward the door. His father came after him, and Arthur drew his left arm out of reach, having had the feeling his father was about to grab it. Arthur went out and down the hall to the front door and out. Norma would forgive him this once, he thought, for crashing in without phoning first.

'Arthur!' Now his father stood on the little front porch of the house.

Arthur trudged back the few steps he had walked. He stood on the front walk.

His father had closed the door. 'That child,' he said in a low voice, 'can be cared for by us, by the girl's family. If you don't persuade her, if you don't insist, it'll be the greatest mistake – one of the greatest mistakes you'll ever make in your life.'

Arthur sighed, wordless and angry.

'You'll never go to Columbia, if you let this happen.'

Arthur had foreseen that. He nodded curtly and went on across the lawn toward Norma's, up her front steps, and he knocked.

Norma opened the door, not at all annoyed by the interruption, because she was only doing some mending in the living room, she said. One of Norma's curtains was spread over most of the sofa where she usually sat.

'Looks the way my house is going to look next week,' Arthur said. 'Mom and Grandma are making a lot of new curtains.'

'I'm just hemming mine. Hem came undone.'

'To tell you the truth, I came over to make a phone call, if I may. Indi, and I'll reimburse you. Okay?'

'Cer-tainly, Arthur. Private, I gather. Would you like me to disappear in the bedroom?'

'Oh, not that private,' said Arthur, though he would have preferred to be alone. 'May I make it now?'

'Go right ahead.' She returned to her curtain on the sofa.

Arthur dialed the hospital number and asked for room eight sixteen.

At this point, Norma went into her bedroom at the back corner of the house, trailing the curtain behind her.

'Hello, Maggie,' he whispered, when Maggie answered. 'How are you?'

'Oh, fine. In bed already.' She sounded cheerful. 'Lovely room. Color TV. Mom's here.'

In the room, Arthur supposed. 'I'm so damned mad that my dad called your folks up. Some so-and-so at his *church* told him, and I didn't know that till one o'clock today. Then – I was out all afternoon working till – just now, when I found out he'd phoned. I'm very sorry. Can you tell your mother that?'

'Don't worry so much. I think my father took care of it.'

'What time's the – that business tomorrow morning?'

Now Norma was coming back, carrying a purple sewing basket, still trailing the curtain.

'Eight o'clock. – Too bad your father's so upset. There's no reason to be.'

Arthur felt much better. Once again, Maggie's fantastic calm worked its magic. She was the one suffering, the one in danger, and she sounded saner than anyone else!

'. . . Now Mom's back. I think she wants to speak with you.'

'Hello, Mrs Brewster. I was saying to Maggie – I'm sorry about my father—'

'I think Warren and I handled it pretty well. Tried to. I'm afraid this family doesn't see eye to eye with yours.'

'I don't either. It's my father, not my mother.'

'Tomorrow it'll be over and we can all forget it. You tell your father that. Want to speak with Maggie again?'

'Hi, Arthur. Now the doctor just came in – so I'll have to sign off.'

'I'll phone tomorrow noon to ask how you are. All my love, darling.'

Arthur turned around and looked at another world: Norma

sewing away with her legs and feet hidden under the curtain. He fished for money in his pocket, and left two singles by the phone, knowing his call would cost a bit less.

'Success?' asked Norma.

'Oh, sure. Thanks, Norma. – Living room's pretty busy at my house lately.'

'Got time to sit down? It's getting on to the official drinks hour, nearly seven. Tempt you to something?'

'Thanks – no.' Arthur didn't want a drink, and didn't want to leave. But his father might be bothering the Brewsters on the telephone this minute! What if his father got the bright idea of *going* to the hospital! Arthur spilled some of the coins he had been clutching, and had to gather them from the carpet.

'Nervous tonight? – I wish you luck, Arthur.'

'With what?'

'Anything and everything,' Norma said, looking at him.

12

His mother and grandmother were in the kitchen when Arthur went back to the house, and supper was imminent. And his father was on the telephone.

'I see. Thank *you*,' his father said in an annoyed tone, and hung up.

If he had been trying the hospital, Arthur hoped that he had been told the Brewsters were accepting no more calls from Mr Alderman, Senior.

His father came in, and they all took their places at the table. Slices of smoked salmon lay on plates before them, and Arthur had to push the cat's front paws off his thigh as he bowed his head for his father's blessing.

'Father, we thank Thee – as ever – for the blessings laid before us. In this moment of – anxiety and wrongdoing, we ask Your patience and forgiveness. We ask You to show us the way. Show us all. Amen.'

Robbie hiccupped so violently, he rose a bit from his seat.

Arthur gave his brother a smile, and opened his paper napkin.

'How was Norma?' his mother asked.

'Same as ever. Sewing,' Arthur replied. 'Mending a hem of a

curtain. Ahem!' He glanced at Robbie, who liked stupid puns, but Robbie might not have heard.

His father chewed his smoked salmon as if it were an arduous job that had to be done, though it was a treat in the household.

'And what did you do today at Mrs DeWitt's?' asked his grandmother.

The women kept the conversation going, and his father continued to look as if he couldn't wait to say something unpleasant, though he didn't say anything. Robbie was also silent. Robbie looked taller on his bench seat. His jaw was growing heavier. Was Robbie going to take his father's side? How could he understand the situation at his age? On the other hand, the young could be bent.

In the interval before dessert, when his mother was up from the table, his father said, 'You spoke with the girl, I suppose, Arthur?'

'Yes.'

'Richard, must we? Just now?' said Lois.

'Later may be too late. However, if later it is—'

The dessert period would have been a torture, except that his mother's hot lemon meringue pie was excellent, and Arthur had an appetite. Then came coffee in the living room. Robbie was gently asked to go to his room, and didn't. Arthur could see his grandmother on the brink of leaving the living room after one cup of coffee, then deciding to stay, which pleased Arthur.

'Well, Arthur, did you ask the girl to change her mind?' his father asked.

'No.'

'Did you try?'

'No, I didn't.'

'It's still not too late,' said his father, who was trying in his own way to be calm, Arthur could see.

Arthur glanced at his grandmother, who was looking into her

coffee cup, and at Robbie, who sat like part of the audience in a movie house.

'They won't accept my calls now,' said Richard sadly. 'But you could reach them, I'm pretty sure. The girl or her mother. I could even drive you to the hospital tonight.'

Arthur winced and rubbed his forehead. 'I don't think Robbie should be in on all this, Dad. Not the people at church either. I don't know how many you've—'

'You went to Norma's house,' said his father.

'I went to phone, but I didn't say anything about *this*.'

There was a knock on the door. Lois got up with an air of annoyance and said:

'Richard, will you let him in?'

His father went to the door. 'Hello, Eddie, come in! Just in time for coffee.' Mumbles. '... still a chance, yes.' His father ushered a slender man of about twenty-five into the living room, with his hand on the man's shoulder. The stranger carried a black briefcase. 'Eddie Howell,' said Richard. 'You know my family. And this is Arthur.'

Arthur nodded, but didn't get up. A church acquaintance of his father's, no doubt, one of the 'young people' his father often talked about. He looked sickly to Arthur, pale-faced, thin, wearing glasses and a dark suit.

'Shall we—' Eddie began, and seemed to suppose that they – he and his father and himself – were to go into his father's study, which Eddie had cast an eye at.

'No, no, sit down, Eddie. Coffee, Lois?'

His mother was already on the way to fetch another cup and saucer.

'I'm not sure Robbie—' Eddie began.

'Oh, he's one of the family,' said Richard.

Really awful, Arthur thought. Eddie had wanted to get him into a room alone, where he could do a job on him with the pamphlets that he probably carried in that briefcase.

'So what's happening now?' asked Eddie with his gentle smile. He had his coffee and sat in an armless chair with knees together and feet in a pigeon-toed position.

'No progress,' said Richard. 'But it's still not too late, as I said to my son. Never too late till the moment itself.'

Eddie looked at Arthur with a bland smile, as if he were regarding some strange organism, Arthur felt, which wouldn't come to its senses and behave right. The man's dark eyes behind his glasses looked puzzled and troubled. That was an act, Arthur thought.

'What're your intentions, Arthur?' Eddie asked.

'My intentions?'

'About the girl. And her situation.'

Arthur sat forward. His empty coffee cup rattled in its saucer as he set the two items aside.

'Richard,' Lois said, 'I don't think right now is the time to go into all this. With so many people—'

'If not now, then when?' asked Richard.

'Maybe Eddie should talk to Arthur alone,' said Lois.

'Yes, I'm willing,' said Eddie cheerfully, and got up.

'Why go somewhere else?' Arthur asked. 'I'm not going to tell anyone what to do – if that's what you're here to talk about.'

'But – you have already,' said Eddie Howell gently. 'The responsibility is yours now.'

Not entirely, Arthur thought. 'Not now,' he said.

'Yes, now. You have created life and now you – you're trying to disclaim responsibility. You're willing to let it be—'

His mother writhed with discomfort in her chair.

'Go ahead, Eddie!' said his father like a cheerleader.

'You cannot just sit by, if you have any power. That would be your real sin, a truly major sin,' Eddie told Arthur.

Robbie, neutral-faced and attentive, kept his eyes on Eddie.

Arthur said, 'I'll do what the girl wants. What her family wants too. I can't understand the meddling.'

'And you don't see your responsibility,' Eddie said, still affably smiling.

Arthur did, of course. Wasn't it equal, his and Maggie's responsibility? 'But not now,' Arthur replied. 'Now the girl has the right to do what she wants.'

Eddie shook his head.

'I do see what Arthur means,' his grandmother put in gently. 'Not that I mean to interfere in this.'

'I'd be pleased to hear what you have to say, ma'am,' said Eddie.

'Considering the girl's age – and Arthur's – Well, I'm sure you see my point. And as far as I know, this family isn't Catholic. The girl's family seems to be taking it – calmly, shall I say? As something that can happen in the best of families. Why not let things be? That's the end of my speech.' Joan threw a quick smile at her daughter.

Eddie nodded slowly, with a frown above his apparently frozen smile.

Eddie Howell was a sick prig, Arthur thought, and so was his father to be sitting there with a solemn face, concentrating on this twit – fifteen or twenty years younger than his father – as if he were God himself or some kind of divine messenger.

'I'd like to speak with you for a minute in your own room, Arthur,' said Eddie. 'Is that possible?'

Arthur shook his head slowly. 'You can say anything you want to right here.'

Eddie took a breath. 'I strongly recommend that you call up this girl – or her family or both – and say you don't want this operation to take place. That you know it should *not* take place. I understand the family's even well off and could take care of the child. That is not the point even.' He raised a forefinger. 'The point is – human life. I know your father has the phone number of the hotel where the parents are. Or we could even go there in my car – speak to them.'

Arthur relished the idea of a fight with this jerk, plus his father, if they tried to push him into a car. Arthur pressed his right fist into the palm of his left hand. 'Sorry,' he began with an effort at calmness, 'but my father's been annoying the family all afternoon, and they're not taking any more phone calls from us.' Sweat zipped down his cheek, reminding him of the hours at Mrs DeWitt's that afternoon.

Eddie opened his briefcase. 'I'd like you to read two things I brought with me this evening,' he said, producing two magazines of different sizes, laying them gently on the coffee table. 'Can you do me that courtesy? Promise me?'

Why should he promise? Shove them, Arthur wanted to say, and if his grandmother hadn't been present, he might have. Twits such as Eddie Howell were anti-Darwin, Arthur reminded himself; in fact they spat on Darwin. This thought gave Arthur fortitude, even a sense of advantage. 'Yes, sure,' Arthur said, and stood up with an air of calling the visit over.

His mother rose also, but drifted to the kitchen. His father beckoned Eddie Howell into his study and closed the door.

'You did very well, Arthur,' said his grandmother. 'Kept your temper. Good for you.'

Arthur shook his head. Robbie regarded Arthur as if he were now the center of the screen instead of Eddie Howell. 'Don't you find this pretty boring, Robbie?'

'Nope. Why should I?'

His father and Eddie oozed back into the living room and toward the front door. Eddie turned and said:

'Good night, Arthur – everybody. Don't forget, Arthur, it is not too late until tomorrow morning. And that gives you a lot of time.' At the threshold of the room he raised an arm high, and smiled. 'God bless!'

'Call you up later tonight, Eddie,' his father murmured in the hall. 'Thank you very much for coming.' When the door closed on Eddie, his father came back and went to the magazines on the coffee table. 'I'll put these in your room,' he said to Arthur.

'There's a funny program on in just five minutes,' his grandmother said when his father came back. 'I think it's just what we need. *I* need it, anyway. Do you mind, Richard?'

Richard didn't. Arthur felt proud of his grandmother. They all watched the program – a sitcom that really was funny. Arthur slouched in an armchair and laughed loudly. His father went off to his study after a few minutes and then returned, hooked on the program himself.

Later, after another shower, Arthur did look at the two magazines or tracts which he had found on his bed. One concerned 'the sanctity of life,' and quoted 'be fruitful and multiply.' The second, which had a bit of blue coloring on its badly printed black-on-white cover, was called 'Think Twice' and concentrated on the physical dangers of abortion, septic poisoning, hemorrhages, then the mental blight of depression which was described as 'a living death.' 'Think Twice' was about illegal abortions, which was the term they used, backstreet abortionists, fatal home efforts, as if legal abortions done by competent doctors didn't exist. Doctors and nurses who performed or assisted at any of these operations were labeled murderers, as were the girls or women who had the operation. It was a more concentrated dose of what he had seen before in the magazines lying around the house. Contraceptive devices were never mentioned. The pregnancy was simply a fact, and the fetus had to be carried to full term and born, and so on. Arthur was still in a mood to laugh, and what he was glancing at was no less exaggerated, and in its way slapstick, than what he had been watching on TV. There was also a sadistic element suggestive of the Mad Scientist: Make women pay. All the articles were written by men with WASP names, and the publishing houses had names like the God's Way

Press or New World College Religious Publications, Inc., based in towns so small Arthur had never heard of them, in California, Illinois, Ohio.

Someone tapped at the door. 'Arthur?'

This was his father. 'Yep?'

His father came in. 'Well, I can see you're looking at that, anyway.'

Arthur tossed the two magazines back on his bed. 'Yes, I said I would.'

'And what's your attitude now?'

Arthur took a deep breath. 'Do you really expect me to change my mind because of this – propaganda?'

His father snorted and took his time in replying. 'Not even old enough to vote, and you hold yourself superior to that. To God's word. Not the Bible there, I admit, but still God's word. I don't know how you can sleep tonight and maybe you won't. – Now Arthur – maybe you'll see the light – before dawn – and do something or try to. I don't want this blot on my family.' He went on more slowly, 'And if you want to go to that hospital – any time tonight – I'll drive you there.'

His father stood facing him with his large head bent forward, his gray eyes not exactly crazy-looking, but changed, as if he had taken a drug. Then he turned and left the room. His figure looked old and tired to Arthur, or maybe his father was simply defeated. That was true.

Nearly an hour later, when Arthur went into the kitchen to get a glass of milk and another piece of lemon meringue pie unless Robbie had finished it, his father was on the telephone. The rest of the family had gone to bed, Arthur thought. His father was still dressed. Arthur did not try to listen, but he heard a couple of his father's words anyway. His father was dictating a telegram. At once Arthur listened hard, because he didn't want his name at the end of it.

'It is not too late. Period. We send you – our blessings. Period. Signed the Aldermans. That's A—'

Maggie and her mother would know it wasn't from him. It would have been more honest of his father to have signed the telegram Richard Alderman.

13

By 10 Monday morning, Arthur was cycling toward the town's main public library, and thinking of Maggie, as he had been since 7 when he woke up. Mercifully, his father had not disturbed him, and Arthur had stayed in his room until his father left for work. No comment that morning from his mother or grandmother about Maggie. By now, at 10, Arthur imagined her coming out of the anesthetic, feeling relieved, feeling hardly any pain at all, maybe none. He hoped that was the way it was.

'Morning, Miss Becker!' Arthur said with a smile to the dark-haired librarian in glasses at the desk.

'Hell-o, Arthur!' she replied, looking up from the book she was reading. 'Nice day, isn't it?'

Was it? The sun was shining, true. 'Yes.' He put four books on her big desk and opened their back covers for her stamping in. What did the E. before Becker on her nameplate stand for, Edith? Elvira? Miss Becker wasn't quite as dull as the Elvira type. She was almost pretty and surely not thirty yet.

'Zoo department, zoo department,' said Miss Becker, stamping. 'Is that all you're going to do this summer, read books?'

'Oh – um – I can think of worse fates.'

Arthur went into the big room full of shelves and partitions with books on either side. He paused by the New Acquisitions display, and chose a book of Searle cartoons and a book called *The New Physics*, which was full of mathematical formulae that he probably would not understand, but which had electronic photographs of things he did understand. These books could be borrowed for only a week. This reminded Arthur, as he drifted toward the science section, that his parents were off soon to California in the car; Robbie was going with them, and Arthur was sure his father wasn't going to invite him. Not that Arthur wanted to go, especially in a car that would be pretty crowded with four, but his father wasn't going to say anything such as, 'Want to join us in S.F.?' if he took a plane, for instance. Rather amazing that his father thought him capable of taking care of the house alone for at least two weeks. To have the house to himself was going to be absolute heaven, Arthur thought.

He chose five books, got them checked out, and had gone through the wide doorway into the lobby, when Miss Becker called:

'Oh, Arthur! Almost forgot something. Talk about the absent-minded librarian!' She laughed and bent to pick up a white plastic bag from the floor beside her. 'This is for you. Little present. I won't be seeing much of you when you go off to Columbia, and I thought maybe you'd be going off somewhere this summer and you'd have time.'

Arthur was quite surprised. He could tell it was a book, a heavy book. 'Thanks very much, Miss Becker.'

'Hope you enjoy it.'

Fantastic, Arthur thought. He'd known Miss Becker since he was about ten, and he remembered her helping him to find certain books whose titles he had brought with him on paper. But to give a book present to just an ordinary borrower! Would this day be full of miracles?

Apple sauce, Arthur thought, when he was halfway home. His mother had asked him to pick up two cans. Arthur turned his bike around.

The house was empty when Arthur got home. His mother and grandmother had gone out to buy more curtain material, Arthur knew, and Robbie was with his friends at Delmar Lake. Arthur had an impulse to telephone Maggie now, at ten past eleven, instead of at noon as he had thought to do, but would she be still groggy, or would they say she was not allowed to speak to anyone as yet? Arthur went into his room and opened the present from Miss Becker. It was gift-wrapped in blue and gold paper. The book was *Life on Earth: Selected Essays*, a collection of the writing of some sixteen zoologists and biologists, most of whose names Arthur knew. A beautiful book! Inside, Miss Becker had written:

For Arthur Alderman. Onward and Upward and enjoy this.

Evelyn Becker

Arthur flipped through it, sniffing its new pages. Ah, bliss! He could have flung himself down and started reading any essay, with the same pleasure as any of the others.

But he'd call Maggie first, and now, while the house was empty. The hospital number had been in the back pocket of his trousers since last evening. He dialed, and asked for room eight sixteen.

A female voice answered.

A nurse, Arthur thought. 'I'm calling – to speak to Miss Brewster.' At that instant, Arthur heard a car door slam in the garage.

'She's right here,' said the female voice, then Maggie said:

'Hello? . . . Oh, hello, Arthur.'

'Are you all right?'

'Yes, sure I'm all right. And it's over.' She sounded a little sleepy.

'Really – everything – It went okay?'

Maggie told him it was okay, everything. Pain? Not worth

mentioning, said Maggie. And yes, her mother was there, and had just gone out to buy some Cokes, because the hospital had run out. And yes, she was coming home tomorrow, and wished she could that afternoon.

'That's just great, Maggie! – Get some sleep now. When can I call you again – and not bother you?'

'Anytime. But not later than eight.'

When they hung up, Arthur jumped several inches from the floor. Marvelous news! And Maggie sounded so calm, as if it were any other day! Arthur composed himself, because his mother and grandmother were in the kitchen, taking things out of bags, murmuring to each other. Arthur joined them.

'Well, Arthur,' said his grandmother, 'we had a most successful morning. And how about you?'

'Nice morning, thanks.' He saw yards of folded red-and-brown material on a chair. 'How's the curtain-making going?'

'Oh – um – rippingly, Lois?'

His mother was not smiling as she took things out of the fridge, starting to prepare lunch. 'I had to do a patch over. Won't happen again, I hope.'

'You're looking quite cheerful this morning,' his grandmother said. 'Maggie's all right?'

'Yes, thanks. Just spoke with her.'

His mother lit the oven. 'So it's over now.'

'Yes,' Arthur said.

'Your father prayed last night, Arthur,' said his mother. 'I want you to realize that – for what it's worth to you. He has his own way of seeing things. He prayed as earnestly as he did for Robbie.'

Was it his mother's way of seeing things, too? Arthur glanced at his grandmother, who was not looking at him. 'About Robbie, Mom – Could you ask him not to talk to his friends about Maggie? I'm sorry he heard all that last night.'

'Oh?' His mother went briskly about her work. 'Fifteen's old enough to know a few things. It would hardly have been possible to hide things from him.'

Not the way his father was talking, Arthur thought. He had a sudden feeling that his mother had turned against him and was taking his father's attitude. 'I mean – the sooner this can blow over, the better, Mom.'

His mother did not reply.

'Maggie's family's not making a big thing out of it, so I don't see why we have to.'

'All *right*, Arthur,' said his mother irritably.

Arthur waited, but nothing more came from his mother. 'So – I'll be pushing off.'

'Without lunch, Arthur?' said his grandmother. 'Haven't you got time?'

'N-no.'

His grandmother followed him into the garage, where his bike was. 'Just wanted you to know, Arthur – I'm very glad Maggie's all right. You're among friends here. Don't forget that.'

His grandmother was his friend, his father certainly not. And his mother? Arthur simply nodded once.

'Your father kept Loey up last night,' his grandmother whispered. 'She lost her sleep.'

'Yep,' Arthur said, feeling awkward. He waved a hand and rode off.

At nearly 4, when there was a lull in business, Arthur asked Tom if he could go out for a couple of minutes to make a telephone call.

'Can't you use our phone? Unless it's very personal.'

Arthur thought, why not? Shoe Repair wasn't home. He reached Maggie within seconds. She sounded wider awake and quite cheerful.

'Your mother there?' he asked.

'Not this minute. She's coming at six to keep me company when I eat.'

'What're you doing, reading? Watching TV?'

'Reading, yes – and thinking.'

'About what?'

'Very different things from what I usually think about. Tell you when I see you next time.'

That might have been ominous, but Maggie's tone was happy. 'What time you sprung tomorrow?'

'Noon. – Oh, I was up and around a lot today. I'm not bedridden.'

Maggie expected to be home by 2 tomorrow afternoon, and Arthur was to call her house after then. At 6:30 that evening, Arthur's spirits were still high. His father came in, looking tired and depressed, and declined even a beer, though his mother and grandmother were imbibing in the kitchen, and Robbie was on his umpty-umpth Coke. New blue curtains hung in Arthur's room, and since he was genuinely pleased by them, he told his grandmother so and kissed her on the cheek.

Robbie had been with his pals fishing all day, and he had a sunburned nose and a bad nick in his right thigh, caused by somebody's fishhook, Robbie said. Their mother changed the messy bandage and applied some of the white cream that Richard used to stop the bleeding of shaving nicks. Robbie sat at the table in shorts and a T-shirt, silent, shoving food in. Arthur expected his father to make some unkind remark, even an indirect one, about Maggie and This Awful Day, but he did not, and even the blessing had been mild, with nothing about wrongdoing. Still, his father looked like a man defeated, and therefore sad, and Arthur thought, what a small defeat, considering all the babies in the world! Would his father have been beaming if he and Maggie had had a baby on their hands in another seven months?

'Going anywhere tonight, Arthur?' asked his grandmother.

'Hadn't thought about it,' Arthur replied. But apart from Maggie, that was all he had been thinking about. He had to get out of the house and hear some music.

During the coffee period in the living room, he telephoned Gus. Gus answered, sounding slow and preoccupied, and in the background, Arthur heard Gus's siblings yelling.

'Sure, come on over,' Gus said.

As Arthur was leaving the house, his father stopped him. 'I'd still like a word with you, when you come home – whatever the hour.'

Again, Arthur thought. They were in the front hall. 'Well – can't we have it now?'

'I think you're a very callous young man.'

Arthur was aware of the heavy lines down his father's cheeks. 'All right. If that's your opinion.'

Arthur waited, but his father said nothing else. Arthur opened the front door. A minute later, he was cycling toward Gus's, inhaling the cool evening air.

The Warylskys' house was no bigger than Mrs DeWitt's, but much better kept. Lights were on in all five front windows, because every room was occupied by the big family. Arthur put his bike up on the front porch, and Gus opened the screen door to greet him.

The house smelled of carrots. Several of the family were watching TV in the living room.

They carried beer cans up to Gus's room. The room was small, with one front window, and Gus kept it in apple-pie order out of necessity. Tennis rackets and duffel bags had to go under the single bed, and there was no closet, just a pole Gus had rigged up for several hangers.

'What was the matter Sunday?' Gus asked.

'Oh – nothing. Just because it was Sunday dinner, my dad wanted me home. – Maybe because my grandma's visiting.'

Arthur drank from a beer can. 'You think we could have a little music?'

'Got a new Beach Boys.'

Gus put the cassette on, not loudly, because his father was already asleep in the next room, Gus said. He and his father had worked from 5 o'clock until dark, setting up a fence in the yard of someone on Eastside. Gus was so tired he dragged his feet.

'Had a good day? You look like it,' Gus said.

'Pretty good, yep.' Arthur wanted to talk about Maggie, and couldn't.

'Saw Maggie?'

'Spoke with her. I'll see her maybe tomorrow.'

Gus sat on the floor, leaning against the bed, his feet near Arthur, who was also sitting on the floor. The soft music sounded perfect; the beer tasted great. Arthur heard a toilet flush somewhere, and a little girl's voice call, 'Night, Mommie!' Maggie might be asleep now, at 9:15. Or was she watching TV, or reading? Was she as happy as he? Maybe she was even happier!

'What do you think of Veronica?' Gus asked sleepily, pushing his frail glasses upward with a forefinger.

It took Arthur a few seconds to replace his vision of Maggie with that of Veronica, a medium-pretty girl with long dark brown hair, not very tall, a girl he had never much noticed. 'All right,' said Arthur. 'You like her?'

'Yeah,' Gus said. 'I dunno, she—'

'Does she like you?'

'I dunno.' Gus's thin lips smiled. 'You can never tell what girls really mean, maybe. I mean the way they really feel.'

Arthur waited, listening more to the music than to Gus. Funny to think of Gus being hung up.

'When you think,' Gus went on, 'I've got four years of college ahead. And I was going to say, I dunno – how long this will last.

Maybe I shouldn't worry about it. Maybe it's better to consider it a short thing.'

'What will last?'

'The way I feel – or she feels.'

'Well, if you have any doubts,' Arthur said, his tone implying that to have any doubts nullified the whole thing.

'Can you expect a girl to hang on, I mean? They're always flirting, playing the field. Veronica not so *much*, I think,' he added earnestly. 'Or are you just supposed to change girls all the time – to be safe? That's a lot of work.'

Arthur thought of asking if Gus had been to bed with Veronica, but thought that might invite the same question in regard to Maggie. 'What does she say?'

'I think she likes me, but maybe because I like her. You see. But how long will it last for her?'

Arthur didn't know what to reply, and what Gus had said depressed him, because it might apply to Maggie, too. How long would Maggie care about him? Then Arthur realized that Maggie had – definitely – liked him in bed. And also afterward. He had been over those fifteen or twenty minutes, in his memory, many times. If she hadn't liked him then, she wouldn't have made another date with him, wouldn't have asked him to her house to meet her family. Everything got back to the fact of bed, Arthur thought. Or at least, that was quite important. Arthur forced himself to return to Gus's situation. 'Is Veronica going to college here?'

'Yep.'

'Well, that makes things a lot easier.'

'Why?'

'You can see her whenever you want to!' It seemed so obvious.

The cassette stopped.

Gus got up to put on another. 'This is called "Lightning."' When the cassette started, Gus stretched, and his fingertips just touched the ceiling. 'Wish I was a good dancer. I'm not even a medium-good dancer.'

A girl's voice sang:

. . . imagine the two of us,
just the two of us the-ere . . .

Gus lay on his bed, his head propped on one hand, and he stared at the floor. In the horizontal, he looked seven feet long. 'I have to wear glasses all the time. Doesn't make a very good impression on girls. I'm not as sure of myself as you are.'

Arthur smiled, loving his friend suddenly. 'But *you* can fix a girl's busted toilet!' Arthur laughed, and got a weak smile from Gus. Arthur's throat closed, his eyes closed, for an instant. Was it the music? No. It was his father. Maybe he was in for another attack tonight. Maybe his father would repeat the no to Columbia, maybe no to any money at all for any college, which meant he'd be stuck at C.U. at best, and Maggie would be even farther away from him. And here was Gus moaning about – what? 'You think I'm sure of myself?'

'Where's Maggie going to college?'

'Radcliffe. Didn't I tell you? Up by Harvard.'

'Yeah, well. Columbia's not so far away, is it?'

'True, true,' Arthur said calmly. He wasn't calm. On the other hand, Maggie liked him, wanted him to call her tomorrow afternoon, and wasn't that everything? Didn't that give courage? It was something he couldn't give to Gus, because it was his own dream, in his head, intangible.

'See this?' Gus asked. He had opened a magazine. The page showed a color photograph of a powerful-looking motorcycle with two black leather seats, a Harley-Davidson, costing a couple of thousand dollars. 'I don't want it,' said Gus, a bit sadly.

Arthur gave a laugh. Then why had Gus shown him the

picture? Why want a motorcycle when you had a car? Was Gus dreaming of being the type who danced well and raced through town on a motorcycle with a girl clinging to his waist? Gus was going to study agriculture at C.U., maybe become a farmer. Arthur drank the last drops of his beer, and asked in a stuffy tone, 'Are you supplied with contraceptives, Gus?'

'Na-aw. – You mean in regard to Veronica? On two dates with her – so far?'

The music sounded suddenly like a mountain of tin cans falling, while the throbbing drumbeat went on.

'You equipped?' Gus asked.

'Why, yes.' Arthur jumped up and produced from a pocket the flat little box of Trojans.

Gus looked at it as if it were an atom bomb or something contraband. 'Yeah, sure, I know.'

Arthur stuck the box back in his pocket. He had not wanted to leave them at home, not even in the back of one of his top drawers. It occurred to Arthur that Gus's family was much more religious than his own. The Warylskys were nearly Catholic, Arthur thought, though he had never asked. He knew Gus's parents went to church every Sunday, whereas Arthur's family had just found religion or the church in a completely different way. Maybe Gus had never been in bed with a girl, simply because it was taboo before marriage, according to his family. Suddenly Arthur felt that his father's attitude was all the more bogus because it was new. The Warylskys spoke little, but practised their religion.

'You use 'em?' Gus asked casually.

'Yes, sure. Otherwise why would I have 'em?'

Gus gave him a lingering, sidewise glance. 'With Maggie?'

Arthur hesitated a second. 'No-o. She doesn't sleep around.' He felt pleased with the answer which both protected Maggie and implied that he had some opportunity with other girls, if he so chose. He dropped his beer can into Gus's wastebasket.

'Another beer, old pal?'

'Thanks, I'd better get moving.' Arthur felt on a crest of confidence just then and thought he had better use it to face his father in the next minutes.

Gus went downstairs with him, and Arthur picked up his bike from the front porch. Someone was still in the living room, watching TV, and in fact it was only a little past 10.

As Arthur entered the kitchen from the garage of his house, his father came in from the living room, dressed but in house-slippers, walking like a slow bear. And just then, Arthur heard a snort from the living room, the sound Robbie made sometimes when he slept, and at once his father turned and said:

'Robbie? Awake, boy? Come and join us. – I want Robbie to hear this, because he's old enough.'

Arthur stood with his back to the refrigerator, hands on his hips. Robbie came in blinking, sleepy-eyed, in pajamas. The house was as silent as if his mother and grandmother were listening from somewhere, but Arthur had the feeling they were in their separate rooms.

'I've had a talk with your mother,' his father began softly, 'and with your brother, too. – Let's all go in and sit down.'

Now his father shepherded them to the living room.

'Those who go against the Lord,' his father said, still softly, 'will pay the price. I'm not so good this evening – after a night of fruitless prayer – last night – at saying to you what I want to, but I'm sure the words will come, just as they come – at our family table when I say blessing.' Now a pause.

Arthur was wondering if his father had tried again to speak with the Brewsters? Maggie's father just might be home by himself this evening. This possibility made Arthur flinch, and he rubbed his palm across his forehead.

'I could have forgiven an adolescent mishap – but for your attitude. You did nothing to prevent what happened today – this morning. I consider it worse than a disgrace to the family. It's a cardinal sin.' His eyes rested sadly on Robbie. 'Robbie thinks so, too. And your mother.'

His father lived in another world, Arthur reminded himself. Arthur tried deliberately to feel miles away from it. 'You talked to my mother? She thinks—'

'You are not being financed by me to go to Columbia or anywhere else.'

'Yes, I think you said that,' said Arthur.

'Well, now you have it again,' said his father with a grim nod.

A faint chill ran up Arthur's spine. Robbie sat tensely on the sofa gazing at him as if he were someone on trial and guilty. The corners of Robbie's mouth turned down a little. His father hadn't finished college, because his family had gone broke just then, Arthur knew. Then his mother hadn't finished, because she had met his father and they had got married. *Pity my mother married a small-minded nobody like you*, Arthur wanted to say. His father had insulted Maggie by talking to people like Eddie Howell, and Arthur was inspired to insult his father in return.

'Nothing to say for yourself,' said his father, as if it were obvious that he hadn't.

Cool it, Arthur told himself. His father was simply in another world. Arthur kept cool outwardly, with his fingers folded on his abdomen, as he slumped in his chair, but his heart thumped as if he were fighting.

'Nothing,' his father repeated.

'What adult,' Arthur said, 'told the story in that yackety church? Did the Reverend tell you who it was?'

'Don't speak in that manner, Arthur.'

Arthur looked at his brother. 'What do you think of that, Robbie? The church people are the gossips – like old women hanging over the back fence.'

'Yackers when they spoke the truth. Gossips,' said his father with a little smile.

Robbie said nothing. His father had already brainwashed Robbie, of course. Robbie believed he was even someone special, Arthur supposed, whom God had chosen to save, in contrast to others God had not chosen to save that particular day or night. Arthur blinked and tried to put on an unangry face. 'You're not telling me my mother thinks the same way you do, are you, Dad? Or my grandmother either?'

'You just ask them,' said his father on a conclusive note.

Was that it? The end of the dusting off for tonight? Arthur stood up and nodded brusquely as if to say, 'I'll do that.' He went off to his room.

14

Arthur was able to talk to his grandmother the next morning, after his father had left for work. His mother had gone off to drive a little girl to the doctor's, because the little girl's mother had no car.

'Dad talked with you and Mom again last night, it seems.'

His grandmother sat on the sofa, sewing small brass rings into a curtain. 'Yes.' She glanced up at Arthur. 'He's overtired – and upset, too.'

Arthur was standing in the middle of the living room. 'I tried to explain – there's nothing to be upset about.' He spoke softly, because Robbie was still asleep, or at least had not put in an appearance as yet. His grandmother's seconds of silence surprised Arthur. Wasn't she on his side? 'He's not giving me anything toward college fees, so maybe that'll give him satisfaction. I frankly don't know what he wants.'

His grandmother twisted a thread around her finger and broke the thread. 'He wants you to say you're sorry.'

'Oh!' Arthur smiled. 'I've said that. I *am* sorry.'

'He thinks you're not sorry enough – as you see.' Now his grandmother sounded more like herself. She threaded her needle and resumed her work.

'Well – am I supposed to crawl around on the floor?'

'No, no, Arthur. – Sit down.'

Arthur didn't want to sit down but he did, on a straight chair rather opposite the sofa.

'I'd lend you the money for college or give it to you, probably,' she went on, 'but that would be flying right in Richard's face.'

Arthur suddenly understood. His grandmother had to 'keep the peace,' too. He was shocked for a moment. Was she going to take his father's side, even *see* his father's side, his grandmother whom he loved even more than his mother, he realized? She had been on his side when he was thirteen and said he was bored with games at school and couldn't a person be just as healthy without them? She had given him wonderful books all his life, usually books for grown-ups, and she had told him to look up every word he didn't know – a rule he had more or less kept.

'Your father thinks you've broken a law of God's – or the church's. That's the way he puts it, Arthur.'

Arthur knew. 'I don't know what's come over him. This is all recent. – Gosh, just a year ago Dad and I went on a camping trip. Two nights sleeping in a tent up north of here. Really fun! – Hard to believe now.' His father now was a different person. Camping out overnight would be a waste of time. 'He's earning a lot more lately. You'd think money would cheer a person up, wouldn't you? If that's their aim in life. You'd think it'd make them less religious – since they say Christ wasn't famous for caring about money.'

Head bent over her work, his grandmother said, 'The church has always been able to reconcile money and religion.'

And politics, maybe. Suddenly he smiled. 'Dad told me he crosses people off his list of clients, if they don't go to church – *some* church. Or if he thinks they're too liberal. He's gone very Republican. Used to be a Democrat when I was little. – What does Mom say to you?'

'Well – she said Richard was very shocked. So he's reacting. And your mother believes in keeping the peace, as you know.' His grandmother gave him a quick glance. 'Your father – What's he now, forty-three? He's trying to make something of himself before it's too late. It's bound to be with his job and the church and the townspeople, that's true. So he's hammering especially hard at you. Hard to take, I know, Arthur. Just be patient – for a time.' Now she stood up, holding the curtain high to get as much off the floor as possible. 'Now you're strong, Arthur – I think.' She extended her free arm.

Arthur put his arm around his grandmother's waist and kissed her cheek, because that was what she expected.

'Hold this side up. You're tall. See what—'

'No, I'm *not*.'

'See what you think. Won't these be pretty? There'll be two of them of course.'

They held the red-and-brown curtain as high as their arms could reach. It did look pretty.

'I'm sure, yes,' Arthur said.

At 3, an hour Arthur felt for some reason to be lucky in regard to Maggie, he telephoned the Brewster house. The telephone rang a long time, and Arthur supposed Maggie and her mother were not back yet from Indi, and then Maggie answered.

'How're you feeling?' Arthur asked.

'Fine. Really. I was downstairs and I came up to get the phone here. I thought it was you. A neighbor's visiting downstairs.' She sounded as if she were smiling.

'Any chance I can see you today? Six-thirty or so?'

Maggie said 6:30 would be fine. Arthur had brought the scarf box to Shoe Repair, hoping for a date after work.

Maggie opened the door for him. She wore the rust-colored slacks that he remembered so well, a white shirt, no makeup, and she looked as if she had just stepped out of a bath. Her eyes were shining.

'Brought you this,' he said, extending the white plastic bag.

She closed the door. 'Can I open it now?'

'Why not?' Arthur wanted to embrace her, to kiss her cheek at least, but somehow didn't dare. And mightn't somebody be in the living room?

There was no one in the living room, only the orange and white cat called Jasper in his usual sleeping spot at the end of the sofa. Maggie opened the box carefully.

'Oh, how pretty! I love it, Arthur.' She held it up as his grandmother had held the curtain that morning, then swung it round her neck and looked at herself in a mirror. 'Maybe my favorite colors.'

Arthur did not take his eyes from her. He felt in awe of her. Had she changed? She must have changed, somehow. 'Maggie, you're not sad?' He spoke softly. 'Feeling funny?'

She glanced shyly at the floor for a second. 'No. Not yet, anyway. My mother asked me that. – I was more depressed before.' She beckoned him into the kitchen. 'To celebrate,' she said, 'let's have a gin and tonic – each.'

Arthur smiled, watching her make them, wearing the new scarf which she had lightly tied and which hung over her shirt collar. His smile became a grin.

Maggie was aware of his staring at her and didn't seem to mind it. She even gave him a mischievous smile. 'And what's your news?' she asked, handing him his drink. 'Cheers.'

'Cheers. – My news is that – it looks like I can't go to Columbia. My dad's not contributing a cent.'

'What? Even with the grant you can't go?'

Arthur explained. His father was livid and had cut the purse strings and for sure. Maybe he could afford C.U., sleeping home. 'Horrible prospect – sleeping home.'

'My gosh, I'm sorry, Arthur. Can't your grandma do something? Persuade him?'

Arthur explained that, too. His grandmother didn't want to antagonize his father. They were now in the living room, and before they had sat down anywhere, Maggie's mother came down the stairs.

'Hello, Arthur,' she said. 'And how are you?'

Mrs Brewster appeared pleasant, but was that only politeness? She wouldn't sit down.

'Again, I'm sorry about my family annoying you on Sunday, Mrs Brewster. It's only my father, not my mother.'

'Oh,' she replied with a shrug. 'People have their views. And Maggie said your father's not a Catholic.'

'Definitely not! That's why I was so—'

'No more talk about it,' Mrs Brewster interrupted. 'See you folks later, maybe.' She went on to the kitchen.

What was he to make of that? Did she detest him? Arthur took a gulp of his drink.

'Your mother. It's a little different from my family.'

'Sit down.'

Arthur sat.

'Want to stay for dinner? My mother said you're welcome to. My dad's not here, by the way.'

Arthur had meant to pay a short visit. He had thought Maggie would be tired or sad or distant, and she was none of these things. He was uncertain about her mother's attitude, however, and this made him uncomfortable. 'Better not, thanks.' He swallowed the rest of his drink. Suddenly he felt awkward. 'I better be going.'

'Already?'

Arthur had stood up. 'I'm so glad you're okay. – Can I call you? See you this week?'

'Sure. Afternoons I'll be mostly in. Mornings are the math course. – I didn't tell you yet about the things I was thinking about in the hospital! The hospital was a great place for thinking, really another world. My idea – or ideas – are about having a course in school – could be high school or college or both. And it could be called just "Life." It'd be to teach people how to deal with all kinds of problems that turn up in everyday life. Could be landlord problems, insurance problems – even abortions – broken legs, children who need help because their parents have broken up – There're so many things. And I think a lot of people don't know how to handle things at all – even if there's some kind of bureau they can go to for help, they don't know about it.' Maggie's face glowed.

'Big order. I know what you mean.'

'Mom and Dad said it would come under sociology. If I had to categorize it. Anyway, I'm enthusiastic. I'll have to see how it shapes up in the next days.'

'In your head,' Arthur said.

'Yes.'

They were at the door. Maggie leaned on him, so that he had to brace himself. He lifted her a few inches from the floor.

'I do love you, darling,' he whispered. 'G'bye.'

She didn't say anything, but that was all right.

Arthur supposed he would be a little late for dinner, but his parents and grandmother and Robbie were watching a TV program which Arthur at once recognized as one of the evangelical shows. A telephone number remained at the bottom of the screen throughout the program, a toll-free number that people could call and give their names and addresses if they wanted religious matter sent to them or if they wanted to join the organization or pledge a contribution. Arthur gave his grandmother a nod of greeting, and leaned against the jamb of the living room doorway, watching. An old cowboy actor, who had been retired since Arthur was a small boy, was now talking out of a slender, weathered, brick-red face. He wore a white Stetson, string tie and an electric blue business suit.

'. . . easy, man, when you know, you *know*, that someone up there, out there, anyway you want to put it, cares about you. You're not alone then. It's as good as havin' a warm, lovin' family around you, even if you're livin' alone in your house or apartment because your spouse has passed on, which may be the case of many of our viewers tonight. But that we are *not* alone – that's what I and my wife found out – at long last – after we had that terrible news delivered to us – by our doctor – about our beloved little adopted daughter Susie. Susie's alive now; you'll see her tonight. She limps, true, because she's got a bone disease. But please notice the expression on her face! It's bustin' with joy, with the . . .'

The screen showed a made-up little girl of about nine with curly blond hair and smiling red lips.

'. . . because she's discovered Christ's charity same as we did . . .'

Then the ex-cowboy's wife came on, Lucy, looking close to seventy in the brilliant lights, heavy with makeup, in a nearly white evening dress. Her waistline looked corsetted and as if it would hurt her to breathe. '. . . in this day and age, when our values are challenged and weakened at every turn in life . . .'

'Oh, no,' Arthur murmured, smiling, and was glad no one in the room heard him. His father leaned forward in his armchair as if to memorize every word. That bit about weakened values was her little wedge, maybe, slipped in slyly to soften up for the hard sell to come: You'd better join the church or buy our book or pledge a contribution or – what? You'll be lost, Arthur supposed, miserable, drunken, alone and shunned. Broke, too. Arthur crossed his feet the other way.

'. . . when my beloved husband Jock and I realized that though we thought we were up against it, God was just testing us – to see if we *would* call on Him. And in my book *Touched by the Lord* I've described the step-by-step . . . but always in the right direction, till that glorious moment when our Susie smiled at us and we knew she was miraculously free of pain.' The old bag smiled more widely, took a tremendous breath of air and sighed.

Arthur drifted into the kitchen. Now he heard the tremolo organ music that indicated the end of the program. It wasn't a church hymn, but a nice old song called 'On the Sunny Side of the Street,' but the way they played made it sound like a dirge.

The family came into the kitchen.

'We've made some changes in our plans, Arthur,' his mother said, as she brought a big salad bowl to the table. 'We're driving to Kansas City Friday, Richard and I and Mama; then Robbie'll fly down a few days later. Not really room for all of us in the car.'

'Then we're driving from Kansas City to San Francisco,' Robbie put in with more enthusiasm than he usually showed about anything, 'through the Mojave Desert and via Santa Fé, where we'll stay a night.'

Arthur caught the note of one-upmanship in his brother's tone. Arthur was going to be stuck at home in the hot mid-western summer, Robbie seemed to say, in disgrace and with not even Columbia to look forward to. 'How nice,' Arthur said to Robbie.

'You could fly out and join us in San Francisco, if you felt like it, Arthur,' said his mother.

They all sat down.

'I'll see. Thank you, Mom.'

The blessing. It was more flowing than usual, as if the TV program had inspired his father.

'Busy day at the shop, Arthur?' his mother asked. 'You're home late tonight.'

'I had a short date after work.'

'There's room for you in Kansas City, Arthur,' said his grandmother. 'I phoned my friend Carol who lives in the same building, and I knew she was going on vacation about now, and she said she'd be very willing for you to have her apartment just to sleep in for a few days. But maybe the idea doesn't sound all that attractive to you.'

It didn't. 'Thanks, Grandma. Not with the job and all.' The idea of putting a distance between himself and Maggie this summer was absurd, and the thought of being anywhere near his father for two weeks or more was odious.

'I told Norma you might be on your own here,' his mother said.

'Why don't you ask Norma over for a drink, Mom? While Grandma's here?'

'Do you know, I asked her this very day, and she declined? Said she was tired or something. She could try going to bed earlier.' Lois smiled, as if glad to have something to smile at. 'I believe she's been here just three or four times in the years we've lived here, Mama. She's very friendly, and we can drop in or call her up and go over anytime, but if we invite her, she's always not feeling too strong, or there's a TV program she wants to watch.'

'She had cancer,' Arthur said. 'Cheerfullest cancer victim I ever saw. We need more like her.'

Here Richard deigned to give him a glance.

Fifteen minutes later, with his coffee cup beside him, Arthur was writing a letter to the head of the Admission Department of Columbia University.

Dear Mr Xarrip:

Due to circumstances beyond my control, I shall not be able to enter Columbia University in September as I had hoped. The expense of $10,450 is more than my parents and I can meet even with the grant, for which I was and am grateful.

Here Arthur chewed his lip and debated writing a second paragraph about the grant being possibly applicable to another college, but thought this wasn't Mr Xarrip's concern. He added

'Yours sincerely' and signed it. He would read it over tomorrow morning, maybe add something and retype it, but tonight he had to get it off his mind.

He hoped his grandmother would knock on his door. But she didn't knock that evening.

15

By Thursday morning, the atmosphere in the house had again changed. His mother made seemingly endless trips from bedroom and kitchen to car, storing the First Aid kit in the glove compartment, sticking a bathing cap into a suitcase already in the back of his father's large and stronger car, which was the one they were taking. One of Robbie's pals had picked him up before 10. His father hadn't gone to work and still wasn't speaking to Arthur, and Arthur felt that his father had tried, and had succeeded, in looking at him without seeing him, which didn't bother Arthur. He was supposed to feel outcast, shunned and wretched, Arthur supposed, but whenever he felt the slightest bit down, he remembered Maggie. He was the lucky one, he thought, with Maggie in his life! By the others, he felt abandoned, meaning his mother and grandmother. Even his mother had barely had a minute to say something to him in regard to college in September, about what he was supposed to do with himself.

'You can find a place somewhere, I know, Arthur, with your good grades. We'll talk about that when we get back, and that won't be long, toward the end of July.'

She had reminded him about locking all doors when he went out and had given him a couple of checks signed and made out to the newspaper deliverer and for the electricity bill which was due.

Friday morning, Arthur awakened to the sounds of voices and bumpings. It was just after 6 and already light. He didn't get out of bed to say good-bye even to his grandmother, because he had said that the night before. Arthur lay with open eyes, listening to the laden car rolling down the driveway, hearing Robbie's 'Bye-bye!' to them from outside. Arthur was thinking, there's Maggie, there's Norma, and there's Gus. People you could count on.

And he had to make up his mind about trying for Chicago University or C.U., the latter being cheaper, because he might not get a penny from his parents, though his grandmother's generosity might return in a few weeks, once she was relieved of his father's pressure.

He put on a bathrobe and house-slippers and went into the kitchen, where he found Robbie leaning against the sink, barefoot in pajamas, drinking from a Coke can. Arthur shook his head. 'Starting early, this corruption.'

Robbie laughed a little, his gray eyes merry, perhaps with the prospect of their running the house alone now.

Arthur made coffee. 'What're you up to today, Robbie?'

'Goin' fishin'.'

'Again?' Robbie liked the phrase 'going fishin',' Arthur had noticed. 'Is that all you do – just sit there all day with a pole in your hands? In a boat?'

Robbie nodded and winced from a belch. 'No, we talk – sometimes.'

Though he slumped against the sink, Robbie looked as tall as himself. The morning sun touched his uncombed hair, making it golden on top, and the sun put a metallic glint in his left eye. His eyes were fixed on Arthur.

'Friends coming for you this morning?'

'Yeah. Round ten,' Robbie said.

'Because—' Arthur said, adjusting the fire under the coffee, 'after I make this, I'm going back to bed without any coffee. I want a couple of hours' sleep. Can you get your own breakfast?'

'Sure. You think I'm a child?'

'Can you turn this off in five or six minutes?'

'Sure!'

Arthur went back to bed, feeling as sleepy as if he had taken a drug. He fell blissfully asleep at once and woke up to a faint and pleasant sound of music. It came from a cassette in Robbie's room. Arthur got up and re-read his letter to Columbia, and decided he would send it as it was. He had thought last night of writing a note to Professor Thatcher in the biology department of Columbia. More than a year ago, Arthur had written the professor, whose name he had found in the Columbia catalogue, to ask a question about the cold light phenomenon of underwater life, and the professor had replied in some detail, with a couple of Xeroxed pages from a scientific quarterly. Arthur had written again to thank him and had said that he hoped to go to Columbia and major in biology. Had Professor Thatcher possibly put in a good word for him at Columbia? But Arthur decided not to write again to Professor Thatcher, because the letter could only be a sad one.

The kitchen smelled of sausages; the skillet had grease in it, and Robbie's egg-smeared plate lay in the sink. Inspired by the aroma, Arthur fried a couple of sausages and an egg and was eating, looking at yesterday's newspaper, when Robbie came in wearing cut-off blue jeans and an old shirt.

'How about if I take a look at your fishing place this morning?' Arthur asked.

'What do you mean?'

'Just take a look for two minutes. Think I'm going to spend all day there?'

Robbie seemed oddly resistant, as if the fishermen were a closed club with private grounds, but it was a public park, Arthur knew, and Arthur said he was riding over.

Arthur set out a few minutes before 10, pedaling slowly, because the sun was already starting to broil down. If Robbie and his older friends passed him in a car, he wasn't aware of it. He was lost in his own thoughts or dreams. And they were pretty vague, he realized. How would the summer turn out? At what college would he be in September? Would his mother get from under his father's thumb long enough to channel some money, somehow, towards college? They had a joint checking account, Arthur knew. He had to find out how things stood, very soon, and act accordingly.

Suddenly he was at the park that surrounded Delmar Lake. Long picnic tables and wooden benches stood here and there, and half a dozen rowboats lay moored at two piers that projected from boathouses. Arthur pedaled along a dirt path toward the first pier, the longer. Three or four rather beat-up cars were parked near the boathouse, and from a distance Arthur recognized his brother, the skinniest figure among a group of five men. Arthur propped his bike against a tree and walked on. Robbie had seen him, but gave no sign of greeting.

'Hi,' Arthur said to one of the men who looked at him. 'I'm Robbie's brother. Arthur.'

'Oh, yeah. We know,' said another man of about fifty, who wore old khaki trousers and a straw hat with holes in it. 'Figurin' on fishin' today?'

Arthur shook his head and smiled a little. 'No, just thought I'd look at your setup here. Pretty neat.' It was anything but neat. The boathouse was falling apart in places.

One of the other men had barely said, 'Hi,' to Arthur, and the two others might not have seen him. Robbie bent over a long wooden box of fishing gear. Arthur saw a couple of six-packs of beer, another of Pepsi, and a couple of baskets containing what he supposed were sandwiches. The youngest of the men was about thirty.

'Robbie, git my good hooks there!' called a paunchy old guy on the pier. 'And the rod with the green on it.'

'You're the fellow we heard about?' asked the first man Arthur had spoken to. 'Ain't got no older brothers, have you?'

'No.' Arthur's cheeks began to sting in a funny way. He was suddenly on guard.

The man nodded and smiled knowingly under the old straw hat and spat to one side.

At least he hadn't spat tobacco juice, Arthur noticed.

The second man came up, hatless, unshaven, wearing dirty green corduroys. 'You figurin' on joinin' *us*?' he asked, as if their club was pretty exclusive.

'No, no. Got a job to go to,' Arthur replied. 'Just wanted to see how my little brother spends his time.' Arthur got no reply. 'Catch any good eatin' fish there? My brother brought a bass home the other day.'

'You got an unusual brother,' said the second man.

'Keeps quiet,' said the first man. 'Got respect. – Nothin' so unusual about you, eh?' He went off into a wheezy guffaw, turned his back on Arthur and motioned to the other man to come with him. Both started talking to the other men who were now unmooring, with Robbie's nimble help, two of the rowboats tied up at the pier. The lake stretched broad and smooth beyond and to the left.

Arthur hated the lot of them. What had Robbie told them about him? And Maggie? Had he mentioned her name? Arthur didn't want to leave as if he had been shooed off, so he shouted, 'Hey, Robbie!'

Robbie straightened up, feet apart. 'What?'

'Have yourself a nice day!' Arthur waved and went back to his bike.

Sinister atmosphere there. Maybe in their sloppy way these men were holier-than-thou types, too? Weren't these old guys married? Or maybe they were transients, wanderers, with cars but no jobs? He might ask Robbie about that.

That evening, Friday, Arthur had a date with Maggie, but not until 9 o'clock or a little after, she had said, because her parents had a woman houseguest and Maggie had to have dinner at home. So Arthur made something for himself and Robbie to eat. Robbie looked sunburned to the point of pain and was still in the same clothes and barefoot, though he claimed to have taken a shower.

'Those old guys,' Arthur said during their meal. 'Don't you find it sort of depressing, spending the whole day with them?'

'No. – Why should I? They tell jokes – sometimes.'

Arthur recalled the fellow in the straw hat breaking up over something that wasn't particularly funny. 'What've you been telling them about me – for instance?'

'About you?' Robbie looked straight at his brother with his cool gray eyes, and oddly it was his head and his hand with the lifted fork that wavered a little. ''Bout what?'

'You know about what.'

'You mean – the girl.'

'Maggie – if you don't mind. I don't mind and she doesn't mind.'

'Yeah, well.' Robbie looked at the table, then back at Arthur.

'They knew about it anyway. What do you mean, what did I tell them?'

Arthur didn't believe that. 'And who told them?'

'Well, a couple of 'em go to the church – Christ Gospel.'

'No kidding?'

'Jeff goes. Sometimes. He's the one you were talking to this morning.'

'The one in the straw hat? – You mean they hear news at the church and then spread it around?'

'No-o, silly!' Robbie squirmed, though squirming was habitual with him, and he looked not at all embarrassed. 'Whole town knows about it, anyway.'

'That is not true,' Arthur said, but suddenly he was unsure himself, and furious at the thought that a handful of gossips, maybe starting with Roxanne, might have created the impression that the whole town knew. Tom Robertson didn't know, or he would have said something, Arthur was pretty sure. Norma Keer didn't know, and she saw a lot of people at her teller's window, and a lot of chatting went on there. 'Come on, Robbie. What did you say to your friends?'

'They knew it! What d'y'mean I had to *say* anything?'

Arthur thought Robbie was lying, and that he wasn't going to get anywhere. He had lost his appetite.

However, when they were tidying up the kitchen, Arthur felt compelled to say, 'You really shouldn't, Robbie – at your age – talk with grown-ups about things like – what we were talking about. You shouldn't spread the yacking. If you were a good brother, you wouldn't do that.'

Robbie was standing in the kitchen, spooning up the last of the walnut crunch ice cream from its plastic container. 'You're not a good brother,' Robbie said. 'Dad says that. He says you're not a good brother to me.'

'Oh.' Arthur shook the suds off his hands and turned around. 'It just could happen to you – someday.'

'Oh, no!' Robbie shook his head slowly.

'If you'd think for a minute, Robbie – nothing awful has happened, if just you and a lot of other people would shut up about it.'

'Your girlfriend had an abortion,' Robbie said.

'And some people have a tonsillectomy – like you.'

'Oh-h – you're tellin' me it's the same?'

'Wait'll it happens to you.' Arthur turned back to the sink.

'It'll never happen to me. I'll get married first. That's the right way to – to do, Dad says.'

Arthur squeezed the sponge and tossed it by the water taps.

Robbie went into the living room and turned the TV up more loudly.

Then the telephone rang.

Robbie got up from the floor and leapt for it. 'That's Mom. She said she'd phone at eight,' he said to Arthur, who was standing in the living room doorway. '... Oh, okay, Mom ... Yep ... Nope ... Nope.' Robbie laughed. 'No, he's here ... Okay.' He handed the telephone to Arthur.

'Hello, Arthur. Just wanted to know if everything is all right there.'

'Yes, fine. Had a good trip?'

'Ah-h – a little exhausting in the heat. But the apartment here is air-conditioned, and we've all just had showers.' She laughed. 'More heat waves due, we heard. We're going on to San Francisco Wednesday morning. I gave you the name of our hotel, didn't I?'

'It's right here by the phone.'

'How's that cut on Robbie's thigh?'

'He didn't say anything about it. Hey, Robbie, how's that cut on your thigh?'

Engrossed in TV, Robbie had to have the question repeated; then over his shoulder he said, 'Okay.'

'Okay,' Arthur reported.

'Mama's out with her partner Blanche now, or I'd have her talk with you ... Well, take care, Arthur, and call us if anything goes wrong, will you?'

When they had hung up, Arthur glanced at his watch. In half an hour he'd set off for Maggie's on his bike. And in a little more than two months he would be eighteen and could drive the car – his mother's – now sitting in the garage, thereby complying with his father's law. He was going into his room when he heard a knock at the door.

'Expecting somebody?' he asked Robbie.

Robbie turned over. 'Nope.'

Arthur half opened the door.

A blond woman stood on the doorstep in a pale summer dress and with a big white pocketbook in her hand. 'Good evening. You're – Is Richard – Mr Alderman—' She looked worried.

'If you mean my father, he's not here.' She was one of the young churchgoers his father talked to, Arthur supposed, though this one looked about thirty. 'My parents took off this morning.'

'No, I—' Her brown eyes glanced nervously sideways and back to Arthur; then she advanced. 'I wanted to see him. Richard. I don't mean to be intruding.'

Arthur stepped back. He left the door open. 'My parents went to Kansas. Won't be back for another two or three weeks.'

She was looking over the partition at the kitchen walls, the ceiling. 'Well, I know,' she said in a gentle voice. 'I just wanted to set foot here again – somehow. Your father has helped me so much. Me and my sister Louise. – Hello, Robbie.' Her very red lips spread in a smile, showing small teeth.

Robbie stood in the living room doorway, his mouth a little open in surprise. 'My father told you not to come here while he's gone.'

'Yes, but – I've just explained – to your brother. He seems nice,' she added, turning her smile on Arthur.

Was she drugged on something, Arthur wondered. She didn't seem drunk, just odd.

'My name is Irene Langley,' she told Arthur in a straightforward way. 'I live with my sister and my mother – who's dying at home. So when I talk to your father – he's very comforting to me.'

'My father said he'd see you when he got back and not to come here,' Robbie said like a soldier passing on orders from a superior. 'I heard him.'

'Been here a few times before?' Arthur asked her.

'Oh, yes. Four or five times – in the afternoons.' She swayed or bent a little, gazing past Robbie into the living room.

Robbie frowned. 'Well, it's no use right now; you can see that.'

'Can I write to your father? Or phone him? I don't think he'd mind that.' She leaned toward Robbie now, and a brown color was visible to Arthur along the left-side part of her hair.

'I think he'd mind it,' Robbie said. 'If he didn't give you his address, that means he doesn't want you to have it.'

The woman seemed not at all offended by Robbie's tone. 'Dear Robbie, what's happened to your *leg*?' She bent closer with concern.

'Oh – fishhook. 'S nothing.'

'Can I give any message from you to my father?' Arthur said, wanting to get rid of her, edging toward the door.

'Just tell him I—' She smiled gently and gazed at the living room ceiling. 'It's such a comfort for me to be here for a few minutes, because Richard gives me such courage. Faith, really. And patience, he calls it. He shows me what to read – which helps such a lot.'

Arthur nodded. 'You have a job?'

'I'm a waitress. Not regular hours. Sometimes at night. It's a diner. Well, a couple of diners, run by the same man.'

The powder on her face looked like paste or dried flour. Robbie scowled in the doorway as if on the brink of pushing her out.

'Well, thank you,' she said to Arthur. 'It's done me such good – being here. It's almost as good as being in a church, because your father has said so many comforting things to me here.'

Arthur moved willingly toward the front door. 'What's your mother dying of?' he asked, curious despite himself.

'Kidney.'

Arthur stood outside on the short porch with the door open. Irene Langley stared into the gathering darkness as if it were some task that she had to face. Behind her, Robbie advanced like a checkerboard piece, ready to oust her.

'G'night, Robbie,' she said, turning as if she had known he was there. Her white high-heeled shoes were worn out, and it crossed Arthur's mind that she might be giving all her extra money to the church, because people at the church had told her to.

'Night,' said Robbie ungraciously. 'I think you better not come here again till my father gets back. What good is it?'

'The aura,' she replied sweetly, smiling at Robbie. 'And we all forgive you,' she added gently to Arthur, 'and bless you just the same. Don't be afraid, because the Lord is with you. That's what your father says.'

Does he, Arthur thought, feeling that he was in the presence of a nut. He walked down the front steps to encourage her departure. She did follow him, slowly.

'Your father thinks he's failed with you, that you've failed with yourself. He told me all about it,' she said with a weak smile that was perhaps meant to be friendly. 'But it's never too late to change. Of course the baby's gone now, but it's not too late for you.'

The baby. A seven-week-old fetus. Hardly distinguishable from a pig's fetus, Arthur reminded himself.

'Do you know,' she began, reaching forth with one hand as she leaned toward Arthur, but he stepped back, 'what strength it takes to watch a mother dying day by day? The hospital just won't keep my mother anymore.' She shook her head for emphasis. 'She can get painkillers galore now, but the doctors say she's happier at home and there's nothing more they can do for her in the hospital. Do you know what it takes to find the strength to face that – calmly?'

The strength that comes from having gone nuts, Arthur thought, at least in this case. 'I can imagine.' He glanced over his shoulder toward Norma's house, just as her living room light came on palely beyond her curtains. If Norma could hear this, how she'd chuckle!

'You're nervous, you feel guilty,' she informed Arthur. 'But all that can go away, if you give yourself into the care of Jesus. You and your girlfriend. But you must repent, and that means, Richard says, just to say you're sorry.'

Arthur nodded and led the way down the walk. 'Did you come in a car?'

'No, I walked.'

'Where do you live?'

'Haskill and Main.'

A mile away at least. 'Your sister has a job, too?'

'No, she stays home and looks after our mother. My sister Louise is fat. Very fat,' said Irene Langley with a laugh that showed more of her small teeth. 'Your father says that's a sin, too – gluttony. But your father smiled when I told him my sister can't resist a candy box. Your father has a sense of humor, you know? And tolerance – such tolerance! I can talk to him better than I can to Bob Cole, though he's pretty good and never closed his ear to me, I'll say that. But your father is warmer – because he's just discovered God himself. His words are new, as he says.'

'You're married?' Arthur asked.

'Now why do you ask me that? – No, but I was married unhappily for about two years. I've been divorced four years now. And I'm *much* happier.'

Arthur saw Robbie on the front steps, watching, and he walked on toward the sidewalkless street.

Now she seemed to realize that he wanted to get rid of her, and she walked suddenly ahead of him, waving, saying over her shoulder, 'Good-bye, Arthur, and bless you!'

Arthur watched her light-colored figure disappear quickly along the edge of the street, under the shadows of the tulip and sycamore trees. He felt a horrible sense of unhappiness suddenly – of her unhappiness. Arthur saw his brother's figure turn and go into the house. He shoved his hands into his back pockets and leapt the front steps.

'You could've been more polite,' Arthur said to Robbie when he had closed the front door. 'What's the idea of talking to a young lady like that? "My father told you not to come here."'

'A young lady?' Robbie replied, gathering himself for combat.

'Yes. Is that the way you treat a friend of Dad's, not even asking her to sit down?'

'He – Dad has his reasons – why he does things, says things.' Robbie clamped his lips together.

'She comes here in the afternoons?'

'Yeah. Coupla times.' Robbie kept his stern face and looked straight at Arthur.

Arthur had the same sense of being excluded that he had felt at Robbie's fishing party that morning. 'When you were here – she came?'

'Yeah. Once anyway. Sure.'

And when his mother wasn't here, Arthur thought. Did his mother know about these religious nuts emoting all over the living room, maybe kneeling on the carpet? 'What does Dad do? Read the Bible to her?'

Robbie shrugged and started to run away as if he had had enough questions. 'No, he asks her – Well, she talks on her own. Then maybe he reads her something or just talks. *She* says it helps her.'

'She's weird, little brother. And you're getting—'

'Don't call me "little brother."'

'You talked to her as if you were her boss. Does Dad talk to her the same way?'

Robbie hesitated. 'You have to. She's dependent, Dad says. At least just now. – She's not weird now. You should've seen her before.'

'Before what?'

'Before a coupla months ago. She was practically a prostitute, Dad told me. She said it, too – to me. Well, she's not now.'

'She still looks like one, to tell you the truth.'

'She sure isn't now. She doesn't drink anymore and she doesn't even drink coffee, just tea. She has less money now.'

'Oh, I can imagine.'

'But she's happier, she says.' Robbie looked at Arthur as if victory was plainly on his side and plainly won. 'Irene's like a saint now – Dad says. But she still needs help or she'll do something crazy. That's why Dad has to speak to her – sort of firmly, the way I did tonight.'

'I see.' And she's goddamn stupid, Arthur wanted to say, not only stupid now but stupid before she found God or the church or Richard. Arthur went into the bathroom and washed his face. He scraped his jaw with his safety razor, though as yet he hadn't much of a beard.

It was at least a quarter past 9, when he got to the Brewsters' house. Maggie answered his ring. She wore a sleeveless dress of light green and darker green sandals.

'We're just having coffee. Want some?'

Arthur walked with her into the air-conditioned living room, where her parents sat, and also a middle-aged woman who he supposed was their houseguest, and a young man who looked twenty or a little more.

'Diane – Arthur Alderman,' Maggie said. 'Diane Vickers and Charles Lafferty.'

'How d'y'do?' said Charles to Arthur from his chair.

Arthur declined coffee, thinking he and Maggie might escape sooner. He assumed she wanted to go out. But who was this Charles? Not Mrs Vickers's son, surely, or they'd have the same name. Charles was the second jolt of the evening. Was he a boyfriend of Maggie's, maybe one she still liked, and approved by her parents? Arthur assessed Charles's medium-good looks, his tan cotton slacks, new tennis shoes, and decided that he had a little money. Always an asset.

'. . . working today, Arthur?' asked Maggie's mother.

'Yes – as usual,' Arthur replied.

A moment later, Charles stood up. 'Thank you, Mrs Brewster – sir.'

'Good night, Charles,' said Diane Vickers warmly, as if she knew him well.

Maggie went with him to the door. Mrs Vickers was looking him over critically with her large made-up eyes, or so Arthur felt. Maggie came back.

'Want to take a walk, Arthur? Or go somewhere?' Maggie asked, as she might have if they had been alone.

'Whichever you want.'

'See you in a minute.' Maggie went upstairs. Arthur heard a car starting outside.

'Maggie tells me you're going to Columbia,' said Diane Vickers.

All the heat of the day seemed to gather and explode in Arthur's face. 'No-no. Things've changed. Just in the last days. I can't go to Columbia. Some other college – but not Columbia.' To attribute this to bad grades or lack of money seemed equally damning. Maggie plainly hadn't mentioned it to her parents, because both of them were politely listening. And of course it was nothing to Betty and Warren Brewster whether he entered Columbia or not, but Arthur felt that he sank further in their esteem. They would assume he was going to a college of lower caliber or maybe no college at all.

Maggie came downstairs with a handbag. Arthur said good night to the Brewsters and to Diane Vickers whose eyes seemed to be looking right through him.

Then he was alone with Maggie, outside in the darkness.

'Go to the quarry?' Maggie said.

'Why not?'

They got into her car.

Arthur rolled his window down. After a while, he said, 'Hey, who's this Charles?'

'Oh – Charles. He goes to C.U. I had a couple of dates with him – a while back. He just wanted to see me again.'

'So – What did you tell him?'

'About what? – Well!' Maggie laughed. 'I told him I had a rather steady relationship now. Words to that effect.'

Arthur smiled in the dark, and rested his head against the seat back, watching Maggie, happy for several seconds until he recalled the conversation with Mrs Vickers. 'Seems you didn't say anything to your folks about Columbia – being out. Anyway I did, because Mrs Vickers asked me. I had to say it wasn't Columbia. Do you think that's a strike against me – with your folks?'

'No, Arthur. Why should they think all that much about it?'

True, Arthur thought. Was he developing an inferiority complex? Paranoia?

Maggie was concentrating on getting the car up the gritty slope beside the limestone slabs, beside the void that was now on their right. She stopped the car and cut the engine. Then she turned to him.

Arthur seized her and kissed her neck, and in that long instant when his eyes were shut, thoughts ran fast through his head. Maggie's unsweet and interesting perfume made him think of the sick, off-putting sweetness of Irene Langley's, which had lingered in the house. *Fight the bastards*, he thought, people like his father, Robbie now, creeps like Irene Langley.

'Ow!'

'Oh! Sorry, Maggie!' He had been squeezing her arm. 'W-want to get out and walk?'

'Yes – if you promise not to fall over the edge again.'

Arthur took her hand and was careful not to squeeze it as they climbed the slope toward the beginning of the dark edge. The air was warmer than the last time, heavier with summer; the stars were all out, though Arthur couldn't see a moon. He felt shaky with a sense of possible failure ahead, failure in every direction. That was just as possible as success, wasn't it? He gulped and asked, 'Diane's a relative?'

'No, just an old friend of Mom's. She lives in the same town as my grandma in Pennsylvania. She's a dietitian in a hospital.'

Arthur half-listened. He was thinking that he couldn't tell Maggie about Irene Langley's visit, though he had thought he might. Irene Langley was too depressing to talk about, to try to be funny about.

'Hey, Maggie! Starting Tuesday I've got my house free to myself. For us. For a couple of weeks at least. My brother's taking off for Kansas.'

16

Robbie was to fly to Kansas City Tuesday morning at 9:30, and Arthur looked forward to his departure. To Arthur, he had become somebody else. If this was growing up, Arthur thought, if his brother was going to become an adult who resembled Robbie at present, then Arthur simply didn't like him. Robbie no longer said anything spontaneous, original, or funny as he had used to. He went around in a slight daze, yet as if on good behavior, a bit stiff-necked, looking as if he were conscious of whatever he was doing, even something as simple as dropping a couple of eggs into a skillet. It crossed Arthur's mind that his parents had left Robbie behind for a few days so that Robbie could try to persuade him into the good path, but there had been no speeches from Robbie. In fact, Robbie's attitude was one of subtle shunning of him.

'You coming to church?' Robbie asked on Sunday morning around 10. He was already dressed in blue trousers and a clean shirt.

'No – thank you. You going on your bike?'

'Guthrie's picking me up. You ought to come.'

Arthur was on the floor in his room, looking over his books and choosing a few to sell. He wore old Levi's and no shirt, because it was another hot day. 'Thanks, my friend, I'm going over to the DeWitt establishment in a few minutes. Work, you know?'

'Sunday's supposed to be a day of rest.'

Arthur was suddenly bored, or angry. 'Parrot!' He stood up with a couple of old paperbacks and instead of slapping them together as he had an impulse to do, he dropped them into the wastebasket.

'You're throwing away books?'

'Yeah. – Sex books. You know? How to make love.' The two he had thrown away were starting to get yellow with age.

Was Robbie blushing? Robbie looked at the wastebasket with interest.

'You wouldn't want to read dirty stuff like that. Sinful.'

A simultaneous knock and a short ring of the doorbell came.

'That's Guthrie,' Robbie said, and went off.

Arthur returned to his books with a dust rag, and after this, he thought, it might be worth it to take the vacuum cleaner to his carpet. His mother expected him to keep the house reasonably clean, because they hadn't a regular cleaning woman.

'*Arthur?*' Robbie's voice had an oddly shrill note. 'Come and meet Guthrie.' Robbie stood in the doorway.

'Can you tell him I'm busy – just now?'

But there was Guthrie just behind Robbie in the hall, a blond fellow in his twenties. 'Hello, Arthur. Glad to meet you,' said the young man, extending a hand. 'Guthrie MacKenzie.'

Arthur extended his hand, hating the feel of the soft moist palm against his. 'Howdy.'

'Not coming with us? – Robbie's told me about you. Like to take you along today, if you're willing,' Guthrie said with a smile. He wore neat blue cotton trousers, a blue shirt and tie under his cotton jacket.

'Just explained to Robbie, I'm going out to work in a few minutes,' Arthur said, and slowly advanced, so that first Guthrie and then Robbie had to back out of his room. Arthur detested them in his room and was determined to herd them into the living room or the kitchen. Robbie, his *brother*, had probably told this one about Maggie, too!

Guthrie walked backward, turned and entered the living room.

Arthur stalked into the living room barefoot, feeling rather proud of his suntanned torso and muscles.

'We'll be off in a minute,' said Guthrie MacKenzie. 'I know – from what your father and Robbie've told me – that you think we're sort of against you. Or we're trying to get you into a club you don't want to join.' He shook his head slowly. 'It's not like that. We have an open attitude. Come to us if you like.' He opened his arms, reminding Arthur of programs he had seen on TV. 'I don't like labels myself. Mind if I smoke?' Guthrie had pulled out cigarettes.

Arthur shrugged. He shook his head when Guthrie extended a pack of Kents.

'Labels give a man a bad name. Give a *church* a bad name, too. I don't even like the label Baptist,' he continued in a pleasant tone, 'though my folks've been that for generations. What we're aiming for is contact, friendliness, happiness. I wanted you to know that you have friends right here, if you want them. You're among friends.'

His grandmother's phrase, Arthur remembered uncomfortably. 'Thank you,' Arthur said.

Robbie was drinking this in.

'You won't join us this morning? You don't have to change your jeans, just put on a shirt. I bet you could come barefoot. Sure! Lots of good men have walked barefoot before.'

Arthur nodded, and hated himself for nodding. 'Yes,' he said, bored and polite. 'If you'll excuse me – Got some things to do before I take off.' He went back to his room.

He found three more old paperbacks to chuck. He tried to damp down his temper, lest he throw away more books than he wanted to.

Guthrie stuck his head into Arthur's room, having suddenly opened the closed door a little, and said a cheery, 'Good-bye! Bless you!'

Finally, the front door closed.

Arthur got the vacuum cleaner and pushed it over the floor of his room, and decided to do Robbie's room, too. Robbie had made his bed in a sloppy way; there were several socks on the floor and a couple of pairs of sneakers, magazines, and cassettes. In the course of clearing the floor of these, Arthur noticed a yellow and blue poster on the wall above Robbie's table: JESUS SAVES, it said, and below the usual Jesus portrait of a bearded fair-haired man with sad blue eyes and pink lips, a photograph of the backs of a crowd of contemporary children had been superimposed. All the children were reaching their arms up toward Jesus. Arthur thought of doing the floor in his parents' bedroom while he had the vacuum out, but he disliked going into their room and decided to put the job off.

He rode off toward Mrs DeWitt's. She had insisted that he have lunch with her today, since last Sunday's lunch had been 'so sadly interrupted.'

His work that day was a breeze: painting a fence green. He mixed some black and white in the green, so the fence would blend with the color of the grass around it. After lunch he worked till just after 4, the hottest time of the afternoon, then turned the hose on himself in the backyard, and rode off in wet Levi's. At home, he took a shower and collapsed on his bed to sleep for a while. Robbie was watching TV. Arthur hadn't a date with Maggie or with anyone that evening, but he had told Robbie he had, because he wanted to get out of the house.

Just after 7, Arthur telephoned Norma Keer, and asked if he could come over. 'I know it's late – the dinner hour.'

'Since when do I keep a definite dinner hour?'

Arthur cut a few roses from the backyard to take to her and went over.

Norma was bringing a big bowl of something to her table, which she had set for two. 'Just some Jell-O,' she said. 'Too hot to eat anything else. Raspberry with banana and cantaloupe cut up in it. Fix yourself a drink first, Arthur, if you want one. My, you look nice. Got a date somewhere later?'

Arthur laughed. 'No.' He made a gin and tonic in the kitchen. Norma already had one.

'And how's your nice girlfriend – Maggie?'

'Oh, fine, thank you. Taking a course at C.U. this summer to brush up on her math. For Radcliffe.'

As the evening went on, Arthur thought Norma didn't know anything about Maggie's stay in the hospital. He was alert for the slightest hint or query.

'More cake, Arthur. Don't be shy.'

Arthur helped himself. Norma made excellent carrot cakes. 'Do you happen to know a woman called Irene Langley? About thirty, dyed blond hair?'

'Langley—' Norma tilted her head back and looked at the ceiling as if she were going through her list of clients at the First National. 'Don't know the name. Who's she?'

'One of the ones that go to my dad's church. She knocked on the door Friday night.'

Norma smiled her tiny smile in her round face and looked suddenly merry. 'I suppose she wanted to drop off a few pamphlets? She didn't knock here.'

'No, she wanted to see my dad, but I'm sure she knew he was out of town. She said my dad talks to her – cheers her up. She's a bit nuts. An ex-prostitute who's found religion.'

'Oh, my goodness!' Here Norma rolled with laughter, and her bosom shook under her low-cut dress.

Arthur had never before noticed Norma's breasts, and he thought now that they looked rather comforting, motherly. He was grinning. 'And Robbie – he knows her. He was furious and asked her to leave. Took quite a while. It's the aura she wanted, she said, the aura in the house there.'

Norma shook her head. 'What's so new about Christ I don't know. When these magazine-peddlers knock on my door and ask me if I know about the Bible, I tell them I read the Bible before they were born!'

Arthur said after a moment, 'What worries me a little is my brother.'

'Oh. Always with those older men, you mean.'

'That's one thing.' Arthur twisted his glass on the table. 'Then his bossy attitude toward this woman Irene. I dunno what's charitable about that. It's just – strange.' There was still another thing, Robbie treating him now as if he were a sinner, and an unrepentant one, but Arthur couldn't say this to Norma. 'Robbie really doesn't like me anymore.'

'Oh, between brothers – Moods, Arthur. Temporary attitudes. Robbie's only fifteen, isn't he? – It won't last.'

Arthur said nothing more.

Eddie Howell turned up unannounced Monday evening at half past 7. Arthur was especially annoyed, because Maggie was there. He had invited Maggie for dinner. Robbie had told Arthur that morning that his friends Jeff and Bill were giving him a send-off party at the house of one of them and that he wouldn't be home before midnight. Consequently Arthur had invited Maggie for the first of what he hoped would be several evenings at his house. Then, just as Arthur was opening the fridge to bring forth cold roast beef and potato salad, the twit was on the doorstep.

'Robbie's out tonight,' Arthur said.

Smiling as ever, Eddie Howell pushed into the hall. 'But anyway you're here and I'd—' He saw Maggie over the partition between hall and kitchen. 'Is this your friend?'

'Yes. Maggie – Eddie Howell. Maggie Brewster.'

'A pleasure,' said Eddie. 'Excuse me for intruding, but I won't stay. I wanted to see how Arthur was. I had no idea I'd have the pleasure of meeting you.'

Arthur wondered about that. 'We were just—'

'I know about the situation of a week ago,' Eddie said to Maggie. 'I'm glad to see you looking so well – because it can be a dangerous thing. And it's always most depressing.'

Maggie exchanged a glance with Arthur. Her polite smile had gone. 'I'm not depressed.'

'Maybe it hasn't hit you yet.'

'No,' Maggie said with her honest air that Arthur knew well. 'It won't. I know by now.'

Arthur saw her brows tremble with annoyance. 'If you don't mind, Eddie – we were just about to eat.'

'Right, and I'm off in a minute.' Eddie Howell's eyes blinked rapidly as he glanced from Arthur to Maggie and back to Arthur. 'I just came to remind you – both – that though you have gone against God's will, you are still forgiven – if you acknowledge what you've done – admit it – and vow to yourself to walk in the right path in the future.'

Maggie took a sip of her drink and set the glass down on the sideboard, just as she might have done if she and Arthur had been alone.

'Do you understand what I'm saying?' Eddie Howell asked Maggie, with a smile.

'Yes,' Maggie said.

'Good.' Eddie Howell nodded cheerfully. 'May I just leave you something?'

'No,' Arthur said, because Eddie was unzipping his briefcase. 'Not tonight, please. Save it for someone else. And while you're—' He glanced nervously toward the living room, then suddenly remembered that he had cleared the living room of religious magazines in preparation for Maggie's visit and had put all the stuff in Robbie's room. 'Never mind.'

'I can see that you're in need of some of the things I have,' Eddie Howell said.

Arthur went to the front door and opened it and stood aside to let Eddie Howell pass him. 'Thanks for the visit, Eddie.'

Eddie Howell moved toward the door, holding his briefcase in both hands. 'Good night, Maggie – Arthur. God bless!'

Arthur closed the door after him and slid the inside bolt.

'Wow,' Maggie said, laughing. 'I thought you were going to throw him out the *door*!'

Arthur spread his arms, then embraced Maggie tightly for a moment. 'See what I'm up against here? You see what they're like?'

'And who's he?'

'Church friend of my father's.'

'Take it easy. They're not worth getting angry about.'

Maggie and her family weren't living with it. But if Maggie wanted him to calm down, he would. He glanced at the fridge, and thought the roast beef could wait a few more seconds. 'And there was one other creep at the door, Irene Langley Friday night before I saw you. Reformed prostitute.'

'She goes to that church too?'

'Yes! My dad makes friends with these people, talks to them when they're depressed. The one Friday night looked coked out.' He told Maggie about Robbie's rude behavior, because it added a comic touch, but he didn't tell her that Irene Langley had frightened him, as an insane person might. He didn't want to tell her either that Irene Langley knew about the abortion.

'Next time they come to the door – just keep the door locked. Tell them through the door your father's out. – Come on, let's eat.'

Later they sat on the sofa, talking of September and school, while a Mozart string quartet played on Arthur's cassette. Tomorrow morning Arthur was going to the C.U. office with his grades from Chalmerston High and his letters of admission to Columbia. He was going to find out the costs and apply for admission, whether he could afford it or not when September came. And the Reagan administration was making student loans harder to get. Maggie had decided to major in sociology as soon as she could at Radcliffe, though her father wanted her to take only liberal arts courses in the first two years.

'I don't mean the social worker house calls kind of thing,' Maggie said. 'I mean finding out why things already exist – conditions and problems. I see the world so differently since those days in the hospital. Funny. Everything's suddenly real, not like a backdrop or a lot of scenery.'

Arthur listened, also aware of Maggie's head resting gently against his cheek. And wouldn't it be great, he thought, if they could spend a little bit of their evenings like this together, once college started, just sitting on a sofa and talking?

''Scuse me.' Robbie's voice had come from behind them.

Arthur saw Robbie standing in the living room doorway.

'Why'd you bolt the front door?'

Arthur stood up. 'I felt like it. Why'd you sneak in? Can't you ring the bell?'

'Wasn't sneaking in; I hadda come in by the garage!'

Robbie had had a few beers, Arthur saw.

'Hello, Robbie,' said Maggie.

'Hi,' said Robbie, still in the doorway.

'I bolted the door because Eddie Howell crashed in, and I don't want any more such,' Arthur said. 'Did you sic him on me tonight?'

After a second, Robbie said, 'No.'

'Don't get mad again, Arthur,' Maggie whispered, putting on the shoes that she had slipped off.

Robbie disappeared into the hall.

It was hardly 11 o'clock, Arthur saw. 'Fine brother I've got, don't you think?'

'Aren't all kid brothers like this?'

Mozart came to a halt. They sat on in the living room, but the atmosphere was not the same. Arthur rode home with Maggie in her car, and then he walked back home, even though it was raining a little.

Arthur knocked on Robbie's door, feeling like one of the intruders, but on the opposing team.

'Yup?'

Robbie was in pajamas on his knees, packing his blue duffel bag. 'Bill's picking me up tomorrow to take me to the airport.'

Robbie had told him that this morning. 'Got your swim shorts? Extra pair of sneaks?' Arthur asked in a bored tone. Their mother wanted Arthur to be sure Robbie had them.

'Yup. I have.' Robbie lost his balance, and his head almost disappeared into the duffel bag.

'Look, Robbie, did Eddie—'

'*I* didn't tell him to come here.'

But Robbie was in touch with the churchgoers, or they with him, Arthur was sure. 'I'd like them to keep away while Dad's gone and you're gone. I don't want them crashing in, understand? Or that other creep Irene crashing in. – Does she ring you up here?'

'No. – Well – yesterday she did.'

'I'm not letting her or any more in.'

Robbie sat back on his heels. 'I know what you're gonna do when I'm gone. Here.' He looked at Arthur with a straining frown under his smooth forehead.

'You think *what* you want.'

'What were you doing on the sofa even – if I hadn't come in?'

'You want to tell something to Mom and Dad? Go ahead! Make something up!' Meddling little rat! Arthur walked out and shut the door.

17

The brief interview Tuesday morning in a room of C.U.'s Administration Building was not as conclusive as Arthur had hoped. He had hoped for a yes or no, the possible no being because the university might be full up, in which case Arthur had imagined them ousting a worse student and taking him in. A Mr Lubbock in shirtsleeves behind a messy desk took a careful look at his papers, paper-clipped them, and said there still were some places for well-qualified students and he could let Arthur know within a week. Could Arthur come in again in a week?

Arthur felt he had reason to be optimistic. En route to his next destination, the public library, he stopped at a used car lot to look over what they had. He saw a lovely two-year-old red Toyota, but the price was out of the question. A boring but reliable-looking Ford was within reason for him, except that he hadn't the eight hundred and fifty dollars it cost.

'Single owner,' said the car lot man. 'Seven years old; that's why the price is so low, otherwise it's a great car.'

It was brown. Arthur had thought of a yellow or red car. 'I'll think it over. Thanks.'

At the library, after returning his books, he went directly to the sociology stacks. The range of the titles, concerning health, migration, employment, baffled him and made it difficult to choose one, or two, but at last he selected one, then went to the science section where the words on the spines of the books looked like a language he knew, and he at once took three from the shelves.

'Now you're reading sociology?' asked Miss Becker, noticing *Changing Tides: Human Migration Since the Second World War*.

'N-n – I just wanted to get a general idea of it.'

'If you want a general idea—' She got up and went to a shelf of new books behind her. 'This one's just come in. It's not on reserve. Want to try it?'

The book was *Sociology and American Social Issues*. Arthur saw from a glance at the contents pages that it covered more ground than the book he had chosen. 'Just what I want. Thanks, Miss Becker.'

'One week on this,' she said, stamping his card. 'When're you off for the east?'

'I'm not. Can't swing the dough, sorry to say. Maybe next year. I dunno.'

'O-oh – I'm sorry, Arthur.'

Arthur nodded, embarrassed. 'I'll be going to C.U., though. I think.'

'They ought to be pleased to have you. At least you'll be around. That's nice.'

Arthur went off to Shoe Repair.

He wrote to his mother that evening at the San Francisco hotel and told her about trying for C.U. He wrote that he was not sure where the money would come from, but he was determined to get a degree and could take a part-time job, and that C.U. was at any rate a whole lot cheaper than Columbia. He added:

> A woman called Irene Langley came to the house last Friday evening. I don't know if she is on drugs or not, but she gave

me the creeps and I had a hard time getting rid of her. Could you please ask Dad to tell his church friends not to barge in like that?

Arthur had a date with Maggie for Wednesday night, and had thought of supper at his house, followed by an open-air jazz concert at the Sky Palace, starting at 10 p.m. The Sky Palace was a former drive-in cinema that had been converted into a roofless theater with a stage, a few seats and plenty of room for parked cars. One didn't have to buy tickets in advance. Arthur wasn't sure Maggie would like the idea, but she did.

Floodlights lit the sky high into the darkness. The amplifiers sounded turned on to maximum. There was a big round dancing area below the stage where the band played, but it looked not worth it to try to get there through the standing crowd, some of whom were dancing where they were.

'Hey, Arthur!'

Arthur looked around. It had been Gus's voice, and amid the half-illuminated figures and faces, Arthur saw Gus's blond head in the distance. Arthur steered Maggie in the general direction.

'Got Veronica!' Gus said, lifting Veronica's hand as if she were some kind of prize.

The girls knew each other from school.

'Gonna *dance*, Gus?' Arthur shouted. Then he said to Maggie, 'Gus thinks he's a lousy dancer.'

They didn't try to get to the dance floor. The girls talked together, and Gus and Arthur. Gus bought hot dogs all round and Arthur beers and Cokes.

'Gus! Let's go to *my* place after this,' Arthur said. 'Got the house free!'

They went finally to Arthur's house. The fridge was full of cold drinks. Scrambled eggs and coffee later, Arthur thought, if people got hungry. He loved being the host, pretending that the house was all his, his and Maggie's, of course. Again the girls stayed together. What did they find to talk about nonstop?

'Veronica *is* sort of pretty,' Arthur said to Gus. Veronica had nice wavy brown hair, a peachy natural color in her cheeks. She was a little overweight and shorter than Maggie.

'Think she likes me?'

Arthur laughed. 'How do I know?'

'Tell me if you think so,' Gus said quietly, and drank from his can of beer.

No one got hungry. Veronica wanted to leave around one, and Arthur was pleased that Maggie showed no sign of leaving. Arthur said good-bye to Gus and Veronica at the door.

He came back to kiss Maggie. 'Nice evening! Wasn't it? For me, anyway.'

'Yes. – What were you and Gus talking about?'

Arthur smiled. '*I* don't know. Nothing.' He hesitated. 'Can you spend the night?'

Maggie laughed as if it were a joke, but he knew part of her laughter was due to shyness. 'Maybe I could, but – as it happens, I've got the curse.'

'Oh. – Well, that doesn't matter. I mean, just stay with me.'

She shook her head. 'Next time. – I'm very glad to get the curse.'

Arthur had been thinking the same thing, that she would be glad. 'I got a sociology book today from the library. Just a sec, I'll show you!'

About five days later, Arthur received a letter from his mother, part of which said:

> Sorry about the Irené visit. Yes, your father knows her and gives himself some credit for having taken her off the drink and off the streets, it seems. I asked Robbie about her visit

and first he said she hadn't come by at all! I think he is a little afraid of her. Then Robbie said you were rude to her. But never mind that. I hope she won't turn up again to bother you. She's a lost soul with a very sick mother and a do-nothing younger sister who just sits at home and doesn't even try to find a job.

Damn Robbie, Arthur thought, lying now.

But Arthur was not inclined to resentment in mid-July, able to see Maggie several times a week, and with a full-time job now at Shop Repair with a higher salary. And there was simply the joy of being alone in the house on West Maple Street, of cutting a few flowers from the back garden and putting them in a vase in anticipation of a visit from Maggie. She stayed over a couple of nights with him, and of course there was time to go to bed together in the evening if they wished, even if Maggie chose to go home to sleep. On the first such occasion, Arthur had told Maggie that he could take some precautions, not knowing how else to put it, and Maggie had said not to worry, because she had taken the pill. Simple! Life could be happy and simple – if not for a few other people. It was lovely to forget for a while that those other people existed.

Then suddenly it was all over, his privacy was over anyway, because the family was due back tomorrow, July 29th. His mother had telephoned from Salt Lake City. And in a couple of days, it would be August, and Maggie was going away for two weeks to Canada with her parents. She was going to a hunting lodge on a lake, and both the lodge and the lake were owned by a pilot friend of her father's. Arthur wished he had been rolling in money or had enough to propose a two-week jaunt somewhere with Maggie, who could probably get the use of the car she drove, her mother's, because the family had two cars. And by September 17th, Maggie would be flying east to Cambridge, Massachusetts.

'Brought you this,' said his mother, holding up a fireman-red shirt of heavy flannel with white buttons. 'Not the weather for it now, but I couldn't resist it in San Francisco, because it looked just your size.'

Arthur was pleased with this. He tried it on.

Robbie, suntanned from head to foot, was prancing around barefoot in jazzy black and white zebra-patterned swim shorts. The family had arrived close to 8 p.m., not 5 p.m., as they had hoped, and Arthur had had time to prepare dinner, for which his mother praised him. His father was rather silent and spoke in monosyllables even to his mother, Arthur noticed.

A Chinese lampshade that expanded into a hollow rectangle had to be installed on the living room's central ceiling light before they could sit down to dinner. This was made of off-white paper. It looked like a box kite.

'And what's your news, Arthur?' his mother asked when they were all at table.

The blessing had been short.

'Tom took me on full-time. Or did I say that on the phone? I forgot.'

'No, you didn't. Isn't that nice, Richard?'

'Um – yes,' said Richard.

'We had fresh seafood every night in San Francisco,' Robbie said to Arthur. 'Fisherman's Wharf a coupla times.' He had put on a shirt at their mother's request.

The telephone rang. It wouldn't be Maggie, Arthur knew, because he had called her at 6, and she knew that his parents were arriving. His father went to answer.

Arthur said to his mother, 'By the way, Mom, I was not rude to Irene Langley. I admit I didn't ask her to sit down. Not sure she wanted to. She came for the aura, as she put it.' Arthur spoke as if his brother were not present. 'You've met her, Mom?'

'Once or twice at church,' his mother said quietly, as if she didn't want to go on with the subject.

Arthur glanced at Robbie who was sitting up straighter than usual, eyes on his plate, from which he forked his food steadily. 'Meet any interesting people on your travels, Robbie?'

'People?'

'You know, those two-legged things?'

Robbie clammed up.

Arthur might have asked him if he had met any nice girls, which would have been a normal question to a brother, but Arthur didn't want to invite any comment about Maggie. Whomever Robbie had met, whatever he had done in the way of surf-boarding and gorging on lobster at Fisherman's Wharf, couldn't equal Arthur's happiness in the past two and a half weeks with Maggie.

'But my dear, it just *isn't* possible,' Richard was saying in the living room. 'I'm pretty sure tonight's no worse – I will. You can count on me. Good night.' Then the click of the telephone being put down.

Richard came back frowning, shaking his head. 'Sorry.'

'Who was that?' asked Lois.

'Oh – um – Irene. Sounding a little upset tonight.' Richard picked up his napkin and continued his meal.

'Is her mother worse?' asked Lois.

'No, no. She herself. Anxious. About what I don't know.' A pause, then he went on. 'Wanted me to come over and see her tonight, or could she come here – walk.' His father shook his head and smiled at his mother. 'Told her it was out of the question.'

'You've got to be firm with her, Dad,' said Robbie.

'That's right,' said Richard.

Arthur looked at his mother, who was listening to Richard.

'A firm attitude, and they're all right – such people. They're *on* the right track,' said Richard. 'Just have to stay on it.'

'Does Bob Cole talk to her at all?' Lois asked.

'Oh, yes. I think he said he went to see her once or twice.'

Richard wiped his lips with his napkin and sat back. The bulge of his abdomen under his untucked pink shirt looked larger than before his vacation. His short, broad nose had a tan that suggested leather. He wanted no coffee, just an early night's sleep.

Arthur and his mother tidied up in the kitchen, while Robbie looked at TV.

'Did you talk to Dad about C.U., Mom?' Arthur asked as softly as he could over the rattle of his own dishwashing at the sink.

'I did, Arthur, and I'm sure it'll work out – with you sleeping here.'

'Because—' Arthur stood on tiptoe to see over the partition into the living room. Robbie was still engrossed in the TV screen. '—I felt guilty even bringing up C.U. to you – Dad being so down on me. But September's getting near.'

'He's not so down on you, Arthur. This trip's done him a lot of good. He's tired tonight, so maybe it doesn't show. And Mama helped. She talked a lot to Richard.' His mother was putting things away in the fridge as she talked. 'Mama just said straight out, it isn't right to punish Arthur by depriving him of college when he's earned it.'

Arthur was surprised, then felt like smiling at the simplicity of it.

His mother pressed his arm and kissed him on the cheek. 'Things'll work out. I'll be glad to have you at home, to tell you the truth. – How's Maggie?'

'All right. Fine. – I was over at her house a couple of times for dinner. Just Maggie and Betty. Her father didn't happen to be there.'

And Maggie's scent was on his pillow. It was from two days ago, and the perfume was fading. He lay face down and inhaled it when he went to bed, and in the mornings, he covered the pillow with the sheet and bedspread as soon as he got up, so as little as possible would escape. When would she next spend an hour with him in his bed, or even half an hour? Now, there was always someone in the house, or the danger of someone. Maggie's house was easier, and she had a wonderful way of saying suddenly, 'My mother's not coming home for another two hours, I know,' when they might be doing a chore in the Brewster yard or snacking in the kitchen.

Maggie'd asked him to come to Canada with her and her family. This was in the Brewster living room one night about five days after Arthur's family had returned.

'Why not join us for a week or so anyway, Arthur, if you've got the time?' her mother put in. 'George's lodge up there sleeps ten people.'

Arthur felt stunned. It was a glimpse of luxury, paradise even, that came like a flash and vanished quickly. A big log cabin, a lake, Maggie, and time on their hands. 'I can't take any vacation this summer – thanks. Also I promised my boss I'd work on till mid-September.'

'Ye-es,' said Maggie with a sigh. 'Arthur still doesn't know for sure if his father's going to pay his tuition at C.U. I told you, didn't I, Mom?'

Arthur thought Maggie had told her mother, but the Brewsters were so comfortably off, her mother probably couldn't imagine his father balking at C.U.'s fees, if he was not even going to board at C.U. 'True, I haven't had a definite promise yet,' Arthur said, feeling awkward. 'Mom keeps saying it'll work out.'

That conversation prompted Arthur to speak to his father later the same evening. Richard was still up in his study when Arthur got home around 11. His father's study door was open, and Arthur saw him in shirtsleeves, standing bent over his desk on which there were a lot of papers and ledgers. The house was hot after the Brewster house. The screen windows had long been up against summer insects, but the screens kept out the faint breeze too.

'Dad?' Arthur said. 'Got a minute?'

'Yes. For what?' His father leaned on his palms on the desk, and some of his straight hair fell forward like antennae over his forehead.

'It's about C.U.,' Arthur said, walking in, trying to appear casual, yet also serious. 'I hate to bring it up, because I'm supposed to finance it myself, I know. But Mom said—'

'Who told you that?'

'Well, I – Not that anybody told me, I just took it for granted. What I'm saying is – I'd be grateful if you and Mom could—' Suddenly all the words stuck, or became confused. 'I'm not sure I can do it all myself, even with a part-time job.'

'Oh, we can help you out,' said his father, and looked down at his papers, as if he wanted Arthur to leave.

'Thanks, but – I—'

'What?'

Arthur faced his father. 'Considering the tuition is two thousand five hundred, about, after I apply my grant, can I ask how much you and Mom might pay?' Arthur felt sweat breaking out all over him.

'Oh – maybe half. How's that?' His father looked at him with firm mouth and jaw.

Arthur nodded. 'Fair enough. Thank you. I had to know something, you know, with September coming up.'

'Depends on your behavior, too.'

What did that mean? Don't sleep with Maggie? Thank God, his father hadn't asked any questions about that. 'Well – what's wrong now?'

'You didn't come to church with us last Sunday,' his father replied. 'For instance. Just begged off. Yard work somewhere. You could do that work in the afternoon.'

'I'm trying to earn some money and save it.' Arthur was a little amused, because sitting on your rear end in church was easier than doing yard work, and lately he was tackling the yard of a neighbor of Mrs DeWitt's, which was nearly as messy as Mrs DeWitt's had been. 'Sorry about the church,' Arthur added.

'And your behavior this spring – I have not forgiven you or excused you.'

Arthur knew. Once more, under his father's stare, Arthur felt as if he were absorbing guilt through his pores, like radioactive fallout. *External, okay*, Arthur told himself. Guilt was supposed to come from inside. He didn't feel guilty, really. 'No, I didn't think you had.'

'And the Brewsters,' Richard went on with faint contempt. 'Are they any better? No. Money doesn't gloss over their – their life-style. Nice clothes, a fine house, doesn't hide anything. And you hang out with them.'

His father was maybe jealous, Arthur thought, as well as off the beam. 'They're certainly not the richest people in this town,' Arthur said. 'I don't think they flaunt their money. Not at all.'

'I'm saying that money doesn't make arrogance look any nicer. What they flaunt is lack of human decency, basic morals. I wouldn't have the Brewsters as my clients. Just tonight I'm looking through my list again, getting rid of two families, one of them every bit as well-off as the Brewsters. I'm suggesting they go to another insurance investment in town.'

That must be losing money for Heritage Life, Arthur thought, but he didn't want to comment. Was Heritage Life, like his father, conducting a purge, making sure its employees went to church on Sunday? Arthur moved toward the door.

'These with-it people like the Brewsters, the jet set, abortions, heavy drinking, never setting foot—'

'That's not true about the Brewsters – heavy drinking. My gosh, Norma Keer drinks more than – Look at the quiet life Norma leads.'

'Norma leads a silly, selfish life in my opinion. Soon to die, she says, and I believe her. And she spends her evening watching TV programs, reading silly books, when she could be – communicating more with the human race, preparing herself by going to church with the rest of us. Small wonder she drinks!'

Arthur supposed his father meant preparing for eternal life in the next world. 'The books she reads aren't all silly. I've seen a few. Philosophy and poetry.'

'Oh, I don't care about her books,' his father said impatiently, 'I would like you to come to church with us this Sunday, Arthur.'

18

The Reverend Bob Cole's sermon on Sunday was on 'Man's Relationship to Woman,' which sounded promising to Arthur. Amid the stuff about fidelity and family unity he thought there might be a useful tip or two in regard to Maggie.

'The other day,' the tall, dark-haired Bob Cole began, 'a young woman – one of us here today, I hope, though I certainly won't point her out or mention her name – came to my office in the middle of the working week and said, "I'm so unhappy. Can you tell me what to do about my marriage?" I began with tactful questions: Was she mistreated; did her husband drink? . . .'

The church was quite full, Arthur noticed, and there were eight or ten people standing at the back. Arthur was in clean blue jeans and clean shirt, but it was too boiling hot even for a cotton jacket. He was off in Mrs DeWitt's direction as soon as his family drove him home after church and he could pick up his bike. The woman in whose yard he worked now gave him Sunday lunch and paid him three dollars an hour.

'. . . didn't talk to her enough. She felt she was married to a stranger, she said. I said to her, "Do you realize your responsibility as a wife as well? Do you try to talk to your husband about *his* work, *his* problems?" – No, she said, she hadn't. I quoted to her a few passages from the Scriptures which I intend to quote this morning.' He bent over his rostrum. 'From Genesis two, verse eighteen. God reveals that he created man first and woman second. Thus: "And the Lord God said, it is not good that the man should be alone; I will make him a helpmeet for him." That means,' said the minister, looking up, removing his glasses, 'that man *needed* assistance from that helpmeet at home . . . '

Robbie scratched a mosquito bite on his ankle. His mother's tan was fading already on her arms. Arthur smelled at least two different perfumes near him, neither his mother's, and it struck him that perfume wasn't appropriate in church, because it was a device for sexual attraction (at least, perfume advertisements hammered that point), just as scents in animals served either as a sexual attraction or as warning to enemies. Funny to think of perfume being a signal to shove off, though in fact some perfumes such as Irene Langley's really did send him the other way. *Ariadne* Maggie's perfume was called, and damned expensive, Maggie had implied, and it was a name Arthur wouldn't forget, and one day soon he'd buy her some, if he had to go to Indi or Chicago for it, because it wasn't obtainable in Chalmerston.

'Now! – *Now!*' the Reverend Cole shouted, jolting Arthur out of his daydream. '*Now* we suffer the misery of which this poor young woman spoke, because *women* lack guidance – from their husbands! Yes, we are *all* bewildered! Both sexes. Woman, the lesser vessel, finds no guidance from her husband! – Why? – Because neither sex knows its function anymore in the system of God. Neither knows its place and its duty. Now we have husbands too busy earning money to listen to their wives; we have wives rebelling, finally, against husbands who come home drunk – who curse and abuse the children, husbands who don't help enough or *praise* enough the backbreaking work of their wives within the household. Hence the so-called feminist movement with its so-called emancipation for women, freedom – to go it alone, to obtain abortions – just by asking for them; *freedom* – they call it, to walk the streets at night, to drop into bars and drink like the very husbands they despise; *freedom* – to quit their homes and children and go out and slave at a job as hard as their menfolk . . . '

Their drunken menfolk slaving? Arthur shifted on the hard pew.

'. . . ask you now is this freedom? No! Both sexes are entirely mixed up!'

In bed, Arthur thought, wallowing together, happy and mixed up. Arthur had to cough. What was going on in the heads of the people around him? Arthur saw only the backs of heads and washed necks in clean shirts, a few fresh haircuts, most of the women in hats. Were they as bored as he, daydreaming, too? They weren't all elderly; lots were under thirty. Most if not all had voted for Reagan, Arthur thought. His mother had voted for Carter and had told Arthur not to tell his father.

The rest of the sermon was predictable. Woman's place was in the home, caring both for husband and children. Man's job was to *lead*. It was a mistake for women to want equal rights, and he put the word rights in quotes, when they had equal rights already, but *different* rights. A mistake for women to fight against their nature, when their hearts and souls were dedicated to hearth and home, just as man's was dedicated to breadwinning and to the protection of wife and family. Easy to see how the message slipped down, Arthur thought, because it was partly true, yet the real message was 'the man is the boss.' Same in the case of abortion, it was men who laid the law down, the Pope for instance, men who dominated the courts who made the laws. Of course he didn't consider himself pro-feminist-movement. They were extremists and sounded nuts sometimes. But women should have the real say about abortion, Arthur thought. Hadn't he just seen the situation in front of his face? And as for being the boss, Arthur loved it when Maggie wanted her way about things, even when she drove the car – after all her own – when he was riding in it, though at first he had felt like a eunuch. Funny, deferring to Maggie, about what kind of car they'd buy, for instance, if they ever did, if they ever got married, would make him feel more like a man rather than less. Bob Cole—

Here his mother touched him gently in the ribs with her elbow. Arthur sat up. He had been slumped in the pew with his arms folded.

Bob Cole was simply a bit primitive, behind the times. Organ music now. The collection. Arthur deliberately hadn't brought a cent, and he didn't glance to see what his father had put in.

Then it was over.

'*Hello*, Lois!' Jane Griffin, one of their neighbors and another worker at the Beverley Home for Children, greeted his mother warmly as the congregation moved toward the door.

Arthur successfully edged through the doorway without having to shake hands with the black-and-purple-gowned Reverend Cole. With the blue sky over his head now, Arthur breathed in the fresh, warm air. Everyone was chattering and smiling in front of the church, as if glad it was over, glad they could go home now and put on comfortable clothes, eat Sunday dinner and relax in the afternoon. Arthur noticed his brother focusing on something and looked in that direction.

His father stood under a curbside tree, talking to a bending figure that Arthur recognized instantly as that of Irene Langley, though the back of her broad-brimmed white hat concealed her face. And his father nearly obscured her with his broad figure made broader by his jacket, which he held open with his hands on his hips. Irene bent appealingly toward him, touched his forearm, and his father stepped back and glanced up at the church steps. Robbie trotted down the steps directly toward his father, stood straight and said something to Irene with the air of making a military announcement. Irene seemed to say, 'Oh-h-h,' and bent the other way.

Arthur looked around for his mother and saw her in a group of five or more people.

'Oh, hello, Arthur!' said a woman whose name Arthur was not sure of. 'How're you? You're looking very fit.'

Kind remarks. Apparent friendliness. Arthur was aware that some of the congregation, he didn't know who or how many, knew about Maggie and him.

'Where's Richard?' his mother asked as they walked down the rest of the steps.

'Stuck with Irene Langley.' Arthur noticed that Miss Langley leaned, then moved away from his father, when she saw his mother and him approaching. Robbie still stood like an arrow by his father.

'Got to go visit her tonight,' Richard said in a grumbling way as they walked to the car. 'Had to promise.'

'What's the matter now?' asked Lois.

'Just that I haven't visited her since I've been back. Means a lot to her.'

Ghastly, Arthur thought, visiting a creep like that with a lazy sister and a dying mother who was probably in bed all the time. Arthur knew the intersection of Haskill and Main. It was probably a small, depressing apartment in an old walk-up building. Arthur was in the backseat with Robbie. Since his father was still grousing as he drove, Arthur said, 'Can't somebody else at the church go to see her, Dad?'

'She says I give her the right words,' his father replied. 'I say the right things. Well, it only takes a few minutes, and she might slip if I don't.'

'Slip?' Arthur asked, curious.

'She used to be a prostitute,' Robbie informed Arthur, when his father hesitated.

Arthur wanted to laugh. Robbie sounded drunk. 'Pro-sti-tute,' Arthur said carefully. 'I thought it was drugs, Dad.'

'Both,' said his father. 'The two things hang together – like everything else.'

'She could be one again – a pros-ti-tute,' Robbie said to Arthur.

'Robbie, that's enough,' said Lois as the car pulled up the drive-way. 'You see what Arthur did with the hedge there, Richard? Doesn't it look nice?'

'Yep, very nice,' said Richard.

'Must say again you did a very good job of keeping the house, too, Arthur. Didn't he, Richard? I do appreciate that.' His mother gave Arthur a smile over the back of her front seat before she got out of the car.

Maggie was to leave on Tuesday for Canada, and Arthur had a date with her on Monday night. Maggie had expected her mother to be out that evening, but her mother's dinner party was canceled, and Arthur, Maggie, and her mother spent the evening in the Brewster house. As it turned out, it wasn't a bad evening. They played records. Betty showed him a few pages of an old family photograph album, laughing at some of the pictures. Maggie as a baby looked like any other baby, but by two was quite recognizable. Arthur felt accepted by the family, even by Warren, who wasn't there. Warren's indifferent attitude to him was simply his way, Arthur had decided, even with people he liked. One evening that summer, Warren had offered Arthur one of his prized Havana cigars, and Arthur had never forgotten that. Warren was to join the family on Wednesday in Canada. Arthur had the address. The lake had an Indian name, and so had the town near it.

Maggie would be gone two weeks, she said, and Arthur supposed a little longer. Even Tuesday afternoon, he felt directionless and blank, and this was the way he would feel, he knew, in September, when she went away east for a longer time. He would be looking at the same walls in his family's house and thinking that Maggie wouldn't be back till Thanksgiving or even Christmas.

On Friday his mother telephoned him at the shop to say that

a Mr Lubbock of C.U. had called up and Arthur was to go and see him today or next week at any time during business hours. Tom Robertson let him off for forty-five minutes that afternoon to go there, and Arthur learned that he had been accepted. Mr Lubbock even said with a friendly smile that it was good to have a local boy with a special aptitude for science.

'Arthur added this news to the letter he was currently writing to Maggie, his second letter to her, but he did not say anything about the brief interview with Mr Lubbock to his parents, leaving it to them to ask, if they were interested. His mother did ask, in the middle of dinner, when he was going to see Mr Lubbock.

'Saw him today,' Arthur replied. 'It went all right. I'm admitted.'

'Oh, wonderful, Arthur! – Isn't that nice, Dick?' At least his mother meant it. Her smile was genuine.

'Well – good,' said his father with a glance at Arthur. 'Yes, that's fine.'

Robbie munched celery steadily, like a bemused rabbit.

The telephone rang, and his mother made a grimace, then smiled again.

'Get that, would you, Robbie?' said their father.

Robbie jumped up. 'What'll I tell 'em?'

'Not here and I'll call back. Find out who it is.'

A few seconds later, Robbie was saying, 'He's not *here*,' for the second time.

'Who is it?' asked Richard, rising, turning around.

'*You* know,' Robbie replied.

Arthur looked at his mother, amused. 'Why doesn't she get a psychiatrist instead of latching on to busy people?'

Patiently, his mother got up and went into the living room. 'Tell her our cat's sick,' she said with a nervous giggle.

Robbie came back stern-faced. 'Old hag! Why's she always bothering *us*?'

'Why does Dad put up with it?' Arthur said. 'After all, she's found God. You'd think she'd use him, wouldn't you?'

Their father returned, frowning. He had agreed to go to see Irene. It was his duty. 'She's weeping. It's worse tonight, I can tell.'

'Is she drinking a little?' asked Lois.

'Not a drop in the house,' Richard said. He went to the front hall hooks for his jacket.

'Say, Dad, could you drop me at Gus's?' Arthur said, getting up. 'It's on the way. Just a minute while I call him?'

His father sighed as if this were a nuisance.

In the car, Arthur and his father were silent for a few minutes; then Arthur asked, not really caring, 'What do you and Irene talk about?'

'Oh – patience. Morale.' His father drove cautiously, as if taking a driving test. 'Remember I used to talk to you about that? How to build and keep morale. Inner strength.'

Arthur's mind jumped to money. Even before Robbie's crisis last May, morale, in the way his father talked about it, was connected with money. It was his grandmother who had talked about patience and doing work that one could be proud of, 'otherwise don't do it.' Arthur asked, 'Has Irene got enough money?'

'No. That's one of her problems. Not that she asks me for any, mind you. I wouldn't yield to that. Yield once and it goes on forever. No, she works now as a waitress in a couple of diners,' his father continued. 'Truck-stop type. Has to go by bus at crazy hours sometimes. I'm afraid she'll yield to temptation and go off with some truck driver one night or day. And he'll give her more money than tips can. So that's a temptation, you see.'

It sounded awful to Arthur, untempting. Imagine going to bed with Irene! Or from Irene's point of view, sleeping with a truck driver who hadn't had a bath or a shave in a couple of days! 'Well – is she demented?'

'No. Why?' His father slowed to let him off at the next crossing.

'Because she didn't seem quite right in the head the night I saw her. – Is her sister any better?'

'Um-m – no.' His father stopped the car.

Arthur got out and said through the open window, 'G'luck Dad. And thanks.'

On a dark sidewalk between Main and Gus's house, where the commercial started to blend into the residential, Arthur encountered a prostitute. She was strolling languidly and said, 'G*ood* evening,' as they passed. What was the world coming to? His father had his work cut out for him.

Arthur rapped on the frame of the screen door at Gus's, and getting no answer, walked in.

'Hi, Art! I'm in the kitchen!' Gus yelled.

Arthur went into the kitchen and found Gus on the linoleum floor near the back door, working on a lawnmower, a small Wolf that ran with gasoline. Gus's mother greeted him. She was slicing orange peel and the kitchen smelled nice.

'Sit down, Art. I won't be long on this. – Want a beer?'

'Not just yet, thanks.' Arthur sat on a straight chair, watching Gus's work.

'What's your news?' Gus asked, blowing on a bolt. He screwed it back with his fingers and picked up a wrench.

'I'm in at C.U. Heard today.'

'Oh – fine. Hear that, Mom? Art's going to C.U. in September.'

'Are you? – Well, nice you'll be around with us, Arthur.'

Arthur nodded. 'Other news,' he said to Gus, 'Maggie's away for two weeks at least. Canada.'

'Oh. Yeah, you said she was going.' Gus stood up and pulled the starter cord. The mower burst into noise and trembling life.

'*Really*, Gus! – You'll make me *cut* myself!' cried his mother, turning around, laughing.

Gus smiled with success and switched the motor off. 'Sorry,

Mom. – Now I'll git this so-and-so out on the back porch for the night.'

Arthur stood up to help, but it was a one-man job. Arthur held the screen door open. Then Gus took beers from the fridge. Gus washed his hands at the sink; then they went up to his room.

'How's Veronica?' Arthur asked.

'Okay, helping her mother put up stuff tonight, she said. String beans and beets.' Gus started to sit on his bed and chose the floor. His jeans had grease spots.

Arthur thought about his father, with that nut Irene this minute, in that nutty household. Did his father pick up the Bible and start quoting?

'Something happen with Maggie?'

'Oh, no! – She invited me up to Canada for a week. But I thought I better stick with my job. – More news, my dad said he'd help out with C.U. Moneywise. Not sure how much, but it sounds like about half.' Arthur knew Gus's family was helping him out, even though Gus would no doubt keep on with his repair jobs, which were quite lucrative. 'Maybe I'll have to take a part-time job. I hate it. I suppose I'm lazy, if you come down to it.' Arthur wouldn't have minded if Gus said he was a bit lazy.

But Gus didn't. He got up and with his back turned to Arthur removed his jeans and put on pajama pants. Then he sat on his bed.

'Can you drive me home tonight?' Arthur asked, worried slightly about the pajama pants, but Gus said:

'Sure. – You walked here?'

'Na-a. My dad drove me. He was seeing somebody at Haskill and Main, one of his church people.'

'You mean he tries to get people to go to church?'

'Well – yeah, but mostly he meets these people *in* church. Young people, he calls them, but this one's about thirty. Irene Langley. Bleached blonde. Used to be a hooker and took drugs too.'

'You met her?'

'Once.'

'So your dad goes over and talks to her – about keeping on the straight path?'

'Something like that. She calls up and whines, wants him to come over. It's creepy.' Arthur wanted to tell Gus about her visit, but was afraid Gus might be bored, and Irene was even depressing to talk about, too.

Gus shook his head. 'Nice of your dad to give her all that time.'

Arthur dropped his beer can into Gus's wastebasket. 'Yeah. A wonder they let her *in* church, because she still looks like a hooker.'

Gus laughed a little. 'Hey, I'm glad you're going to C.U. – I know you're not. – Thank God, I don't have to worry about French anymore, majoring in agriculture. Y'know, my French was just like my dancing; it just got so good and no better. Never would, never will.' Gus put on a cassette, not too loud, because there was always somebody sleeping in a nearby room.

They drank their second beers; then Gus drove Arthur home. The garage doors at Arthur's house were open, but his father's car was not there. Gus declined to come in, both because of his pajama pants and that he had to be up by 6:30.

Arthur found his mother in the living room with one of the thick books she sometimes took from the Home, a book on child care, pediatrics.

'Gus drove you home? – Thought it was Richard for a minute.'

Arthur looked at his watch. Ten to 11. He stretched, suddenly sleepy. 'I'm turning in.'

'I wish Richard was. He needs his sleep, and I *don't* feel like calling that woman up, even if I had her number, which I haven't.' She laid her book aside.

'I bet I could find it. We could call up and remind Dad of an early morning appointment.'

'He may well have one,' said his mother, lighting a cigarette.

'Have you met the sister?'

His mother shook her head. 'Weighs over two hundred pounds, Richard says, sits around nibbling all day and doesn't bother looking for a job. Who'd have her? – Oops! That's Richard's car now.'

Doors slammed. Then Richard came in with his arms-hanging attitude, smiling tiredly at both of them. 'Whew! – That was tough. She hadn't paid her electricity bill. No money. I was trying to go over her finances – income with her, but she says the tips vary so much.' Richard shook his head. 'I didn't offer her a loan, anyway.'

'Good,' Lois said smugly.

'Sister sitting there' – Richard removed his jacket – 'eating candy bars while she listened to us.'

'Must be depressing,' said Lois.

'Oh-h – she tells me about the characters she meets where she works. About the offers she's turned down to travel places. Ha! She was even invited to Cuba, she says. Havana.'

Arthur was bored. Even Havana with its good cigars sounded boring, if Irene had anything to do with it. 'G'night, Mom. G'night, Dad.'

19

On his first day at Chalmerston University, Arthur noticed a girl who much resembled Maggie. This was perhaps the most jolting of his experiences. She was among a couple of hundred students in a corridor of Johnson Hall. Her hair was the same color and cut the same way; she was taller than Maggie and her mouth was wider, but she had the same erect posture and air of energy. She and Arthur were walking in opposite directions.

Arthur's mother had contributed two hundred dollars, which she implied his father wouldn't miss from their joint bank account; Arthur had twice that, and his grandmother had sent him five hundred with a nice note in early September. His fifteen-hundred-dollar grant had been applied, so Arthur was more than in the clear for half the year, which gave him a good feeling. The other feeling he had about C.U. was a fuzzy and disturbing one: Everyone seemed to be specializing instantly in something, agriculture in Gus's case, biology in his, or statistics, or in some detail of electronics. He had imagined a wider range of required subjects, such as English composition and a foreign language (French for him), the study of which would be lifted to some higher plane where classes were smaller, standards higher than those of high school. However, English composition and

French were still demanded for the A.B. he was aiming for, besides the chemistry and physics that went with specializing in biology. In a burst of extravagance, Arthur decided to add philosophy, which was not required.

At home, his father continued the cool treatment, saying 'Morning,' with a faint smile as if Arthur were a stranger on ship, and 'Good night, Arthur,' over his shoulder sometimes. But no matter, because his mother beamed at him often. Arthur carried his books and notebooks in a brown leather briefcase with three compartments and two zippers and with both handle and strap, which Maggie had brought him from Canada. 'Strap's detachable,' Maggie had said, 'in case you think it's feminine.'

At C.U., there was Gus and Veronica, and other faces familiar to Arthur from senior classes in high school. He had a locker for a spare raincoat, boots, and old umbrella, with a good combination lock, because there was a lot of thievery, he had been warned. He had bought the secondhand brown Ford.

As the autumn came on, there was a letup in Irene Langley's telephone calls, Arthur noticed. At least, his father seemed to be home most evenings. Arthur now refused to go to church, claiming that C.U. demanded all his time, which was certainly true if he scanned even half of the 'suggested reading list' for English and philosophy, not to mention biology, as Professor Jurgens was always adding titles of his latest fancy to his mimeographed list.

Maggie wrote in October:

> Just finished a swat at math. Can you believe that I still have to spend extra time on it? Exam coming up even and if I don't pass they can warn me in January and throw me out next spring!
>
> It's as you said, the older boys date all the freshmen as if they've never seen girls before, but so far I've had just two

'dates' and these were in groups. Twice as many fellows as girls, so you're not really dating anybody . . . I miss you.

All my love, M.

She was coming home for Thanksgiving. That was something to look forward to.

After a long period of abeyance, Robbie's tantrum fits returned over a square dance party to be given in the high school gym on Halloween. All the kids were to come in costume. And Robbie had announced one evening that he was going and was taking a girl named Mildred. Robbie had said he wanted a costume of black tights, maybe with a white skeleton painted on it, and he was going to look for it. His parents and Arthur were all pleased that Robbie intended to go to something 'social.' They asked about Mildred.

'Oh, she's just a girl,' Robbie replied.

Then, the evening before the event, Robbie got cold feet. He wasn't going, he said, and no, he hadn't told Mildred.

'Look,' Arthur said, 'you can't just stand a girl *up*! Unless Mildred can go on her own or something. You'd have to be in the hospital—'

'I'll talk to him,' their mother said.

A few minutes later, when Arthur was in his own room, he heard Robbie's voice rise to a screech, as it had used to before his voice changed. Arthur got up to close his door, found it already closed, then heard his mother say:

'No one's *making* you go, Robbie. What do you mean?'

'It makes me sick,' Robbie replied, 'and I'm *not going*!'

What was the hitch now, with little Robbie? Arthur went into the living room, because he wanted Robbie to go to this party. Little Robbie, now half an inch taller than he, had no social life at all.

'Now what's up?' Arthur asked, with a genial air of someone who had been only slightly disturbed by the loud voices. His father's study door was closed. 'You're not going – why? That's a good-looking outfit, by the way.'

Robbie was in the pants part of the skeleton suit, and the shirt part dangled from one hand. He shifted about the living room, naked from the waist up, red-faced. 'It's silly and I'm not gonna wear it!'

'Then wear your blue jeans!' their mother said. 'Nobody'll care, Robbie. Wear your skull mask—'

'I'm not going at all!'

'Shy about Mildred maybe,' Arthur said.

'You shut your trap!' Robbie retorted. 'The hell with her, I just don't want to go to this goddamned *thing*!'

Lois put her hands over her ears for an instant, and Richard opened his study door.

'What the dickens is going on here?' Richard said.

'Robbie doesn't want to go to the party tomorrow night.'

'Not only don't want to, I'm *not* going,' said Robbie. He started to shove his tights down, then ran off to his room to do it.

'Robbie!' said Richard in his best baritone.

Robbie stopped and turned.

'Why aren't you going to that party?' Richard asked. 'It's a school party.'

'I don't feel like it; I think it's silly, and I don't know why I have to go.'

'You have to go, because *I* tell you to go,' said Richard, advancing on Robbie. 'Your mother sees that you get the – the right stuff to wear; you've got a date to take – and you back out? *No*, boy. You're going.'

Robbie hesitated, crumpled, bowed his head, then turned and fled before anyone could see a tear.

Arthur looked at his father, amazed. The argument was over. Robbie was going tomorrow night. In the old days, Robbie would have written on the floor with clenched fists.

Richard said to Lois, 'He's going.'

'I can't – understand it,' Lois whispered. 'I mean the way he's acting.'

'Neither can I. But he's going. Do him good.' Richard went back to his study.

As Arthur returned to his room, he heard a choked sob from behind Robbie's closed door.

A couple of days later, Arthur said to his mother, at a moment when they were alone in the house, 'What was Robbie afraid of about that party? Taking a *girl* with him?' Robbie had returned with a grim air of having done his duty in regard to the party.

'Well – maybe,' his mother replied, 'because Mildred asked *him*, I gathered. Robbie's—'

Arthur burst out laughing. That made sense. Arthur couldn't imagine Robbie taking the initiative and asking a girl.

'I think he wanted to go, but by himself. That's the way I see it. He came back saying parties like that were silly and not grown-up.' His mother added, 'Maybe we should be glad he's not sniffing coke.'

Arthur knew his brother was still consorting with his Delmar Lake chums, who were now hunting instead of fishing, the season having changed. Robbie hadn't his own gun, because their father forbade it, but Robbie shot rabbits and wild ducks with the guns of others, he had told the family.

In the corridors, and sometimes on the steps of the C.U. library, where students stopped to talk and smoke a cigarette, Arthur saw the girl called Aline Morrison, who looked so much like Maggie, and his heart gave a jump each time. His eyes were apt to linger, but twice the girl had noticed him, and Arthur had at once looked away. She wasn't, of course, a duplicate of Maggie. Her nose was more pointed. But the way she held herself was like Maggie in a good mood. One day in the library, when Arthur had taken some books from the stacks and sat down to do an hour's work, he glanced across the long table and saw the Morrison girl directly opposite him.

She looked at him at the same time, then back to what she was writing.

Arthur slowly gathered his books and notebooks, as if moving slowly would make him less conspicuous, and left the table for another. He forgot about the Morrison girl, and then as he was checking out books at the desk, he saw her standing by the exit door.

'Hello,' she said. 'I don't know your name.'

'Arthur.'

'I was wondering – well, why you looked at me and then left that table.' She smiled, almost laughed. Her brown eyes had darker brown flecks in them, a little like Maggie's which were, however, an odd mixture of blue and brown and green.

They were walking on slowly.

'It's nothing. It's just that you remind me of someone I know.'

'Somebody here?'

'No, she's at another college.'

'Remind you pleasantly?'

'Yes, sure. – Sorry if I annoyed you. Didn't mean to.'

'You didn't annoy me. Why don't you join us in the lunch hall some time? We're usually back corner right.'

Who was we, Arthur wondered. 'Thanks. I'm only a freshman.'

'Sophs are allowed to talk to freshmen. Anyway, you don't look like a scared rabbit type.'

'Thanks.' Arthur smiled and walked on. He had no desire to make a date with the Morrison girl, he realized. Was he afraid of her somehow? No. He had Maggie, so why make a date with the Morrison girl?

Three days before Maggie was due home for Thanksgiving, Arthur had a telephone call from her. Maggie said she had chicken pox.

'Unbelievable, isn't it? Hundred-and-four fever at six this evening and I'm in quarantine. I can't come home for Thanksgiving. The doctor says it'll take a week—'

'Gosh, I'm sorry!'

'So'm I. Now it'll be Christmas before I see you!'

Arthur told his mother, who was in the living room working over a big file of letters from the Beverley Home.

'Oh, dear! That's a nasty business at her age. What tough luck, Arthur – for both of you.'

'Her mother knows, but I think I'll call Betty anyway.' Arthur dialed the Brewster number, but nobody answered. He went to a shelf in the living room, and pulled out the Merck Manual. 'Did I ever have chicken pox, Mom?'

'You certainly did. Robbie, too, at the same time. It's not serious when you're small. – Maggie must've come in contact with a small child with it – somehow.'

As Arthur was reading about pustules, his father came in, unexpectedly, because he had gone out after dinner to visit a client and the client had stood him up. His father's presence, plus the rotten news from Maggie, inspired Arthur to leave and go straight to the Brewster house.

A dim light was on in the Brewster living room, but no one answered the doorbell. Arthur had brought a philosophy text and a flashlight and sat in his car reading.

Betty Brewster's white Volkswagen Polo arrived in less than half an hour.

'Hi, Betty! – You heard the bad news?'

'About Maggie? Yes, this afternoon. – Come in, Arthur. How long've you been waiting? You must be freezing!'

Arthur was happy to come into the house. He had visited Betty at least twice since Maggie had been gone, and once Betty had called him to ask news of Maggie, suspecting that Maggie wrote to him more often than to her. Betty had asked him to visit anytime he chose. Now she made old-fashioneds in heavy glasses.

'I wrote a note to Maggie,' said Betty. 'I'm afraid to try to call her, in case she's not near a phone. I reminded her *not* to scratch, now or later. Quite a big rash, you know, all over the face and the torso even.'

Arthur felt increasingly alarmed. 'Maybe you should get her into a hospital here?'

Betty laughed. 'No. I had a friend who caught it. A grown-up. Four rotten days, but you're hardly in bed, just fever. Then these little pustules break. Highly unpleasant.'

The grandfather clock ticked in the hall. Betty asked him about college, about his brother. Arthur was reluctant to leave.

'Come and have Thanksgiving dinner with us, if you feel like it, Arthur,' Betty said. 'Just Warren and me and another couple – middle-aged, sorry to say, but easy to get along with.'

Arthur was tempted, because the dinner would be in Maggie's house. 'Thank you. I suppose my folks'll expect me to be home.'

'We have our dinner in the evening. You can eat two dinners, can't you?'

Arthur grinned. 'I suppose I can. Thank you, Betty. I'd like to come.'

'Six-thirty. – Any time between six and seven doesn't matter at all.'

Robbie's contribution to Thanksgiving was a rabbit freshly shot by himself in the Delmar Lake woods with 'the men,' as Robbie called them. For some reason, Arthur thought of a chain gang when Robbie said this. His mother, of course, was going to bake a turkey, and nobody in the family cared for rabbit except Richard.

'Can't we put it in the fridge or the deep freeze till after tomorrow?' Lois asked.

This was the day before Thanksgiving Day, and Arthur was

home when Robbie came in with the rabbit in a slightly bloody newspaper at noon.

'Sure, but I gotta skin him and clean him first. Want to watch me skin him, Arthur?'

'Not particularly,' Arthur replied. 'I suppose it's dead and not just half-dead?'

Robbie's macho bored Arthur. He now wore green rubber boots too big for him, somebody's hand-me-down hunting jacket with pockets for bullets and small game, and a murderous-looking knife in a leather sheath fastened to the jacket belt. Robbie stalked out with the bloody bundle into the backyard, via his father's study door, and proceeded to skin the animal with the knife. This involved cutting the head and feet off first, Robbie had informed Arthur and their mother. She had a plastic bag in which to put these items for disposal, plus the skin, but no, Robbie wanted to keep the skin, he had said.

Arthur went back to his room, vaguely disgusted. The hide, wherever Robbie put it, was going to be of interest to Rovy the cat. Arthur had considerable homework to do during the five-day Thanksgiving holiday. And he wanted to go to the post office before 4 p.m. that day, so his latest to Maggie would get off. He added to his letter:

> You give me so much morale in this boring life here. I wish I could give you half as much.

20

At Christmas time, Arthur arranged with Maggie's mother that he would pick Maggie up at 4:30 at Indi Airport and drive her home. He saw her before she saw him. She was waiting beside the revolving luggage belt.

'Maggie?' She was still Maggie, with longer hair now, which made him aware of all the time that had passed, and not a bit like the girl called Aline, of whom Arthur had dreamed once, to his annoyance, because he so rarely dreamed of Maggie.

'And what do you think of my – splotches?' She ducked her head with the shyness that Arthur loved.

'Hardly noticed 'em!' But he had, a dozen or more pink and red dots all over her cheeks and forehead. *I warn you it's disgusting,* Maggie had written in her last letter. Arthur carried her suitcase and duffel bag. 'Wait'll you see my car. – Not much to look at, even though I cleaned it today in your honor.'

Maggie said the car looked fine, and she didn't mind its color.

'Anyway, it's ours,' Arthur said.

They started off for the hour's drive to Chalmerston.

'My mother wants you to come for Christmas dinner,' Maggie said. 'I don't know if she told you.'

Why hadn't she said something more personal, Arthur

thought. Or for that matter, why hadn't he? He hadn't even kissed her, and that wasn't because of the pink splotches.

'Did Mom tell you?'

'No. Thanks, Mag. I accept – with pleasure. – Know what's happening at my house? Dad wants this Irene Langley and her sister to come Christmas and my mother's dead set against it.' Arthur laughed.

'You mean the one you told me about who goes to their church?'

'None other. And if her sister comes – she'll break any chair in the house, she's so fat. According to Dad. Well – my grandmother arrived yesterday, and she said can *you* come for Christmas dinner. So why don't you do what I did Thanksgiving, my place first and a repeat performance at your house, because your folks eat dinner later – don't they?' How could he go on yacking like a fool, with Maggie just inches away, touchable, *here*?

'I'm not presentable. My face. I told you.'

'Oh, *Mag*! It's not as bad as you said it was. And it gets a little better every day, doesn't it?'

After a while, she said, 'How's your social life?'

'Are you joking? – I see Gus. All his classes are in different buildings, though. – And how about your social life?'

Maggie said she had been to one football game, followed by a dance, and she hadn't liked that enough to want to do it again. She mentioned Larry Hargiss, a medical student, and Arthur supposed he was one of the ones much older, possibly a post-grad student already twenty-two. She said she quite liked a girl called Kate, who was also majoring in sociology and was from Chicago.

Arthur stopped the car in Maggie's driveway and carried her luggage to the door, but declined to come in. 'Get yourself unpacked. Call me later if you want to. I'll be home. I wasn't sure you'd feel like doing anything tonight.'

'I dunno – but I'll call you. After I talk with Mom.' Her mother's car was not in the garage, Maggie had seen by looking through the garage window. 'I'd better not say yes to Christmas dinner at your house. You know how your father is – about me. Tell your mother thanks though, would you? Just say I have to stay with my folks.'

Arthur felt pained and ashamed. 'S-sure, Mag.' Now she had the door open. 'Want me to carry these upstairs for you?'

'No!' She smiled. 'I'm not an invalid.'

Arthur seized her shoulders, kissed her cheek, then her lips quickly, and ran off to his car.

He had been awkward! Off on the wrong foot again. He'd have to make up for that. It was cold enough for snow. One lot of snow had come and gone. He hoped it snowed for Christmas.

At his house, Arthur found the conversation about Irene and her sister still in progress, or it had resumed. His father stood in the living room, having recently come out of his study apparently, because the study door was wide open. His grandmother sat on the sofa, and his mother was just carrying from the kitchen a bowl of popcorn whose aroma filled the house.

'Robbie, do you have to use that word – over and over?' Lois asked.

Arthur had paused in the kitchen, and his mother, on her way to the living room, had not seen him. Arthur scraped up the remaining kernels in the popcorn pot on the stove and chewed them.

'Can't we, Richard, take them a Christmas *box* on Christmas Day? Fruit cake and candy – maybe a gift for their house?'

'But I've told you I *invited* them,' Richard replied. 'So call it my fault, if you like, *my* mistake.' He said it in a tone implying that an invitation at Christmas could be a mistake only in the eyes of the selfish and stingy. 'I don't know how I can undo it – in all conscience.'

Christmas was two days off. Arthur rinsed his hands at the sink, then drifted into the living room.

'Hel-lo, Arthur,' said his grandmother. 'And how is Maggie?'

'Fine. Complaining about the spots on her face. She thinks she looks like somebody who caught some buckshot, but really – it's not so bad.'

'Poor girl! If she doesn't touch it, she won't have a mark though. – Arthur, I *think* there's an old-fashioned for you in the fridge, if you happen to want it.'

Arthur went to get it. It was one slightly sweet drink he didn't mind, not as sweet as his father's silly Alexanders.

'Seems to me if we propose an alternative,' his mother was saying gently, 'like the day after Christmas – turkey buffet supper? Christmas comes but once a year, and Mama's here, and if I can speak plainly – I just don't care to think of Irene's face across the table from me at Christmas. Christmas is a family affair.'

His father glanced at Arthur from under lowered brows as Arthur returned to the living room. 'A gift or a buffet the next day isn't the same as Christmas in a real home. And I feel these two are in need.'

His mother sighed. 'Well, let's stop it now for Mama's sake, for Arthur's sake.'

'*Arthur's* sake?' said his father, feigning surprise.

'Dad says Irene can make good fudge, Mom. Maybe she could bring some.' This from Robbie.

Arthur saw his mother look at Robbie and expected her to say she wouldn't eat a piece of Irene's fudge if her life depended on it, but his mother said nothing.

Ludicrous, Arthur thought. Really like a mad soap opera. Who the hell cared about Irene and her fat sister or whether they came to anything? Maggie was in town, just about a mile away! Arthur gave his grandmother a big grin. She patted the sofa beside her, and Arthur went and sat down. His grandmother managed to change the subject, but Arthur's mind, not for the first time, was on trying to foresee when he might have the house free to ask Maggie over, so they could go to bed in his room. His father went back to work the 27th. Would his mother and grandmother go off somewhere one morning or afternoon or even for a long lunch? Would Robbie, by chance, be off hunting with the men at the same time? Would Maggie's house be a more likely venue, since her mother was only one person, and Maggie had said her father might not be able to come home even on Christmas Day, and she didn't know his schedule afterward?

Maggie rang up just after 7. Her mother wanted her to stay in, because she thought Maggie looked tired, but Arthur could come over anytime and also have dinner with them. So Arthur decided to do that.

And the Langley sisters did come for Christmas dinner. His mother had said beforehand, 'Not more than two hours, I hope, Richard. You ease them out, would you?' Richard solemnly promised.

The eight-foot-high tree in the living room had been decorated by his mother, grandmother, and Arthur himself, Robbie having backed out, unwilling. Crazy, Arthur thought, at his age, to feel excited by the smell of fir needles and his memories of the old-fashioned red-and-white torchlike ornament that had always graced the very top of the tree, and which Arthur remembered from when he was small. Maggie came over for a few minutes Christmas Eve Day, with a box of candy for the family and a present in a small package for Arthur, which he did not open then. He wanted to open it alone, and besides it was a tradition in his family that presents were opened on Christmas Day morning. He had two presents for Maggie to take, the more important one being a slender gold chain bracelet.

Christmas Day morning arrived: cold white wine and egg nog in a silver punch bowl from his grandmother's family. Christmas carols rang out on the TV while they unwrapped presents, all eyes on the unwrapper until the surprise was disclosed, admired, and it was someone else's turn to unwrap. The weighty book from his grandmother turned out to be *A Dictionary of Science Terms*. His mother gave him a navy blue pea jacket with slash pockets, like a Navy jacket but with a cut of higher fashion.

The dinner hour of more or less 1 approached, pleasantly delayed by chatter in the kitchen. His father went off to fetch the Langley sisters.

'Did you decide on the strongest chair yet, Mom?' asked Arthur, laughing merrily.

His grandmother had been pleased with the pale blue and purple silk scarf Arthur had given her, and was wearing it now. Arthur had given his mother a black case like a briefcase but smaller, with an address book and a writing pad in it, which he thought she could use for her work at the Beverley Home.

The gaiety in the kitchen subsided as Richard's car rolled up the driveway, and Robbie marched forth to open the door.

'Don't let all that cold air in, Robbie!' Lois said.

There were a couple of inches of snow outside, enough to make the scene white, and it was still coming down lightly.

Rovy, who had been hovering around the warm stove, interested in the smell of turkey, fled as the trio came into the kitchen. Louise Langley bumped both sides of the kitchen door, and turned a little sideways to let herself through.

Richard introduced everybody.

Irene had a bunch of orange gladioli clasped in both hands along with her purse strap. Her sister Louise looked half-asleep and wore a fixed smile broader and more open than Irene's, showing her upper and lower teeth. She was taller than Irene, which made her bulk formidable, rather like a piece of furniture that one had to walk around. She moved slowly and from side to side.

'Yes, these gladioli were brought by a neighbor this morning,' Irene said for the second time, 'but I wanted the Alderman family to have them. – It's so kind of you to have us.'

His grandmother stood near the living room door observing all this with a sharp eye, Arthur noticed.

'Take yer coats!' Robbie said brusquely but politely, extending his arms for Irene's coat, then Louise's.

Richard halfheartedly proposed drinks. Irene said she would have just a little old-fashioned, if Richard had the makings.

'Egg nog for me,' said Louise, smiling more broadly. 'Got a sweet tooth, I have to admit – My, you've got a pretty house here, Lois!' She stood on tiptoe and looked around. Her wide hips were covered by a loose black satin skirt that she must have made for herself, and her blouse was also of satin, white and full of ruffles.

Richard led the sisters into the living room, followed by Robbie.

'Whee-yoo!' Arthur whispered.

His grandmother laughed softly.

Robbie was back. 'Mom, any more of those tollhouse cookies?'

'First breadbox on the left there,' said his mother.

The bench at the table creaked when Louise sat down on it. Her hair, Arthur observed as they bowed their heads for the blessing, was a natural color, judging from the parting, a dark brown. Louise's eyebrows were darkened with makeup and surprisingly thick, while Irene had plucked hers to a hair's breadth.

'It's so – pacifying to have a blessing by a man,' Irene murmured. 'Don't you think so, Lois?'

'Yes. – It is.'

Crabmeat cocktail. Then Richard carved.

'Yum-yum!' said Louise, and giggled like a child at the sight of the plump and well-browned turkey.

Irene continued to sway gently, even seated. Louise's mouth seemed to be visibly watering. Robbie yawned while waiting for his plate to be served, as if the Langley sisters came every day.

'How is your mother doing, Irene?' Joan asked. 'If I may call you Irene.'

'She's – Oh, of *course* you may call me Irene. My mother – is a very sad case. She's not going to get any better. Though we do pray, both of us.' She glanced at her sister.

'Cancer,' said Louise to Joan.

'Oh, dear,' said Joan.

'If that's my plate, can I have more cranberry sauce, Dad?' said Robbie.

Richard wore a green-and-red-striped shirt in honor of the day and had turned back his cuffs before he began carving. Lois was serving the vegetables. There were candied yams, creamed onions, and green peas.

They ate, and somehow talked as well. In no time, though she did not seem to be rushing, Louise's plate was empty and she was ready for seconds.

'You said you wouldn't gorge, Louise,' Irene announced in a flat tone, as if she said the same thing at every meal.

Arthur thought he ought to say something, so he came up with, 'Have you some friends in the neighborhood – to help out with your mother?' His last words were almost drowned in a flood of negatives from both sisters.

'No, we are shunned,' Irene told him. 'Most people don't care at all about their neighbors. That's what Richard says. That's why my sister and I so appreciate . . .'

Arthur saw his mother take a deep breath.

Louise drank her white wine as if it were water, and outdid herself on the dessert, which was two kinds of fruitcake with or without pineapple sherbet. One fruitcake was homemade by his grandmother. Robbie belched, which evoked from Arthur the only real laugh at the table.

Then there was coffee in the living room. Louise took one of the two sturdy green armchairs and seemed to sink and sink in it, as if the springs had collapsed and she might be sitting on the floor. Arthur, in euphoria after the good meal and with the anticipation of seeing Maggie later, of opening her present which was in his room, was seized with near-hysterics and had to go into the hall on the pretext of a fit of coughing and nose-blowing.

His mother was already trying to ease them out, with some gentle assistance from his grandmother. Lois was not standing, though she sat on the edge of the chair, saying something about her family being obliged to visit another house in the neighborhood.

'I'm sorry this can't be a *longer* afternoon,' his mother said.

'Oh, I quite understand, Lois,' said Irene, leaning forward but not getting up. 'I did want to say about Arthur – before we leave—' Irene looked at Arthur with the awful, red-lipped smile meant to be gentle and understanding.

At that moment, Louise struggled up from the depths of the green armchair and gave her attention to Arthur also. 'Could you show me where the John is, please?'

Arthur escorted her down the hall. She must pee like a cow, he thought.

'... Christ does forgive. This is his very own day. Gloria in excelsis, I think people say,' Irene was murmuring. 'This is a time for – redeeming—'

'Redemption,' said Richard, fiddling with his unlighted pipe, frowning.

Arthur noticed that Robbie had the blank but attentive expression that came to his face in church, or when his father talked at the table about the spiritual side of man. Irene, Arthur realized, was talking about the physical side, about 'sinning,' about him.

'... young people have made a mistake, they must realize it and face it – and say they're sorry. That way ...'

His mother gave a nervous shake of her head and glanced at her mother. Arthur frowned at the floor for an instant.

'If you'll excuse me,' his mother said, standing up, 'we must be leaving soon. I'm sure Richard can drive you both home.'

'Or Arthur can,' said Richard. 'Are we in such a rush to—'

'I'm sure Irene and her sister would prefer you to drive them, Richard,' said Lois, turning on the sweetness. 'Wouldn't you, Irene?'

'Well – I suppose we would.' Reluctantly, though still smiling, Irene got to her feet. She wore very high-heeled black shoes. 'Thank you – all. You have been so kind. This is a household of the Lord. Isn't it – Louise?' She looked at her sister, who was just then returning from the hall.

'What?' said Louise.

Robbie fetched the coats. Thanks and Merry Christmases, and then Richard went with the two out the kitchen door to his car.

His mother opened the kitchen window at the same time as Arthur opened a living room window. Just a minute, Arthur thought, we'll get their stink out in spite of the cold! His mother came into the living room.

'My *goodness*, their vulgarity!' she said to both her mother and Arthur.

Robbie came in quietly behind her.

'Dear Loey, we'd better think of it as funny – the way Arthur does,' Joan said. 'I thought you were going to explode there, Arthur!' His grandmother laughed heartily.

Robbie was standing with one hand on the back of the armchair where Louise had sat. He was not smiling. He looked at Arthur levelly with his gray eyes that were more like Richard's than were Arthur's. Robbie's brow was as smooth as if he gazed out on Delmar Lake on a quiet afternoon of fishing. He looked at his grandmother and said, 'They have to be managed. That's what Dad says. Otherwise they'll fall. Or stray like sheep.'

'Sheep.' Arthur smiled. 'The sister, too?'

'What do you mean, managed?' Joan asked.

'They need someone to talk to them – 'specially Irene, to make sure she does the right things. She's not so good at deciding things for herself.'

'Such as what?' asked Joan.

'Oh – Dad said she was going to buy a new fridge when she hasn't even the money to pay her electric bill. So Dad stopped that. Then there's a danger Irene might start to sell herself, because she's a waitress in a truck-stop diner.'

Arthur broke up again and bent over. 'Who'd buy her?'

His grandmother went on talking with Robbie, and Arthur drifted away, into the hall, to his room. He closed his door, seized Maggie's present, then opened it with care. The sleek little white box under the wrapping contained a gold chain, longer and thinner than the one he had given Maggie. In its middle a small gold disc was suspended, a nearly flattened sphere, smooth on both sides, with nothing written on it. Her card said, 'For Christmas, with my love. M.' The chain was soft as silk, not too thick or thin. Arthur felt that he had been presented with a Rolls or a yacht. He held it around his neck and saw in the mirror that it would hardly show if the top button of his shirt were open. Exactly right! Arthur fastened it, and tugged his shirt collar up. Very likely his family would not notice it this evening. Arthur suddenly realized that his father hadn't given him a Christmas present. And who cared? He had given his father quite a nice pen and pencil set with a cheerful card warning him to hang on to the pencil, because his father was always complaining that the pencils got lost. Robbie had received, among many other things, a new suit.

The following Monday, Arthur's mother and grandmother were invited to a buffet lunch at Jane Griffin's house, and Robbie had an all-day date with 'the men.' So Arthur invited Maggie for lunch at a quarter to 1. Bliss again to have her in the house, to know that they could be alone for two hours! Arthur made scrambled eggs mixed with pre-cooked crisp bacon. Lovely to take it easy, to know that after lunch and leaving dishes on the table, they could go to bed together in his room. His room had a key. Maggie went to take a shower. And she would have taken the magic pill! And the books Arthur had perused stood him in good stead. No rushing. Don't do everything the same way every time.

'I'm glad you didn't put on clean sheets. I like them like this,' Maggie said.

Arthur wore nothing but his new neck chain, and Maggie her gold bracelet. And girls could often do it twice, Arthur had read. Amazing, but true. And afterwards, it would also have been bliss to fall asleep for a few minutes, but Arthur reached for his wristwatch. When his mother and grandmother came home around 3, Maggie had departed five minutes before, and the kitchen was on the way to being tidy again.

Robbie was much in demand by his sportsmen chums that holiday season. Surely some of them had teenaged daughters, Arthur thought, though Robbie had never mentioned any. The night before New Year's Eve, Robbie was invited to a stag party, and he fairly strutted when he announced this to his family.

'No girls allowed. No women,' Robbie said in his deepest voice, looking serious.

'Filthy creatures, anyway,' Arthur said, which provoked a laugh from his grandmother. 'Don't tell me one of these hunters is getting married.'

'No,' Robbie said. 'Why?'

'Stag parties are usually the night before you get married. Supposed to send the bridegroom off in terrible shape.' Arthur blew smoke toward the ceiling. 'Aren't some of those fellows married?'

'Sure. Some of 'em, maybe. I don't know,' Robbie replied, as if he couldn't care less.

'Haven't they got kids around your age? Do you ever meet any? Any girls?'

Robbie squirmed. 'Is that all you ever think about?' he asked, frowning, then turned and left the living room.

His grandmother was sitting on the sofa, knitting a cap out

of dark green wool that she had found in the house, not enough wool for making anything but a cap, she had said. 'He is a funny one,' she said, not looking up.

Arthur smiled. 'Yeah. These – men—' He looked behind him, never knowing whether Robbie was lurking or not. He moved closer to his grandmother. He had told her about meeting some of the men down at Delmar Lake. 'I bet they're the type who go to a cathouse sometimes in a group. They're always together, acting like professional hillbillies. – I think they have a contempt for girls and women. Do you know what I mean, Grandma?'

'Yes. I think I do.' She did not look up from her knitting. 'But maybe Robbie's jealous of you. That's pretty likely, you know, Arthur? Normal.' She glanced up at him. 'Maybe he'll make some new friends soon – starting with boys his own age. He's as tall as you, I noticed.'

'Yep.'

'And if he's so interested in keeping Irene on the straight and narrow, maybe he gives more thought to the opposite sex than you think.' She chuckled.

Arthur nodded, unsatisfied.

'But don't tease him, Arthur. He's in a period of hero worship for these older fellows – and he's flattered, of course, that they've taken him up. I talked to your father about it. Richard thinks it's harmless. Outdoor activities, and he's learning things.'

The night of Robbie's stag party, Arthur invited Maggie and Gus and Veronica to his house, the rest of his family being out somewhere. They rolled the carpet back, played cassettes, and Maggie gave Gus a dancing lesson, lasting hardly ten minutes and ending in laughter.

Then came Maggie's last day in Chalmerston before flying east. Maggie and he would have the whole day together, except for an interval around 5 p.m., she said, when she wanted to pack to get it off her mind. They spent the morning walking in the woods on Westside. Norma Keer had invited them for lunch, because she was taking the day off 'for medical reasons.' And after lunch, Arthur had his house free again. His parents were out at their work, and Robbie was with 'the men,' who were taking him to a government building in town where people obtained hunting permits. This was a very special afternoon, Arthur felt, because he wouldn't see Maggie again until Easter, and at Easter there was a possibility that she would go with her parents to Bermuda, unless she insisted on staying in town alone in the house.

When he and Maggie had been in his room for an hour or so, there was a knock on the house door, rather like a *bam-bam-bam* of somebody's fist pounding.

'Who the blankety-blank hell is that?' Arthur said. It was not even 3 o'clock.

Bam-bam-bam!

Arthur picked up his bathrobe from a chair.

Maggie was lying in bed with a half-finished cigarette. 'Robbie?'

'Doubt it.' Arthur meant to yell through the door to whoever it was to hold on for a minute, but as soon as he unlocked his own door and went into the hall, he heard Robbie's voice shouting:

'Hey, Art! Lemme *in*!'

Arthur yelled down the hall, 'Just a minute, would you? Take it easy!' He couldn't tell if Robbie was at the front door or the kitchen door. He had bolted both of them.

Maggie was calmly getting dressed. Arthur did the same, pulling on trousers without underpants. He shoved his feet into house-slippers.

Robbie was banging again, loud and slow.

'Damn him,' Arthur muttered. 'Mag, turn the key in the lock and take your time.' Arthur slipped out into the hall.

At that moment he heard a splintering sound, as if Robbie had forced the kitchen door bolt.

This was exactly what he had done, and Robbie stood wild-eyed in the kitchen with blood running down his upper lip.

'What's the idea of busting in? Can't you wait a minute? Look at that mess!' Arthur meant the kitchen doorjamb.

'I was in a fight. I hadda get in!' Robbie splashed water onto his nose at the kitchen sink. He jerked his head toward Arthur. 'You got that girl here; that's why you locked the doors.'

'You mind your own damned business, Robbie.'

'Her car's outside! – I was just fightin' about – about something like this.' Robbie flicked water from his fingers into the sink.

'You were *not*, you goddamn liar!' Suddenly Robbie was on the floor. Arthur had picked him up in two hands and dumped him.

Robbie wobbled up, holding to the sink edge. 'I'll tell Dad about this! About *you*!'

'You go right ahead!' Arthur had his fists ready.

Robbie stormed past him and went to Arthur's door. He knocked, then tried the knob. ''S locked!' he said to Arthur.

'You get the hell away!' Arthur seized him by the front of his clothes and shoved him against Robbie's closed door.

Blood now flowed over Robbie's chin, the color spread by the water. Robbie went into the bathroom.

'Maggie,' Arthur said at his own door. When Maggie turned the key, Arthur went in and locked the door again.

Maggie was dressed, combing her hair at Arthur's mirror. She had even pulled the bedcovers up, so the bed looked as usual.

'Christ, I – He's been in a fistfight somewhere and he's gone nuts!'

'Oh – so what? Take it easy, Arthur. He's just a pesty kid brother.' She smiled at Arthur in the mirror.

'Little son-of-a-bitch twit's going to tell Papa, he says.'

'That I'm here? Well – so what?'

Arthur pushed his bare feet into loafers. Maggie and he went into the hall.

Robbie was on the telephone in the living room. 'Okay, good. G'bye.' He hung up.

'Hello, Robbie,' Maggie said.

'Hi. – Dad's coming over. You better stay,' Robbie said to Arthur.

'Oh,' said Arthur noncommittally, and took Maggie's coat from a hook in the hall and took his windbreaker for himself. He was going to see Maggie to her car. 'Great house, isn't it?' he said to Maggie. 'Friendly atmosphere.'

'Try to cool down, Arthur. Want to come to my place?' Maggie asked as they walked across the snowy lawn to her car.

'If my dad's really coming over – I better stay and stand up to him.'

'They're the ones who're – funny.' Maggie said it in a tone that sounded as if 'funny' meant mentally odd. 'So what if I was in your room?'

Arthur couldn't reply. 'See you around seven?'

'Yes, sure. – Keep calm. Just say we were listening to a cassette.'

Arthur pressed his lips against her cheek, and turned back to the house. Her car was moving off before he reached the front door.

Robbie was again in the bathroom, still washing, with the door open. Arthur went back to his room. He whistled a tune and opened the door of his closet. His grandmother had pressed his green corduroys, he recalled as he saw them, and he'd wear those tonight. He put on socks. He heard the front door close. He had not heard a car. A couple of minutes later, there was a slow knock on Arthur's door.

'Yep?' said Arthur.

His father came in, pink-cheeked from the cold, but he had removed his overcoat. 'Well, well – I understand from Robbie that you've had your girlfriend here this afternoon – for – for the usual purposes?' His father's voice trembled. 'Doors bolted?'

'We had a date, yes. Lunch at Norma's.' Arthur's heart had begun thumping already.

'Lunch at Norma's. That's why you locked and bolted the doors? – This house is not a brothel, Arthur, not *my* house,' said his father with a glance at Arthur's bed.

Arthur thought of the orgies he'd heard about since entering C.U., fellows and girls on the living room floor, not particularly caring whom they made love with, lights out and disco tapes blaring.

'Nothing to say for yourself?'

'That's it. Nothing,' Arthur said.

'Then you're out. You're not sleeping under my roof or eating my bread any longer. You can pack.'

Robbie stood behind his father in the hall, listening.

His father went out and closed the door.

21

Arthur stood where he was for a few seconds. To pack meant to pack now. And where was he to sleep tonight? Maybe at Gus's. And later there might be room for him in one of the dorms at C.U., because he had heard about three fellows sharing a dorm room meant for two. But that cost something, and he might as well assume that his father would not let his mother give him another extra cent.

Through his closed door, Arthur heard his father's rumbling voice and Robbie's slightly higher-pitched barks.

Arthur hauled a suitcase from the bottom of his closet. Trousers, a couple of sweaters, and socks went in, also several textbooks.

He heard a car pass and realized that it was his mother's only when he heard the kitchen door close and heard his parents' voices.

'Oh – Richard!' said his mother in an anguished tone.

Arthur decided to face it again, now. He walked into the hall, then the kitchen, where his parents were. His mother was removing her coat, and Arthur took it for her and put it on a hook.

'—when a girl is *dead*,' his mother said in a breathless voice.

'Yes, well. These things,' said his father, 'they happen.'

'I'm going to make some hot tea. I need it. Anybody else?' She went to the stove and picked up the kettle. 'Hello, Arthur. – I'm distracted today.'

'Hi, Mom.' Arthur noticed that Robbie was lurking just inside the living room. 'I'll be leaving tonight. I suppose Dad told you.'

'Yes, he did.' His mother spoke over her shoulder, as if she had other things on her mind.

His father looked about to go off to his study, but he didn't. Arthur watched his mother light the fire under the kettle. She was frowning. 'Some girl's dead, did you say, Mom?'

'Eva MacNeil. I think I told you about her. Came to the Home about a month ago – asking for help. Pregnant.' His mother glanced at Arthur. 'We heard this afternoon she killed herself – sleeping pills and gin. Somebody found her in her room this noon.'

Arthur vaguely remembered his mother saying something about a pregnant girl a couple of weeks ago. The Home hadn't been able to help the girl. 'She didn't want the child, wasn't that it?'

'She tried to get an abortion and couldn't. And we couldn't raise the right money – at the Home.'

His father frowned at Arthur, as if Arthur were intruding on a conversation between him and his mother. 'I'm packing now, Mom – and going out to Maggie's tonight for dinner.'

His mother glanced at him with the same pained expression on her face. 'I'll come in and see you in a minute, Arthur. I just want some tea, I'm frozen through.'

'When are you leaving?' Robbie asked Arthur.

Arthur did not answer and went back to his room. A minute or so later, his mother brought two cups of tea, handed Arthur one, and sat down on his straight chair.

'Dad wants me out.'

'I know.' In the sad lines of her face, Arthur saw that she wasn't going to fight for him with his father.

'I don't want you to try to make him change his mind,' Arthur said. 'The atmosphere here's too awful. I'm sure I can sleep at Gus's tonight. I can look for a room in town.' Arthur flipped the suitcase lid down, though he hadn't finished his packing.

'Arthur, I'm sorry, I'm not myself today.' His mother's eyes met his for an instant, then she set her cup and saucer aside and bent her face into her hands. 'I so wanted to help that *girl*!'

'I know.' Arthur understood suddenly. It could have been Maggie, if Maggie or he hadn't had the money. 'My father would say – it's just what she deserved. Death – for her sins.'

'Oh, no! He wouldn't if he'd known Eva.'

'Why not? It's the principle. – I don't want to stay in a house with a man like my father – or Robbie.'

'Robbie?'

'Just the same. Can't you see it?'

The telephone had been ringing. His mother got up.

In the hall, Robbie said to his mother, 'Mom, it's for you.'

Arthur put his suitcase and a duffel bag into his car when he drove off at 7 for Maggie's house. He still hadn't called Gus. He told Maggie what had happened after she left, including his mother's being upset about the suicide of the girl called Eva MacNeil.

'Maybe I'll sleep at Gus's tonight, look for a room in town tomorrow. Maybe a cheap dorm at C.U.?' Arthur shrugged. 'I dunno.'

Maggie looked stunned. 'My gosh, Arthur! – Won't your mother talk to your father—'

'I – don't – want to beg,' Arthur said softly, though Maggie's mother was in the kitchen and out of hearing.

'Have to get something from the kitchen.' Maggie got up.

There was a nicely crackling fire in the fireplace. The orange and white cat Jasper was sleeping where he always did, at one end of the sofa.

Maggie came back with a plate of canapés – smoked oysters, black olives. 'Forgot these. – Mom says you can sleep here tonight.'

Arthur drew his hand back from the plate. 'I told you *not* to tell her. It's a goddamned mess!'

'There's a guest room here,' Maggie said.

At the dinner table, Betty said, 'Maggie told me about the difficulties today, Arthur. So you're most welcome to stay with us tonight. And tomorrow night, too, until you get settled. It's an awful feeling, not knowing where you're going to put your head down at night.'

So later that evening, Arthur was shown into a guest room bigger than Maggie's bedroom, with a double bed, two windows on the yard at the back, a commodious chest of drawers and a closet. He had taken the *Herald* up with him to look at rooms for rent, but found only one to share with '40-ish woman,' while the apartments were out of his price range. Still, he fell asleep in the big bed almost as content as if Maggie had been sleeping beside him.

The next morning, Arthur drove Maggie to the airport. He felt shaky, on the brink of cracking up – whatever that was – and was glad Maggie made the parting quick. One kiss and she was gone, with a promise to write him soon. Arthur went at once to a telephone booth and called Gus's house. One of his brothers answered and said Gus would be home at noon.

It was a quarter past noon when Arthur got to Gus's house, and the family was in the kitchen, at least four of them besides Gus, and his mother seemed to be preparing various hot lunches plus sandwiches. In that chaos, it was easy for Arthur to tell Gus, without being heard by anybody, that he had been kicked out by his father and had spent last night at Maggie's house.

'Ho-wolly cow!' said Gus, properly impressed.

'You don't happen to know of a cheap room I could rent somewhere,' Arthur said.

Gus pondered, his blond eyebrows frowning above his glasses. 'Well, there's that dump on Pine Street run by Mrs Haskins. Four or five rooms and only one bathroom in the house.'

Arthur knew the place, because he had been there once to meet somebody. It was a cheap and rather noisy rooming house.

'Too bad there's not a room to spare here,' Gus said sadly. 'But we've got an army cot, and you're welcome to stay in my room.'

Arthur imagined Gus and himself trying to study evenings in Gus's small room and shook his head. 'I don't want to bother you. But that's nice of you, Gus.'

'Come out with Veronica and me tonight. You look down in the mouth. We're just going to some roadside place for a couple of beers. After dinner? 'Bout eight?'

Arthur agreed. Gus would come by the Brewster house in his car, and Arthur could take his car tonight or not, 'And I might take you up on that army cot deal – for tonight. I'm shy about bothering Maggie's mother.'

When Arthur got back to the Brewster house, he let himself in with the key. 'Betty?' he called. No answer, but because the garage door was shut, he hadn't been sure whether she was out or in. Now he opened the front door again, took a white envelope from the mailbox, and laid it on the hall table. It had no stamp. Then Arthur noticed that it was addressed to him c.o. Brewster. Typewritten. Arthur opened it and read:

Dear Arthur,

I regret my anger yesterday but not my decision. It is intolerable to me and I think it would be to most parents to shelter a son or daughter who so deliberately mocks the principles by which his parents live. It is regretable that the young girl concerned is no different from you, and it seems that neither of you learn from experience or care a whit about the feelings of others. I believe it is only by shocking you to reality that you will ever learn anything. Your mother and I ever wish the best for you.

Your father,
Richard

P.S. I had little more schooling than you now when I was forced to quit college and earn a living for my mother and myself.

Arthur noticed that his father had spelt *regrettable* with one t. Well, well. Tonight, at any rate, he had a bed at faithful old Gus's.

He went upstairs to his room and again packed his suitcase and duffel bag. Then downstairs again to look up the number of C.U.'s Administration Building. A woman answered, and Arthur asked to speak with someone in charge of dormitory places.

'What is your problem?'

'I want to know if there's any room left for this coming semester. I'm a day student now.'

'The person to tell you will be on duty tomorrow or Friday. The university is not officially open until tomorrow.'

Ah, well, tomorrow. Arthur went to the kitchen, where the coffee machine's light showed red, and poured a cup. Then back to his room, where he pulled out a couple of books. One was *Do You Really Speak English*, required reading for his English class. Before he settled down, he crossed the hall to Maggie's room and opened its door halfway. He looked at its single bed, its beige and blue curtains at the two windows, at her writing table on the left, slightly untidy with two books taken from the row at the back now lying on the table, and a piece of white paper underneath one. He closed the door again.

Betty came home around 6, and gave him a shout. 'Busy?'

'No!' He tossed the English book on the bed and went down.

Betty was in the front hall, hanging up her coat. She rubbed her knuckles against her palm. 'Wow, it's nippy. Have you made any plans? Because I spoke with Warren today. He called from California.'

'I can stay at my friend Gus's tonight. Tomorrow – well, at the end of this week I can see about a dorm room, I just found out.'

'You'd prefer to go somewhere else tonight? Because I told Warren the situation, and he thinks it's pretty awful. Warren says why not stay here for a few days till you get your bearings. If you find something in a couple of days, fine. Or if we annoy each other, I'll ask you to leave or you'll leave on your own.' Betty smiled. 'All right? So you don't have to leave tonight unless you want to.' She went off to the kitchen. 'I need a hot coffee. Are you in tonight, Arthur?'

'Gus is picking me up at eight.'

'If you want something to eat before, help yourself to the left-over steak in the fridge. It's very good. I'm going to have a bowl of soup and go to bed. Two hours I was driving around with a couple of the protection committee people, looking at houses that need – repairs and such. And trees that have to be felled.' She lifted her cup of coffee to her lips. 'Make yourself at home, Arthur. Don't tie yourself in a knot.'

Arthur managed a smile, but something made him quite speechless. Maybe gratitude.

Gus arrived just before 8, and Arthur decided to leave his car and go in Gus's. Arthur sat in the back. He told Gus and Veronica about Betty Brewster's offer to let him stay a few days until he found a place.

'I think your father's being pretty grim,' Veronica said in her slow, thoughtful way. 'I think my family's pretty old-fashioned, but I honestly don't think they'd act like *this*.' She looked over her shoulder at Arthur. 'I was saying to Gus just now, I know a girl who invited her boyfriend to stay in the house and sleep in her room over the holidays. Family didn't mind.'

Arthur said nothing. The wind through Veronica's window, open just half an inch, hit him right in the neck and he didn't care. Gus was driving rather fast, but Arthur didn't care about that either, because he trusted Gus.

They stopped at a roadside bar-restaurant called Mom's Pride, which had disco music on the jukebox, and served beer, hamburgers, steak sandwiches and the usual. Arthur went to the bar-counter and ordered three french fries and three beers and paid for them, then he dropped some coins in the jukebox, one of them for 'Hot Toddy,' a favorite of his and Maggie's. Gus and Veronica went off to dance; then Arthur danced with Veronica.

'Gus's dancing improving?' Arthur shouted.

'What?' asked Veronica, hopping up and down as lightly as a bubble opposite him.

'Yeee-owrrr! Shamazz!' some male idiot roared in Arthur's ear for no reason.

The lights turned into polka dots, blackened, came back to pink.

A little after midnight, they were rolling along toward town, Arthur in front beside Gus, and Veronica reclining on the backseat, sleepy. Ahead, on the left side of the dark road, Arthur saw a silvery, box-car shape, glowing like a nocturnal insect.

'Hey, Gus! That's the Silver Arrow diner, I think. Where Irene works. Remember I told you about Irene Langley? Shall we drop in? For a last coffee?'

'Sure, old pal,' said Gus, and signaled for a left pull-over.

Their shoes crunched on the frozen pebbles in front of the place. Three enormous eighteen-wheel trucks were parked facing the diner, dwarfing it, looking ready to attack it.

Irene was on duty, Arthur saw at a glance. Her peroxide hair and red lips caught the eye at once under the fluorescent lights, and even every cigarette butt that had been dropped on the floor gave Arthur the feeling of looking at them through a microscope. Ten or more men sat hunched on the counter stools, wearing caps and heavy jackets, and more of them, with a woman or two, sat at the booth tables. Besides Irene, there were two other waitresses behind the counter, and all wore white uniforms with silvery collars and caps and broad silvery belts. A jukebox played, but not so loudly as at Mom's Pride.

Arthur gave Gus a discreet nod, to indicate that the blonde was La Belle Irene. They took three stools at the counter, one man moving over for them so they could sit together.

'Ah-hah-hah! Naughty fellows you all are!' Irene yelled with a merry laugh to someone far on Arthur's right.

The truckers were grinning, Arthur noticed, focusing on Irene.

'What time y'off tonight?' one asked.

'Seven o'clock in the *morning*!' Irene bent with her giggle and spilled coffee from mugs she held in a cluster.

'Make it earlier if you want to, I bet!'

Irene leaned toward Gus, Veronica and Arthur, with eyes swimmy from fatigue or the glare. 'Good evening, and what'll you folks have?'

'Coffee,' said Gus.

'Same,' said Arthur.

Veronica didn't want anything.

'*Mac* didn't say that!' shouted one of the truck drivers at Irene, as she drew coffee from the machine farther to Arthur's right.

'She goes to your church?' Gus asked Arthur.

'My church? My dad's church,' said Arthur.

Gus shook his head. 'Looks like a hooker if I ever saw one.'

Irene returned with the coffees. 'Oh – it's *Arthur*! Oh, goodness! I heard about – Richard turned you out, didn't he?' Her eyes looked a little more awake.

'News travels fast,' said Arthur.

'That's true.' She pronounced it *tree-you* in her genteel manner. 'I said to Richard – *I* could take you in and would. To be Christian. But *he* said that you had to learn the hard way – and repent.' She had put on a frown.

'*Irene*! Two beers for number three!' another waitress called out. 'And four burgers with for the rail, tell Cookie!'

Irene moved.

'Get a load of that,' Arthur said to Gus with a smile, and got up from his stool. 'Back in a sec.' He went to the men's toilet, which had a lot of graffiti on the walls, drawings, phone numbers and C.B. code numbers, some circled in red and blue crayon. *Head jobs*, Arthur read. *Hot patootie massage*. Arthur washed his face in water so icy, it sent a chill all over him.

On the ride home, Veronica's house being the first stop, the three of them talked about several things, but not Irene. She was too depressing, Arthur supposed, to be even funny.

22

When Arthur went downstairs in the Brewster house the next day, he saw an unstamped letter on the hall table addressed to him in his mother's handwriting. Betty, who had gone out an hour ago, hadn't wanted to disturb him, Arthur supposed, because he had said he had some work to do before afternoon classes.

Dearest Arthur,

Phoned Gus and he said he thought you were still at the Brewsters'. Can you come for lunch today, Thursday? Am home alone. Didn't want to bother Betty B. by phoning.

Love from your
Mom

It was ten to twelve. Arthur telephoned. 'Sure, I can come, Mom. See you in about fifteen minutes.'

Earlier that morning, Arthur had helped Betty shift a bookcase to another wall of a room, which had involved taking all the books out and putting them back in the same order. Arthur had been happy to be of use, especially since Betty had been so grateful. Warren got bored at the mention of such jobs, Betty said.

Arthur left his car at the grass edge in front of his house.

'Hello, Arthur, how *are* you?' She kissed his cheek.

'Fine. Why not? – And Betty said I could stay at her house till I found something.'

'*Isn't* that nice of her? – I didn't see her this morning, just dropped the letter in the box. Must call her and thank her. Is Warren there now?'

'No, but Betty talked with him on the phone. It's even his idea that I'm – *could* stay a few days till I found somewhere.' Arthur enjoyed saying that, because Warren Brewster's attitude was so different from his father's. 'However – I'm inquiring about a dorm room this afternoon.'

They were in the kitchen, and Arthur smelled corned beef and cabbage, one of his favourite dishes. He took a beer from the fridge at his mother's suggestion.

'That's what I wanted to talk to you about, the dorm idea,' his mother said cheerfully. 'I spoke with Mama Tuesday night. Told her – you know. So we agreed, Mama and I, that we could see about your dorm fees and the tuition, too. The important thing is not to worry,' his mother finished in a rush, as if she was embarrassed.

Arthur felt a little embarrassed. 'Thanks, Mom.'

'So if your father wants to make such a fuss' – she slid cabbage onto a big white platter, around a rosy mountain of corned beef – 'he'll just have to make it all by himself.'

'Does Dad know?'

'Yes, because I told him straight off Tuesday night after I'd spoken to Mama. He thinks we're spoiling you, *but* – I just want you to know we're not all such stiff-necks in this family. I'm glad my side of the family can come through. – Now let's talk about something else.' She smiled at him.

They sat down and began their lunch.

'Oh, Mom, last night I went by the Silver Arrow with Gus and his girlfriend. You know, where Irene works? Truck-stop? You bet!

Really a pretty tough place. All the truckers kidding with Irene. Trying to make a date with her.' Arthur laughed.

'Really, Arthur? That bad?' asked his mother, looking amused.

'And Dad's trying to save her soul. Question, has she got a soul to save? – Hello, Rovy!'

The cat had jumped onto his bench seat.

'I went to Eva MacNeil's funeral this morning.'

'This *morning*, Mom?'

'Yes. Not many people, because her family's in Chicago. Five of us from the Home, I'm glad to say. Very touching somehow – a girl of twenty-two. And Richard just can't understand my feelings. The world's full of such girls, he said, as if she were a delinquent – which she wasn't. And what about the young man involved, I said to him. Seldom a mention of them, good or bad. Well—' Here his mother took a few seconds. 'I must say her boyfriend wasn't at the funeral. I understand this was one of those accidents, a short affair. I know she didn't try to reach the boy. I think he was from out of town. Eva even went to work the same day she took the pills. She didn't tell anyone she was so depressed.'

Arthur could imagine it: one night in bed, or afternoon, or any time, then pregnancy, then death. It suddenly struck Arthur that his father would consider suicide a sin, also.

'Sacredness of life, Richard talks about. Here's a good place to – show it or uphold it, one would think. Young girl "in trouble," as they used to say. – Sometimes Richard's attitude seems so like the Catholics', I get worried. I shouldn't say Catholic, I'm sure, but I don't know how else to describe it.'

'Fundamentalist,' Arthur replied promptly.

After lunch, his mother found a spare suitcase and a couple of sturdy plastic bags, and into these they put more of Arthur's belongings. He took the 'Jupiter' Symphony from the living room, a present from his grandmother at Christmas, because Betty had a record player, and at any rate he wanted it with him. He took also

Mozart's string quartet in D Minor, belonging to him. His mother said he should feel free to come to the house whenever he wanted to, and she gave him back his keys, one to the front door, one to the garage door, which were on the same ring.

Then his mother had to leave, because she was late already for the Home.

Arthur stayed and washed the dishes, so that his mother would have a pleasant surprise, a clean kitchen, when she returned around 6 this evening. The telephone rang. Arthur didn't answer it. It was a half-friendly house, a half-hostile house. Very odd. Arthur whistled 'Sunday, Sweet Sunday.' Sweet Sunday, with nothing to do. When would he ever have that, with Maggie?

That afternoon, Arthur learned that he could move into a C.U. dorm, sharing a bedroom-study with one other freshman, for a hundred and fifty dollars a month with breakfast and dinner. Toilets and bathrooms were 'down the hall,' the woman informed Arthur, and there was a swivel telephone which served two bedroom-studies. Arthur had seen one of the cramped rooms once, when he had visited a student. It was the cheapest lodging; he knew he would have to take it, but he hesitated. 'Can I confirm this tomorrow? There's more than one room like that free now?'

'Oh, yes, and this semester a lot of students drop out or they've been asked to leave and haven't told us as yet.'

At dinner that evening with Betty, Arthur told her that there was a place for him in a dorm and that his family – specifically his mother and grandmother – had offered to pay his bills. While Betty was out, Arthur had prepared dinner.

'I don't know why,' Betty said, 'you particularly want to live in a dorm, when you could stay here. I know the dorm's more convenient because it's on the campus. But since you've got a car – Well, it's up to you, Arthur.'

Of course Betty's house was preferable! It had space; it was civilized. To live in the house was a little like being with Maggie.

'Of course I'd prefer to be here,' he said finally. 'I'd also want to pay you something. – That's normal.'

'We'll figure something out. Warren's coming home tomorrow morning. *He* said – I didn't even tell Warren you can cook! He thinks it's a good idea if someone's in the house with me, since he's away so much. He suggested thirty dollars a week, all included.'

'Thank you. – Very reasonable,' Arthur said, trying to look as calm about it as Betty appeared to be, but he was thrilled.

'Reasonable, I suppose, but you're a help around the house, and that's something.' She smiled quickly at Arthur, the corners of her mouth went up, like Maggie's. 'Try it for a week. You may want to change your mind. But Warren says with housebreakers and so on – when *I'm* out so much—'

Arthur had a brief fantasy of tackling three armed robbers with his bare knuckles, knocking them senseless to the floor. He would relish that, protecting the house.

Arthur phoned his mother that evening from the living room telephone. Betty was upstairs. He told her about the arrangement with the Brewsters.

'I spoke with Betty around three this afternoon on the phone. She didn't mention your staying.'

Arthur laughed. 'She didn't tell me you'd phoned. I suppose *you* phoned?'

His mother had. 'Behave yourself, Arthur. And I'm very glad about this. Give Betty my – greetings and thanks, would you? I feel that you're all right, there at her house.'

Maggie wrote to Arthur twice in January, but not to her mother. Arthur was to pass on her news, if any, she wrote, though every Sunday noon Maggie rang up, keeping a promise she had made to her mother. Maggie wrote that she was not sure she would come home for Easter. This surprised Arthur, since Maggie would have a week off at least, and economy couldn't be a factor, because the family traveled free on Sigma Airlines.

In February, even with a heavy schedule of work at C.U. and a house project at the Brewsters', preparing the cellar walls for whitewashing, Arthur found himself counting the weeks before Easter. Surely Maggie would come home. At any rate, it made Arthur happier to believe she would. When he asked Betty what she thought Maggie's ideas were, Betty said she never knew what was up with Maggie until the last minute. Arthur worried, about her possibly having met someone else she liked, invariably an older fellow in Arthur's imagination. On the other hand, her letters reassured him.

> . . . You ask if I think of you in bed. Sure I do. And by the way what are you doing, free as the wind there? Here we have to check in by midnight, and no fellows allowed in the dorms after 10 p.m. But I'm not exactly complaining about that.
>
> Glad your father's keeping quiet, and that your mother is so understanding and helping with the checks! Mom says you're being useful around the house and says Dad's glad you are there.
>
> The color of my bed? Well, it is beige, sort of like darkish oatmeal. How romantic!
>
> Now I have to memorize a couple of stanzas of Byron, whom I quite like. He is really romantic, sometimes witty.
>
> Yes, I think of you a lot, since you ask. Love always,
>
> Maggie

Arthur kept all her letters in chronological order in a folder. Sometimes Maggie neglected to date them, so he did it.

Betty Brewster was out for dinner at least once a week, and perhaps once a week she had someone or several people to the house for dinner. Arthur helped on the latter occasions by setting the table and doing some cooking, helped serve drinks, then tactfully disappeared, unless Betty expressly asked him to eat with them. He found the Brewsters' friends more interesting than those of his parents, and Arthur realized that his parents, even his mother, were not inclined to entertain. Arthur thought this was true of most of the town.

One evening in early March, when Betty and Arthur were having their after-dinner coffee at the table, they heard a car door slam in the silence, then a second door.

'Wonder who that is?' said Betty.

Arthur got up. Now he heard steps, and somebody knocked. 'Who is it?'

'Robbie.'

'What's the matter, Robbie?'

'Nothing! Can't you open the door?'

Behind him, Betty said, 'Your brother? He can come in, Arthur.'

Arthur opened the door but not widely, and Robbie marched in, followed by another person, Eddie Howell.

'Evening,' said Eddie Howell, removing a deerstalker cap. His fixed smile was on. 'Excuse me, Mrs Brewster. My name is Eddie Howell. We just wanted to ask how you are, Arthur.'

'Good evening,' said Betty.

'My brother Robbie,' Arthur said, frowning, annoyed by their oozing toward the living room. 'You might've phoned first, Robbie.'

'Then you would've said no about us coming over,' Robbie replied. He was at last removing his coonskin cap. He wore his long hunting jacket and unfastened galoshes.

'You've got a lovely house, Mrs Brewster,' said Eddie.

'And what can I do for you – both?' Arthur noticed that Eddie Howell had his briefcase.

'There's nothing that you have to *do* for us, Arthur. Your father's interested in how you're doing – what you're doing.'

Was he? Arthur saw pink dots in front of his eyes.

'Won't you sit down?' asked Betty. 'I'm glad to meet you, Robbie.'

Robbie nodded awkwardly. 'Me, too.'

'We don't want to keep you,' said Eddie Howell, at the same time glancing around as if trying to decide between the other sofa and an armchair as a place to sit.

'Take your coats off?' asked Betty.

'Oh, no, thank you.' Eddie Howell seemed definite about this at least. 'No, I can say what I have to say very quickly. It's that Richard, Arthur's father, is concerned about how his boy is doing. Whether he's happy – making progress.'

'Doing all right, thanks.' Arthur stood with folded arms.

Betty sat on the edge of a sofa.

Eddie Howell sat carefully at the end of the other sofa, and Robbie took an armchair, dangling his coonskin cap between his knees.

'Arthur has been through so much – last year,' Eddie Howell said, addressing Betty. 'It isn't easy for a young man to endure such experiences. Or a young woman,' he added. 'Sets a soul in turmoil.'

But Howell's phony smile could settle that turmoil, Arthur supposed. Robbie's face looked blank and neutral, as if he weren't even listening. He was looking at the big watercolor landscape over the fireplace.

'... wants to know if you've come to terms with what happened, if you've examined your own conscience and – if you can feel – or begin to feel at peace with God and yourself. *If*, your father asks.'

Arthur glanced at Betty, blinked and said with deliberate calm, 'I'm doing all right at C.U. now. And I don't know – what's worrying him.'

Eddie Howell was silent.

'That you're living *here*,' Robbie put in. 'In this very house.'

Arthur took a breath. 'I have to do some work tonight. Mrs Brewster, too.' He addressed Eddie Howell.

'I won't take long,' said Eddie with his pink-lipped smile. 'Your father's a little upset – understandably, I think – because you're staying in this house. He says it's wrong. With all due respect to Mrs Brewster,' he conceded with a nod to her, 'for her kindness and charity.'

'Charity?' Betty asked, smiling. 'Arthur's quite a help in this house, Mr—'

'Howell.'

'Mr Howell. I invited Arthur. He didn't come begging.'

'No, I—' Eddie Howell looked at Arthur. 'You feel no guilt, no need to say, "I'm sorry"?'

'I've said that. Why should I go on repeating it? T-to whom?' Arthur thought of his father, smug with his sense of revenge. His father had thrown him out of the house. 'If my father's trying to bollix C.U. for me – somehow – he – can—'

'Arthur.' Betty was on her feet. 'Easy does it.'

Eddie Howell also stood up and tilted his smiling face sideways. 'Your father's not trying to interfere with your schooling, Arthur. We want you back – back to the church and the friendly arms of the people who really care about you. This includes Christ, the greatest forgiver of them all.'

Friendly arms of his father? Eddie Howell's words seemed to imply that Betty's arms were not friendly.

'I do think, Mr Howell,' Betty said, 'that Arthur's doing pretty well now. He works hard; he's happy at C.U. I'm *very* glad to have him in the house here. So maybe you could tell Mr Alderman that?' Gracefully she moved toward the door.

Eddie Howell was not quite finished and stood his ground. 'You won't be truly happy, Arthur, until you realize profoundly what has happened, until you decide to give yourself into the care of God and Christ.' At last he moved. 'Good night, Mrs Brewster and God bless you.'

Arthur did not listen to the mumbled words at the door. He

wiped moisture from his forehead. The solid closing of the front door was a pleasure to hear. Betty came back.

'Well – now you see it,' Arthur said.

Betty gave a laugh. 'Come on, Arthur. They mean well. They think they mean well. – Let's forget about that visit. Stop frowning!'

'Okay.'

'I think a half scotch wouldn't hurt you, Arthur. Neat. Let's be – um – sinful.' She went to the bar cart in the corner of the room. 'They really are boring, aren't they?' Betty suddenly doubled over with a laugh.

'The line that killed me – my *father's* welcoming arms—'

'Cool it, Arthur,' Betty said, smiling at him.

Maggie had inherited her calm from her mother, Arthur thought. 'Yes, ma'am.'

23

Some ten days before Easter holidays, Arthur received a letter from Maggie. It said:

Dearest Arthur,

Now I have some news which I know you may take hard. It is also very hard for me to write. It is not just that I met somebody else, but it is more important than that. There is someone, and that is Larry Hargiss. But I also have changed a lot since last September and also last summer. Maybe you have, too?

So I am not coming home for Easter. And I hope really that you can manage to forget me without too much pain. I know what we had was important – for both of us. But we were like children then compared to now, don't you think? At least it *helps* to think of it that way. I will always care for you in a very special way, because you are important in my life. But there is a long tough way ahead for you, more years of school, and for me, too, very likely more than three years if we both go on to graduate schools.

My mother I know would still like to have you stay with

her. But I will understand if you don't feel like it. I know you are very serious and this may upset you.

With very much love,

Maggie

Arthur had read it quickly, standing in his room in the Brewster house, and now he felt faint, though he didn't sit down. So it was Larry Hargiss after all, the medical student of Harvard. The name had stuck unpleasantly in his head since Maggie had uttered it on the ride homeward from the airport at Christmas. Now here it was. Damn the bastard! And Maggie was probably spending Easter vacation with him either at his parents' house or at some resort. Did Betty know about Larry? Maybe, because Maggie had written 'My mother I know would still like . . .' Betty would have waited, of course, for Maggie to break the news. And at Christmas? Maggie hadn't been pretending to him at Christmas, Arthur was sure. What had happened since Christmas? He stared at her letter with the feeling that it had been written by another person, but the handwriting was hers. Arthur put the letter on the table near his typewriter. It was twenty-two minutes past noon.

He had no classes till 2 p.m., which was why he had come back to the Brewster house for lunch and an hour's reading (English). He felt he was not going to make it to English class at 2, or to Bio at 3 and French at 4. Certainly he could afford to cut, as his attendance record was close to perfect. And of all things to think about, whether he could afford to cut!

Betty was out, for how long Arthur didn't know, maybe till 6. Arthur went down to the kitchen to get a cup of coffee.

He would have to move at once from the Brewsters' into one of the dorms. Impossible to think of living and sleeping here now. Suddenly Maggie's room with its writing table and books upright at the back of it against the wall, her typewriter with its green felt cover, her dressing table on which stood a few bottles of perfume, eau de cologne, mysterious little boxes – all this, he realized, had been a private display, a little like a portrait of Maggie that he could look at when she was gone. Now the same picture seemed to shut him out, like the unfriendly face of a stranger. One day she might open her room door to Larry Hargiss.

After half a cup of coffee, Arthur went quickly upstairs to the bathroom and threw up into the toilet. Then he washed his face with a cold towel and brushed his teeth.

It'd be a good idea to meet his classes this afternoon, instead of falling apart, he thought. He drove early back to C.U., and wandered around under the trees of the campus, over an arched footbridge, keeping his eyes on the ground, until time for English class. In the middle of the second class, microbio, he sneaked out when Professor Jurgens was writing something on the blackboard.

Arthur walked to the Administration Building. He was told that there was a place in Hamilton Hall which he could share with one other male student.

'Nothing in Creighton?' Arthur asked for no particular reason, except that a bio student whom he rather liked, Stephen Summer, lived in Creighton.

'Creighton's full, I know that.'

'Then I'd better take the Hamilton. Can I confirm that tomorrow? I didn't bring my *c-c*—' He hesitated between cash and checkbook, and it took one or the other to clinch it.

The woman said she would reserve it through tomorrow, and Arthur didn't leave before he had it written on a piece of paper that he had an option on room 214 at Hamilton.

Write today off, he told himself. He wanted to see Gus. Meanwhile, he had to pack up his things and explain to Betty. So he drove back to the Brewsters' house. Betty was still not in, and Arthur took a couple of plastic bags from the broom closet and went upstairs and started his packing. Several minutes later, when he was almost finished, he heard the faint thud of the front door closing, and minutes after that, Betty's voice calling:

'Arthur? Would you like some tea?'

Arthur went to his door. 'Yep! Thanks. – See you.'

'I thought you had classes this afternoon,' Betty said when he came down. She was in the kitchen, and the electric kettle had just started to boil.

'Wasn't feeling so well today.'

'Not getting flu, are you? It's around, I heard today.'

'I had a letter from Maggie. It seems she's met somebody else.'

'Oh? – Who?'

'Somebody called Larry?' Arthur tried to sound casual.

'That medical student.'

'So you knew about it,' Arthur said.

'No, I didn't, Arthur. She mentioned him a couple of times in her letters. I knew he liked *her*. – Let's go in. Can you carry that?'

Arthur carried the tray. He was thinking that Maggie had sounded quite as usual the last time she had telephoned on a Sunday, and he had been able to speak with her for a minute, after Betty.

'Arthur, I *am* sorry. Maybe it'll blow over. Who knows?'

Arthur set the tray down on the coffee table. 'Maggie doesn't say something she doesn't mean.'

Betty poured the tea and cut two pieces of cake. 'Maggie may get over this Larry in a month! – But I can imagine what I say doesn't make you feel any better just now.'

Still, Arthur hung on her every word. 'I've heard,' he said, stirring his tea, 'girls always prefer fellows a little older than they are. I can't do much about that.'

Betty extended a plate of cake to him. 'Have this – I insist. And eat it. – It's not the end of the world, Arthur. Even if Maggie – even if it lasts for a while. Is this Larry the person Maggie's going to spend the rest of her life with? You're both eighteen. It's hard to plan a whole life at eighteen.'

Was it hard? Arthur was planning his life in biology, maybe specifically microbiology, and he felt he was on the right track. He wasn't suddenly going to become an architect. He had felt on the right track with Maggie. 'Half my life's just gone,' he said. 'Maggie is half my life.'

Betty shook her head. 'It just seems that way today!'

'Yes.' It seemed to Arthur as true as anything he had ever seen under a microscope or seen proved by logic. 'So I thought I should get out of the house. I can definitely leave tomorrow, if that's all right. Even tonight, if I sleep at Gus's.'

'Not necessary, Arthur,' Betty said slowly. 'You're as welcome here as you ever were.' She poured more tea for both of them. She had strong but graceful hands, much like Maggie's.

'This is so much Maggie's house – to me. Tomorrow I know I can get a dorm room, because I asked today.'

Betty sighed and took a cigarette. 'I understand. – It might even be good for you to try to forget her for a while. See what happens. You can't just mope for the next many weeks, Arthur; your class work would go to hell and you don't want that!'

Before 7 that evening, Arthur telephoned Gus, and asked if he could come over, knowing Gus and his family wouldn't mind if he crashed in while they were having dinner. Then Arthur knocked on Betty's half-open door and told her that he was going over to Gus's for a while.

'Good idea, Arthur! See you later, maybe.'

At Gus's house, it was twenty minutes before they could go up to his room, and during this time in the kitchen where dinner was in progress, Gus's mother insisted on giving Arthur a plate of something at a corner of the table.

'Maggie's met someone else. Older guy. Wouldn't you know,' Arthur said, when Gus had closed his room door.

'Oh, yeah? – I had that feeling tonight, looking at you.'

'You did?' It sounded like a pronouncement that he even looked dead to other people and was still somehow walking around. 'Jesus!' Arthur bent his head, put his face into his palms and wept. He held his breath.

'Yeah, yeah,' Gus said. 'It happens. Boy, yeah – I heard of it. A lot.'

Arthur laughed and looked at Gus through wet eyes. 'Not to you, ol' pal, I hope. Not *you*!'

'Na-ah – yeah. Little bit when I was sixteen. But you and Maggie – well, I was hoping it would last. Y'know what Veronica would say?'

'What?' asked Arthur, eager for words, thoughts.

'Meet somebody else. Even if it's short. Yep, you know she was saying something like that the other day about a girl she knows. The girl got left high 'n' dry and was talking about suicide.'

'Well, I ain't thinkin' about *suicide*!' Arthur said with a laugh.

Gus ran down to the kitchen and was back in a flash with two beer cans and two Coke cans. 'Tonight you got a choice.'

'I'm moving out of the Brewster house,' Arthur said.

'I can understand that.'

'So now I'm a man without a country.' Arthur hoisted his beer. 'Without a home, anyway. I can go into Hamilton Hall dorm tomorrow, by the way. I asked this afternoon.'

The following day at the lunch hour, Arthur moved into 214 of Hamilton Hall, having paid a month's bill in cash taken from his savings bank. His roommate or study-mate Frank Costello was not in. The room was not large, and its area was square, its walls originally creamy white but now soiled with fingerprints and odd smudges. In opposite corners stood two single beds, and against opposite walls, two writing tables, so that the table-users would have their backs to each other. One scruffy carpet, not very big. On an old-fashioned trunk with metal corners, no doubt

Costello's, stood a hot plate with one burner, and Arthur had just been told that hot plates were not allowed. Costello's bed was unmade, and the other bed's two blankets had been carelessly thrown over the bed, and there was no pillow, Arthur noticed. A carton of empty Coke bottles sat by the trunk. The one window on Arthur's side looked onto the campus and at least had a view of tall and handsome trees. There was a tiny fridge on the floor near Costello's trunk, and in the wall there, the swivel telephone, now swivelled toward the next room, and its convex container had the words YACK BOX pencilled on it. Arthur went over and turned it. A gray telephone, filthy with fingerprints, came into view. What would *that* show up under a microscope in the way of germs, and was it even safe to hold it anywhere near one's nose or mouth?

Arthur gave a laugh like a yelp that brought tears to his eyes, sent a shiver over him, and after the crazy laugh, he felt better, but was glad Frank Costello hadn't walked in and heard him. He set his suitcase, duffel bag and typewriter closer to his bed, and now he noticed a minuscule chest of drawers beside his bed. The top of it served as a night table, Arthur supposed. He returned to the swivel telephone, because he wanted to call his mother before she left for the Home. He pressed the O button and had to identify himself before he was given permission to dial.

Arthur's father answered, one of the rare days he was home for lunch, but Arthur didn't give a damn today.

'Mom there?' Arthur asked.

'Just a minute. Lois?'

His mother came on.

'Hi, Mom. Just wanted to tell you I moved into Hamilton Hall at C.U. today.'

'Oh? – Why this decision?'

'Well, to put it quickly – Maggie's sort of said good-bye to me.' Arthur stood up straight and looked at the ceiling. His mother sounded thoroughly shocked. '*Yes*, Mom, but don't say anything to Dad, will you? Please . . . Oh, it's nothing great but quite okay. Thanks to you and Grandma, I suppose I can afford it . . . Yes.' He gave his mother the number, reading it from the dirty telephone base. He had to assure his mother he wasn't unhappy and had to promise to telephone her at the weekend and come for a meal. Arthur promised only the telephone call.

Then he unpacked, making use of a tiny closet, and left a note on Costello's bed, saying he was the new room-sharer and would be back at 5:30. He went off for afternoon classes, followed by a stop at the town's main supermarket where he bought some fruit, Cokes, beer and milk. While he was putting these things away, some into the little fridge, a slender dark-haired fellow came into the room, and showed no surprise at seeing Arthur.

'Hello. Arthur Alderman,' Arthur said. 'You're Frank?'

'Yup.' Now Frank frowned. He had a couple of books under one arm and a brown paper bag in one hand.

'Just bought a little stuff,' Arthur said. 'Wrote you a note.' He nodded toward Frank's bed. 'The dorm people didn't tell you I was coming in?'

'Nope. Didn't hear from 'em. Didn't see 'em today.' Frank let his books fall on his bed. Then he pushed off his desert boots, carried the paper bag to the fridge area, pulled out a six-pack of Coca-Cola and cut its cardboard with a bread knife. 'Want one?'

'No, thanks. Just bought some.'

'I'm not here too much. Goin' out tonight,' said Frank.

Arthur was still on his knees by the fridge. 'Where you from?'

'New York.' His dark brown eyes were pink-rimmed.

Arthur doubted that, for some reason, but it was of no importance. Frank went out with his bathrobe and returned in it, carrying his clothes, a few minutes later as Arthur was going out to sample the Hamilton Hall refectory. The dining hall was cafeteria-style and not crowded, though already rather noisy, and the food was what Arthur had been told it was, boring but ample.

When he returned to his room, Frank had gone, and Arthur sat down to write a letter to Maggie. He wrote it in longhand.

> Today I moved from your house to room 214 in Hamilton Hall of C.U.

He didn't mean that she should write to him and didn't ask her to in the course of the letter.

> ... My bedroom-study-mate is a fellow named Frank Costello which sounds like the Mafia, but I have heard this can be an Irish name, too.
>
> Your mother was very nice as usual and asked me to stay on. But you can imagine how I feel. I do still love you; there is not a bit of a change there, and if that's a mistake, I don't know why it is. And so I hope you are happy – really.
>
> All my love, ever,
>
> Arthur

About two minutes after he had stamped the airmail envelope and was pulling on a jacket to go out and mail it, Arthur was seized again with nausea and had to get to one of the toilets down the hall.

Back from the letter-dropping, Arthur studied for half an hour. But every few minutes he thought about his letter to Maggie. It hadn't been exactly right. It was friendly, polite, calm. But it wasn't at all the truth. The truth was something awful. He felt that he had no reason for living now, though he didn't feel like killing himself. The jangling music (inferior rock) that came faintly from somebody's room down the hall did not even annoy him, because it seemed part of the general madness and ugliness of his life just now. He would have three more years in a room such as this, unless a miracle happened, and miracles usually didn't.

At 1 in the morning, after about an hour's sleep, Arthur woke up and found his forehead cold with perspiration, though the room was even overheated. Arthur shivered. His chest was sleek with sweat. He put on a bathrobe and went down the hall. Some students were still up. Arthur didn't know any of them. He had brought his towel, and he leaned over a basin, wiping his face in cold water. Was he hot or cold? When he went back to bed, he couldn't get to sleep and his heart beat rather quickly. He deliberately breathed slowly, as he had often told Robbie to do, he recalled, when Robbie was furious about something. The dawn was showing before he fell asleep. Then Frank Costello came in, either a bit drunk or very tired, turned on the central light, then his table light, kicked off his shoes and fell into bed after removing his trousers, turned off his table light and left the central light on. Arthur didn't bother getting up to turn it off.

And so it went even at the beginning of Easter holidays, when classes stopped, and only a few students stayed on at the dorms, because they had nowhere to go. Frank Costello went 'home' – his parents were separated, he said – to Wisconsin, not New York. Frank took angel dust, Arthur had discovered, as it was certainly no secret, and Frank didn't care whether he got passing grades this semester or not. 'My folks're paying, but they keep me on short rein. Look at this dump!' Frank had said. 'These shits here can kick me out when they want to. I couldn't care less.'

Frank Costello's life was drearier than his own, Arthur realized. Arthur had his microbiology to hang on to, but what joy did Frank get except five or six highs a week? Professor Jurgens of microbio liked Arthur and in January had invited him to dinner at his house, which Arthur knew was unusual. Still, he could not talk with Professor Jurgens about Maggie. And the cold sweats at night continued, not every night, but two or three a week. His trousers became looser at his waist. Arthur went to Norma Keer's house for dinner one evening, ignoring his family's house next door, as if it belonged to strangers. Before he left, he told Norma about Maggie's being interested in someone else now, and Norma had been as sympathetic as Betty Brewster, saying, 'Everyone in the world has this happen to them once or twice, Arthur. Now don't let it get you down for long.' But what, after all, could Norma or anyone else do about it?

Maggie wrote him a short letter, saying that she was glad he was 'not taking it too hard,' for which Arthur stoically congratulated himself.

During Easter vacation, Arthur visited the Brewster house four or five times. Warren had a few consecutive days off, quite by lucky accident, Warren said. Arthur tried to keep a cheerful air, feeling that people would smile behind his back if he looked melancholic. Betty told him his room was still empty, and they invited him to stay for a couple of days, if he wished, and there was yard work to be done besides. Arthur did several hours of work in the yard, some of it with Betty, but he never stayed a night. If he ate small meals, his food stayed down better, but Arthur knew something had to be done or he would end up sick in a hospital or at a psychiatrist's. And what would he tell a psychiatrist? 'The bottom's fallen out. There's nothing under my feet now.' Something like that.

On the second day of return to regular classes at C.U., Arthur had a cheerful idea. It was an idea to cheer himself up, he realized, and quite simple. He would invite Gus and Veronica and a girl called Shirley something, whom Veronica had introduced Arthur to a week or so before. He would invite them out for drinks and eats, as if it were his birthday. So Arthur, running into Gus on the campus that day, proposed Friday night for the get-together. Gus said Friday would be fine for him and probably Veronica.

'Can Veronica get Shirley? They're together in some classes, aren't they?'

'I didn't think you liked her,' Gus said. 'That's what Veronica told me.'

Arthur could hardly remember Shirley. 'I don't *dislike* her. I just thought it'd be nice to – Maybe Mom's Pride? That's sort of fun.'

As it turned out, Shirley wasn't free, but a girl called Francey McCullough was. Veronica had produced her. Francey was a soph, about five feet five with short, curly brown hair and a friendly but absent or distant manner. They went in two cars, as Gus wanted to take his, and Arthur as host wanted to drive his own car. Arthur picked up Francey at Gus's house, the meeting place, and they drove to Mom's Pride.

The jukebox at Mom's Pride was throbbing, and the place looked full. Arthur hadn't reserved a table, if that were even possible, but after a ten-minute wait with beers at the counter, they got a booth for four. Francey looked like a dud compared to Maggie, Arthur thought, even compared to Veronica, whose homey charms Arthur had begun to see. But Arthur felt it was his evening; he was determined to be a good host, which meant being sure everyone had what he or she wanted and that he paid for it.

'I know a girl who likes you a lot,' Francey said to Arthur when they were dancing. 'Aline. Remember her? Short brown hair?'

Arthur certainly did. Aline was the one who resembled Maggie, and he thought of Maggie at the same time he heard the name Aline. 'Yes, sure. Met her once.' He hoped Veronica or Gus hadn't told Francey about Maggie having abandoned him. Nothing he could do about it now, if they had.

Old Gus's dancing was improving, or he was more at ease with Veronica than he had been with Maggie. Arthur smiled at the sight of them, Gus tall and lanky and Veronica dumpier than Francey, bending and twisting in unison a yard apart from each other.

'You do boxing?' Francey asked.

'*Do* boxing? – No, I – Never in my life. I'm a sports snob!'

'No kidding! You're so strong; you could do wrestling.'

Arthur laughed, feeling his couple of beers in a pleasant way. There was a slow number, the lights dimmed, as at a disco, and people on the floor groaned and laughed. Francey held him round the waist. Not since Maggie had he held a girl like this, and that had been – around New Year's, so long ago! Arthur realized he was becoming excited and drew back a little; Francey pressed herself against him, then drew back also, and their eyes met for an instant in the semi-darkness. She was not smiling.

The music ended; the lights came on, and some people clapped their hands.

Arthur checked Gus and Veronica and Francey for further orders, then went to the counter for two coffees, one beer, another hamburger for Gus, and a double order of french fries.

'Make that two beers!' Arthur said, and paid.

They dipped french fries into ketchup at the edge of the big plate.

'How's dorm life, Arthur?' Veronica asked him.

'Just elegant,' Arthur said, thinking of Frank Costello's dirty socks and shorts on the floor.

'Sorry about—' Veronica squirmed, and her brows frowned quickly. 'You had to leave the Brewsters'.'

'Didn't *have* to,' Arthur yelled over the music, 'but I couldn't camp there forever.' Gus and Francey didn't seem to pay attention to what he had said, and so much the better. Francey sat next to Arthur in the booth. She was leaning back in the corner, smoking a cigarette slowly, eyeing him, Arthur felt. He asked Veronica to dance.

'Francey likes you,' Veronica said on the dance floor.

'She said that?'

'No, I can see it.' Veronica smiled at him with her curiously sleepy eyes. 'Just now – she hasn't got a boyfriend. You might give it a *thought.*' Veronica had to shout to make herself heard.

Arthur wasn't thinking about it, wasn't planning. By 1 o'clock, he was in a happier mood. 'Hey, Gus! Coffee nightcap at the Silver Arrow? Remember that night? That hooker Irene?'

'What's the Silver Arrow?' Francey asked.

'Truck-stop diner,' Gus said. 'Sho, boy. I'm gettin' tired of this place. You gals gettin' tired of this place?'

They pushed off for the Silver Arrow, Francey again in Arthur's car.

'What's so great about this diner?' Francey asked.

'Absolutely nothing. Well – there's a woman behind the counter who's pretty tough. The whole place is tough.'

'A woman you know?'

'No-o.' Arthur laughed. 'Well, I met her once or twice. Am I a patron, no.'

Again a couple of giant trucks stood outside the diner and half a dozen cars besides. A man in a windbreaker and light-colored trousers, who didn't look like a trucker, was drunk and making a fuss because a waitress was refusing to serve him a beer.

'You're gonna get *thrown* out if you don't *get* out!' yelled one of the waitresses behind the counter.

And there was Irene with her phony blond hair under her silver cap, grinning at the altercation between the drunk and her colleague.

'That's the one,' Arthur said to Francey, and nodded his head toward Irene, who hadn't noticed his group.

There was no room for all of them together at the counter, so Arthur sat with Francey on two stools, and Gus with Veronica farther down. All the booths were taken. The jukebox played 'Tuxedo Junction.' Arthur yelled an order for four coffees.

'Really is a tough place,' Francey said to Arthur.

'Slice of life, as they say,' Arthur replied with a languid air.

Arthur and Francey got their coffees, served by the middle waitress. Irene still hadn't noticed Arthur, and in fact her eyes looked unfocused, despite her big smile. Maybe the lights of the place damaged people's eyesight after a while.

A trucker, trying to clown but plainly enjoying his superior muscle power, ejected the drunk who fell down the couple of steps outside the door.

'Who's driving *that* guy home?' a woman yelled.

'Let him walk!' Laughter.

Gus came over to Arthur, smiling a little, his hands stuffed in the slash pockets of his jacket. 'Hey, Art,' he said in Arthur's ear. 'Veronica thinks your blond friend's pregnant.'

'No kidding!' said Arthur, amused. 'Pretty likely, I s'pose.' If so, his father's counsel had been in vain.

Gus went back to Veronica, but after a minute, he and Veronica were able to take stools next to Arthur and Francey. Meanwhile Arthur had been looking at Irene. Was her waistline bigger? Possibly. But it wouldn't have caught Arthur's eye. Did pregnant women start getting heavier at the waistline or below it?

'Oh, hello, Arthur,' a voice said near him, just as he had turned to Francey.

Irene leaned toward him, and Arthur glanced at her hands which were so near his coffee, red nails and a fake gold ring, and somebody's check between two fingers.

'You all right? Being a good boy?' she asked.

'Oh, sure.' Arthur saw for an instant that crazy mixture of intense concern and mental fuzziness in her eyes that so disturbed him. 'And you? I hope—'

Irene was summoned by a loud male voice at the food window.

'Amazing, no?' Arthur said to Francey. 'She goes to church – every Sunday.'

Francey put her head back and laughed, hardly making a

sound, and lit a cigarette before Arthur could pull out his lighter. Arthur liked the way she laughed, as if she enjoyed it.

Arthur was to drive Francey home. The couples said good night outside the Silver Arrow.

'Great evening, Art. Thanks a lot,' Gus said. 'See you soon. Come by my house *anytime*.'

'Come by my joint anytime,' Arthur said, 'but I can't promise any privacy.'

In the car, Francey said, 'I'd like to see your joint. Can we go there?'

Arthur wasn't surprised. He had been about to propose the same thing. 'Sure. My roommate's not even in tonight – or even tomorrow night. He's in Wisconsin.' Arthur was suddenly reminded of an overheard remark at Ruthie's party last year, when Maggie had been out of town for the first abortion: '. . . roommate's out and won't be back till four,' a fellow from C.U. had said, trying to persuade a high school girl to go off with him.

'This place isn't too bad,' Francey said when she entered 214.

The Residence Assistant had not been at his desk downstairs when Arthur had sneaked Francey in. In fact, sneaking girls in was considered no problem, Arthur had learned. The problem was the other way round, if a girl wanted to have a fellow in her room after 11 p.m.

'To tell you the truth, I straightened it up a little. Doesn't always look this neat.'

But Francey remarked that he had a view out the window instead of looking on a wall and that he had only one roommate, whereas some people had a second who slept on another jammed-in bed. So Arthur felt better suddenly about his living arrangements. When he turned from the fridge, whence he had been taking two beers, Francey opened her arms. Arthur put the beers down. He held her tightly. And now it didn't matter if he became excited. They kissed. Then Arthur stepped back.

'D-do you – This beer—'

'Have you got a short whisky?'

He had, a hardly touched half-bottle of Ballantine's which he had bought because it reminded him of Betty Brewster's well-equipped household. Arthur fetched it from his suitcase in the closet. They each had two neat ones, and then Arthur escorted Francey down the hall to a shower room. One fellow saw them in the hall and whistled. The shower room was empty, and Arthur waited holding Francey's clothes, while she stepped under the water. He had brought his bathrobe for her. By now it was nearly 2 a.m. He took Francey back to his room; then he went and had a shower. When he came back, Francey was in his bed.

'Bring the whisky,' she said.

He brought it and their two glasses.

Then they were in bed, with the door locked, the lights out, the whisky on the night table forgotten. Arthur was gentle, but reached a climax so soon, it was embarrassing. There was of course a next time. The second and third times he did much better. And the girl was perfect. To Arthur, she was no longer Francey, but *a girl*, or *the girl*. She was also not in a hurry. The dawn was showing at the window, when Arthur was aware of a pleasant drowsiness. He raised up on one elbow. The girl was looking at him with half-open eyes.

'Who would have thought,' she said, 'you'd be so nice in bed? Well, I would. – I did. – Can you reach a cigarette?'

Arthur had to get out of bed for them, but he could see well enough not to turn the light on. In those couple of seconds, as he reached for the red and white pack on his writing table, he realized that he was cured, suddenly, as if from a disease. He was cured of his depression over Maggie. Was that the same as being cured of Maggie, the same as his love for her ending? Just erased, dead, gone? He wasn't sure as yet. He simply realized that he was one hundred percent happier. And in those few seconds, he realized that this had nothing to do with hanging on to Francey, or being in love with her, or even trying to start an affair with her.

He lit a cigarette and handed it to her. Then he pulled on his pajama pants. 'Shouldn't we get some sleep? Have you got things to do today?'

'What's today?' she asked sleepily.

'Saturday!' Arthur laughed.

She went off to the showers, by herself, and Arthur made cups of instant coffee, strong and black without sugar, as he had noticed Francey had taken her coffee in the Silver Arrow. The world was changed, as if he had been reborn, and thinking of the born-again Christians, Arthur laughed out loud. Great, if he stood up in church and shouted, '*I* am a born-again, because I slept with a nice girl – and out of wedlock, too! I experienced a miracle!' They'd throw him out by the back of his neck and the seat of his pants!

Francey returned and got back into bed. 'What're you smiling at?'

Arthur brought the coffees. 'The born-again Christians! My father goes to a born-again church here and that blonde in the diner last night goes to the same church. And last night Gus and Veronica thought she looked pregnant. I happen to know she's not married.'

'Hm-m. Pregnant.' Francey gave a short laugh. 'Must say she looks like a floozie.'

'Doesn't she?' Arthur laughed. 'I had a fight with my dad about the whole thing. Well, not about her but about something – similar. Holier-than-thou bastards! Irene was asking last night if I was being a good boy! – They're all *sick!*'

'Yeah, and what they're doing politically is not so funny. They're trying to run the government and they've got a good start. They've got a shit-list for liberals. Making sure they don't get elected, you know? They've even started book-banning. The hell with all of them. It's only the individual who matters – finally.'

'Yes. – And how can I thank you, *thank* you – for last night and this morning?' Arthur made a bow.

'Arthur, you're still a little drunk! Drink your coffee; come back to bed and sleep a while.'

'After a shower.'

Arthur took a shower. Then they slept till nearly noon.

24

Saturday afternoon around 1, Arthur drove Francey McCullough to a house in Varney Street, in town, where she had a date with a girl student to do some work for a dramatics class.

'See you again maybe. Thanks for the lift,' Francey said as she got out of his car. She had just given him her telephone number at a women's dorm on campus.

Amazing, Arthur thought. Fantastic. Francey was so casual with her good-bye wave – just as he preferred her to be at that moment – and she had wrought a transformation in him overnight!

He drove back to his dorm room, and spent half an hour dreamily tidying up everything. What did last night mean?

What did Francey mean, with her few words to him? And last night? Did it mean that Maggie was really cut off, that he didn't love her anymore, just like that? Arthur couldn't believe that. But the pain Maggie had caused him was gone. That was why the word 'cured' had occurred to him at dawn. Very strange, because he couldn't with any honesty say he was in love with Francey or even much attracted to her. Maybe he'd spend another night with her, and maybe not. Maybe she wanted to see him again, and maybe she wouldn't, when he telephoned her. She'd talked about her present boyfriend. 'A kind of a quarrel, but maybe we'll get back together, I don't know.' Arthur had forgotten the boyfriend's name, but he was a senior at C.U.

Arthur treated himself to the most pleasant of his assignments, reading a couple of stories from Joyce's *The Dubliners*, followed by some bio; then the telephone rang around 4, when he was snoozing on his bed. Nobody answered in the next room, so Arthur got up and swivelled the telephone toward him.

'Hello, *Franky*!' said an excited voice, male.

'No. Frank's not here.'

'Where is he?'

'Home, he said. Wisconsin.'

The caller groaned. 'If he comes in, can you tell him there's a party tonight in Cranleigh, room number – one sixty-one. Any time after eight. Tell him John called.'

Arthur wrote this message and put it on Frank's bed.

Then he had a happy inspiration to see his mother this evening. He dialed his house number, and Robbie answered. 'How're you, Robbie?'

'Okay.'

'Is Mom there?'

'Yep.' Robbie let the telephone drop hard on the table.

'*Hello*, Arthur!' said his mother.

'I was wondering can I come over tonight? If you're home?'

His mother was delighted. Of course he could come over and have dinner with them, and did he need anything like sweaters or shirts so she could get them ready?

Just before his family's dinner hour, Arthur drove to the house on West Maple. Norma Keer was trimming her hedges. Arthur put his car in the driveway and waved hello to Norma. 'You getting very far with that little thing?' Arthur asked, because Norma was using secateurs instead of hedge-clippers.

'Getting the *dead* branches out!' she called out. 'Better visit me soon or I'll forget all about you!'

Arthur knocked on his front door and heard his mother's steps, fairly running.

'Door's *open*! Hello, Arthur!' She kissed his cheek. 'You're looking – pretty well. How long's it been? A month?'

'*No*, Mom! Two weeks,' Arthur said, smiling. 'Hi, Robbie.'

Robbie leaned against the living room doorjamb, eyes on the TV. 'Hi,' he said over his shoulder.

Arthur hung his jacket in the hall and saw from a glance into the living room that his father was in his study, whose door was half open.

'Nothing special to eat tonight, just pork chops,' said his mother. 'You're thinner, Arthur. Are you getting enough to eat at that – dorm?'

'The food is *not* as good as yours. And I had a cold about a week ago.'

They chatted. The kitchen was as usual more pleasant than the living room for Arthur. His mother asked when he had last written to his grandmother, and Arthur replied truthfully two weeks ago.

'She phones me sometimes, you know, always asks about you. I told her about Maggie. Hope you don't mind, Arthur.'

'No-o. Well – these things happen – they say. – I don't look as if I'm collapsing, do I?'

Lois shook her head and smiled. She grabbed his sweatered left arm for a moment and pressed it. 'Can't tell you how glad I am you're here tonight!'

Robbie had gone farther into the living room, nearer the TV with its voices and sounds of gunfire and explosions. Then Richard emerged from his study.

'Hello, Arthur,' said his father.

'Hi, Dad.'

His father said nothing more and entered the kitchen with the air of wondering how soon dinner would be ready.

The dinner period was no less sticky, with his father and Robbie silent, he and his mother being the life of the party, if the party could be said to have any life. His mother asked him to remind her that she had clean shirts ready for him in the hall closet and had he brought any dirty shirts? Arthur had forgotten to.

'By the way, Dad, how's Irene?' Arthur asked in a silence. 'Is she still going to church?'

'Sure she is. – As far as I know.'

'I was at the Silver Arrow last night. One of my friends thought she looked pregnant. I hope it's not true.'

'Who told you that?' asked his mother.

'Nobody told me. It's just that Veronica – Gus's girlfriend – thought she looked pregnant.' Arthur was aware of Robbie's gray eyes lifting from his food to his father. 'I don't suppose it matters. You said she used to – well—'

'She is pregnant, yes,' said his father, twiddling with his napkin at one side of his empty plate. 'Funny, it – Well, long enough, I suppose, for somebody to notice.'

Robbie looked like a soldier on the alert. His torso and head didn't move, but his eyes shot from his father to his mother, bounced off Arthur, then returned to his father.

Irene had fallen, and abortion was out of the question. If his father was still counseling Irene, he would counsel against it. What a mess! And poor Irene had half a brain, to be generous about it. 'And who's the father?' Arthur asked. 'One of those truckers?'

'Arthur! – Don't joke about a thing like that.' But his mother was smiling slightly.

'Didn't mean to be joking,' Arthur said.

'We don't know. Not the point.' His father got up, removing his own plate and Lois's, too.

Wasn't it some kind of point, Arthur thought, a matter of some interest, anyway? Was she plying her trade again, Arthur wanted to ask, but instead he said, 'She's got a boyfriend? Must have.' Had she initiated Robbie? And wouldn't that be a funny twist? Arthur set his teeth to keep from smiling.

'Well—' said his mother, rising to remove Arthur's plate. 'Nobody knows. It's sad.'

'So what's she going to do?' Arthur addressed this question to both his parents.

Richard was returning to the table with four dessert plates. 'What do you mean? She'll have the baby, of course.'

Arthur lit a Marlboro. He was aware of a small pleasure, perhaps nasty of him, in seeing his father in a bind: His protégée Irene had kicked the traces and got herself pregnant. Ah, the pleasures of the body!

'. . . hard sauce to go with this fruit cake, Arthur. I hope you'll like it,' said his mother, trying to fill in the silence.

His father had reseated himself.

'Who's going to take care of the child?' Arthur asked.

'Why, she will,' his father replied. 'Who else? She's got her sister there at home to help.'

His father's matter-of-factness surprised Arthur. Wasn't this a catastrophe, Irene pregnant? At the same time, the situation seemed funny: that gross sister, sitting around eating candy, giving the baby its bottles, while Irene went back to work at the Silver Arrow. Funny and bizarre, just as bizarre as Robbie's steely earnestness on his left. Robbie maintained his forward-leaning attitude, attentive to every word. 'You mean,' Arthur said, spooning hard sauce onto his cake, 'Irene won't tell you who the father is? Or does she even know?'

'Arthur – can't we change the subject?' said his mother.

Arthur glanced at his mother. 'Just that the father could help in the situation. They haven't much money, Irene and her sister, from what I've heard.'

His mother sighed. 'Well, Irene's not quite right in the head, poor girl.'

'She's insane,' Robbie said, looking at Arthur. 'I told you that the day she turned up here – last summer.'

Robbie's grimness amazed Arthur. It was the ugly side of virtue, he supposed, feeling superior to dimwit sinners like Irene. 'Girls do sometimes get pregnant, Robbie,' Arthur said gently, 'and don't forget it takes a fellow to make them pregnant. You must forgive. Isn't that right?'

'Ar-thur—' said his mother.

Robbie said nothing.

After dinner, Arthur and his mother took their coffee into Arthur's room, while Richard and Robbie stayed in the living room in front of the television. Arthur wanted a couple of things from his room.

'Do you think Maggie will stay with this new boy?' his mother asked.

'I dunno. – May as well assume so.' His voice sounded hollow, even scared. He wound a brown belt around his hand, then decided to buckle it on over his trousers and sweater. The empty feeling had come back.

'You look better in the face – your expression. But I'd like to see you put on a pound or two. I was quite worried about you a few weeks ago. – You're not just pretending now, are you?'

He knew what his mother meant, pretending to be of good cheer when he wasn't. Arthur shook his head, feeling suddenly angry for no reason. He avoided looking at his mother's eyes. 'Hey, Mom,' he said in a low voice, and glanced at his closed door. 'Why's Robbie so concerned about this Irene mess?'

His mother drew a deep breath. 'It's a disappointment – for Richard. You know? And Robbie understands that. Richard thought Irene was doing so much better, that she was happier and on her feet again – and now this, she's – What is it, four or five months pregnant. That means she was putting on an act all this time.'

So it happened in December or January, Arthur reckoned. 'Mom, if you could see the guys in the Silver Arrow! – And she sort of leads them on. No wonder nobody knows who the father is. And in fact who cares?' Arthur gazed into his open closet. He took his navy blue Viyella shirt from a hanger and remembered the afternoon he had bought it, on the occasion of his first dinner at Maggie's house. 'Is Dad still giving a tenth of his income to the church?' Arthur asked out of the blue.

'Ye-es, I'm pretty sure. And a bit more.'

Arthur closed the closet door and started folding his shirt on his bed. 'Reminds me of a piece I read in *Time* in February. All these rich churches are connected – not like a business partnership, but they're all spouting the same thing. It's like a gas. You can't see it, but it's there, in the atmosphere. We've all got to breathe it – because the Moral Majority says so.' Arthur felt vaguely angry again, but he had managed to keep his voice calm. 'These churches are off the income tax hook, and they're rolling in dough. Like the Worldwide Church. They publish *Plain Truth*. Like the Moonies. The big shots live in luxury, and they say, "This is the way our people like to see us." Looking rich, I mean.'

His mother made no reply. Arthur knew she was thinking about something else. He had expected her to say that Richard and she didn't look exactly rich, did they, nor did the Reverend Bob Cole. That wouldn't have daunted Arthur in his argument. It was the leaders of these churches who were rich, and their followers broke, a lot of them, and just about as gullible as the gullible blacks who had followed Jim Jones to death in Guyana after being fleeced by him. That story had made a big impression on Arthur. Many of the American blacks in his group, and a few moonstruck whites, too, had been handing over regularly their Social Security checks to go into Jim Jones's bank account. Arthur felt spoiling for a fight, but not with his mother.

His mother changed the subject. How was Gus; how was Veronica? And had he gone along with the two of them the evening they had been to the Silver Arrow? Here Arthur was able to say something a bit more cheerful, that he had had a date with a girl called Francey, just last night when they had gone to the Silver Arrow after Mom's Pride. And Francey was not his new girlfriend by any means, because she had a steady boyfriend, Arthur had been told.

'Whatever it is – tonight you look a lot more cheerful. You know, Arthur, if Maggie's stuck on this other fellow, you've just got to get over her. I don't want to see you unhappy.'

Arthur opened a lower drawer, looking for things he might want. *Get over her.* He hated phrases like that. There would never be another girl like Maggie; it was as simple as that. Arthur could have cracked up at that moment, and he was about to excuse himself to go into the bathroom for a minute, when his mother proposed that they ring up Norma Keer and see if they could come over.

So Arthur telephoned, and ten minutes later, he and his mother were sitting in Norma's living room; coffee was brewing in the kitchen, and Norma in stockinged feet bent over her coffee table, fussing with cups. When she asked Arthur how Maggie was, he was able to reply:

'Very well, I think. She'll be majoring in sociology.'

But when Norma made cheerful remarks about seeing Maggie when summer vacation started, Arthur had the feeling that she was talking to a ghost, that the ghost was himself. Norma suggested a small brandy to go with their coffee, and Arthur accepted, though his mother didn't.

'And Robbie?' Norma asked. 'He hardly says hello to me any-more when I'm out in the yard. I always give him a hail.'

It occurred to Arthur that Robbie shunned Norma, because Robbie knew Norma was rather a friend of his. 'And your health, Norma,' said Arthur, thinking both to change the subject and perhaps make the atmosphere more depressing, even though to inquire about a person's health was surely a polite thing to do.

'Good news Monday. I was saving it to tell you – case you asked.' Norma sat down in her usual sofa corner, sitting a bit more upright than usual. 'Doctor said Monday, "Great progress." Meaning I'm no longer on death row.'

'How marvelous, Norma!' Lois said. 'Why didn't you call us up – Monday?' Lois laughed with pleasure.

'Oh – Just saving it. Don't I look happier? Doctor had the results of a couple more tests – I can't keep track of 'em all. Anyway, he said, "Two big problems conquered." He thinks I have nothing to worry about. So all the pills and the X-rays really did accomplish something.'

Yes, it was a miracle, Arthur thought. He had never expected to hear such words from Norma. He felt as happy for her as if she had been a member of his family – his grandmother, maybe. 'Cheers, Norma!' Arthur lifted his little glass. As he tipped his head back he was aware of the Italian Renaissance table beyond him and on his right, the sturdy one that Maggie had admired. Would Maggie ever look at it again, here with him? Smile at him as she had that day, with the fingertips of her right hand, he remembered, touching the top of that table? He was glad that his mother declined a second coffee.

Then he was standing with his mother in the driveway beside his car; his mother was telling him to drive carefully, and Arthur realized that he hadn't said good night to his father or to Robbie, and that he didn't care.

'You keep happy. And call me soon!'

The next day, Sunday around 4 p.m., Frank Costello got back

from Wisconsin. Arthur had known his privacy couldn't last forever.

Frank tumbled duffel bags and what looked like a guitar in a canvas case onto the floor near his bed.

'Nice trip?' Arthur asked, because Frank hadn't even said hello, or was maybe too out of breath to do so.

'Yeah. Not bad, thanks. Makes a break.'

'One message for you there. It's on your bed.'

'Oh, yeah. Thanks.'

Now the atmosphere was different, more tense. But the happy thing was, Arthur thought as he settled himself on his bed to read the remaining required pages of Alfred Whitehead, that he had pulled out of his slough of depression. Nice word, *slough*, suggesting mud or a quagmire. How did one pronounce it, sluff or sloff? Was it safe to base his cure on Francey McCullough? That meant that any girl could do it. Girls were interchangeable, he had read somewhere in a novel. Of course, just for going to bed with, that was true. And what else did he know about Francey? He decided he would call Francey up Tuesday. That would not be rushing things. Maybe she'd tell him straightaway she was back with her boyfriend. Get back to Whitehead! Whitehead was boring. Nothing but platitudes.

Still, on Monday morning Arthur found himself hoping as usual that there might be a letter from Maggie at the desk downstairs. There was nothing for him. And as usual, he imagined Maggie preoccupied with Larry Hargiss, probably seeing him at least three times a week. Why not, since their universities were so close, and maybe Hargiss had some classes at Radcliffe? And maybe Maggie was thinking that it would be better, wiser or something, if she didn't write again. Arthur had written once again after his first post-Hargiss letter, and he was sure she hadn't lost his dorm address, unless she wanted to lose it.

On Tuesday around 6 p.m., Francey telephoned Arthur.

'Why didn't you phone me?' she asked.

Arthur heard her badly, because Frank had a cassette on. 'I was *going* to phone you in about ten minutes!'

'. . . doing tonight? Want to come to my place? . . . Ellsworth three eleven.'

Francey had her dorm apartment free, and she had food for dinner. The apartment, though small, had two bedrooms, a bath and a tiny living room with a TV set. Luxury!

'How've you been?' Francey asked.

What to answer to that? 'Okay.'

'You're so serious!' Francey said, unsmiling, and she grabbed Arthur round the waist. 'I'm depressed. So why don't we eat and drink – and relax.'

The telephone rang while Francey was making rum drinks. She didn't answer it. Francey was frying hot dogs and toasting buns. She asked Arthur to make the green salad.

'These boots – drive me nuts,' Francey said, removing a pair of furry beige boots from near the door, throwing them into a closet. 'Not my boots, Susanne's.'

They ate at a bridge table, to music by Cole Porter, 'Ridin' High' and other old stuff that Arthur liked, and 'It's All Right with Me,' which he thought a fitting song for both of them.

'Are you forgetting your boyfriend with a new fellow every night?' Arthur asked.

'I'm not forgetting him,' she said a bit sullenly. 'Maybe I ought to. Life's tough, isn't it? I wish I didn't fall in love so hard.'

Less than an hour later, they were in bed, in a bed that smelled like a perfume factory, though Arthur was sure Francey hadn't doused it in perfume deliberately. The making love was strange, like a duty to be done, as when he carried sacks of weeds at Mrs DeWitt's, and his body obeyed his will. By the same token, the pleasure at the end was not so much a pleasure but a finish.

Francey said, 'Oh!' Francey was pleased. She could have done it again, when he couldn't.

'I wish I were in love with you,' she said.

Arthur said nothing. Did he wish that? Francey was easy to be with, the kind of girl who didn't make trouble. And she had saved him from a collapse. Did that count for something? Was that enough, and enough for what?

'Now I have to throw you out, because it's ten to ten and Susanne might come back from a movie any minute. She's the type to lodge a complaint, as they say, if a fellow's actually *in* bed. You can be here if you're up and dressed.'

Arthur got dressed. He thought he should leave.

'Call me again?' Francey said.

For some reason, Arthur didn't want to telephone Francey the next day or the next. By Friday, he felt quite depressed again, without knowing why. Around 6 p.m., Frank offered him, not for the first time, some of his angel dust. Arthur declined. The cocaine might have been fun for a few minutes, if he felt anything at all from it. The couple of times Arthur had sampled coke, not from Frank, he hadn't felt anything, and someone had told him it was because he didn't sniff enough. Arthur was sure Frank would give him enough, but Frank also depressed Arthur.

'Pick y'up,' said Frank. 'Do you good. Better for you than alcohol.'

'Since when am I drinking a lot of alcohol?' Arthur asked in a good-natured tone. Angel dusters, Arthur had observed, always had a bad word to say about alcohol, even a couple of beers, and when Arthur had asked a coke-taker why he wouldn't drink, even one beer, the fellow had replied, 'Because if I start on alcohol, I can't stop. I finish everything in sight.' That thought was depressing, and so was the prospect of Frank's presence until the end of the school year. Frank had even told Arthur days ago that he had been 'dismissed' from C.U., but Frank lingered on, using the room as a place to sleep, and C.U. was not throwing him out, Arthur supposed, because no other student was going to rent Frank's part of the room this late in the school year. Before 7, Frank and his pal John departed.

Arthur went to the swivel telephone and dialed Betty Brewster's number.

She was in. 'Hello, Arthur, how *are* you?'

'Pretty much okay – thanks. And you?'

'Same as ever. Warren left the house five minutes ago. What a pity, because I know he'd have wanted to say hello to you.'

'Is – I haven't heard from Maggie in – in quite a few days. Is she okay?'

'Oh, far as I know. She phoned us last Sunday. Warren was here, which was nice. I know she's studying pretty hard. I'll tell her to write to you, if she's being forgetful.'

'Oh, don't *tell* her.' Arthur's face grew suddenly warm.

'Well – the house isn't the same without you – Warren said. He said, "Get Arthur back, *I* don't want to do all these little things."' Betty laughed.

Arthur had stinging eyes when he hung up, and he flung open the fridge door and reached for a beer. He could of course go back to the Brewsters' house tomorrow, tonight, which would be a hell of a lot more aesthetic than where he was, but he would feel as if he were sitting there waiting – and hopelessly – for Maggie, or else making use of the Brewsters' kindness.

He had an impulse to call up Francey and repressed it. Nice to know she was there, however.

The next morning, as if prompted by a long-distance thought wave from Betty, a letter from Maggie was at the desk for him. Arthur was aware, as he opened the envelope, of his hope that Maggie had got fed up with Mr Hargiss, of his hope for even a hint along this line. The letter was dated 19th May.

Dear Arthur,

Am writing this before I start out on a regimen of work so I can pass the finals. Maybe you are doing the same? Math is still my toughest and I still have to pass a fresh exam to make minimum requirements. On the other hand, am taking a basic one-semester sociology course and I like my Prof. Robert Pinderley, very much.

Whatever you might be thinking, I don't go out much. Nobody does here, as the atmosphere is rather strict and we all have so much work to do. Before exam times, they give us coffee and sandwiches in the dorm corridors around 11, because lots of us are studying till after midnight.

My mother says (again!) that she misses you. So I hope with your decision to live in those C.U. dorms you aren't too unhappy. I suddenly wish we could take a walk by the quarry and feel free again! High school work was never like this, no?

Maybe you're happier now – than you sounded in your last letter? Maybe you've met somebody you like or who at least can cheer you up? I hope so.

Please write another note when you can.

With very much love,

Maggie

This letter gave Arthur a lot of instant thoughts pro and con, but the negative won out. No mention of Mr Hargiss, but that was Maggie being tactful. Had his last letter sounded so glum? And despite mentioning the quarry, she *hoped* he had met someone else. What could be more negative than that? It added up to 'let's be friends,' which to Arthur was horrid.

He set off for philosophy class at 9 a.m. Boring Whitehead, and even more boring Plato. Everything they said seemed so obvious – why had they taken the trouble to write it all out? – and also unconsoling. Wasn't philosophy supposed to help you to live? Maybe extremists were better, people like Nietzsche, even Cotton Mather, the latter surely a soulmate of his father's, all hellfire and damnation and no sign of tolerance. 'Jesus!' Arthur said aloud, like a curse.

He thought of phoning Gus this evening and going over to the Warylsky house for an hour. Or maybe he'd run into Gus on the campus today and ask him. He never encountered Francey, though he never especially kept a lookout for her on the campus. He didn't want to call on Norma tonight. In fact, he didn't want to see Gus, not merely because he was too depressed to inflict himself on a friend, but because he knew Gus couldn't really help. Nobody could help.

By 6:30 that evening, Arthur was saying on the telephone to Francey, 'Come over. Can you? Frank's out and I don't know when he'll be back.'

Francey hesitated just a couple of seconds. 'Why not?'

'Pick you up in five minutes!'

Arthur did. They played the radio, which belonged to Frank. They tuned in to dance music, for atmosphere, though they didn't dance. Arthur produced a dinner of sorts, slightly aided by Francey who was not much interested in dinner. She sipped his scotch and looked dreamy and distant and a bit sad. Then they went to bed. Around 1 o'clock, Arthur said:

'Has it ever occurred to you to be my girlfriend?' He waited, hoping she would say, 'Why not?'

She was smoking a cigarette. 'I don't want to *be* anybody's girlfriend. I just want to be.'

That sounded like philosophy. 'Do you have to be in love? Does everybody – have to be in love?'

She laughed. 'I *am* against it. – But I still say you're nice.'

Arthur thought it best to let it go at that. Francey was going to stay the night. He would love that, to wake up in the morning and find her there. And if he found that bore Frank also in the morning, to hell with him. Nothing could wake Frank in the morning, anyway.

That pleasant night and early morning with Francey set him up for the next many days, enabled him to study with a level head, and even made him believe he had found, by accident, a new philosophy: Take life as it comes. Enjoy and be grateful. Not grateful to God, but to luck and chance. Tread carefully, speak carefully, and hang on to what you've got. Be polite to what you've got. When the word *polite* occurred to Arthur, he sent flowers to Francey McCullough's dorm room, having ascertained at the florist's shop in Chalmerston that his card would be attached to the bouquet and that the flowers wouldn't be just dumped downstairs but put into the hands of either Miss McCullough or of her roommate in room 311. They were pink roses and blue carnations, a crazy combination, Arthur supposed, but he had fancied that mixture. He had written on the card:

To my non-girlfriend with quite a lot of love and thanks.

A.

If she received it, she didn't telephone that evening, but Arthur didn't mind that. He had to study for what Professor Jurgens called a 'preparatory exam' in microbio. Again Arthur was alone in his dorm room, oblivious of the mess in Frank's half of it. He studied until after 1 a.m.

On the following afternoon, the class took Jurgens' special exam, and Arthur was sure he passed and would score high, maybe the highest. The marks were not to be put on a bulletin board as at the finals, but the papers returned to each student individually. Since he hadn't seen Francey in over a week, he decided to call her and ask her for a date, not necessarily for that night but for during the coming weekend.

A girl answered and said Francey was under the shower and to wait a minute. Then Francey came on.

'Hello? – Oh, hello, Arthur.'

'Hi. I was wondering when I could see you? Maybe Friday? Saturday?'

'Well—' She sounded slightly breathless, as if she were drying herself with a towel. 'I made it up with my boyfriend. So I'm sorry to say I don't think we should see each other again. Not for the moment. You understand? – Sorry. But that's the way it is.'

'Yes, sure I understand. Yes, well—'

'And thanks for the flowers! They're still here. Looking nice.'

'Yes, well – I wish you lots of luck, Francey.'

Then they hung up. Arthur felt as if he had been shot in the stomach or the chest. He took a shower and put on different clothes to change the atmosphere, if he possibly could. He was trying not to think about anything, certainly not Francey. However, to think of Francey was unavoidable, and he thought: What had he lost? A girl who was willing to go to bed with him, or maybe anybody, a girl whom he hardly knew, and who he knew had been in love with another fellow, and therefore he had known that exactly this might happen.

Still, it was awful. Not only Maggie was gone, but Francey, too. The bottom had really fallen out. But this phrase reminded him of what he had felt when Maggie had written the letter about Larry Hargiss. That had been the bottom falling out, not Francey now.

For a few seconds, Arthur was scared stiff. He went down the hall to the toilets, thinking he was going to be sick. His stomach tightened, but he didn't retch, and in fact there was nothing in his stomach now, he realized with some relief. He wasn't sick at all, he told himself, and looked at himself in the mirror and ran his comb through his hair. Beads of sweat stood on his forehead like condensation on cold glass.

The thing to do was take a walk, he thought, so he put on his favorite old sneakers, turned out the lights and departed. He had remembered to take a pocket flashlight with him. When he finally looked up at a street marker, he found that he had walked a long way southward, or so he thought. The street names S. Morgan and Tweeley didn't mean a thing to him, but the glow of the light, which meant the center of town, was behind him, and he could tell north from south by the very visible position of Vega and its attendant diamond-shaped constellation. For want of any other objective, he started back in the direction of C.U. and his room.

Suddenly he found himself standing beside his own car, as if the brown Ford had been his objective. And where to go? Arthur looked at his watch and saw to his surprise that it was ten past 11. He had been walking for more than three hours.

'God's sake,' he murmured, and leaned his head on the roof of his car. His hands were in his pockets, and he had the keys with him. He got in his car and sat for a minute, then started the motor. The Silver Arrow would be a fitting place tonight, he thought, those brutal lights, the cruddy customers, that female clown Irene, so full of virtue. That had amusement value! Arthur drove with deliberate calm, taking every corner in second gear, because the image of an impact had come to his mind. He had not thought of a car accident, but of an impact against his chest. He suddenly remembered himself at thirteen, crashing into the chest, the abdomen of a big fellow who had stepped into his path to block a door. This had been when he had run off from home and caught a bus to New York, with fourteen dollars in his pocket, he recalled. He had left a note on his bed saying: 'Don't worry. Back in four days,' or something like that, but his parents had guessed that he had gone to New York, because he had been there a couple of times with his parents and the city had fascinated him. So his parents had alerted police there, and when Arthur in the evening of the second day had inquired at a modest-looking hotel for a room for the night, the man behind the desk had asked his age, and Arthur had bolted for the door and encountered a security guard or some employee of the hotel. End of that adventure.

Second gear again. *Ritual*, he thought, kept people on an even keel. He remembered thinking this in the days just after Maggie's letter of good-bye to him, remembered making himself do things in the same old way, when he really felt like breaking something, maybe a piece of furniture. He remembered thinking that ritual kept people calm and that it was a major part of religion, the getting up and sitting down in church, the singing of hymns when nobody bothered to think much about what the words meant. Outward form. And what was inside half the time? Misery, hell and confusion. And why didn't people face it? Because they couldn't.

And there was the Silver Arrow glowing on the right side of the road ahead. Arthur slid up between two ordinary parked cars this time, though at least one mountainous truck stood out in front with its blunt nose pointed toward the boxcar-shaped diner.

Arthur went in. There was a steamy smell of onions and bacon, and a girl's voice sang on the jukebox. A woman in one of the booths laughed loudly.

'Make it *three* coffees!'

'. . . *with* a slice, I *said* that!'

Arthur headed for an empty stool at the counter. There were two waitresses behind the counter, in silver caps, neither Irene. Rather promptly, he was asked what he wanted. 'Hamburger medium and a coffee, please,' Arthur said.

'With or without a slice?' asked the girl.

'With.'

She had set a glass of water in front of him, and Arthur sipped this, looking around for Irene. It would be rather nice if she weren't here, he thought. Then suddenly she appeared on his left, coming through a doorway which was out of his range of vision, though he saw part of the door when she opened it. She looked in high spirits, smiling, carrying paper napkins that went into the metal containers, and from the way she walked, he knew she was wearing high heels. And her waistline! Yes, there could be no doubt now, and how soon would she have to stop working, in fact? What would the other two girls behind the counter be thinking these days as to who the father was? Or did they bother to wonder? The girls looked pretty tough themselves, though both were younger than Irene.

The waitress with coppery hair delivered his hamburger in its steamy brown-topped bun and thumped a mug of coffee down beside it. Arthur opened his little cream container and dumped it into his coffee.

Irene hadn't seen him. She was yelling something through her smiling mouth at someone several stools down on Arthur's left, and then she rocked back, laughing. She had bright rouge on her cheeks this evening, really like a clown.

Arthur bit into his hamburger and chewed it as if it were sawdust, though there was nothing the matter with it. If he ate slowly and thought about something else, it would stay down, and that was all to the good. He couldn't afford another tailspin now, just before the final exams.

Irene spotted him and reacted with a start of surprise. 'Well, Arthur!' she said, taking a second to lean toward him. Each of her hands gripped two mugs of coffee. 'How've you been? – You're looking a little down tonight. Gotcha friends with you?' Her eyes flitted somewhere behind Arthur.

'No.' Arthur thought her smile looked wild and demented.

She came back after delivering the coffees somewhere. 'And I suppose you notice I – Well, you oughta know.'

She had glanced down at her waistline, and Arthur realized with embarrassment that she was talking about her pregnancy. He shook his head and gulped. 'Didn't know.'

'Your father's. Yes.' She nodded with the same dazed smile and somewhat unfocused eyes. Then she gave the counter in front of Arthur an absent wipe with a damp cloth. 'He didn't tell you?'

'*Irene*!' yelled one of the other waitresses with urgency. 'Scrambled ready to go there!'

Irene swung around and went to the open window on the kitchen to Arthur's left. Plates of eggs and bacon steamed on the windowsill, and Irene bore these away to some booth behind Arthur.

What did she mean, his father's? That his father had made her pregnant? Was she spreading that story around? Arthur frowned and pushed his plate nervously away with the back of his fingers. He wanted to ask Irene a little more. But what? Irene was nuts. She'd say anything. 'Hey!' Arthur said, as Irene flashed past, moving to Arthur's right. She'd have a miscarriage if she kept up this mad pace, Arthur thought with sudden amusement. What should he ask her? What his father *said* about the situation? Would that enlighten him, or would Irene come out with some falsehoods, fantasies? '*Irene!*'

Irene paused and gave him her attention.

'What does my father say about this?' Arthur asked, aware of the presence of a man on either side of him, but the place was noisy and they didn't seem to be listening.

'I think he's pleased,' Irene replied.

'And my mother?'

Irene shrugged. 'Not sure she knows.' There was a flash of mischief in her face before she hurried away to the coffee taps.

Absolute crap! It really put the icing on the cake tonight! And suppose people started believing it! Suppose she said it to the Reverend Cole at the First Church of Christ Gospel, that fountainhead of gossip? Well, at least she wasn't claiming it was Jesus' child or God's! Arthur smiled wryly, seized his coffee mug and drank it all. His bill was a dollar seventy-five, and he left two singles and went out to his car.

Now it was ten to midnight. Arthur had an irrepressible urge to phone his mother, to see her tonight. He had wanted to use the telephone booth in the Silver Arrow, but had not wanted Irene to see him using it, though he supposed it was doubtful whether it would have occurred to her that he was calling his parents. He could call from some other roadside place or a side-walk booth in town, but what if his father answered and said no to a visit?

Arthur drove to his parents' house. By the time he got there it was a quarter past midnight, and the house was dark. Only old Norma had a dim light on in her living room. Arthur went up the front steps and knocked gently.

After several seconds, he heard shuffling footsteps which he recognized as those of his father in house-shoes.

'Who's there?'

'Arthur.'

His father opened the door slightly. 'Well, it's a bit—'

'I know. Sorry. I want to talk with Mom for a minute.'

'Your mother's tired tonight,' said his father.

Then there was his mother behind his father, turning on the hall light. 'Arthur! Something the matter?'

'Oh, no, Mom. Can I talk with you a minute?'

'Of course, Arthur. Come in.'

'Just something personal,' Arthur said as he went in, hoping to get rid of his father.

His father had to back up in the narrow front hall; then he turned and went to the bedroom, as if to get back to the serious business of sleeping.

Arthur saw from a vertical streak of light in the hall that his father had not shut the bedroom door. His mother turned on a lamp in the living room, but this wasn't private enough, either.

'Let's go to the garage,' Arthur whispered.

His mother followed him.

'I just saw Irene,' Arthur said in a voice hardly above a whisper. 'What's this about her saying – about her pregnancy—'

'What's she saying? – To *you*?'

'Yes! Well, she's saying that Dad is responsible for it.' He could tell that his mother had heard it before. 'She's full of crap, isn't she?'

'Now calm down, Arthur.'

But Arthur couldn't and he opened the kitchen door quickly to see if his father was standing behind it, listening. The kitchen was empty. 'You heard it before. – Well, what's Dad doing about it?'

'About—'

'About the story. It isn't true, is it?'

'Well—'

'Mom, for gosh sake!' He grabbed his mother's forearm, realizing that he was absurdly upset himself. 'Mom, *is* it true?'

'I don't know.'

'Well – holy cow! What does Dad say?'

His mother's shoulders twisted. She didn't look at Arthur. 'He said – Oh, I don't want to talk about it, Arthur.'

'I don't either. But – I mean, if she's putting out a story like that, somebody's got to do something about it, no? – Are you saying it's possible that it's *true*?' How could anyone come near Irene, Arthur was thinking, except a drunken truck driver?

'No, I'm not. But Richard said he did spend – some time with her. Not whole nights, I mean, but – because she was upset and wanted him there. But Richard—'

'Oh, f'Chris'sake!' Suddenly it did seem just barely possible. 'Well, Mom, it's either yes or no, isn't it?' He seized his mother's wrist, because she was swaying as if she might faint. 'Lean against the car, Mom!' Arthur whispered.

'Don't say anything to Robbie about this, will you?' She glanced at Arthur.

'I had the idea the other night Robbie knows something already.'

'No. He just knows she's – in the state she's in.'

Arthur reached for his cigarettes. 'Here, Mom. Want one?' Arthur lit both their cigarettes. 'When did she start yacking about this?'

'Oh – last month. That's when I heard. She spoke to me on the phone.'

'Oh, my God, Mom! – Didn't you just ask Dad, one way or the other?' Arthur asked, aware of a mean satisfaction that his father was in this pickle, whether he was responsible or not, because his father had made his life wretched under the same circumstances. 'Surely he'd tell you the truth.'

His mother drew on her cigarette and stared down at her house-shoes. 'Richard says it's possible. He said he – one or two evenings – Oh, it's so awful, I really can't believe it, Arthur!' She began to weep.

Arthur groped for a handkerchief, found none, and reached into the pocket of his mother's dressing gown. He found a paper tissue and handed it to her.

'Irene calls here – sometimes – and we try to answer the phone before Robbie does. But of course if he ever hears any of this, he'd just say Irene's insane. He's always saying that. Well, she *is* insane.'

'Yes. So,' Arthur said, enjoying his cigarette, 'the next question is, has she got a boyfriend or two? Doubt if she'd have anyone steady, but these one-night stands?'

'Oh, she denies that completely, I know!' his mother said at once. 'Since going to church, which started – last summer anyway. She swears it, Richard says.'

Rather good of his father to say that, Arthur thought. 'She sure flirts, Mom!' Arthur said with a laugh.

'S-sh!'

'There's such a thing as – lying in bed with a girl,' Arthur began more softly, and at once wished he hadn't begun, because he didn't know how to finish. 'My father must know—'

'What?'

'Whether it's possible or not that he got a girl pregnant. So Dad says it's possible. Christ! Who could get anywhere near her – even to be polite?'

'Let's go back in. Richard'll think it's funny if we're out here so long.'

'Tell him I was talking about Maggie. Or Francey; that's better.'

'Okay.' His mother opened the kitchen door gently and went in. 'I feel like a cup of tea, warm as it is. Tea's comforting,' his mother murmured, as if to herself. She put the kettle on.

The light had been on in the kitchen, and the single light was still on in the living room. Arthur looked into the hall. His parents' bedroom door was now closed, he saw by going a little farther into the hall. So was Robbie's door closed.

'Robbie sleeps like a log,' his mother whispered when Arthur came back.

Then his mother changed her mind. She would make hot toddies, if that was agreeable to Arthur.

Arthur couldn't have cared less. It was an insane night, and hot toddies with the temperature in the lower eighties didn't seem especially more crazy. The fact was seeping in that his mother simply didn't want to say outright that his father was responsible for Irene's child-to-be.

'Mom, the child's going to be born, isn't it? – Since Dad's anti-abortion and – of course it's awfully late now.'

'Oh, abortion never was in the picture,' his mother said over her shoulder, whispering. 'Oh, no, she seems to want it.'

Arthur had to stand near his mother to hear. 'Is Dad going to acknowledge it?' He knew this question would further agonize his mother, but he had to get at some facts.

'I know he's going to deny it,' his mother whispered. 'It doesn't matter what she says around town, because everybody knows she's a bit off. And Richard *doesn't* know – for sure.' She busied herself suddenly with boiling the water.

That answered one question, and raised another. If his father wasn't sure, didn't that mean Irene had a boyfriend or two? But suppose the child was the image of his father and Irene kept on with her story? Arthur saw his mother's hand slip nervously as she poured Four Roses into the two glasses, followed by hot water, sugar and lemon.

'Here,' she said, handing him his.

It tasted good. The first couple of swallows went straight to Arthur's head. 'I'll bet Dad wouldn't have minded an abortion in this case,' he said softly, and laughed.

'Don't be so cruel, Arthur.'

Cruel? He cruel about abortion? Slightly hysterical amusement rose, but he kept a straight face. It was what the girl wanted that mattered, he remembered thinking last year, and now Irene wanted this child.

A door latch opened sharply in the hall, and Arthur braced himself for his father, but it was Robbie, standing suddenly in bare feet and droopy pink pajamas in the doorway, very upright and frowning. 'What's – what's going on? What's he laughing about?'

'Laughing?' said Lois. 'Maybe we were a little loud. I'm sorry, Robbie – that we woke you up.'

'Is Arthur laughing—' Robbie's frown became intense, and he wiped his eyes with the back of his hand vigorously. '—laughing about Irene?' Robbie spoke softly.

'No, Robbie, no,' said their mother. 'Goodness, what's funny about her?'

'Nothing,' said Robbie. 'She's mentally sick. Well – what were you laughing at?' Robbie addressed his brother.

'I forget – now.' Arthur folded his arms in an attitude of boredom at his brother's presence.

'Like a glass of milk, Robbie?' asked Lois.

'No. That chocolate cake, if it's still here,' said Robbie, advancing toward the refrigerator as if the chocolate cake were an objective that he might have to fight for.

Their mother had the cake plate out of the fridge first and found a fork for Robbie.

'How's the hunting going, Robbie?' Arthur asked.

'Not the hunting season now,' he replied, frowning, eating. 'I'm busy. School and stuff.'

'Robbie's going around sometimes with Richard,' Lois said. 'Calling on people, you know?'

'Insurance clients?' Arthur asked.

'N – well, not so much, but the church people. Old people and young people who just want to talk or who have problems,' his mother said.

Silence.

Robbie surely hadn't been with his father on the nights when he crawled into bed with Irene for half an hour, Arthur thought, and just now he didn't feel like smiling at the idea. Did his father keep most of his clothes on? It was disgusting to imagine! And it was absolutely creepy to imagine Irene's whining voice saying, 'Won't you get into bed for me just for a few minutes,' or maybe she'd turn on the tears and say, 'I'll just kill myself or go out on the street if you don't stay with me a little while tonight.' Did prostitutes have real sexual desires? Was his father supposed to give her an orgasm? 'I'll push off, Mom.' Arthur set his glass on the drain board.

Robbie had finished his cake and disappeared.

'Must you, Arthur? Have another half one. The water's still hot.'

Arthur declined.

'You could stay the night,' said his mother. 'Why not, it's so late. Your bed's made up same as ever.'

'No, Mom, it's easy to drive back.' Arthur couldn't bear the atmosphere of the house. If he and his mother had been alone in the house, it would've been a different matter.

His mother went out with him, glancing shyly to right and left as if someone might see her in her dressing gown on the front walk, though the tree-lined streets were deserted and almost black. Even Norma's house light was out.

Then Arthur drove off. His mother had pressed his hand and looked as if she wanted to say something important to him, but she had said merely 'Good night and take care.' Arthur too had wanted to say he was worried about what Robbie might do to Irene. He had had a few seconds ago a premonition that Robbie would hit her in the face with something, or worse.

25

At a quarter past 4 that morning, Arthur was still awake in his bed. He had got up at 3 to drink a can of beer, usually a slight soporific, but he knew that it was one of those nights when he wouldn't sleep at all, even though Frank Costello was not in and probably wouldn't be.

Arthur's thoughts were a mixture of Francey, his father's mess, and Maggie, but the thoughts of his father and Irene were strongest. His mother hadn't wanted to say outright that his father was responsible, yet she certainly had said as much in the course of their talking. It wasn't funny now; it was a tragedy, or a social tragedy or shame, Arthur supposed. One night a few months from now, he and Gus might stop for coffee at the Silver Arrow and Irene wouldn't be there, because she'd be in some hospital, giving birth to a baby who would be his half-brother or half-sister!

This sickening thought made Arthur blink and stare at the ceiling. The corners of his room were becoming visible. He imagined the infant, male or female, a half-wit, frowning with gray eyes, like his father or Robbie. He sat up and turned his bedside lamp on, picked up a chunky microbiology text, and for several minutes flipped the pages, looking for details that he thought might be asked on the final.

The dawn reminded him of waking up here with Francey, or of staying awake with her. What did Irene do in bed? Arthur writhed and put the book down, recalling her awful perfume, and she was thirty if she was a day, but of course thirty would be young to his father. Could his father possibly have been attracted to Irene? How could he have had an ejaculation if some kind of attraction hadn't been there? Incredible! While her sister slept behind some other closed door? Or partition?

His father would deny the child, his mother said, but what was his mother going to say to his grandmother if there was any talk about the child? Arthur imagined a court scene: Irene screaming that Richard Alderman was the father of her child, and a pair of cops strong-arming her out, somebody else putting a straitjacket on her, maybe. It was mad. But could it happen? And if his father was saying to his mother, 'I was in bed with her a couple of times . . .' and not going on from there, then his father was being cowardly. If he wasn't guilty, why was he being vague? His father would know if there had been any men in Irene's life lately, because his father kept such an eye on her and Irene told all her troubles and sins. His father knew, yes or no. That was Arthur's conclusion.

'Oh, Maggie!' Arthur said, and turned over to try to sleep. He had no class until 10.

He awoke to the ringing of the telephone, which seemed part of a dream.

'Hello, Arthur, it's Betty. I'm phoning you early before you go off to classes. Can you come for a drink tonight – or tea, dinner? Or all of those things?'

Arthur glanced at his wristwatch and saw that it was just past 8. 'I'd like to, but just now it's exam time. I'd better stay in tonight, thanks anyway.'

Then he made some strong instant coffee on the hot plate, having fetched fresh water from Frank's empty fruit juice bottles.

Around 9:30, he parked his car deliberately far from the building where his class was, hoping a walk would clear his head.

'Hey! – Hey! You in a daze, Art?' Gus approached him on the steps of Everett Hall.

'Oh, hi, Gus,' Arthur said.

'Had some bad news?' Gus asked. 'Something about Maggie?'

Arthur shook his head. 'Na-a. Just can't wake up this morning.'

Gus invited him to come for dinner on Sunday night, if he felt like it. It was Gus's birthday. Then he loped down the steps on the way to another building.

At just past 5, after his last class, Arthur went to a booth in a downstairs hall and dialed Betty's number. He asked if he could change his mind and come over.

'Of course, Arthur! Soon? Now?'

'Half an hour, all right? . . . Thank you, Betty.'

Arthur drove to his dorm, had a shower and put on a clean shirt. This didn't pick him up much. The day was hot and breezeless, with a faint promise of rain that didn't come, like yesterday. Then Arthur was walking up the curving flagstoned front path of the Brewsters' house, aware of the tall blue spruce to his left on the lawn, of the climbing red rosebush that he had used to tend, now blossoming and looking as happy as ever under Betty's care, or maybe she'd found a part-time gardener.

'Hello, Arthur, come in!' Betty said at the door.

She had set a pitcher of iced tea and half a three-layer chocolate cake on the coffee table, reminding Arthur of Robbie's hunk of cake last evening. Betty asked his news, and Arthur confined his replies to class work and exams.

'And how're your folks?' Betty asked. She wore an embroidered pajama suit of black satin, which Arthur had complimented her on, because it was pretty.

'All right, thanks. Saw my mother last night.'

'And – your brother?'

Maybe Betty had forgotten his name. 'Robbie. Same as ever. Skinny and getting taller. – He doesn't talk much.'

'I remember you saying that. – You're not looking very cheerful, Arthur.'

'Maybe it's the heat. It's great to be here for a while.' He meant in the Brewsters' air-conditioning, and he was sure Betty understood.

'You know, if that dorm's getting you down—' Betty smiled. 'I've heard about those dorms! You really are welcome here. Think about next fall. Long way off, but think about it.'

Betty's words felt like a prison sentence: next fall. And the year after that. Arthur had hoped to get a small lift from merely entering the house, but he hadn't. The staircase with its pretty banister, every picture on the wall, recalled Maggie and at the same time shut him off from her.

'Why don't you stay for some dinner, Arthur? Just a cold snack, potato salad and some cold meat. It'd do you good. I think you've lost weight.'

'I did, but I'm gaining it back.'

'Any plans for this summer?'

Arthur at once thought of diving into some cool lake and not coming up. 'I'll find a summer job – set some money aside. – Haven't been thinking too much about it.' He rolled his glass between his hands, feeling awkward.

'I'm such a fool! Where're you even going to *be* this summer, Arthur?'

'There's a dorm arrangement students can make. Not difficult.'

Betty continued to look at him with concern.

'How's Maggie? What's she doing this summer?'

'Ah. Well, Maggie's decided not to come home till mid-July. She's going somewhere in Massachusetts. With her new friend. For two weeks, anyway, she says. We'll see.'

Arthur felt as if another missile had hit him. His ears rang, as if they were full of little bells. That was a prelude to a faint. 'Yep,' Arthur said meaninglessly. He started to get up, sat down again, then stood up. 'I really should be taking off.'

'Now I've said the wrong thing. But you asked about Maggie.' Betty had not risen from the other sofa opposite the coffee table. 'Now listen, Arthur.'

These things happen, Arthur expected.

'You've got good friends – in me and Warren. How do we – all of us – know what Maggie's going to do? Finally?'

She's no doubt sleeping with Hargiss since Easter, Arthur was thinking. Arthur pressed his nails into his thumb and stood listening politely.

'There're other girls in the world. It never seems as if there are, I know. You mustn't torture yourself, Arthur.'

He nodded, and moved toward the door.

Then Betty got up.

Arthur thought, with a blaze of shame, that it would be a matter of weeks, maybe only days, before the Irene story got around town.

Betty's hand was on his left shoulder. 'You won't change your mind and stay? Please?'

He shook his head. 'Thanks, Betty. And thanks for the tea.'

He went to his car and didn't look back at the Brewster house. He went back to the dorm, where as luck would have it, Frank was in, with his cassette blaring rock.

The added annoyance of lousy loud music just didn't matter that evening, and the music was going to go on until Frank's departure for the night's fun, probably 10 p.m. The room smelled of pot. Arthur took still another shower, put on pajama pants, and settled down on his bed to try it for another hour: facts. He reviewed DNA, a pet subject of Professor Jurgens, and Arthur paid attention to spelling because Jurgens was a stickler. After twenty minutes, Arthur's thoughts had changed, and for the better. He was going to pass his exams with ease. Half the students at C.U. were plain lazy, Arthur had noticed, variations of Frank Costello, and *they* passed. Arthur had braced himself for higher standards. 'Minorities' simply couldn't be flunked out, Arthur had been told by other students, and he also had observed it himself. Students who showed the minimum of effort or will were allowed to scrape by, even praised.

This made him think of his grandmother. What had she written in her last letter? Something quite cheering. He had forgotten her exact phrases, her nice adjectives, but the idea was that she thought he was doing well and that she was proud of him. Arthur remembered: '. . . a pity Richard can't be a more concerned father now when you need one, instead of spending so much time with those drifters and failures whom he may never help to any extent . . .'

Arthur's first exam was physics on the Friday of that week. He rated himself as passing, and pretty well. At half past 5, when Arthur had been in his dorm room for about fifteen minutes, the telephone rang. The fellow in the adjacent room answered before Arthur could. Frank Costello was face down asleep on his bed.

'Who?' Arthur heard the next room say. 'Oh, yeah, just a minute.'

The swivel platform turned toward Arthur.

'Hello, Arthur, it's me,' said his mother's voice. 'Are you all right?'

'Sure, Mom. And you?'

'I sup-pose. Just wanted to know if you got through your exam all right. You had the first today, didn't you?'

'Physics. Just got out. – You by yourself?'

'Yes.'

Arthur could tell she was worried about something. 'What's the latest? Any more peeps out of – you know, Irene?' He said the name softly, hating it.

'No, not a word.'

'Good. And Robbie – He still doesn't know?'

'Arthur, it's not a matter of knowing – for sure. How can anyone believe what she says?'

'All right, I meant her story,' Arthur replied rather sharply. 'You can believe what Dad says, yes or no. Can't you?'

'Things are not so simple.'

Why weren't they, Arthur wondered. 'Where's Robbie?'

'Oh, tonight's his poker night, and he got started early. He went over to Jeff's to have dinner. The game's at Jeff's tonight. Why not come over here for some dinner, Arthur?'

Arthur hesitated. 'Well, Dad's there, isn't he?'

'He will be, yes.'

'Then I don't want to come, Mom, thanks.'

When Arthur hung up, he had a few minutes of black depression.

Saturday afternoon, Arthur had a glimpse of the fellow he supposed was Francey's boyfriend. This was in a snack place called The Dungeon on a street near the campus, popular for its hamburgers and doughnuts and because it stayed open till 1 a.m. Arthur had entered and walked down its two steps onto its floor, when he saw Francey in a booth on his left, smiling at a fellow with short, wavy blond hair, whose face Arthur couldn't see. Her radiant expression, her bright eyes – extra bright then – reminded him of a few happy moments with her, just after they'd made love, even. Arthur turned and left The Dungeon, glad that Francey hadn't seen him.

Frank had slept for something like sixteen hours and wanted to engage Arthur in conversation. 'What's all this studying *about*? – When you come out, y'know – and there's no jobs and – Why make life more boring? Grinding away like you?'

At that moment, life was boring, even maddening, and not just because of Frank Costello swaying pink-eyed in the middle of the room. 'Yep,' said Arthur, leaning back in his straight chair to ease his shoulders.

'Don't you ever think about it? I start – feeling on the side of the blacks. *They* know what they're in for – nothin'. *But*—' Frank said with the air of someone about to make a big pronouncement, 'they've got music, no? That's something and that's plenty. They're geniuses at *that*. When I piss outa this factory here, I'm heading for New York – maybe just for two weeks, till my five hundred bucks runs out. That's all I can get out of my dad, I'm sure, but I'm gonna try my luck there – doin' something hangin' around music. Y'know?' Frank was barefoot and topless, wearing pajama pants now. 'Mind if I sit down?' he asked, indicating Arthur's bed.

'I do just now – because I have to keep on with this stuff here, honestly.'

Frank nodded, disappointed. 'Mind if I take one of your beers? I can replace it.'

'Help yourself,' Arthur said, and bent over his notes again.

Frank popped the can open and swigged. 'Mm-m. – Good when it's cold. – I'm sorry I said you were old-fashioned. I didn't—'

'Oh, never mind,' Arthur mumbled, hoping Frank would just go away. Frank had never called him old-fashioned, except by implication, whereas Arthur thought Frank was unbelievably old-fashioned, the rah-rah college type that had died out with the dinosaur, even before his father's generation.

Luckily, Frank elected to go out that evening. There had been much telephoning, and Arthur had feared Frank was organizing a little party to be held in the room, but finally he departed. Arthur relaxed, stood up and stretched, and decided to go down to Hamilton Hall's 'living room,' where there was a TV. He wanted to forget about microbiology for ten minutes. The news was on, and it was about Reagan's big budget demands for armaments, defense. Arthur had heard it before, and it seemed to get bigger every time he heard it. Some students, perhaps political science majors, were taking notes. Arthur went out for a short walk, ate something in the dorm cafeteria, and was back at his books when the telephone rang at 10. It was the third time the phone had rung since Frank's departure, and Arthur supposed it was again for Frank.

'Hello, Arthur. Me again – bothering you,' his mother said.

'No, Mom. You're not bothering me. Frank's out tonight, which is nice. How're things with you?'

'Oh-h – the same. Richard's out this evening and so's Robbie – again. Not enough poker *last* night, it seems.'

'Dad's with a client?' Arthur had a vision of his father calling on Irene Langley, bringing a small bouquet, maybe a religious magazine, too.

'Yes. Two clients, he said. – I don't suppose you'd like to come for Sunday dinner tomorrow.'

'Are you going to church?' Arthur thought he might visit his mother while his father and Robbie were at church.

'Not sure. Once in a while I duck out, you know, because I really do have work to do for the Home. Not sure about tomorrow. Anyway, we're home by twelve-thirty, as you know.'

Arthur certainly did not want to come for Sunday dinner with his father staring into space and Robbie hostile. 'Well, Mom, frankly – what fun is it?'

His mother's silence was painful to him.

'I could invite *you* out for lunch Sunday, Mom.'

'Oh, not now with your exams coming up.'

'Sure, Mom! Please. Of course I can spare a couple of hours!'

But that didn't work out. His mother was in the habit of preparing Sunday dinner, after church, Arthur didn't have to be reminded of that, and it was like an ironbound duty.

'Next Friday's my last exam, Mom ... Yes, two on Tuesday. After Friday life'll be better.'

Arthur drifted to the hot plate on the fridge to boil water

for coffee. He felt uneasy, because his mother was uneasy and unhappy. His grandmother ought to visit again soon, because her visits always picked his mother up. His grandma could smile at Robbie and his father, though maybe behind their backs. Anyway, Joan didn't let them get her down. The next time he wrote his grandma, he would ask how soon she could come for a visit. And why not write her tonight?

The words sped off his typewriter, and it was the happiest break of the day.

> . . . Mom seems depressed, don't know from what. Maybe she's tired. But I know a visit from you would cheer her up and me too!
>
> I wonder how many are in your school now? 80?
>
> Exam time just now. I am anxious, but some people say anxiety is healthy. I think I'll pass everything, even French.
>
> Love from your diligent (just now)
> grandson Arthur

Arthur felt better, though he hadn't mentioned something that he might have mentioned to his grandmother: that he didn't know what he was going to do with his summer or even where he would be living. He might visit his grandmother, because she had a spare room in her apartment. He might be able to find a summer job in Kansas City, or he might work for his grandmother, doing odd jobs for which she wouldn't have to pay him, though she probably would. At any rate, he didn't want to hang around a ghostly campus all summer, knowing that he would have to look at the same scene next September.

26

Arthur slept late on Sunday morning. Frank's bed was empty and unmade. He hoped Frank stayed away all day.

Gus Warylsky phoned just before noon. Would Arthur like to come over at twelve-thirty for lunch? Then go swimming with him and Veronica in the Grove Park pool? 'Do ya *good*! I'm taking the whole day off.' It was Gus's birthday, Arthur remembered. Arthur was tempted, but he had the room alone now, and his swim shorts were at home. He declined, but promised to turn up that evening for dinner.

Then he felt guilty, as if he'd done the unfriendly thing to Gus.

By 4, Frank still hadn't come in, and Arthur had done a good four hours' work on three subjects. He took his biological terms book to his bed and lay browsing in it until he fell asleep.

The telephone awakened him, and he leapt up, staggering.

'Hello, *Arthur*,' said his mother. 'What're you doing? – Can you come over?' Her voice shook slightly.

'Well – yes, Mom. What's the matter?' For an instant, he imagined that Irene had turned up, that his mother couldn't handle her, or that his father wouldn't throw her out of the house.

'I'm worried.'

'Irene's not there, is she?'

'No! Oh, no. But can you come?' Her voice was soft, as if she didn't want to be overheard.

'Now.'

'Yes, now.'

'Absolutely, Mom. See you.' He hung up, and put on his sneakers.

Maybe Richard and Robbie were having a quarrel, but about what, since they always agreed with each other? Or were they both arguing with his mother? More likely. Or had his father spilled more beans? Or was he overanxious, Arthur thought, as he turned the last curve into West Maple.

Just as Arthur pulled his handbrake in the driveway, he heard two loud noises – *blam-blam* – and his first thought was that a couple of his tires had blown. But the sounds had come from the house. Arthur ran to the front door, which he found unlocked. He heard his mother – and it was a short scream that he heard.

'Arthur!' His mother ran toward him from the living room.

Arthur caught the scent of gun smoke. His mother grabbed his hand.

Robbie stalked across the living room with a shotgun upright in his hand, and he clumped its stock once on the floor. Robbie looked blank-eyed and grim. 'S-s – f—' Whatever he was trying to say, he couldn't get it out.

Arthur went past Robbie toward the study, dragging his mother with him, because she still clung to his hand. He saw his father on his back on the floor of the study. His jaw and neck were red with blood, as was the top part of his striped shirt.

'Dad!' Arthur bent over him, but drew his hand back before he touched him. The front of his father's throat looked torn away, and also part of his jaw. Blood flowed into the green carpet.

Spatters of blood on his father's desk caught Arthur's eye as he straightened.

'We've got to call a doctor!' said his mother.

'He's dead, Mom.' Arthur turned away from his father's fixed gray eyes. 'Useless, Mom.'

His mother snatched her hand away from Arthur's. 'They were arguing here for half an *hour*!'

Arthur looked at his brother, who was still standing in the middle of the living room floor, his gun butt down on the carpet, his right hand gripping the double barrel. Robbie was breathing through his mouth, looking at Arthur, but with no expression at all on his face.

'Is he dead, Arthur? Shall we call the doctor?'

'Oh, Mom, he is dead. But I'll call a doctor, sure!' Arthur led her past Robbie to the sofa, but his mother would not sit.

There were three quick raps at the front door.

Robbie snuffled and wiped his nose with the back of his hand.

Someone came in. It was Norma Keer.

'Hello, Arthur! What happened? I thought I heard a gun go off!' She glanced at Robbie and frowned. 'Say, what's going on?'

'*Telephone!*' said his mother to Arthur. '*Get* somebody!'

Norma came into the living room, and Robbie walked past her toward the hall, as if he didn't see her.

'My father was shot,' Arthur said.

Norma's bulging eyes got rounder. 'You don't mean it! Where is he? You mean in the yard?'

'No. In there, yes,' Arthur said, because Norma was walking toward the study which had a door onto the backyard. 'Mom, let me go! I'll phone.'

'Oh, my goodness! – Oh, dear *heavens*!' Norma cried.

Arthur went to the study door where Norma stood, as if drawn by some need to see his father's corpse once more, to be sure he was dead. Now Arthur noticed that his father's blue trousers were damp between the legs. 'I know he's dead. I should call for an ambulance, shouldn't I, Norma?'

'Oh, yes, Arthur, yes. – Two shots! I heard them! – Shall I phone for you, Arthur?'

'No. Thanks.' Arthur went to the telephone, too shaken to look for the nearest hospital's number, but EMERGENCY was printed on the first page of the directory, and Arthur dialed the number beside it. 'Hello, I need an ambulance. Now.'

'Name and address, please?'

Arthur gave this information.

Still trembling, his mother stood listening to him. Then, when he put the telephone down, she turned to the study door, walked past Norma and knelt by his father's body. She put her hand on his shirt-front, over his heart. Her other hand pressed his father's left hand, which lay on the carpet. 'He's even cool, I think,' his mother said. 'They say – Maybe a blanket—'

'Oh, *Mom*!'

'The gun went off by accident?' Norma asked Arthur in a whisper. 'What happened?'

'Robbie shot him,' Arthur said.

Norma's mouth fell open. 'You don't mean it!'

'Didn't you hear them quarreling?' his mother asked. 'They were quarreling half an hour. Yelling finally!'

'Didn't hear them,' said Norma. 'But then my TV was on.'

They were in the living room now, but near the study door. Arthur took a step farther from the study door and glanced toward the hall, anxious, even afraid of Robbie's return. Robbie had a gun, and he was out of his mind. Was he reloading his gun back there in his room?

'Back in a minute, Mom.' Arthur went off quietly to the hall.

Robbie's room door was closed. Arthur knocked, twice and slowly, acutely aware just now that Robbie detested him.

'Who's there?'

'Arthur.'

Robbie didn't answer.

Arthur did not want to retreat, to leave it to somebody else to open the door, so he turned the knob and took a step in.

Robbie was sitting on the edge of his bed with the gun lying across his skinny thighs, his right hand gripping the wooden stock.

'Did you load that thing again?'

'No.' Robbie looked at Arthur, frowning.

Arthur heard the distant whine of a siren. He lunged forward suddenly and seized the gun at the middle of its long barrels, and as Robbie held on to the stock, Arthur jerked it away from him. 'You gone *nuts?*'

'Dad deserved it!' Robbie replied, looking straight at Arthur with his pale, metal-like eyes.

'Oh?' Arthur suddenly understood or thought he did. 'Y-you talking about Irene?'

'Yep.'

Arthur was holding the gun in a position to fend off Robbie with it in case he jumped up and tried to take it from him. He went out with the gun and closed the door.

Through the kitchen window, Arthur saw an ambulance pulling up to the edge of the lawn, a long white car with a blue light on top. Arthur set the gun in a corner in the hall, left of the row of hooks that held jackets. 'I'll get it, Mom,' he said, and opened the front door.

'This right? Alderman?' said a man in white trousers and white short-sleeved shirt.

Arthur nodded, stepping aside.

Another young man, also in white, came briskly up the front walk, carrying a doctor's bag.

Arthur made a gesture to indicate the direction of the study; the first intern went in and stooped beside his father's body and felt for a few seconds for a pulse in the wrist.

'How did this happen?' The intern was addressing Arthur and Norma who stood in the doorway. 'Accident? Suicide?'

'He was shot,' Arthur said.

'Family thing?'

'Yes,' Arthur said.

'Got to get the police, so we can't move him for the moment,' said the black-haired young intern, and went past Arthur and Norma into the living room. 'No stretcher yet!' he shouted toward the front door. 'Got to get the police. May I use your phone?'

'Sure,' said Arthur.

Norma said to Arthur, 'Maybe you want me out of the way, but I'll stay just a minute.' She beckoned Arthur toward the kitchen. 'Where's your scotch, Arthur? Your mother could use a little. It'll calm her.'

Arthur opened the lower left cabinet door, where there was always a bottle of something. He found some Cutty Sark and poured some into two glasses, then a third, for himself. He took one glass to his mother, who was still standing in the living room, looking glassy-eyed and helpless in a way that wrung Arthur's heart. She was listening to the intern, or at least looking at him; then the intern put the phone down.

'Really drink this, Mom,' Arthur said. 'And sit down.'

'What's Robbie doing?' she asked.

'Just sitting on his bed.' Arthur looked at his mother's pale and stricken face. 'I got his gun away. Don't worry, Mom.'

His mother winced at the sharpness of the straight scotch. Arthur drew her toward the kitchen, because the interns were going back and forth in the living room, and another was on the telephone now.

'Sit down, Lois.' Norma pulled out a straight chair from the table. She had to press Lois's shoulders to make her sit. 'What on earth got into *Robbie*?' Norma asked in a whisper.

Lois shut her eyes tightly and did not answer.

'Where is he? In his room?' Norma looked at Arthur.

Arthur was glad Norma was with them. 'In his room – just sitting.' Arthur looked at Robbie's room door, which he could barely see, and had a sudden impulse to go in and beat Robbie to a pulp. But the cops would take care of that. Little Robbie was going to be whisked away, in just a few minutes.

The police had arrived. These were two men in short sleeves with guns on their hips. They spoke to the interns as if they knew them personally, before they crossed the living room to look into the study. A third policeman entered the house. They had left the front door wide open. One of the first two policemen came into the kitchen and pulled a notebook from a back pocket.

'Afternoon – ma'am,' he said, not knowing which woman to address.

'My mother,' Arthur said, indicating Lois.

'Family quarrel?' asked the policeman. 'Who's re—'

'My brother,' Arthur said. 'He's in his room. There.' Arthur pointed toward the hall.

The cop looked suddenly more alert. 'Is he still armed?'

'No. Has he got another gun there, Mom? – Mom?'

'I don't know,' said his mother.

'How old is he?' asked the cop.

'Fifteen.'

The policeman went to consult with his colleagues in the living room.

Arthur heard the clicks of a camera working in his father's study. Now he saw a man in plain clothes rising to his feet after having measured something on the floor with a tape.

Then two policemen went into the hall. Arthur pointed out the door. The first policeman had drawn his gun; the second had his hand on his gun. The first policeman knocked with his free hand and at once tried the doorknob. The door was not locked. Arthur heard some of their words.

'... okay, do you want to come with us? ... Yes, Louey, go ahead ... What's your name?'

'What's this for?' Robbie murmured.

'... tell us your name?'

Click. Handcuffs, Arthur thought, and that was true, he saw, as the three came out of Robbie's room, one cop in front of Robbie, the other behind him. Robbie's wrists were locked together in front of him, and Robbie scowled. Then there was an awkward moment as the three of them had to back into the living room to let the interns pass into the front hall with his father's body on a stretcher. One gasped with the weight or the heat, and they bumped the stretcher against the partition between hall and kitchen. The body was in a gray sack. The interns carried it out into the sunlight and away.

The policeman with the notebook entered the kitchen and informed Arthur and his mother that Robert would be taken to juvenile detention center today, not a prison, because he was under sixteen.

'We'll leave you the address and telephone number. Just now, I have to ask you a few questions.' He looked more hopefully at Arthur. 'You were here when it happened?'

'No. I'd just got here – got to the driveway. Then I heard the shots.' Arthur saw, behind the policeman, another policeman bending toward the shotgun that leaned against the hall door.

'That's right,' Norma said. 'I live just next door. I heard the shots and I looked out my window. I saw Arthur just getting out of his car in the driveway.'

The time? Arthur and Norma estimated twenty past 4. Witnesses? Lois confirmed that she had seen her son fire the gun.

'Tommy?' the policeman with Robbie interrupted. 'Any idea how long you'll be?'

'Oh, five minutes. Go ahead with him.'

The policeman with Robbie urged him toward the front door.

Robbie squirmed, but looked hardly more annoyed than when their mother asked him to wash his hands before a meal.

Lois jumped up suddenly. 'Robbie!' But she didn't touch Robbie, as if the policeman's presence somehow prevented her. 'Robbie, *I* just can't believe this has *happened*!'

'Well, it did. – My father told me the truth,' Robbie said. 'He told me because I asked him.'

'You'll be able to talk with him later, ma'am,' said the officer with Robbie.

Lois looked confused. 'Doesn't he need—'

Arthur took his mother's hand and held on to it. 'They'll give him whatever he needs, Mom.' She had been going to pack a kit for him, Arthur supposed.

Then Robbie was out of the house, and the policeman in the kitchen sat down at the table where Robbie usually sat. The policeman asked what Robbie and his father had been quarreling about, but asked it in a way that sounded as if it didn't matter too much. He got no answer from Arthur's mother, at any rate, because she said she didn't know.

'Then after a few minutes,' Lois told the policeman, 'Robbie went to his room and came back with his gun. I saw him, but it was too late. I couldn't stop him. I'd already called my son – to come – because I felt something awful was going to happen.'

The policeman took his parents' names, and Robbie's and Arthur's, even Norma's plus her address. Then the policeman asked his mother to come with him into the study. Arthur drifted into the living room, but did not go farther, because they wanted his mother's answers. He watched his mother pointing to where Robbie had stood and saw the policeman turn his gaze to the shotgun pellet marks in the wall. The policeman carefully avoided treading on the stain on the carpet. The plainclothesman, who Arthur supposed was a detective, and the cameraman were still at work. Then the policeman told Arthur and his mother that the body would go to the city morgue, and that tomorrow morning Mrs Alderman would be free to make funeral arrangements.

'This is the morgue number you can call, ma'am, and if you don't by noon tomorrow, we'll call you. – Would you like us to get a doctor for you now to give you a sedative? Something like that? Sometimes helps.'

Lois didn't answer, and Norma said: 'I'll stay with her for a while. If she needs anything, we'll telephone Dr Swithers.'

Then the front door closed, and the house was empty except for Lois, Norma and himself. Norma said something about making tea and found the kettle. Arthur crossed the living room to his father's study, whose door was open. He had meant only to close the door, so his mother wouldn't have to look at the carpet, but he stood for a few seconds looking at the spot where his father's body had lain on its back, with right leg bent at the knee, arms splayed, with the sunken disaster where his throat and jaw had been. The wall to Arthur's right showed four or five little pits in its cream-colored wallpaper from the buckshot. Robbie must have been standing on the other side of his father's desk; his father must have been standing, from the height of the wallpaper pits, and then his father had probably taken a couple of steps toward the study door and fallen backward. The patch of dark blood on the green carpet had well-defined edges and its shape reminded Arthur of the outline of France or maybe Alaska. This was something he could take care of, he thought, and went to the kitchen for a bucket and a floor rag.

Norma was urging Lois to sit on the bench; his mother was talking, almost weeping, and Arthur supposed that was all to the good.

He drew cold water at the sink, then returned to the study to attack the carpet. The blood seemed to double itself, and the water in the bucket became deep red. Arthur changed the water in the bathroom tub and started again. The edges looked blurred, but it was hopeless, they'd have to get rid of the carpet, but he supposed what he was doing was an improvement, better than letting the stain stay here for his mother to see and soak into the wood below. The carpet was tacked down. He wiped dried blood from the wood of his father's desk. Arthur changed the water again, forgetting if it was the second or third time, and finally he rinsed the rag and left it in a bucket of cold water in the garage.

'Tea, Arthur. Do you good,' said Norma. 'Another little whiskey, too? You look a little pale.'

'No, I'm fine,' Arthur said, determined to keep on his feet in the kitchen, though his ears were ringing. The blood's *gone*, he told himself, down the drain. A second later, the floor seemed to be moving under his feet, and then he blacked out.

Norma held a wet dish towel against his forehead and wiped his face with it.

'Just lie there for a minute, Arthur. Don't try to get up,' Norma said. 'Perfectly normal,' she added to his mother. 'Poor boy's been . . .'

Arthur wobbled to the living room sofa. Norma insisted that he stretch out and saw to it that he sipped some sweetened tea.

His mother looked pale, refused to lie down anywhere, and kept asking Norma what sounded like unfinished questions:

'Tomorrow? – What time did he say? – I don't think Robbie knew what he was doing, do you? . . . Do you think I should phone my mother, Norma?'

'Not tonight, Lois, honestly. Not now.'

Arthur felt better and sat up. It dawned on him like a miracle that the house was empty of both Richard and Robbie, of Richard permanently, and of Robbie for an undetermined length of time.

'Mom, I'll stay here tonight. Don't you worry. I'll go back to the dorm and get my stuff. Now.'

'You sure you feel all right?' asked Norma, still on her feet in her house-shoes.

'Yes, and I'm going now,' Arthur said, and went to his room. He knew he had an old duffel bag that held quite a lot, and he found this at the back of his closet. 'See you folks in – less than an hour. You'll be here, Norma?'

'You bet I will,' said Norma.

Arthur drove to Hamilton Hall. Frank was not in, which made packing easier, but necessitated a note to Frank, Arthur supposed. He scribbled one and left it on Frank's bed. He looked at his empty half of the room and found himself smiling. He was going home to a house that he loved, to his mother whom he loved, and maybe it was not nice, not normal to be happy with his father gone, dead, and his brother gone, locked up, but he felt happy enough to fly. As usual, the Resident Assistant, a senior student, was not at the desk downstairs, but tomorrow he could tell someone in the Administration Building that he would be living at home for the rest of the school year, a matter of a few days. He got into his car.

At home, Norma told him that one neighbor had called at the door; another had telephoned to ask what was the matter, having noticed the ambulance and the police car.

'They were waiting a decent interval maybe,' said Norma, who seldom had a good word for the neighbors. 'They'd ring the fire department maybe an hour after they saw your house was burning. – Now your mother called up your grandmother, because I couldn't stop her. And you two are to come over to my place for something to eat. Your mother wanted a bath, so that's where she is. See you in a few minutes.'

Arthur carried his things into his room and began to unpack. His writing table was even dusted, he noticed, and no doubt his mother kept it that way. Ah, how sweet to put his American dictionary back in its usual place, to set his Harrap's French dictionary next to it! And at the back of the table his fossilized sea urchins sat in a row as usual.

From the bathroom, Arthur heard occasional splashes, as if his mother were dreamily sponging water onto her shoulders. Arthur took off his T-shirt and washed at the kitchen sink, drying himself with his towel that he had brought from the dorm room. He put on a clean shirt from among the shirts left in a drawer.

Then he and his mother went across the lawn to Norma's house. His mother seemed quiet and thoughtful, but not sad, Arthur thought, not weepy, and not in a daze either. Norma had her table laden with cold cuts, pickles, olives and salad, arranged as for a buffet.

'We can sit or take the plates over to the sofa, as you folks like,' Norma said. 'Iced tea? Beer?'

It was like a party, a surprise party, Arthur felt. He served his mother and made sure she had what she wanted. Arthur found himself laughing loudly, as were Norma and his mother, and an instant later he couldn't recall what they had been laughing at. Amazing, too, that it was already 10 o'clock.

There was a noise at the door, audible through their voices.

'Was that a knock?' Norma asked, and hauled herself from the sofa. 'Who's there?' she called through the door. There was some reply, and Norma opened the door a little.

'Is Richard here by any chance? Richard Alderman?'

Arthur recognized the voice and stood up. 'No,' he said, walking toward the door. 'He's not here.'

Eddie Howell was already inside the door, his smile on. 'Hello, Arthur! I'm Eddie Howell,' he said to Norma. 'Sorry to bother you, but I have a date with Richard tonight, and I saw his car there and lights here, so I thought – Good evening, Lois.'

Lois was on her feet by the sofa.

'My father's dead, Mr Howell,' Arthur said.

Eddie Howell's mouth formed an O-shape.

'He was killed,' Arthur said. 'Around four this afternoon.'

'Killed? – Are you serious?' asked Eddie.

'Yes, it's true,' said Lois behind Arthur. 'My husband was shot. He's dead.'

'Now, Lois, you don't have to deal with this,' said Norma gently.

'Shot by whom?' asked Eddie.

'Robbie shot him,' Arthur replied, and deliberately stood up straighter. 'They had an argument.'

'Argument about what?'

'About Irene Langley?'

'Arthur, do you and Mr Howell want to sit down?' This was from Norma.

'Don't think so, thanks,' Arthur said. 'You know Irene Langley, don't you, Eddie?'

'Yes, sure, she goes to our church.'

'Then you know what she's been talking about – maybe?'

Arthur could see that Eddie did, though he wasn't admitting to it at once. 'Well, I heard – But she's not to be believed all the time, poor woman. She spoke to Robbie?' Eddie asked in a tone of surprise.

'Maybe my father did. So you know about it. Did my father tell you?'

'Oh, no, no, no. – But I sometimes see Irene. I call on her – visit her.'

What a lot of visitors Irene had! 'You sure should've kept it from Robbie,' Arthur said. 'You're a big influence on him. Don't you feel a little responsible for him?'

'No,' said Eddie, looking at Arthur, frowning now. 'He's Richard's son. I had no idea they were quarreling! Richard never said anything about it.'

'Yes, if it weren't for you – people like you,' Lois began.

'Lois, I'm so *sorry* to hear this news!' Eddie extended a hand toward Lois, but didn't quite touch her. 'I spoke with Richard just this morning at church! Robbie, too. They seemed just as usual.'

'If it weren't—'

'Lois, now take it easy.' Norma was hovering uneasily.

Arthur had a glimpse of his mother's taut face, of her eyelids twitching with anger or with the start of tears.

'Robbie was under your power! Like a madman!' Lois said.

'My power?' said Eddie, looking baffled.

'*Somebody's* got to say it,' said Lois. '*You* know what my son was angry about. The same thing you and Richard *and* Robbie, yes, were angry about – about Arthur last summer. Arthur may have got a girl pregnant, but I mean – is it worth a death? That's what it amounts to. *You* should go and talk to Robbie! He thinks he did the right thing!' Lois's voice went shrill, and she shook with sobs, but she still stood upright.

Norma put her arm around Lois's shoulders. 'Lois – now you cry it all out. Won't hurt you.'

'I don't know what *I've* done to cause this,' said Eddie, almost recovering his usual smiling calm.

'Get the hell out,' Arthur muttered to Eddie.

Eddie took a small step backward, toward the door. 'Where is Robbie?'

'Police took him away,' Arthur said. He went past Eddie and opened the door for him.

Eddie hesitated, then called, 'Good night, Lois. Night ma'am,' and went out.

Arthur closed the door after him.

His mother stood with Norma by the sofa, holding a paper napkin to her nose, but she was not weeping.

'Asking me where Robbie is!' said Arthur.

Norma persuaded his mother to sit down. His mother had forgotten her cigarettes, so Arthur crossed the lawn to get them for her from the house. Their telephone was ringing, but Arthur didn't bother answering it. If Norma didn't know about Irene's part in his father's death, she would know now, Arthur thought. And about a girl in connection with him. Would she assume the girl was Maggie? It didn't matter somehow, because Norma was a friend and her friendship was stronger than the rest. Arthur expected a question or two from Norma that evening, but she asked none.

27

The next morning, Monday, the telephone began ringing early. Arthur answered one call around 9.

'This is Bob Cole,' said a rich tenor voice. 'Is that Arthur? . . . Eddie Howell called me last night and told me the sad news. I'm very shocked and saddened, Arthur. Could I possibly have a word with your mother?'

'Yes. Just a minute, I'll call her.' Arthur did, and his mother came in from the bedroom. 'The Reverend Cole now,' Arthur said.

Arthur went out to the backyard, not wanting to hear what his mother said. This morning, he had woken up early, found himself in his familiar old bed, and thought, 'My God, I'm home!' and had imagined his mother coming in with coffee around 8, which was exactly what had happened. His grandmother had telephoned earlier this morning, and she was arriving at 8:30 this evening at Indi Airport. That would be to the good. The detention place where Robbie was being held had telephoned also. They wanted Lois to come this morning and sign some papers, and Arthur had offered to go, but the police wanted his mother. Arthur had taken another look at the study carpet and realized that it had to be thrown away.

'Arthur!' his mother called.

He ran from the toolshed to the back door, which caused him to cross his father's study again. He pulled the study door on the living room shut behind him.

'Betty Brewster,' said Lois, holding the telephone toward him.

'I heard about yesterday from a – a woman friend you don't know, I think,' Betty said. 'I'm absolutely shocked. – As I said to your mother, I'm calling to ask if you need any help. If there's anything I can do. Services.'

'Thanks, Betty. I don't know what my mother said. Can't think of anything. I'm staying here, and my grandma's coming tonight.'

He was glad that Betty didn't ask any reason for Robbie's deed. His mother was still not back from the trip to the place of detention when Arthur left the house at half past 12 for his exam at 1. In Everett Hall, where the exam was, he kept his eyes on the corridor floor as he walked, and was glad that no one he knew approached him or spoke to him. And even this afternoon, the notice about his father's death might not be in the *Herald*, maybe not until tomorrow. When he reached the room where the exam took place, no talking was allowed. The students sat two seats apart, to discourage cheating. Arthur's eyes met those of a boy he knew, who grinned quickly and gave a thumbs-up at Arthur.

Five minutes later, Arthur was in another world. This was the Introduction to Philosophy exam.

Leaving Everett Hall at nearly 4 p.m., Arthur caught a glimpse of Francey, trotting in calf-length cut-off jeans and a red shirt toward a car whose door someone inside the car was holding open for her. The sight of Francey had no effect on him at all. That was just as well. That was even progress.

And tonight his grandma would arrive. That was something to be happy about, fetching her at the airport. Early that morning, his mother had spruced up the spare room, cut some day lilies and put them in a vase, in case the rest of the day would bring too many chores for her to take care of details. Arthur found a note at home.

Back around 5:30. Can you get three steaks out of freezer? In mad hurry at after 1.

His mother had gone to the Home this afternoon as usual. Rovy was making gentle noises in his 'I am hungry' voice and rubbing his length against Arthur's legs. Arthur fed him, then took three steaks from the freezer and put them on a big wooden chopping board which he stuck in the oven, out of Rovy's reach.

'Rovy, do you realize we're alone, alone, *alone*?' Arthur said to the cat.

No reply from Rovy to this. His hunched, brindled body jerked as he dived into his food.

At half past 5, his mother's car crept up in the driveway. What were they going to do with his father's car? Sell the damned thing, Arthur hoped, though it was the best of the three cars now. Arthur didn't want to touch it or drive it, ever. His mother came into the kitchen by way of the garage door.

'Hi, Mom! I just made coffee. Want some?'

'Yes. Whew!' She had two big blue ledgers from the Home in her arms.

'How was it? Why'd you go to the Home today, Mom? – Did you see Robbie?' Arthur was curious about Robbie, despite himself.

'Yes. Must wash my hands.' She went off to the bathroom.

Arthur poured the coffee.

'Yes, Robbie,' his mother said, coming back. 'He was in a room with three or four other boys – reading magazines.'

'Well,' Arthur said. 'Magazines. – Where is this place?'

'It's a building behind the main police headquarters here. This is temporary. Then he'll go to another place near Indi.' His mother spoke carefully, stirring her coffee.

Arthur waited patiently for her to say more.

'At the other place, they'll have some kind of hearing in something like a juvenile court. Maybe even at this place, I don't know.'

'Well – did Robbie say anything more to you?'

'No, almost nothing,' his mother replied promptly. 'He seemed not the least bit sorry, you know? Or even sad.'

Arthur could imagine.

'Then I went to where Richard is,' said his mother, staring at the table, and now tears started in her eyes. 'I had to go there – after seeing Robbie.'

Arthur writhed. 'Mom, why didn't you phone me this morning and I'd have gone with you? I was here!'

'I didn't have to *see* Richard, but I had to sign some papers. One of them was for the funeral home – Gregson, you know. And I agreed that the funeral should be tomorrow. At eleven. I spoke with them. I really don't feel like notifying anybody.' She bowed her head.

'Don't drink any more coffee, Mom. Go and take a nap. I can make dinner – start it before I go off at seven-fifteen for Grandma. – Don't worry about anything.'

'I don't think we have to send a telegram to Richard's brother Stephen, do you? I'll write to him. They weren't – close.'

'No, Mom.' Arthur hardly remembered his uncle Stephen whom he had met when he was about ten and who lived in Washington State. Suddenly Arthur thought of the *Herald*, which must have been dropped in the mailbox as usual around 2 p.m.

Just then, the telephone rang, and Arthur answered. It was a woman whose name he vaguely knew, offering her sympathies. Arthur said that his mother was resting now and thanked her on behalf of his mother. Then he went to the mailbox beside the front door, which held two letters and the *Chalmerston Herald*.

His father's picture was on the front page, in a single column at the bottom, an old picture of him looking about thirty-five in a white shirt and tie and dark suit, square-faced, sturdy, faintly smiling. Where had they got that picture from?

> ... insurance and retirement benefit representative of Heritage Life was fatally shot Sunday afternoon by his son Robert, 15, according to police, in his home on West Maple Street ...

From the way it was written, it might have been an accident. Arthur took the newspaper to his room, hoping his mother wouldn't miss it and ask for it. His mother had gone into the bedroom to rest, but when he looked through the half-open door, he saw his mother stooped by the chest of drawers.

'I wanted to put away some more of Richard's things before Mama comes.'

'Mom, you put away enough this morning! – Now stop, so you won't feel tired later.' Arthur watched her drift toward the double bed and wilt. She lay on it face down, and Arthur closed the door gently.

The living room already looked slightly different: His mother had removed his father's old tweed jacket, which so often hung on a straight chair near the study, and his pipe-rack, which he seldom used. Arthur set the table in the kitchen. The telephone rang as he was peeling potatoes.

'Damn,' he said, and went to answer it.

'Hello. It's Irene,' said a wailing voice. 'I just wanted—'

'We're busy here just now. Sorry, I've—'

'Can I speak with your mother? I'd—'

Arthur hung up. Then he lifted the telephone off the hook, so his mother's nap wouldn't be disturbed. It was time he left the house for Indi Airport.

'I most certainly will go and see Robbie,' his grandmother said as they were driving toward Chalmerston.

'I hope he's pleasant to you,' Arthur said.

'To me? What do you mean?'

'He's all clammed up now.' Arthur frowned at the road as he drove.

'What were they quarreling *about*? Do you know?'

'I don't know,' Arthur said. 'I wasn't there.'

At home, the scene was almost convincingly cheerful for several minutes. Hugs and kisses, his grandmother opening her suitcase in the spare room, then drinks in the living room while Arthur carried on making dinner.

'... quarreling. This was Sunday afternoon,' his mother's voice said. 'Well, I may as well tell you now, because Robbie will. Do you remember Irene Langley? Christmas with her sister?'

Arthur tried not to hear it and deliberately tossed a big cooking spoon into the sink, making a clatter.

'Oh, *no*, Lois!' said his grandmother.

Arthur put the steaks on, looked at his watch, then went into the living room.

'But what did Richard *say*?' His grandmother was sitting on the sofa, upright with attention.

'I found him vague,' his mother replied. 'I know I – I don't want to believe it.'

His grandmother shook her head. 'And how much is she going to talk around town? – That's a very unpleasant side of it.'

Arthur gave his grandmother a sign that dinner was ready.

Joan got up and put an arm around Lois's shoulder, kissed her cheek. 'Lois, darling, what a time for you! Arthur says dinner's ready. Let's forget all about this for a few minutes.'

After dinner, though it was rather late, his grandmother proposed coffee in the living room, as usual.

'You've got to turn in early, haven't you, Arthur?' his grandmother asked. 'Exam tomorrow?'

'Yes, two of 'em.'

'Happy to be home?'

'Oh – *am* I!'

Then his grandmother frowned as she sipped her coffee. 'I can see Robbie before eleven, don't you think. Loey? No difficulties about seeing him, are there?'

'Shouldn't think so.'

'Maybe he'll want to come with us to the funeral? Would that be allowed?'

Lois hesitated. 'Hadn't thought about it. I'm sure it would be allowed—'

The telephone rang. Arthur let his mother answer, because it was probably one of his mother's friends. Arthur didn't even listen as his mother said a few phrases. Then she said:

'Arthur? It's Maggie.' His mother extended the telephone toward him.

'*Maggie?*' Arthur took the telephone. 'H'lo?'

'Hello, Arthur.' Maggie seemed to sigh. 'My mother just phoned me. She said your father – well, that—'

'Yes.' Arthur shut his eyes and was glad his mother and grandmother had drifted off to the kitchen.

'She said it was in the paper that Robbie shot him. How awful, Arthur! It was an accident?'

'No.'

'My *gosh*! – I won't ask why just now, but I wanted to say that I'm very sorry. – You're home now? Staying?'

'Yep.' Arthur wanted to cut through the rubbish and say, *I love you, Maggie, the same as always*, even though she might reply, *I'm sorry about that*. 'Y-you're not coming home this summer, I heard.'

'Probably not, that's true. Maybe very late this summer, the way things look ... Will you give my love to your mother and your grandmother, too? Your mother said she's there.'

When they hung up, he had still not said *I love you*, for which he reproached himself, then in the next instant he wondered if it hadn't been wiser that he hadn't said it? Mightn't it have bored her? Girls always knew anyway, he had read somewhere. His grandmother did not come in to see him at bedtime. She and his mother were talking quietly in the living room until very late.

The next morning, Arthur left the house before 9 for the microbio exam, which began at 9:30. His mother and grandmother had already gone, on their way to Robbie's present place of detention, and this was to be followed by the funeral at 11. Arthur was glad that his grandmother hadn't brought up his attending the funeral, maybe by trying to postpone his exam, which might not have been possible anyway. Arthur simply didn't want to go to his father's funeral and listen to a lot of phony words from Bob Cole. He thought it more than likely that Irene Langley would turn up at the service in the First Church of Christ Gospel, then ride in one of the limousines to the cemetery called Greenhills on the west side of town. Arthur spat into a hedge before he leapt up the steps of Everett Hall.

When he returned home at nearly noon, his mother and grandmother were not back. They would have had to linger and talk after the funeral, he supposed. Arthur dearly wanted a beer and there were plenty in the fridge, but he was afraid of being sleepy or muddleheaded for the French exam at 2 if he drank one, so he took a shower instead. Under the shower, he thought, while he had been writing a paragraph on DNA at 11:30, his father had been lowered into the grave, the clods of earth had begun to fall on the coffin top. His father had talked so much about a soul, yet his body of course had to be disposed of like anyone's else's, like a dog's or a cat's, and eventually the worms would get at it, despite the quality of the coffin. But that wasn't the important thing: His father had died in disgrace, or at least for a disgraceful reason. Even his mother must have been thinking, as his coffin sank into the ground, that Richard's death needn't have been, except for Robbie's anger and the reason for that anger.

By the time Arthur had dressed in the bathroom, the two had returned. And it occurred to him suddenly that there was usually food and drink after a funeral at the house of the deceased. Wasn't there? But not in his father's case.

'Hello, Arthur. – And how was the exam?' His mother asked in a tired voice.

'Went okay.'

His grandmother was silent. She wore a purple summer dress and a black shawl around her shoulders, which she had probably put over her head in church and at the funeral. She removed the shawl and folded it twice.

'And the funeral – did you take Robbie?' Arthur asked.

'He could've gone. He didn't want to go,' said his mother.

There were a few seconds of silence.

'Well – shall I do something about lunch, Mom? I have to take off just after one. French this afternoon.'

'I know, dear. I'll fix something for us. – Just want to get out of these shoes first.' She went to the bedroom.

Arthur set the table for three, not caring if he ate a bite standing up. 'Hope Irene wasn't at the funeral,' Arthur said softly to his grandmother.

'She was. Weeping. Real tears, I saw them. Still – as I said to your mother, I had the feeling she hadn't talked all over town. Didn't you think that, too, Lois?' she asked as his mother came back.

'You wouldn't be able to tell. People wouldn't let on – not at the funeral.'

'You saw Robbie, too, Mom?' Arthur asked.

'For a minute. Then Mama talked with him in his room. I think Mama's a little surprised.'

'He was so cold,' said his grandmother. 'He's like a changed boy. And then maybe he isn't.'

'Just said, "I don't want to go to the funeral"? Something like that?' Arthur asked.

'Yes,' said his grandmother. 'And he said he thought – what he had done was right. Was *right*. He is a changed boy.'

Arthur sipped a glass of milk and glanced at his wristwatch. He felt sorry for his grandmother.

'And he doesn't seem to mind at all being where he is,' his grandmother said. 'He talked about joining the Marines later.' She tried to smile.

'How long's he going to be where he is, Mom?'

'Couple of days, I gathered. Something about a psychiatrist talking to him; then there's a hearing.' His mother was putting some warm corned beef hash on the table.

'He told me,' said Joan, 'that your father made a confession to him about Irene. And then he knew what he ought to do.'

Arthur felt a shock, as if he had not known this before. 'Sunday?'

'Yes, after midday dinner. Robbie told me Irene spoke to him on the telephone Saturday, but she'd told Richard long before.'

Arthur looked at his mother. 'Robbie didn't say anything to you Saturday?'

'No!' said his mother. 'I remember now, Richard and I were out for a couple of hours shopping Saturday afternoon.'

'And he went to church on Sunday?' Arthur asked, amazed, but only for an instant, because his brother of course would go to church, no matter what.

'Yes,' said his mother, 'and I didn't notice any difference at all the – in the way he acted with Richard.'

Arthur slid around the bench seat, past the place where Robbie usually sat. 'Better be going, Mom – if you'll excuse me.' Arthur tapped his pants pocket to make sure he had his car keys.

'Yes, and you know Robbie told me, Arthur,' said his grandmother, looking at him, 'that what his father had said was so awful, he didn't want to tell his mother. So he just gave him the correct punishment, he said.' Then she crumpled, or her face did, and she closed her eyes to stop the tears.

In his grandmother's chin, illuminated by the sunshine that came through the kitchen window, Arthur saw little hatchlike wrinkles that he had never noticed before. He ached for her, because there was nothing he could do, no words he could say that would make the facts any easier to bear.

'I feel that I've lost a grandson, that's all,' said his grandmother. 'And it's very sad.'

28

The Reverend Cole was due to arrive at half past 5, his mother told Arthur, when he got home after the French exam.

'Bob said he was going to see Robbie this afternoon, too. And Gus phoned as soon as you'd left. Really the phone's been ringing all afternoon.'

Arthur had seen Gus and talked with him just a few minutes ago.

'And Robbie's hearing is on Friday morning. I'm allowed to be present, which they implied was unusual, but nobody else is – of the family.'

'I see.' Arthur's last exam was on Friday morning. 'Where's Grandma?'

'Having a nap. She wants to go back to Kansas City Friday afternoon, then come back next week to help me out with things. She came here on such short notice, you know – she has to do a few things at her school before she's free.'

Arthur knew there was paperwork for his mother, though she had said something about a woman from his father's office coming to do that. He went to his room, put on old Levi's and a T-shirt, and went out into the backyard. The light of the declining sun struck his face and felt delicious. He took the spade from the toolshed.

When his mother called to him, nearly an hour later, he was grimy and sweaty. He walked toward her, swinging the spade by its handle. 'Mom, I don't want to see that guy,' he said softly and firmly.

'Please, Arthur. – Five minutes? He knows you've been busy with exams. He gave a very nice speech at Richard's – before the funeral, in the church.' His mother wore a fresh summer dress.

He knew he had to put in an appearance if his mother had told Bob Cole he was here. 'Okay, Mom. In a minute.'

Then Arthur took his time, lazily washed his hands, wet his head, and spat out water from the backyard faucet whose handle was hot to the touch. He was hoping the minister would be on his feet and on the way out when he went in.

Not so. The minister sat solemn-faced with a full glass of iced tea in his hand when Arthur entered the living room. Arthur accepted a glass of iced tea from his mother, but declined to sit, saying his Levi's were too dirty.

'Arthur, we're all of us extremely sad and shocked by what has happened,' said Bob Cole, sadly smiling. 'I'm just here to say a few words of friendship and sympathy.'

Arthur waited. Was he going to mention Irene? Had he already?

'... hard for us all to realize that a quiet boy like Robbie could've done such a thing. It's a time when we all need all the inner strength we can muster. But that can come with love, forgiveness and neighborliness.' His dark eyes moved past Arthur's grandmother, who was sitting on the sofa, past his mother sitting on the edge of an armchair, and returned to Arthur.

'Have a coconut cookie, Arthur, they're very good,' said his mother.

Arthur took one to please his mother. He was remembering when the Reverend Cole had spoken to his father about him and

Maggie. Now the minister was extending sympathy to his family about his father? 'Robbie thought he was doing the right thing, you know.'

'Arthur, I don't think we need to go into that,' said his mother gently.

Arthur could see in Bob Cole's suddenly more alert expression that he knew Irene's part in this story. 'If you talked with Robbie, he probably said the same thing to you.'

'Ye-es, he did,' said the minister.

'And you've probably talked to Irene,' Arthur said.

'Now, Arthur,' said his grandmother, 'we all – Do sit down. Your jeans aren't all that dirty.'

Bob Cole looked into the distance and cleared his throat. 'It's not appropriate for me, Arthur, to talk about what members of our congregation tell me in confidence.'

'But she talked with you, I suppose. So you know why my brother was angry.'

The Reverend took a deep breath. 'But she's not always to be believed. – She's still rather disturbed mentally,' he informed Joan, 'though a lot calmer than she used to be.'

'But my brother believed her story,' Arthur went on, 'and according to Robbie, my father said it was true. – That's what I'm talking about.'

'Arthur—' His mother seemed not to know how to go on. 'Arthur's had a trying day today, Bob. Two exams, morning and afternoon.'

Bob Cole nodded calmly, as if he understood. 'No matter what Irene told me, Arthur, I cannot tell you – or the general public. That would be a breach of confidence, unfair to everyone and to myself, my vocation.'

This brought Arthur back to what he had been thinking seconds before. 'This reminds me of last year – the abortion.' He moistened his lips nervously. 'I remember you heard it from someone and spoke to my father and evidently to a few other people such as Eddie Howell. Anyway – it seems to me that was making it sort of public – I think.'

Bob Cole looked at his grandmother with a faint smile, as if to say that they had to be patient with the young. 'That was for your own good, Arthur – in the long run.'

A platitude and an evasion, Arthur thought. 'The whole fuss last year was over whether my f-friend should have an abortion or not, though she wanted one and got one. Now that something's really happened – you sort of back out. You're not interfering.'

'How so?' the Reverend asked earnestly. 'We are all *most* concerned. And – we are concerned about abortion, yes. We all know that Irene is not married, but abortion was always out of the question and she will have that child *and* – our church is going to help financially. And that's something.'

Yes, it was something, Arthur realized, in the church's favor. But a child from an insane mother? 'You said a minute—'

Arthur was interrupted by the Reverend's suddenly sitting forward. 'I think it's time I took my leave.'

'I was going to mention insanity,' Arthur said, setting his tea glass down on the coffee table. 'When an insane or mentally disturbed person – as you called Irene Langley – gets pregnant, she has the baby, too?'

'Yes,' replied Bob Cole. 'I've no doubt she'll have that baby. Because she wants it.' He smiled sweetly, as if he were christening the baby at that very minute.

'And suppose she's telling a lie?' asked Arthur.

'About what? Having a baby?' Bob Cole's smile spread.

'About my father being responsible,' Arthur said, aware that his mother's hands writhed in her lap.

'Well, is that the point of anything?' asked Bob Cole. 'What *she* says? Who can prove it or disprove it?' Now the Reverend stood up. 'Human life is the point, Arthur. Everyone knows Irene's a little strange. Had a hard life, too – unbelievably hard. That's why we all try to help her in every—'

'The point is, that's why my father's dead, why Robbie shot him,' Arthur said.

'That *is* true, Bob.' Lois stood up, looking at Bob Cole as if she were half afraid of what she had just said. 'It's true, because Robbie believed what his father said. And he was so shocked – Robbie, I mean. I couldn't calm him down Sunday. He had such an idea that sex – anything to do with physical relations outside of marriage – was so evil. Really evil. But as I said to Arthur – no, to Eddie Howell – is it worth killing somebody over, after all? But he learned that at the church. He never used to be like this, when he was ten and twelve, honestly. And there was Richard – not giving me any help at all!' Lois gasped and tossed her head back, as if determined not to cry.

'Loey,' said Joan, getting up. 'Just for today try—'

'I'm sorry, Mama, but I have to say – I don't care if Richard is responsible or not. He's dead. That's what matters to me.' Then she couldn't speak anymore.

Bob Cole, still upright, put his hand on Lois's arm. 'There, there. I understand, Lois. I really do.'

Arthur stood with his hands on his hips, repressing an impulse to fling the Reverend's hand off his mother. Keep your goddamn 'secrets,' Arthur wanted to say, and if not for his grandmother's presence, he would have said it.

His mother and grandmother saw the Reverend to the door. Much mumbling of comforting phrases.

'Two-faced bastard,' Arthur said as soon as he heard the front door close. He headed for the fridge and a cold beer. 'Evasive, don't you think, Grandma?' Arthur said over his shoulder.

'Yes,' said his grandmother firmly, and she gave Arthur a quick smile. The smile was more sad than amused.

*

Friday morning, Arthur took his last exam, during which time his mother attended the hearing on Robbie. His grandmother had gone with her, intending to wait in the car or in a nearby café, if there was one, his grandmother had said. Her plane was at 1:45 p.m., and his mother was to drive her to the airport.

Arthur was home when his mother arrived at 3. For once she had taken the afternoon off.

'He's got to be in a boys' detention place for six months,' his mother said. 'It's near Indianapolis, a place called Foster House. For boys up to eighteen. They have schooling there, and gardening – carpentering—'

Arthur had expected something like this. 'But what did they *say*? – How many people there at the hearing?'

'Oh – five or six. They said he'd been influenced by his father. Overly influenced, I mean, which of course is true. They said he was obsessive. You know – those phrases.' She leaned against a cupboard, untied the scarf at her neck and yanked it off so quickly it made a snapping sound.

'Sit down, Mom. Want a coffee? – Was Robbie there?'

'For fifteen minutes or so, yes. Then they took him out. He said – his father had admitted to a sin and he said what it was.' She glanced at Arthur, then sat down on a straight chair.

Arthur winced, imagining his mother's feelings. He was making instant coffee for her.

'And I had to say, because it's true, that Robbie had all this influence in the last year. And in a way I think that helped in his defense.'

Arthur listened to the water getting hot. 'And what happens after six months?'

'They'll see how he's doing and if he can come home.' His mother smiled suddenly. 'He mentioned joining the Marines! But I thought a boy had to be seventeen. Nobody made any remarks in the hearing.' She laughed. 'He'll be sixteen soon, and I was afraid they'd put him behind bars somewhere, which of course wouldn't do him any good at all. This Foster House – it sounds like the next thing to a summer camp. – Thanks, dear, for the coffee.'

Arthur was sick of Robbie. He didn't care if Robbie was behind bars, in a room with one other delinquent or a dorm with forty others with beds in a row. 'When's Grandma coming back?'

'She said probably Tuesday. – Oh, the woman from Richard's office is coming this evening to take some of Richard's papers.'

That sounded dismal. 'I might go over to Gus's tonight. After supper.' He stood up from the bench seat. 'And I'm going to tackle that carpet now.'

'What do you mean, tackle it?'

'Get it up. Hopeless to clean, Mom.'

His mother did not remonstrate, and he went to the study and did what he could with his hands first, then fetched a claw hammer and pliers. His father's desk was heavy, and he lifted one side at a time and shoved the green carpet under it with a foot. Finally he had the carpet in a heap by the backyard door. He had wanted above all to get the fuzzy-edged stain out of sight, but there it was again, sharper-edged and still like France, on the beige wood of the floor. He swept the floor, and for what it was worth, attacked the spot again with soapy water and a brush. This yielded no visible pink. He put newspapers over the wet place on the floor. Then he slung a rope around the carpet, pulled it onto the lawn and into the garage, and with a couple of heaves got it into the hatch of his father's car. He took his father's keys from the hook in the kitchen and backed the car out.

Arthur drove to the nearest public dump he knew, ousted the carpet, and turned at once homeward. It was the first time he had driven his father's car, and he detested it. It had a loose, uncertain steering. Play, it was called. The wheel suggested phoniness, evasiveness and double meanings.

By a quarter past 8, Arthur was at Gus's house. All Gus's family seemed to be in the kitchen.

'We were so surprised by that news!' Gus's mother said. 'How is your poor mother? . . . And where is Robbie now? . . . Give your mother our love, would you, Arthur?'

Gus and Arthur went upstairs to Gus's room with Cokes and beers.

'Jesus!' Gus said, shaking his head.

Gus was looking at him as if he were someone returned from the moon, or so Arthur felt.

'Mighta gone to the funeral that morning, Art, but I had an exam,' Gus said.

Arthur gave a laugh. 'So did I. I didn't go.'

'What *happened?*'

Arthur told him about Sunday afternoon.

Gus popped open two beer cans. 'What'd your brother *say* to you?'

'*Say* to me? Or anybody! Not a damn thing! I took the gun out of his hand! He was sitting in his room with it – maybe two minutes after he fired it. He just takes the attitude he did the right thing.'

'What d'y'mean?' Gus was still standing in the center of his small room.

Arthur sat down on the floor, his back against a leg of Gus's table. 'Well, if you haven't heard – You haven't heard? About Irene at the Silver Arrow?'

'No. What?'

'Well, she says my dad was responsible for her being – um – pregnant.'

'You're *kiddin'*!'

'I am not. She said it to me too last Friday night when I went to the diner by myself. I didn't believe her, y'know? Then I found out she'd said the same thing to my mom – and then Robbie—'

'You mean it's true?'

'Could be. I think so.' Arthur glanced at the closed door. It was going to come out, Irene's story, and he had preferred to tell Gus himself. 'You won't say anything to your folks, would you? No reason for it to get any more spread around.'

'No, no, sure.' Gus had sat down on his bed. 'What does your mother say?'

'I know she doesn't want to believe it. But I think she has to. – Because my father the same as said it! I didn't hear him, of course; I wasn't there.' Arthur stared at Gus's carpet, then looked up at Gus. 'Pretty awful to imagine, isn't it? Coming anywhere near Irene.'

Gus nodded thoughtfully. 'Y'know, just a couple of days ago I read in the paper about a fourteen-year-old fellow in Texas shooting *both* his parents dead just because his father wouldn't let him take the car. Imagine that. – But Robbie's re-eally weird. I can even understand the Texas guy better.'

Gus had more questions. How long was Robbie going to be where he was? And could his mother afford to keep the house? Arthur said he wasn't sure. Gus went down for more drink, and Arthur put a cassette on, with the volume very low.

'Got a joint. Mary Warner,' Gus said when he came back. 'Want to share it?'

They knelt on the floor and smoked by the open window. Gus said his parents had noses like foxes. Arthur tried to believe he was getting a big kick from the joint. He wanted to feel floating, going out into space, able to float anywhere.

'There's one,' said Gus, grinning, pointing out the window at the darkening street below. 'Pot her!' Gus pointed a finger. 'Bang-bang! Gotcha!'

Arthur suppressed a wild laugh. A woman was walking along the sidewalk in an interestingly languid way, by herself, under the trees. 'One place I don't want to go to tonight.'

'Where's that?'

'Silver Arrow.'

'Hah!'

Arthur drew the last of his share and handed the rather soft cigarette to Gus.

29

Arthur stood in front of his parents' closet in the bedroom, pulling his father's clothes off hangers, making a heap for the Salvation Army. He hated the chore, and his mother had given it to him, he supposed, because the clothing was 'men's things.' The chest of drawers yielded shirts, sweaters, several mufflers, scarves, handkerchiefs. Arthur was to put aside what Robbie might use – shirts and sweaters, Arthur supposed. Arthur felt baffled and depressed after ten minutes, wanted to ask his mother if she could finish the rest, but she was at the table in the kitchen answering letters of condolence she had received, which seemed to number fifty, or sixty, so Arthur kept at it.

It was Saturday afternoon and raining lightly, when Arthur would have liked to be fooling around in the backyard. That morning his mother had gone to visit Robbie, this time taking him a few of what she thought were his favorite books, one of Jack London's and one called *Woodlore* with a gaudy cardboard cover that made it look like a book for ten-year-olds, which it probably was. His mother had also taken Robbie a jar of homemade strawberry jam from last year. Robbie was to go to Foster House on Monday.

Arthur went to his father's study and took several stamps and a couple of stamp books that he remembered were lying on a corner of his father's desk. He put these on the table where his mother was writing. 'Coffee, Mom?'

'Yes, please. – Some of these letters are so sweet,' said his mother. 'Listen to this one. Where is it? From Cora Bowman at the Home. You remember her?'

Arthur did not.

'"Richard always had time for people and the kindness to say a sweet word when they needed it." That's a happy thought, isn't it?'

'Yes,' said Arthur. He thought his mother looked tired. She had washed her hair after lunch; it was nearly dry, and she hadn't combed it out. 'Mom, can't I do some of that answering for you?'

She remonstrated, saying the letters were addressed to her, but Arthur won her over by saying surely some of them were 'mixed.' So Arthur got a pen and set about answering the first letter he opened. This was from Myra and Jack O'Reilly, whom Arthur didn't know from Eve and Adam. Arthur wrote:

> On behalf of my mother and myself, I write this to thank you for your words of sympathy in our days of grief here . . .

As he went on with other letters, varying his words but not the idea, the blatant phoniness that he felt in himself disappeared. He was doing the right thing. What he wrote and signed had nothing to do with himself. His house was supposed to be a house of grief now, but it was a more cheerful house already than it had been in more than a year. In fact, how sincere were all these letter-writers? After nearly forty-five minutes of this, Arthur dropped the pen and telephoned the Salvation Army. The Salvation Army promised to come and collect before 9 on Monday morning.

'We might change Robbie's room around. Don't you think so, Arthur?' his mother asked. She was standing at the threshold of Robbie's room.

'Sure.'

'It'll be more cheerful for him – different, when he comes home. The bed could go against the opposite wall with the head near that window.'

Arthur saw what she meant, but was not interested. Worn-out cardboard boxes cluttered the corners of the room, some holding childhood games, Arthur knew, and maybe some held ammunition. Robbie had always hoarded things. 'Mom – the carpet for the study. Let's think about that.'

On Monday morning, after the Salvation Army's coming and going, Arthur and his mother went to a department store in town and chose a sturdy carpet material of a color called simply 'light oak.' A couple of men arrived Tuesday morning to lay the carpet, and on Lois's instructions they set the desk in a different place, against the inside wall. This would cause pictures to be rehung, which inspired Lois to think of new wallpaper. New wallpaper was obligatory in Arthur's opinion, because of the shotgun pellet marks in one wall, which his mother oddly seemed not to see, though Arthur was always aware of them.

'White!' Lois said. 'I want this room to be light and cheerful. And I'm sure I can tidy up that desk and make it useful.' She was smiling.

Arthur nodded. He could certainly clean up the desk one afternoon when his mother was at the Home and give her a nice surprise. The desk was oak and needed some hand-sanding and then furniture polish. Arthur wanted every piece of paper that had belonged to his father out of the desk, so that the desk could start to belong to his mother. He began this job after his mother left for the Home that day. He put the curling tablets, the old folders of probably useless and obsolete business papers (otherwise the woman from the office would have taken them) into a big plastic shopping bag, and stuck it in the garage. What a mess when people die, Arthur thought.

And later that afternoon, Arthur met his grandmother at

Indi Airport and found her in much better spirits than last week. She asked questions, mainly about his mother, as they drove homeward.

'Any more news from what's-her-name? Irene?'

'No, thank God.' Arthur had a vision of her, more pregnant than ever, swinging coffee mugs at the Silver Arrow.

'And when is that offspring due?'

'September?' Arthur said hesitantly. 'Who knows exactly?'

'And what about your exams? Have you had the results yet?'

'Friday,' Arthur said. 'I go in Friday and take a look at the bulletin boards.'

At home, dinner was under way and his mother had put on pale blue slacks and a white shirt. His grandmother had been in the house hardly two minutes when his mother said:

'Oh, the new carpet, Mama! Come and look!' Lois led her mother to the study.

The new light-oak-colored carpet, clean as if no one had as yet set foot on it, stretched into the four corners of the room. The desk now sat on the left, with a space between it and the wall for a chair, so that someone at the desk would face the backyard wall with its big glass door. The boring gray metal files Arthur had wanted to chuck, but his mother meant to use them, once Arthur painted them white. Arthur's eyes as usual were drawn to the spatter of little holes in the wall to his right.

'Wallpaper comes next,' said his mother as they went out of the room. 'We might do that this week, Mama.'

After dinner, during coffee, his grandmother said, 'Now about this infant-to-be – Thank you, Arthur,' she interrupted, because Arthur had sprung to light her after-dinner cigarette. 'What's your attitude going to be, Loey? That's important.' She pulled a pillow behind her in a corner of the sofa.

'I'm not a hundred percent sure it's – you know, what that woman's saying,' Lois replied.

'Yes, Loey,' Joan said with a glance at Arthur, 'but if she asks you for total or partial support—'

Arthur hadn't thought of that.

'I'd say no, I swear,' said his mother.

'And if she wants to put the child in the Home? Not when it's tiny, but when it's about two – or less?' his grandmother asked.

His mother sighed. 'She'd be allowed to do that. Yes. – Don't forget Bob Cole said the church was going to give her some money.'

No one spoke for a few seconds.

'And if the baby turns out to be very much like Richard, what's your attitude going to be, Loey? – Best to be prepared.'

His mother reflected. 'I'm going to ignore it.'

There was another silence, but a better one, Arthur felt. The baby would be his father's; the resemblance might be beyond any doubt. But at least his mother had begun to form 'an attitude.' But where would ignoring the child get her in Chalmerston? The church people, and his mother's friends, they would all be interested in that baby and what it looked like.

'I could ask to have a blood test made,' his mother said. 'That just might clear Richard.'

His grandmother said, 'Yes, dear, and it might do the opposite. I'm concerned with your stance.'

Arthur said quietly, 'My dad had Type O. I remember that from somewhere. The commonest type. Forty-five percent of people have Type O.'

30

Joan pronounced the carpet in Robbie's room worn out and said she would make him a present of another. She and his mother went off Wednesday afternoon to look for wallpaper and the new carpet. His grandmother considered herself a good paperhanger, and with a little help from Arthur, she said she would do Robbie's room and the study too.

On Thursday Arthur was sent to town to buy another wide paste brush, a bucket and plaster of Paris. He bought these things at Schmidt's, the biggest hardware store in town, realized that he was only a block away from Shoe Repair, and decided to say hello to Tom Robertson.

Arthur was surprised to see the front of the adjacent store demolished, workmen banging away with hammers and another pushing a wheelbarrow of cement up a ramp. Shoe Repair's rather primitive but neat sign was still in place over the door and front window, however, and Arthur saw that the shop was doing business today as usual. He went in. The right-hand wall of the shop had been knocked out.

'Hell-o, Arthur!' said Tom, in shirtsleeves and perspiring. 'How're you, boy? What d'y'think of this?' He gestured toward the torn-down wall. 'I'm spreading out. I bought the next property there. Ground floor only.'

'Really? Business that good?'

'Maybe I'm one of the few these days,' Tom said with a satisfied smile. 'What're you up to? It's been a year, hasn't it? College—' Then he looked as if he had thought of something unpleasant. 'Your father – can't tell you how surprised I was to read about *that*, Arthur. How's your mother doing?'

'Pretty well, I think, thanks. My grandma's visiting now and that's a help.'

'I'm sure it is. – And what about your brother?'

Arthur felt shame, and hated it. 'He's in a place called Foster House – for six months. Near Indi.'

Tom shook his head slowly. Then he said, 'If you want a summer job – or maybe you don't.'

'Well, yes, I might!' Arthur smiled.

'You could be my manager!' Tom turned to listen to a woman customer. 'They're down there on the lower right, ma'am. All the patent leathers.' He again addressed Arthur. 'You could help me ordering stock, display – Got one boy—' He looked behind him. 'Nice enough boy as a salesman, but you'd make a better manager. Regular salary if you can work a full day. Say two hundred a week?'

That sounded good. 'Fair enough. Can I tell you for sure tomorrow? I'd like to work here, Tom. Thanks.'

'Sure, no big hurry, but—' He looked at the open wall bordered with jagged plaster on his left. '—the sooner the better. I've ordered a lot of new stock.'

Arthur went away cheered. Why had he even hesitated? Maybe because his mother's and grandmother's financial reckonings might make them decide that the Alderman family, what was left of it, should sell the house and move, maybe move out of town. They were going over the insurance papers this minute.

Once home, Arthur was put to work scraping at the remnants of old wallpaper in Robbie's room. He disliked the thought that he was working on the walls for Robbie, but he reflected that it might be a long time before Robbie lived in the house again, probably a lot longer than six months.

As they were starting dessert that evening, his grandmother said quite casually, 'I don't see why you can't go to Columbia in September, Arthur, if you still want to go.'

Arthur had his mouth full of cake. 'Oh?' He was amazed, having thought that the household was going to have less money now, not more.

'Yes,' said his grandmother. 'There's the insurance – considerable. Your mother's pension as a widow. Not to mention that I feel free to contribute something now – so I hope that cheers you up, Arthur.'

'Certainly does.' He was thinking that a renewal of his grant for next year could contribute something, too, but didn't want to mention this until he was sure of it. 'Some other good news today, Mom. Tom Robertson offered me a job full-time. As manager, he calls it. How about that? Two hundred a week. Tom's bought the space next door – you know, where there used to be a little electrical appliances shop?'

'Really, Arthur? And you took it?'

Arthur saw from his mother's happy face that she assumed he had. 'I will take it. I told Tom I'd tell him tomorrow.'

That evening, Arthur and his grandmother worked until after midnight and got more than half the walls in Robbie's room papered. Arthur played a couple of his Brandenburg cassettes to cheer them as they labored.

On Friday morning, Arthur drove to the Administration Building of C.U. in whose basement the grades of the entire student body were displayed for all to see. The bulletin boards were well lit with little lights above them, but the corridors suggested dungeons, and students shuffled along, stiff, anxious and silent. Some stared at the bulletin boards as if frozen by terrible shock. Arthur came upon Philosophy P 112 first, and saw that he had got a B-plus. Encouraging and better than he had expected. He sidled past a clump of students in jeans and T-shirts who were yacketing and laughing, maybe with relief. French was next with a B-minus. That too could have been worse! He ran into Gus.

'Passed bugs,' said Gus with a tired but happy smile.

'Oh, good.' Arthur knew Gus had been worried about this course which demanded a prodigious memory. 'Veronica here?'

'Helping her mother out with something. Wants me to get her grades for her.' Gus held up a notebook he was carrying. 'So far no failures.'

'Come by the house some time. My grandma's with us. We're doing wallpapering. I don't mean you have to work.'

'Okay. Call you first, though.'

Physics 126. Arthur had a B-plus. Another success. Then he deliberately sought out the Biology corridor in the labyrinth. Microbiology 310. His name was near the top of the alphabetical lists and easy to spot. There was an A-plus beside it. Arthur felt his face grow warm, as if someone were with him and he were blushing. No other name had an A-plus beside it, he saw at a glance, and there were only two other A's, one for Summer, the boy Arthur liked. Arthur didn't look at the fellows around him as he moved away from the board. He was not much interested in his English results, but sought out the board and found a B-plus. Very respectable if not quite tops.

As he was leaving the building, Arthur saw Francey in her faded, cut-off jeans, a shirt with tails hanging out.

'Lousy C-minus in Drama,' Francey said to him with the start of tears in her eyes. 'It's incredible! That instructor's nuts! C-minus doesn't make sense, not with the *work* I did!'

Arthur frowned. 'Sorry, Francey.' A second later, she was gone.

When Arthur got home, his grandmother told him that his mother was out at the supermarket.

'Look at the progress here!' His grandmother was on her knees in the study, cutting lengths of white wallpaper with the aid of a yardstick. 'All measured and ready to go. – How were your grades?'

Arthur told her, capping his list with the A-plus.

'Isn't that marvelous! Never heard of an A-plus. – Are you the teacher's pet?'

Arthur laughed, blushing again. 'Yes, maybe.'

'You be sure and write to Columbia today, as you said you would.'

'Yep.'

'Your mother and I are going to visit Robbie this afternoon. Don't suppose you'd like to come.'

It was utterly depressing, the thought of going to see Robbie. 'No, Grandma. Tell him hello – I suppose. – I don't see what good it would do if I went.'

Arthur felt awkward as he left the study. In his room, he looked for the letters he had had from Columbia, and found two. He had had a fear that he might have thrown them away in a fit of anger after one of his set-tos with his father. He had addressed the envelope to the Admissions Department, when he heard his mother's car, and went out to help her unload the groceries.

There were more titbits for Robbie. Smoked oysters, a certain kind of sausage which Arthur particularly disliked, a container of vanilla ice cream big enough for him to share with his roommate, if he had one, his mother said. During their short lunch, his grandmother mentioned his college grades, and his mother did seem pleased for a few seconds, but Arthur could see that her mind was on Robbie.

While the women were gone, Arthur wrote a first draft of a letter to Columbia's Admissions Officer, reminding him of his admission last year and of his grant which he had had to apply to C.U. Arthur respectfully asked if he might be given a grant for the coming scholastic year. It crossed Arthur's mind that Professor Jurgens might put in a good word for him, so he wrote a short letter to Professor Jurgens and was about to put a stamp on it when it occurred to him that he could deliver it to his house now. Arthur looked up the professor's address, 121 Cherry Street, and drove there. Arthur put the letter into the Jurgens' tin mailbox and turned the red flag up to indicate that something was in it.

'Hello? – Oh, Arthur!' Professor Jurgens stood on his doorstep. 'Leaving me a note? Come in!'

Arthur took the letter from the box and explained his errand.

'But of course, Arthur, with pleasure. I can write it now, if you'd like to wait a minute or two.'

'Oh, no, thank you, sir.' Arthur thought it would be rather rude to stand around or sit in the living room while the professor wrote a letter about his qualifications.

'Well then, I'll do it straightaway and send it off myself. I'm sure you're in a hurry.' Professor Jurgens smiled, and his small blue eyes lit up behind his glasses. 'Columbia's what you've been wanting, I know.'

'Yes. Now it looks like I can make it – financially. If there's room for me.'

'I should think they'll make room,' the professor said cheerfully.

Arthur walked back to his car elated. The professor had just shaken his hand. He had also paid him high compliments. The handshaking impressed Arthur more: There was something that implied equality about that. As Arthur moved his car off, he realized that Professor Jurgens hadn't mentioned his father's death, or rather his father's murder. Maybe Jurgens hadn't even noticed the item in the newspaper. That would be typical of Jurgens!

At home, Arthur telephoned Tom Robertson to say he would be very happy to take the job.

Arthur felt in a mood to have a party that evening and realized that it might have to be a party for one, in his own head, if his mother and grandmother got back in a depressed mood, due to something new they had heard about Robbie. This was more or less the way it was.

When they returned, his grandmother disappeared for 'a quick cool shower,' while his mother washed her hands and face at the sink with the aid of a paper towel. Arthur asked the news.

'They gave me a written report – if you'd like to see it.' She took a white envelope from her handbag.

Arthur began reading it, while his mother got ice cubes from the fridge.

'They didn't suggest that he's going to get any worse,' his mother said, 'and they don't talk about him as if he were a criminal.'

They wouldn't, Arthur supposed. The Xeroxed one-page form he was looking at showed twenty or more check marks indicating yes or no and variations. Potentially violent was checked yes, so was obsessive, religious, introvert, asocial as opposed to gregarious and antisocial, and indifferent in regard to opposite sex as opposed to active, interested, inhibited or anti, which Arthur would have checked. There was also a Xerox of a typed page.

'He doesn't seem unhappy,' his mother said. 'Seems almost the same as ever, to tell you the truth. Reconciled, Mama called him.'

'Well – good.' Arthur was reading prose that combined jargon with clumsy English, something strangers had written about his brother whom he knew so well. Or did he?

> . . . who reacted violently to a situation in his immediate family circle. The subject was unusually emotionally dependent on the victim, namely his father, and would seem to have excluded all other relationships apart from a few older men whom the subject knows outside the family and who collectively and not individually form his only social circle. Absence of guilt-feeling notable. At the same time, subject expresses regret of father's absence now. Marked indifference as to how others in family or society evaluate his act.

His grandmother came into the kitchen. They were making tall drinks. Arthur read the last few lines with little interest, as if doing a duty. He had learned nothing new.

... probably respond best to well-organized environment ... emotionally retarded. Unable to reason well in new situations (see Test 9) ...

That evening when Arthur and his grandmother were finishing Robbie's room, she said, 'I've never seen anything like it. No sorrow – really. No *pity*. He just looks at us with a ghost of a smile, quite as usual, you could say.' His grandmother looked behind her at the half-open door, but Lois was sorting papers in the living room now. 'It doesn't occur to him that other people don't accept so easily what he's done.'

Arthur was on the ladder, and he took from his grandmother's hands a strip of wallpaper and stuck it at the top against the paste-covered section. He didn't want to talk about his brother, but he said finally, 'And after six months?'

His grandmother gave a rare derogatory laugh. '*If* they decide to release him, the army might suit him well. Or the Marines, where it's tougher, or so I've heard.'

Ritual. Drill. Like the church, Arthur thought. Robbie could again take a pride in doing the right thing. Possibly killing people instead of rabbits. Uniforms and a word of praise. Promotion.

'Take this, Arthur.'

Arthur reached for the damp rag.

31

Display was Arthur's first assignment Monday, which meant the longer front window and to some extent the interior, though Tom still wanted his bargain counters. A couple of extra stepladders kept getting in Arthur's way, as the workmen were not quite finished with the ceiling lights, and these gave Arthur an idea for the front windows: stepladders with a shoe and the price on each step.

Betty Brewster asked Lois and Joan for tea at her house, and Arthur was invited too, but couldn't go because of his job. Gus and Veronica came for dinner one evening, and Gus said casually to Arthur afterwards in the living room:

'I noticed – what's-her-name wasn't at the Silver Arrow the other night. Veronica and I were there and I asked about her. Baby's due in August, one of the waitresses said.'

'August,' Arthur repeated, surprised.

His mother, grandmother and Veronica were then in the kitchen. Later that evening, when Arthur and his mother were alone, Arthur told his mother this.

'Yes, I heard too. From Bob Cole,' his mother replied, and at once showed the nervousness that the subject of Irene always brought. 'Bob Cole says she comes to church almost every day. There's someone there to unlock the doors for her. And she's got someone to drive her, a neighbor, I suppose. – Bob went to see Robbie last Tuesday. Did I tell you that?'

'No.' And Arthur wasn't interested.

'I had a nice note from the man called Jeff,' his mother went on. 'One of Robbie's Delmar Lake friends. Belated note, I must say, but still nice of him. They're going to visit Robbie, they said. That'll pick Robbie up, I know.'

Amazing they hadn't visited Robbie before. Would Foster House let them in? Those fellows were the type the guards would frisk first. Arthur had been in a sour mood ever since his mother and grandmother had come home from the tea at Betty's. He had asked them if Betty had had any news about Maggie, and his mother had reported that Maggie was spending the summer on the East Coast and would come home for a week or so in early September before she went back to Radcliffe. So Arthur supposed all was going blissfully well with Larry Hargiss and family. How tall was Mr Hargiss? That didn't matter. Arthur imagined walking up to him one day, maybe when Hargiss was with Maggie, socking him in the jaw with a hard right, and Hargiss would fall to the ground somewhere, unconscious. Another tea invitation Arthur more regretted missing was that from Professor Jurgens, whose wife telephoned one evening. The date fell on a working day, and Mrs Jurgens hadn't proposed any other date.

Arthur still went often to the public library, and he was able to tell Miss Becker that he was going to Columbia in September. A letter had come from Columbia, saying he had been accepted as a dorm student, and as an added bonus or compliment, or so Arthur felt, Columbia had enclosed an application form for a $1,500 grant, 'which may be possible for this academic year but perhaps not for the next.' Arthur knew the Reagan administration was economizing. But Columbia wouldn't have sent the grant application form unless they thought it likely he would get a grant for this year.

His grandmother had been gone for ten days and had left the

house transformed: His mother's bedroom had a new double bed with a blue and gray counterpane; Robbie's room was re-arranged, his old scratched table replaced by a handsome one that his mother and grandmother had found at a secondhand place. His mother talked of taking a full-time job as a secretary in September. Her typing was excellent, and she had bought a book on shorthand. His grandmother had offered to pay fifty percent of his Columbia bills, Arthur had learned, and if she said that, she would do it and a bit more. When he graduated and started earning, Arthur thought, he would repay his grandmother, so what she would give him he liked to consider a loan. He would have to continue his schooling somewhere, maybe Columbia, for two more years after the usual four. The future spiraled in Arthur's mind into a nebulous and distant point, like one of the third-dimensional diagrams in physics. How high would tuition fees be in *five* years?

Would his mother ever remarry? She was only about forty-three, not exactly old. But there were no prospects around that Arthur could see or imagine. He wished his grandmother could come and live with them, but her life and her dance school in Kansas City was bound to be more interesting than Chalmerston. Arthur tried to take cheer from the fact that he was free of his father's harangues and disapproval, that September meant the East and New York. But he still missed Maggie and it hurt, like a disease that he could not get rid of. Francey had not cured him. He wondered, in fact, if Francey had had any effect at all in regard to Maggie? Gus had introduced him to a blond girl called Leonora, half-Polish and half-French, who was visiting relatives of Gus's family in town. She had been interesting and attractive, but she hadn't struck a spark; it had simply been a pleasant evening.

His mother drove to Foster House every four or five days to visit Robbie, and Arthur still declined to go. Arthur gathered that Robbie never asked about him or expressed any wish to see him. His mother returned from his visits with an air of optimism: Robbie was obeying all the rules and didn't seem to mind them. Robbie said the food was good. He had a different roommate now, because Robbie had made some remarks that the Puerto Rican boy had complained about. Racial remarks, Arthur gathered.

'So he's going to get out when the six months are up? – He'll start back in school here?'

'It depends on his behavior, they said. So far, it's considered quite good. I talk with Mr Dillard every time I go, you know.'

Mr Dillard was one of the superintendents, Arthur knew. Robbie was presumably coming home in December, on probation.

When his mother returned from her next visit, the news was not so good: Robbie had got into a fistfight with his new roommate, who had accused Robbie of breaking a toolbox, while Robbie had said that someone else had come into the room and done it. 'Each boy is making a toolbox, I mean,' his mother explained, 'and they take the boxes to their rooms in the evening till the next carpentry lesson.' Robbie had broken the boy's nose, and Robbie was walking around stiffly with his ribs strapped in adhesive tape. The other boy was bigger and had retaliated.

Arthur made hardly a comment.

He was doing an errand for his mother in J.C. Penney's on a Saturday morning in early August when he saw Maggie. Arthur was at the 'novelties' counter with his mother's list in hand, waiting for a salesgirl, when he happened to look to his left. At first, he didn't believe it was Maggie, but someone rather like her, because this girl's hair was longer, quite to her shoulders and brushed back and held by a clip or a ribbon. His heart seemed to stop. The girl *was* Maggie. Now she leaned forward, talking to a salesgirl across the counter. She appeared to be by herself. There were lots of people between them, coming and going.

'Help you, sir?'

'Th-this,' Arthur said, handing the piece of paper to the

salesgirl, as if abandoning the idea of reading it to her, and in fact he didn't understand the numbers on the list which had to do with thread weights. He looked again at Maggie, who stood with her left foot extended and resting on the heel. That was just like Maggie!

'Yes, here you are. This the color you mean for the yellow?' The girl had three spools on her palm already, two white, one yellow.

'I'm sure that's okay,' Arthur said, fishing money out.

There was time. Maggie hadn't finished at the counter.

Arthur got his little white bag from the salesgirl and walked toward Maggie, hesitated, then went on.

Maggie lifted her eyes from the counter and looked at him, and smiled uncertainly or shyly. 'Oh – Arthur!'

''S really you! I couldn't believe it.' He crushed the top of the paper bag, which was weightless, in his fingers. 'Thought you weren't coming back till September.'

'I changed my mind. – Mom—'

Someone bumped into Arthur and passed him. 'What?'

'Mom says you're going to Columbia in September.'

'Right. Yes.'

Now Maggie had to give her attention to the salesgirl, and took her purchase, in a larger bag.

They started to walk slowly toward an exit.

'You're staying the rest of the summer?' he asked.

'Till the seventeenth of September.'

Arthur nodded and took a breath. 'Walk you to your car?' He wondered if Larry Hargiss was with her, maybe holding the car somewhere.

'I have to buy one more thing. Somewhere else.'

They were out on the sidewalk. She was walking in another direction from Shoe Repair, where he was due back now, because he had asked Tom's permission to run out on a quick errand for his mother. What a lucky little errand it had been! Arthur felt stunned, hypnotized even, by the fact that Maggie was beside him, so close their arms almost touched, Maggie whom he could seize now like a madman, if he chose, and whose body would be firm and real. If he didn't ask now, he thought, he was gutless. Or a fool.

'Can I call you sometime, Maggie?' he asked in a firm voice.

She smiled again, more at ease than a minute ago. 'Sure, Arthur. Why not?'

'Okay.' He stopped. 'I have to go the other way. Now. I'll call you, Maggie.' He turned and walked away, trotted, looking at the pavement. It was like a dream! Yet her voice was still in his ear: *Sure, Arthur. Why not?* How long had she been in town? Five days? Longer? Had Mr Hargiss just departed from the Brewster house? Why would she say *why not* like that unless she still liked him?

Arthur felt elated, though puzzled, all the rest of the day. He was selling now, as well as being manager in name. His elation, he told himself, must be based solely on the fact that Maggie was in town, geographically near. But if she was still tied up with Mr Hargiss, she might also have said *why not* in the same manner, Arthur was thinking by 5 p.m. It would be stupid to build himself up for a letdown.

Nevertheless he was inspired to ask his mother out to dinner that evening at the Chowder House, a place that served excellent seafood.

'What puts you in such a good mood?' she asked. 'Don't tell me Tom's given you a raise already?'

'Not quite yet. I just thought it'd be nice to go out for a change.' He intended to mention Maggie during dinner. Or he might decide not to mention her at all.

Arthur was midway through delicious fried scallops and was about to begin, 'By the way,' when his mother said:

'I saw Jane Griffin at the Home today. She'd heard also that the church was going to pay Irene's hospital bills – when that child arrives.'

Dismal subject. Ruining the evening, Arthur thought. But since it was on his mother's mind, he knew he had to share it with her. 'Well, well. Did the minister announce it from the pulpit?'

'No-o, silly! Bob mentioned it to Jane, because Jane's a full-time employee now at the Home. Where that child might go, you know, finally.'

Arthur was not enjoying his food so much now. 'Did she say anything about who the father might be?'

'Well – she said she'd heard the rumor. Because Richard often visited her, but Jane made light of it and said they – meaning people – might as well be talking about Eddie Howell or Bob Cole who also visit her.'

Arthur was laughing. 'Eddie Howell! That stallion! – I suppose Jane was fishing – for you to say yes or no about Dad?'

His mother shrugged. 'Maybe. – But I didn't rise to the bait. Everyone knows the rough company Irene meets where she works.'

Arthur wanted to change the subject, and couldn't. 'Did Jane connect any of this with what Robbie did?'

'Didn't seem to. No hint of that. – Robbie still doesn't want any of his father's clothes.'

Arthur could have told his mother that the day he had sorted out the sweaters. His mother had been sad the day she got back from Foster House and Robbie had rejected the clothes, but his mother had left the sweaters and scarves at Foster House to be given to the other boys. Since then his mother had tried again with some more items that had belonged to Richard.

Now to make the atmosphere a little more cheerful, if he could, Arthur said, 'I saw Maggie today.'

'Maggie? She's in town?'

'Yes. She was shopping and I ran into her.'

'Why didn't you tell me before? So that's why you're in a good mood. – Are you going to see her again?'

'I said I might call her, yes. – What would you like for dessert, Mom?'

That night, Arthur had a vivid dream about Maggie taking a boat somewhere, and he was seeing her off. She had a stateroom to herself, and there were lots of people around, all strangers. Maggie said she was going to the Arctic, and Arthur could not find out why. She was going to be gone a long while, she said, and he was miserable at the prospect. Her hair was much longer, down to her waist, and then as he was waving good-bye to her – from some place remote from the ship but not the dock – her hair became shorter and shorter until it was as it used to be, and Maggie flitted into her stateroom and closed the door. Arthur awoke with damp eyes and a forehead wet with sweat.

He rubbed his chin with a clenched fist. My God, just a *dream*, he thought. Maggie was here in town! And she wasn't going to the Arctic!

That day, Arthur telephoned the Brewster house during his lunch hour.

Betty answered in a cheerful tone and passed him to Maggie.

'Art,' he said, though Maggie never called him that. 'You said I could call you up, so I am. Any chance of seeing you?'

A few seconds later, he had a date to come to Maggie's house around 6:30 'for a Coke or something.'

Arthur fully expected to run into Larry Hargiss, so he paid attention to what he wore. After a shower at home, he put on clean blue jeans and shirt, and a summer jacket not absolutely clean but not dirty either. A particularly pretty peachy rose was in full bloom in the garden, but he decided against bringing this in hand, in case Mr Hargiss was present.

Mr Hargiss was at least not in the living room when Arthur arrived. Betty greeted him warmly and remarked that she hadn't seen him in more than a month.

'You kids have what you want. I'm going upstairs,' Betty said.

Maggie made a gin and tonic for Arthur. She wore a pale green shirtwaist dress, white sandals, and looked especially pretty, Arthur thought. The gold bracelet he had given her was still on her right wrist. Had she been in bed with Mr Hargiss, wearing that? Arthur thought at once, he had been in bed with Francey, wearing Maggie's chain around his neck; Francey had even praised it. Did that make them even? Did it matter?

'What're you frowning about?' Maggie asked.

'I dunno.'

Arthur was prepared for Mr Hargiss to come down the stairs at any moment, but decided not to ask if he was here, not to say or ask anything about him. But the minutes went by and Mr Hargiss did not come down the stairs. Maggie talked about Radcliffe and how much she liked her sociology course which she had been able to take in her second semester. She told him about a field project she and another girl student had been given. They had visited employment agencies in Cambridge and had made a survey of their successful and unsuccessful clients with regard to age and education with graphs to illustrate the findings.

'What about race as a factor?'

'I know!' Maggie laughed. 'Wasn't supposed to *be* a factor in this particular survey.'

A vision of a half-black baby in Irene's arms danced before his eyes. How much did Maggie know of the story Irene was putting out?

'I *am* sorry about your father, Arthur.'

Arthur rolled his glass between his hands. 'Well, I'm not – terribly.'

'Don't say *that*!'

Arthur hesitated. 'Well, look what he did. To you – to us. The way he acted. You think I appreciated that?' He blinked. 'You've no idea how much pleasanter life is at my house now. You ought to come over and see. Two rooms done over. Mom and I've got space! Peace and quiet—'

'Oh, yes, Robbie's gone.'

Arthur gave a laugh. Again he glanced toward the staircase, but maybe Mr Hargiss really wasn't here. 'Gone, yes, till December at least. He's at a place called Foster House near Indi. Full of juvenile delinquents like him. Up to age eighteen.'

Maggie asked what was going to happen after December. Probation anyway, then maybe the Marines, Arthur told her.

'When would you like me to push off?' he asked.

'No hurry. I haven't got a date tonight.' She was sitting on the opposite sofa, forearms crossed on her knees, and frequently she glanced at the carpet, as if she were shy with him.

'Then maybe you'd like to go out to dinner somewhere.'

Arthur took her to Mom's Pride. The air-conditioning was on, and the jukebox sounded fine. Heartened by the first half of his hamburger, Arthur broke his resolution and asked:

'And how is Mr Hargiss?'

'Oh – all right – I suppose.'

'You came home sooner than you said you would. That's why I asked.'

'Well, true, I am back earlier.'

He shouldn't ask anything more just now, Arthur thought. Maggie wouldn't like being quizzed. 'Feel like dancing?'

It was better, dancing. Arthur could relax. During a slow song, he held her in his arms. The magic was still there, for him. And in Maggie? He was not sure.

When they were sitting in the booth again, he said, 'Did your mother say anything to you about Irene Langley?'

'No. – Is she that blond woman—'

'Yes. The one I told you about last summer. Goes to my father's church. Well – you haven't heard. I may as well tell you before you hear it from someone else. She's pregnant – and she's saying my father is responsible.'

Maggie's brows frowned. 'Wha-at? Saying it to your mother?'

Arthur nodded. 'And to me, too. So when Robbie heard – this, he really turned against my dad. That's when he shot him, when my dad—'

'Oh, Arthur, I didn't know *that*!'

'Yes – well—' He nervously downed the last half inch of his beer. 'And now – I mean, not now, but when he was alive, it seems my father admitted it to my brother.' There it was, and Maggie was going to start drifting away tonight, now. She'd be polite. But she would be going to the Arctic.

'It's not true, is it? – Or is it?'

'Maybe it is true. My dad was seeing Irene quite often, not—' He began again. 'I don't mean he ever stayed the night with this old bag, but he went to see her the same as he went to see a few other people who go to that church. Irene works at a diner. She's an ex-prostitute, really awful to look at.' Arthur scowled at the table.

'Well, do you believe it?' Maggie's tone didn't sound as earnest or heavy as he had feared.

'I have to. Yes. – What a family! Brother in jail, father in – in disgrace. Baby's due this month. Hope it's half black, as I always want to say to Mom and don't.'

Maggie's gaze rested on her empty glass that she slid back and forth on the table. She declined Arthur's offer of another scotch and water.

'I thought I should tell you all this, because if I didn't – it'd be like seeing you under false pretenses. Something like that.' If she wanted to tell her mother, he thought, there was nothing he could do about that, and maybe her mother had already heard it from somewhere and had chosen not to say anything to Maggie?

Arthur wanted another beer and got up to get it. As he was standing waiting at the busy bar counter, he realized that he couldn't burst out tonight with a cheerful speech about what he wanted to do, what he intended to make of himself by the time he was twenty-three. A scientist! He meant to have a doctorate degree by twenty-three or so and an interesting job somewhere, and if a fixed job were not interesting enough then, he'd be on some exploratory trip or doing research work where he wished. Respected among his colleagues! Dreams! But why couldn't he make them come true? Yet how could he say any of this tonight without sounding as if he were boasting, full of hot air, trying to compensate for what he had just told Maggie? The image of a hot volcano came to his mind. That was himself! He grabbed his beer and tossed down a dollar bill. He even recognized the volcano picture: It was one he remembered in a book of von Humboldt's voyages that his grandmother had given him when he was about ten.

They lingered on till midnight at Mom's Pride and talked of other things. Arthur looked for a change in Maggie, because of what he had told her, but he did not see any. Could it be that the sins of the father weren't always visited upon the son? When Arthur drove Maggie home, she didn't ask him to come in, but Arthur didn't mind.

'Kiss you good night?' he whispered. It was like a yes or no question about Mr Hargiss. He kissed her. And a second time. He went off to his car, sure that he would see her again.

Had Maggie parted with Mr Hargiss? Maggie wasn't the type to announce outright that she'd given someone the brush-off. He'd have to court her again, even if she had. He rather liked the idea.

32

'To see Robert Alderman,' Arthur said to a guard in the front hall of Foster House.

'Your name? . . . Can you sign in here, please?'

Arthur signed his name in a ledger, and the guard filled in the date and time. The guard looked into the paper bag Arthur carried, then stepped to one side of a doorway through which Arthur had to walk. This was a metal-detector device, and it registered with a buzz: Arthur had his car keys and some change in the left-side pocket of his Levi's. That was all right.

'Straight ahead. Tell the other guard down there.'

A second guard was silhouetted in an open doorway. Arthur walked down a barren and rather wide hall of the one-story building. There were rooms to right and left, half of them with their doors hanging open. His mother had been urging him to 'pay a visit' to Robbie, and here he was at 10:30 on a Sunday morning when he would rather have been sleeping till about now, because he had been out late with Maggie last night.

'Alderman? He's out there somewhere, I think,' said the second armed guard. 'If not, he's in his room.' He looked at a list. 'That's room seventy-two.'

Arthur walked out into the hot sun. At least thirty boys were wielding spades and hoes in a rather vast expanse of land. Arthur saw rows of tomato plants and half-grown cabbages. The boys wore khaki shorts or trousers, and some were stripped to the waist. At a glance Arthur could see that the boys weren't knocking themselves out at their labors. He hesitated, then realized that a blond-looking head and skinny body really belonged to Robbie. Arthur walked on a narrow path between rows. The big yard was bounded by a heavy wire fence with a top part that slanted inward, composed of barbed wire.

'Hey, Robbie!'

Robbie looked up, then leaned on his hoe. 'Yeah? – Hi.'

'Just visiting. – How are things?'

Robbie tossed his hoe down with an air of annoyance and walked toward Arthur. His first step hit the center of a young cabbage, mashing its leaves. Evidently Robbie was allowed to walk off, because he did, and Arthur followed him back into the hall. Robbie paused at a drinking fountain and rubbed a handful of water over his face.

'Room's here,' said Robbie, heading toward a certain door.

The room walls were of the same pale blue as the corridor. There were two narrow iron beds, a single table in the center of the room, two shelves that held books covered in transparent plastic. Robbie sat down on his bed.

'Mom gave me these to give you,' Arthur said, extending the paper bag he had been carrying. He knew what was in it, a hunk of fruit cake wrapped in wax paper, two issues of *Newsweek*, chocolate bars.

Robbie rummaged quickly in the bag, frowning, and put the items out on his bed. His movements reminded Arthur of those of an animal.

'Where's your roommate?'

'He has kitchen duty this morning.'

'You get along with him all right?'

Robbie shrugged. 'He bores me.' He was avoiding looking at Arthur.

'Looking forward to getting out in December?'

Robbie gave his brother a frowning glance. 'Yeah, maybe. But I don't want to go back to that kooky high school again.'

'Don't want to live home again? Why not?' Arthur realized that he was merely curious about this.

Robbie put on his clammed-up look. He stood up suddenly and folded his arms. 'Those high school kids are boring dopes. I'm not going back to *that*, no *sir*. They don't understand anything. They're zombies.'

'I see. – Well, don't try running away from here. They'll just catch you and put you in for longer.' Arthur realized that he was trying to sound friendly and chummy and that he didn't feel in the least friendly and chummy towards the sullen-faced figure in front of him. 'Any messages for Mom?'

'Nope. Can't think of any.'

Arthur moved toward the door, which was closed. 'Well, what do you want to do, Robbie? Once you're out in December. Got any cheerful ideas?'

Robbie shrugged again. 'Why should I tell you? – I don't care where I am. Maybe I'll join the Marines. That outfit—'

'Can you get in at sixteen?'

'Or maybe I'll live in the boat house on Delmar Lake all year round. I got friends there, Bill and Jeff and all the others. I don't have to go back to school if I don't want to. I don't give a shit if I'm on probation, okay, but they can't stop me from living where I want to.'

Arthur thought they could, but didn't say anything.

'My friends'll stick with me. I could work for *them* down at the lake – or anywhere. Once I'm out of this shithouse.' Robbie swung an arm to indicate the walls, the whole building.

Three loud bongs sounded in the hall.

'Is that for lunch?' Arthur asked.

'Church in five minutes,' Robbie said with the same sourness.

The door behind Arthur burst open, and a dark-haired boy in khaki trousers and shirt with the tails hanging out hurtled past Arthur and yanked out the bottom drawer of a small chest.

'Fucking kay dee, fucking *gar-r-bage!*' the boy yelled as if to himself, snatched off his dirty shirt and shook out a fresh one. Then he noticed Arthur and looked utterly amazed.

'Just taking off,' Arthur said. 'Robbie – take care of yourself, will you?' He was afraid of a sneer from both of them if he told Robbie to keep in line so he'd get out sooner. 'Bye for now.'

Now the hall was noisy with adolescent boys murmuring, laughing, moving in the opposite direction from Arthur. Organ music quivered from somewhere.

'Hey! – Sir!'

Arthur had to sign the ledger again to get out. It was a pleasure to start the car and head for home.

When Arthur got to the house, his mother had just come back from church and was still in her Sunday finery, including a dark blue straw hat which Arthur rather liked.

'How was church?' Arthur asked with deliberate cheer.

His mother gave him a sidelong look, as if to say, 'Same as ever.' She relit the oven, then removed her hat gently. 'And you saw Robbie? How was he?'

'Fine. All tanned. Working in the vegetable garden there – till it was time for church.'

'I hope he was friendly at least.'

'Ha! Well – he remembered me, I suppose.'

'But what did he say? – What's his attitude?'

'Mom, do you think he talks to me? – He doesn't want to go back to high school here.' Arthur took a can of beer from the fridge. 'Maybe you know that. He seemed pretty definite about it.'

His mother was opening the top of a new box of salt. 'Did you talk to Mr Dillard?'

Arthur felt both guilty and annoyed. He hadn't wanted to look up Mr Dillard and ask how Robbie was 'doing.' 'No, Mom. I didn't. – Want me to do something?'

'Make a little salad, if you will. – I spoke to Jane after church. She said Irene's in the hospital.'

Arthur felt a small shock. He had realized that his mother was nervous and had supposed it was because of something she had heard at the First Church of Christ Gospel. 'Does that mean it's going to be born today? Or is it already?'

'Certainly likely, I'd say,' replied his mother, inspecting the oven.

Was his mother expecting a call from someone, telling her whether the baby was boy or girl, black or white? Arthur wasn't going to ask. The rest of today was ruined too, he realized, and it was worse for his mother than for him. He at least had a bright spot to look forward to, a date with Maggie at 5 p.m. to do a little work in her backyard, and as far as he knew, she was free for the evening. Maggie was working on a project for her sociology course, collaborating with another Radcliffe girl who lived in Chicago, and they were not to communicate by telephone, according to the rules of this assignment, but by letter, and emerge with a 'coordinated study.' This occupied some of Maggie's days. Arthur poured the dressing over the lettuce leaves. Their meal was ready and Arthur took up the carving knife and fork. He felt ravenous. He sought for something comforting or cheering to say to his mother. *I hope it's born dead*, he wanted to say, and couldn't. At 5, Arthur was at Maggie's house, in Levi's and tennis shoes and an old denim shirt. He had brought a clean shirt which he left in the car. Betty Brewster was sitting in a sunny corner of the big backyard, writing letters. She wore shorts and a halter and broad-brimmed hat, because there was still a strong sun.

After ten minutes, Arthur removed his shirt. He was clearing a strip with a fork and a spade, lifting out pieces of turf which

Maggie was carrying to another spot. Daffodils were to go in where Arthur was digging, but it was still too early to plant them.

'You saw your brother this morning?' Maggie asked.

'Yeah,' Arthur said, smiling, and he plunged his fork in. 'Do you mind if I don't talk about that?'

'No-o,' Maggie drawled with her air of patience. 'But I'm interested. What kind of a place is it? – Was he friendly?'

'Mom asked the same thing. I wouldn't call him friendly. Not to me. – Place is like a prison.' Arthur paused to wipe a gnat out of his eye.

'You don't have to work so fast, Arthur!' Maggie lifted more turf pieces into a broad basket carrier.

Betty brought out cold lemonade and cookies. 'I'm sure this won't spoil anybody's appetite for dinner. My, Arthur, that's progress!'

He had dug a strip a foot wide half the length of the backyard, almost, and furthermore its line was straight. Arthur was rather proud of the black streak of freshly opened earth.

An hour or so later, under the Brewsters' shower which Arthur knew well, Arthur washed even his hair and turned the water on cold at the last. He felt very well. And how was Irene feeling, he wondered, as he pulled the wadded towel across his torso and examined his chest muscles and biceps in the mirror. Was even now his half-brother or half-sister breathing the air of this world, the same air that he was? That was really crazy, yet maybe true! Arthur drew on a pink oxford cloth shirt with button-down collar.

It was Mom's Pride again for dinner. Maggie had liked the place. Gus and Veronica were due to turn up later. Gus was at Veronica's house this evening, looking at her mother's sewing machine, which he was supposed to fix if he could. Maggie and Arthur ate hamburgers and french fries.

'And Mr Hargiss,' Arthur began casually. 'You're going to see him again when you go back east?'

Maggie took a breath. 'I'll see him – because he takes a chemistry course at Radcliffe.'

'I meant—' Arthur was sure she knew what he meant. This was their third date since Maggie had returned, the second having been a film, and he hadn't felt like asking about Hargiss that evening. 'I meant, are you in love with him?'

'No. Not any more.'

'Oh.' But she had been, of course. 'You mean you broke it off?'

Maggie looked down at her nearly finished plate. 'Well, yes. I didn't like his family so much.' She looked up at Arthur. 'I thought they were bossy. We had to do certain things certain days, Larry and I. Everything planned days in advance. There was a yacht club there – all very nice – but it was a little – interfering. I could see it was going to go on forever – like that.'

'Stuffy.'

'Not stuffy the way they dressed or anything. It was what we had to do.'

Arthur felt relieved. Mr Hargiss had been eliminated:

Later, when he was dancing with Maggie and feeling especially confident, Arthur had an impulse to tell her that today, maybe this evening, Irene's baby would be born. But he decided against it, because he wouldn't be able to say it lightly enough. Or perhaps the fact was, it wasn't a light or funny subject. It was better to look into Maggie's smiling eyes as they danced some distance apart, to be in another world with her alone, with all the gyrating figures around them nothing more than part of the walls.

'There's Gus!' Maggie said.

Arthur looked behind him and raised an arm.

There was room for the four of them in the booth. Gus and Veronica ordered beers, Maggie and Arthur salad and more beers.

'Got the sewing machine fixed?' Arthur asked.

'No,' said Gus, hanging his head.

'You *did*,' said Veronica. 'I swear it was working when we left the house, Arthur! I don't know what Gus is talking about.'

'See if it works tomorrow. I'm not convinced,' Gus said.

'Perfectionist!' said Veronica. 'Tell me about Radcliffe, Maggie. I'm dying to hear details.' She brushed her long hair back and leaned forward expectantly.

'Details of what?' Maggie laughed.

'The rooms, for instance. Do you have to be – I mean, how many times a week can you go out in the evening, say?'

Arthur gave a laugh.

'All you want, I suppose,' Maggie said. 'Unless your grades are pretty bad. Then they might—'

'What time do you have to be *in* at night?' Gus asked in a girlish way.

'Oh, stop it,' said Veronica. 'I mean, the rooms, yes. Private rooms?'

'Thinking of going there?' asked Gus.

Each girl had her own room, Maggie said. Veronica wanted to know how big they were. And how about the bathrooms?

'How about 'em?' said Gus. 'Does a maid come with each room?'

'Telephone?' asked Arthur. 'Color TV?'

'Alderman! – Anyone here named *Alderman*?'

Arthur heard a man's voice yelling this through the music and chatter, and he stood up to see better. 'Here! Yep!' His car, he thought first, but how would they know his name from his car?

''Scuse me,' he said to the others.

'Telephone call,' the busy waiter said to Arthur, and went off. 'First booth on the right.' He pointed.

Arthur walked to a corner near the front of the place where there were two booths, one occupied, the other with its receiver off the hook. 'Hello?'

'Hello, Arthur,' said his mother in a breathless voice. 'You said you might be there, so—'

'Well, Mom, I *am* here.'

'Irene's just had a baby girl. I thought I should tell you.'

'I see. Well.' Arthur was pressing a palm against one ear in order to hear.

'Bob Cole phoned me around seven, just before the Griffins got here. Irene's at the United Memorial Hospital.'

Arthur didn't give a damn where she was. His mother sounded shaky. He knew that his mother had invited the Griffins for dinner, and he assumed they had left now. 'Well, Mom, don't *you* worry. – Are you okay?'

'Of course I'm all right,' said his mother promptly.

'Okay, stay that way. – I won't be late tonight, Mom.'

As Arthur walked back to the booth, he noticed Roxanne at the table far to his left, laughing giddily as usual, with a big group. He'd heard that Roxanne had got married and left town. Maybe a false rumor. Arthur realized that he was glancing around for faces he might know or who might know him. He saw at least two, acquaintances from C.U., who were paying him no mind. He sat down again next to Maggie.

'Anything wrong?' Maggie asked.

'No, no.' Arthur had an impulse to blurt it out. Everyone would know tomorrow or the next day, anyway. Gus and Veronica were looking at him. 'Well, that was my Mom. She said Irene's had a baby girl.'

'Well, well,' said Gus. 'I think I'll have another beer.'

'The one at the diner,' Veronica said calmly.

'Yes.' Arthur supposed that Gus had told Veronica that Alderman Senior was suspected of having sired the child. Or had Gus? *I suppose I have a half-sister now,* Arthur thought of saying, but that was going too far; that was too awful.

Maggie patted Arthur's hand, which rested on the bench seat between them. Arthur had clenched his fist, but he opened it and took Maggie's hand, and with his other hand rubbed his eyes, then reached for what was left of his beer. The baby was going to live. It hadn't been born dead. And what would its blood type be? Arthur reminded himself that he had decided not to care. He realized that he did care. He glanced at Maggie and swallowed his beer as if it were a lump of something. 'What the hell?' Arthur said, addressing all three.

Maybe he wasn't heard across the table in all the noise.

'*State* gonna take care of that kid?' Gus almost shouted the question.

'The *State*? I really dunno. The church a little bit – I heard.' Arthur managed a weak laugh.

Their beers finished and more on the way, they all got up to dance. Old Gus looked happy this evening, more sure of himself. Gus wasn't thinking about Irene's bastard. Dancing with Maggie, Arthur could forget everything except her and the music, the drums, the *tings* of the cymbals. They had a life together, for now at least. The rest of the world was something apart, distant even, when he was with Maggie.

33

Arthur was home by just after 1 a.m. His mother was in the kitchen, washing up some pots at the sink.

'Still at it, Mom? Can't I finish those for you?'

'I'm only late because I was watching a film on TV.' His mother seemed tense and did not look at Arthur.

He wanted a final beer and reached into the fridge. He had just said to Maggie, 'I wish I could spend the night with you, upstairs in that narrow bed,' and he had thought it might be possible, if he had left early in the morning. It would have been possible, Arthur knew, but for Betty's presence in the house, though Maggie didn't say so. He was sure that one of these evenings Maggie would come out with, 'My mother won't be back till one in the morning, I know,' and consequently Arthur felt quite cheerful at that moment. And with a pleasant future dancing in his head, he was supposed to concentrate on Irene lying in some hospital bed with a tiny infant girl by her side, because his mother was thinking of that.

'Well, did—' Arthur began. 'Did the Griffins say anything about Irene?'

'They didn't say a word,' his mother replied over her shoulder. 'Almost ominous. Ha!' She turned and looked at him.

'Maybe they don't know. What's so fascinating about Irene's offspring? Don't take it so seriously, Mom.'

His mother dried her hands on a paper towel.

Arthur pressed the cold beer can against his forehead and tried to continue. 'Bob Cole went to the hospital?'

'Yes, because Irene wanted him to come. He said the baby had a little blond hair.'

So would a child of his father's, Arthur realized with disgust and annoyance. He and his brother had had 'a little blond hair' when they had been born, Arthur had heard. 'And why did he take the trouble to mention that?'

'Oh – Bob talks on and on. – He said Irene wanted me to come and see the baby.'

'Oh, f'Chris' sake!' Arthur felt like flinging his beer can at the sink, but he set it atop the fridge and took his mother's hands in his, something he had never done before. 'Mom, you've got to let it roll off you. Ignore it! – If you don't talk to people you know – and if they don't ask you questions – or if they do, just brush it off! Let Irene handle it. And give her the brush-off, too. If—' His mother was listening, looking straight at him with rather sad blue eyes, and Arthur suddenly and shyly released her hands. 'Mom, if I could only give you some of what *I* feel tonight. Everything's going so well! I'm going away in September, and Maggie – Everything's all right there, I'm sure. I'd like you to be—' Happy or happier, he wanted to say, but things were not going well for Robbie, and Robbie was part of his mother's life, too. His mother couldn't turn loose of Robbie as easily as she might wash her hands of Irene. 'I had an idea tonight.'

'What?'

'We should move to another town. Maybe some place in New Jersey. Pennsylvania, maybe. Change your life, Mom! Sell the house here – Mom, have you considered getting married again?'

'Married again? No, Arthur, why?'

'Well, why not? Companionship. And you're still pretty!'

'Any prospects in mind for me?' His mother laughed as if the idea were an absurdity.

'No, because I haven't given it much thought. In this boring town? – Anybody but the Reverend Cole, Mom! Holy cow!' Arthur rocked back, laughing. Bob Cole was a bachelor and without the least sign, which Arthur had looked for, of being gay. Arthur suspected him of playing the field carefully with girls some distance from Chalmerston.

'Arthur, I think you're a little drunk.'

'I think you're a little right. But – I'll say the same thing tomorrow. It's a good idea if we move. If we sold this house—'

'And Robbie?'

Arthur looked into his mother's eyes again. 'Robbie's not coming back, Mom. Not here – to this house. I'd bet my life on that. He doesn't want to.' And there was the study in this house, reminding his mother that his father had died there.

'This house is sad, Mom.'

His mother bent her head. 'Ye-es, I know.'

Arthur kissed his mother's cheek. 'Go to bed, Mom. But think about what I said. Sleep on it.'

Arthur's first thought on awakening the next morning was *moving.* Settling his mother in another town, maybe in northern Pennsylvania, as he had said last night. The East Coast was more expensive than the area where they lived now, but the next house need not be as big as this, perhaps. He could look for a house in early September, in the weeks before Columbia classes began. He could drive his car east, as he had not thought of doing before, sell it finally for a couple of peanuts in New York or in some small town, since a car in New York was useless and a drain. Then his mother could keep her own car and find a secretarial job in the town where the new house would be, if she wanted or needed to take a job. Why was that such an impossible dream?

The sunlight came through the window on Arthur's left, beautiful, cool and warm at the same time on the white sheet that covered him. It was almost 8. 'Ah-h,' Arthur said, because the world seemed good at that moment.

His next thought was not so pleasant: Irene and her offspring. He sat up on the edge of his bed. A birth announcement might be in the *Chalmerston Herald* today, and if not, certainly tomorrow, because all births and deaths got at least a two-line mention. Miss Irene Langley standing by itself after 'born to' would make the announcement look as if she'd had the child by some kind of parthenogenesis! She would probably have given the little thing a name already.

His mother tapped on the door. 'Coffee is served!'

'Ah, most welcome! And good morning, madame,' said Arthur holding the door. 'Did you think about what I was saying last night?'

'Yes. And I think it's a good idea. I'll ask Mama what she thinks.' His mother looked at him, and her eyes seemed already happier, younger, merely with the thought.

'Leave it to me. I'll scout around. East Coast. Can't think now till I've had my coffee, you know.' Arthur picked up the mug and sipped.

Arthur called Maggie from Shoe Repair just after noon, as he had promised to do, and told her about his idea of his mother moving to another town in the East. Maggie said she thought it was a *very* good idea, because the present house 'must be so sad for her.' In Maggie's voice he heard a sympathy that struck deep. Maggie said there were some brochures on real estate in Pennsylvania and New Jersey in her house, six months old but maybe still useful, because her parents had been thinking last winter of moving to the East Coast. Arthur made a date with her to come to her house that evening after dinner.

Maggie gave him the pamphlets and brochures, which had a lot of photographs of houses that were not out of his and his mother's price range. Arthur told Tom Robertson of his intention. This meant he would work only the first week in September in the shop, not the first two weeks. Tom said he was sorry – mainly at the idea of Arthur's moving out of Chalmerston – but he gave Arthur his blessing. He used the word blessing, and Arthur recollected that Tom was one of the few who knew him and who did not seem to have heard of Irene Langley's connection with his father.

One day in early September, just before Arthur was to head east in his car, his mother said:

'I saw Irene pushing a baby carriage this morning on Main Street. I must say, it was that fat sister who caught my eye. I thought it was a tent swaying from side to side in the breeze!' His mother paused to laugh. 'Then I blinked and I recognized Louise in a wide blue dress, ambling along eating an ice-cream cone. And beside her, Irene – pushing a baby carriage.'

Arthur gave a one-sided smile. 'Did you have a look at the infant?'

'Well, I confess I did. At the risk of being noticed by Irene and talked to, but she was walking along as if in a trance – and her sister was concentrating on her ice cream. I was behind them, so I walked ahead and turned back. The baby looked asleep. I didn't see any blond hair, now that I think of it. I'll just have to take Bob Cole's word for that.'

The damned thing existed! His mother had seen it. His half-sister. Arthur realized he had forgotten to look for any birth announcement in the *Herald*. 'Well, if Madame Irene is walking around already, I suppose she can go back to work soon. Maybe she's already back at the Silver Arrow.'

'Yes, why not? The sister could look after the baby.'

Arthur noticed that his mother looked a bit nervous. That

would pass in a few minutes. He was glad his mother had actually *seen* the thing, because it made the infant less of a ghost, made it flesh and blood, fated to die one day, just like the rest of humanity. 'Speaking of Irene going back to work – wouldn't it be funny if she went back to her old profession – you know – streetwalking.'

His mother's shoulders bent with a laugh. 'Oh, Arthur!'

'Without the church to guide her,' Arthur went on, and at once thought, without his father to guide her. The Reverend Cole was supposed to be doing the job now. Would he? Could he? Arthur tried to be serious. 'There really is more money in street-walking than in the Silver Arrow,' he said in a solemn voice.

The Talented Mr Ripley

PATRICIA HIGHSMITH

The Talented Mr Ripley is one of the most influential, groundbreaking crime novels ever written. Tom Ripley travels to Italy with a commission to coax a prodigal young American back to his wealthy father. But Ripley finds himself very fond of Dickie Greenleaf. He wants to be like him – exactly like him. Suave, agreeable and utterly amoral, Ripley will stop at nothing – not even murder – to accomplish his goal.

The Talented Mr Ripley serves as an unforgettable introduction to this smooth confidence man, whose talent for murder and self-invention is chronicled in four further Ripley novels.

'I'm a huge Highsmith fan. If there's one book I wish I'd written, it's *The Talented Mr Ripley*'
Sarah Waters

'I love [Highsmith] so much . . . what a revelation her writing was'
Gillian Flynn

'Ripley, amoral, hedonistic and charming, is a genuinely original creation. It is hard to imagine anyone interested in modern fiction who has not read the Ripley novels'
Daily Telegraph

The Tremor Of Forgery

PATRICIA HIGHSMITH

'Highsmith's finest novel'
Graham Greene

Howard Ingham, an American writer, is in Tunisia working on a screenplay; but when the film's director fails to arrive, he feels stranded. The erratic mail eventually brings news of his suicide. For reasons obscure even to himself, Ingham decides to stay on and work on a novel, but a series of peculiar events – a hushed-up murder and a vanished corpse – lures him inexorably into the deep, ambivalent shadows of the Arab town; into deceit and away from conventional morality. Ultimately, what is in question is not justice or truth but the state of his oddly, quiet conscience.

'Highsmith is a giant of the genre. The original, the best, the gloriously twisted Queen of Suspense'
Mark Billingham

'No one has created psychological suspense more tensely and more deliciously satisfying'
Vogue

The Birds

Short Stories

DAPHNE DU MAURIER

'How long he fought with them in the darkness he could not tell, but at last the beating of the wings about him lessened and then withdrew . . .'

A classic of alienation and horror, 'The Birds' was immortalised by Hitchcock in his celebrated film. The five other chilling stories in this collection echo a sense of dislocation and mock man's sense of dominance over the natural world. The mountain paradise of Monte Verita promises immortality, but at a terrible price; a neglected wife haunts her husband in the form of an apple tree; a photographer steps out from behind the camera and into his subject's life; a date with a cinema usherette leads to a walk in the cemetery; and a jealous father finds a remedy when three's a crowd.

'One of the last century's most original literary talents'
Daily Telegraph

'At her best, in a story such as "The Birds", there is an intense and exhilarating fusion of feeling, landscape, climate, character and story. She wrote exciting plots, she was highly skilled at arousing suspense, and she was, too, a writer of fearless originality'
Guardian

Don't Look Now

Short Stories

DAPHNE DU MAURIER

'The child struggled to her feet and stood before him, the pixie hood falling from her head on to the floor. He stared at her, incredulity turning to horror, to fear.'

John and Laura have come to Venice to escape the pain of their young daughter's death. But when they encounter two old women who claim to have second sight, they find that instead of laying their ghosts to rest they become caught up in a train of increasingly strange and violent events. The other four stories in this chilling collection also explore deep fears and longings: a lonely teacher investigates a mysterious American couple; a young woman confronts her father's past; a party of pilgrims meet disaster in Jerusalem; a scientist harnesses the power of the mind, to chilling effect.

'One of the last century's most original literary talents'
Daily Telegraph

'Daphne du Maurier wrote two of the most menacing tales of the 20th-century fiction – "The Birds" and "Don't Look Now" . . . Deeply unsettling as these films are (a line of birds on a climbing frame, or a glimpse of a little girl's red coat), the stories can be equally chilling on the page – if not more so'
Guardian